PENGUIN BOOKS

THE SMOKE THIEVES

4 4 0016807 2

SALLY GREEN lives in Cheshire, England. She began writing in 2010. Coffee drinker, runner, Lancashire accent of sorts.

Books by Sally Green
HALF BAD

HALF WILD

HALF LOST

Short stories (ebook only)
HALF LIES

HALF TRUTHS

Follow Sally on Twitter, Instagram and Tumblr
@Sa11eGreen
#SmokeThieves

SALLY GREEN

THE SMOKE THIEVES

PENGUIN BOOKS

PENGUIN BOOKS

UK | USA | Canada | Ireland | Australia
India | New Zealand | South Africa

Penguin Books is part of the Penguin Random House group of companies
whose addresses can be found at global.penguinrandomhouse.com.

www.penguin.co.uk   www.puffin.co.uk   www.ladybird.co.uk

First published 2018

001

Set in 9.75/14.5 pt Sabon LT Std by Jouve
Printed in Great Britain by Clays Ltd, St Ives plc

A CIP catalogue record for this book is available from the British Library

PAPERBACK
ISBN: 978-0-141-37539-7

All correspondence to:
Penguin Books
Penguin Random House Children's
80 Strand, London WC2R ORL

MIX
Paper from
responsible sources
FSC® C018179
www.fsc.org

Penguin Random House is committed to a
sustainable future for our business, our readers
and our planet. This book is made from Forest
Stewardship Council® certified paper.

For Indy

It is illegal to buy, trade in, procure, obtain by any means, inhale, swallow, or use in any fashion the smoke from demons.

Laws of Pitoria, V. 1, C. 43.1

CASTLE
TARASENTH
FIELDING
BRIGANT
SEA
OF
BRIGANT
BRIGANE
ABASK
CALIDOR
CALIA
PITORIA
N

THE
NORTHERN
PLATEAU

● PRAVONT

RIVER ROSS

● ROSSARB

BAY OF
ROSSARB

● DORNAN

GOLDMINSTER

● CHEAMSTER

SEA

PITORIA

WESTMOUTH

GORGANT

RIVER CHAR

CHARRON

TORNIA

ILLAST

SAVAANT

Tash

NORTHERN PLATEAU, PITORIA

'Everything ready?'

'No. This is a figment of your imagination and I've been sitting on my arse all day eating honey.' Tash was adjusting the rope so its knotted end was a hand's breadth above the bottom of the pit.

'A bit lower,' Gravell said.

'I'm not blind!'

'You need to check it.'

Tash turned on Gravell, 'I know what I need to do!'

Gravell always got serious and pernickety at this stage and it only now occurred to Tash that it was because he was scared. Tash was scared too, but it didn't help to think that Gravell wasn't far off shitting in his pants as well.

'Not nervous, are you?' she asked.

Gravell muttered, 'Why should I be nervous? You're the one it'll catch first. By the time it's done with you I'll be long gone.'

It was true, of course. Tash was the bait. She lured the demon into the trap and Gravell finished it off.

Tash was thirteen and had been demon bait since Gravell bought her from her family four years ago. He'd turned up one sunny day, the hugest, hairiest man she'd ever seen, saying he'd heard that they had a girl who was a fast runner, and told her he'd give her five kopeks if she could run to the trees before the harpoon he threw hit the ground. Tash thought it must be a trick – no one would pay just to see her run, and five kopeks was a huge sum – but she did it anyway, mostly to show off that she could. She wasn't sure what she'd do with the money – she'd never had more than a kopek before and she'd have to hide it before her brothers took it off her. But she needn't have worried; she left with Gravell that afternoon. Gravell gave her father ten kroners for her, he told her later. 'A bit pricey,' he teased. No wonder her father had been smiling when she left.

Gravell was her family now, which was to Tash's mind a lot better than the previous one. Gravell didn't beat her, she was rarely hungry, and while she was sometimes cold, that was the nature of the work. And from the first day with Gravell she had been given boots. Yes, compared to her previous life, this one with Gravell was one of luxury and plenty. The money from selling demon smoke was good, although demons were rare and dangerous. The whole process of killing demons and selling smoke was illegal, but the sheriff's men didn't bother them if they were discreet. Gravell and Tash usually managed to catch four or five demons a season, and the money lasted the year; when they were in towns they stayed at inns, slept in beds, had baths, and, best of all, Tash had boots. Two pairs now!

Tash loved her boots. Her ordinary everyday boots were of thick leather with sturdy soles. Those were good for walking and hiking, and didn't rub or pinch. She had no blisters and the smell from them she considered to be a good smell, more leathery than the stale sweat that Gravell's boots oozed. Tash's second pair, the pair she was wearing now, she'd got when they were in Dornan a few months earlier. These were her running boots and they fitted perfectly. They had sharp metal spikes in the soles so she could grip hard and set off fast. Gravell had come up with the design and he'd even paid for them – two kroners, which was a lot for boots. As she put them on the first time, he'd said, 'Look after them and they'll look after you.'

Tash did look after them and she definitely, absolutely refused to be ungrateful, but what she wanted, what she coveted more than anything in the world, were the ankle boots she'd thought Gravell was going to give her when he told her he was treating her to something special. She'd seen the ankle boots in the window of the cobbler's shop in Dornan and mentioned them a few times to Gravell. They were the most beautiful, delicate pale grey boots of suede, so soft and fine that they looked to be made from rabbit's ears.

When Gravell showed her the spiked boots and told her how he'd come up with the idea for them, she made a good job, she thought, of looking delighted. Tash told herself not to be disappointed. It would all work out. The spiked boots would help in this hunt and with the money from the demon kill she'd be able to buy the grey suede boots herself.

And soon they'd have their first demon.

Gravell found this demon's lair after only a week. He'd dug the pit, though these days Tash set up and checked the escape mechanism and, in fact, wouldn't let Gravell near it.

Gravell had taught Tash to be careful, to double-check everything. She went through a test run now, walking back from the pit a hundred paces, then jogging through the trees, picking up speed where there was little snow on the ground and into the small clearing where the snow was deeper but where she'd trampled it down to compress it so that it had hardened to a crisp, going at full speed now, pumping her legs, leaning forward, her spikes giving her grip but not holding her back, and then she was leaping over the edge of the pit, hitting the icy floor with a crunch, absorbing the drop with her knees but immediately getting up and running to the end and . . . waiting.

Waiting. That was the hardest part. That was the real shit-in-your-pants time, when your mind was screaming at you to grab the rope but you couldn't because you had to wait for the demon to come down, and only when he was on the way down, just as he touched the bottom of the pit and screamed and screeched and slid towards you, could you grab the rope and release the pulley mechanism.

Tash pulled on the rope, bearing down on it with all her weight, her right foot resting on the lowest, thickest knot. The wooden release gave and Tash flew upwards, as natural and lazy as a yawn, so balanced that her fingers were barely touching the rope, and at the apex of her flight she stopped, hanging in the air, totally free, then she let go of the rope, leant forward and reached for the fir tree, arms out to hug the branches. She held herself there before casually sliding down. A pine cone scratched her face and she landed almost knee-deep in the pile of snow she'd banked there.

Tash walked back to reset the trap. Soil and footprints surrounded the pit; she'd have to clean the base of her boots to make sure they didn't get clogged with dirt.

'You're bleeding.'

Tash felt her cheek and looked at the blood on her fingertips. Demons got more excited when they smelt blood. She licked her fingers and said, 'Let's get on with it.'

She grabbed the ropes and set the pulley back into place, satisfied that she'd done everything properly. The pulley was working smoothly. It was a good pit. Gravell had dug it over three days, making it long, thin and deep, and last night he and Tash had poured water down the steep sides until there was two hands' depth in the bottom, which had frozen nicely to a hard, smooth ice. It was still possible to climb out of the pit – demons were good at climbing – and Gravell had over the years tried different ways to get the walls covered with ice too, but it had never been that successful. So they would do what Gravell had always done and paint the pit walls with a mix of animal's blood and guts. It smelt strong and disgusting and was enough to distract and confuse the demon, giving Gravell time to throw his harpoons. Gravell had five long harpoons, though it usually only took three to finish the demon off. They were specially made, each with a metal tip and teeth so they couldn't be pulled out. The demon would scream and screech. The noise was horrible and Tash always had to remind herself that the demon would gladly do worse to her if he – it – caught her.

Tash looked up; the sun was still high in the sky. The demon hunt happened at the end of the day. She could feel her stomach begin to tighten with nerves. She just wanted to get on with it. Gravell still had to coat the walls of the pit, then take cover in the nearby bushes and wait. Only when he saw the demon leap into the pit would he move forward, harpoons in hand. Timing was everything and they had it down to an art now, but it was Tash who risked her life, Tash who attracted the demon, Tash who had to know when to start running to draw the demon after her, Tash who had to outrun the demon, jump into the pit and, at the last possible moment, grab the rope and be hoisted out.

True, the demon could avoid the pit and attack Gravell. This had happened only once in their four years of demon hunting together. Tash wasn't sure what had happened that day and Gravell didn't talk about it. She'd leapt into the pit and waited, but the demon hadn't followed her in. She'd heard Gravell shout; there was a high-pitched demon screech, and then silence. She hadn't known what to do. If the demon was dead, why wasn't Gravell shouting for her to come out? Did the screech mean the demon was wounded? Or was it the screech it made as it attacked and killed Gravell? Was the demon silent now because it was feasting on Gravell's body? Should she run while the demon was drinking Gravell's blood? She'd waited and looked up at the sky above the pit walls and realized she wanted a piss. She'd wanted to cry too.

She'd waited, holding on to the rope, but she was too terrified to move. Finally she'd heard something, a shuffling in the snow, and Gravell shouted down, 'Are you going to come out of there this year?' And Tash had tried to release the pulley but her hand was so cold and so shaky it took a while and Gravell was swearing at her by then. When she got out she was surprised to see that Gravell wasn't wounded at all. He'd laughed when she'd said, 'You're not dead.' He went quiet and then said, 'Fucking demons.'

'Why didn't it come into the pit?'

'I don't know. Maybe it saw me. Smelt me. Sensed something . . . whatever it is they do.'

The demon was lying fifty paces from the pit with just one harpoon in its body. Had Gravell run or had the demon run? She had asked and all Gravell had said was, 'We were both fucking running.' The other harpoons were speared into the ground at different points around them, as if Gravell had thrown them and missed. Gravell shook his head, saying, 'Like trying to harpoon an angry wasp.'

The demon wasn't much bigger than Tash. It was very thin, all sinew and skin, no fat at all; it reminded Tash of her older brother. Its skin was more purple than the usual reds and burnt oranges, the sunset colours of the bigger demons. Within a day the body would rot and melt away, the smell strong and earthy for that time, and then it would be gone, not even leaving a stain on the ground. There was no blood; demons didn't have blood.

'Did you get the smoke?' Tash had asked.

'No. I was a bit busy.'

The smoke came out of the demon after it died. Tash wondered what Gravell had been busy doing, but she knew that he'd come close to death and saw that his hands were still trembling. She imagined that he must have killed the demon and tried to hold the bottle to catch the smoke but his hands had been shaking too much.

'Was it beautiful?'

'Very. Purple. Some red and a bit of orange to start but then all purple right through to the end.'

'Purple!' Tash wished she'd seen it. They had nothing to show for all their work, weeks of tracking, and then the days of digging and preparation. Nothing to show except their lives and stories of the beauty of the demon smoke.

'Tell me more about the smoke, Gravell,' Tash had said.

And Gravell told her how it had seeped out of the demon's mouth – after the demon had stopped screeching.

'Not much smoke this time,' Gravell added. 'Small demon. Young maybe.' Tash had nodded. They'd lit a fire to get warm and in the morning they'd watched the demon's body shrink and disappear, and then they had set off to find another.

Today's demon was the first of the season. They didn't hunt in winter, as it was too harsh, the snow too deep and the cold bitter. They'd come up to the Northern Plateau as soon as the deep snows began to melt, though this year spring had arrived but then winter returned for a few weeks and so there was still deep snow in the shade and in hollows. Gravell had found the demon's lair and worked out the best place for the pit. Now Gravell lowered the pot of blood and guts into the pit and climbed down the ladder to paint the walls. Tash didn't have to do this; Gravell had never asked her to – it was his job and he took pride in it. He wasn't going to mess up weeks of work by failing to do this last task properly.

Tash sat on her pack and waited. She wrapped a fur round herself and stared at the distant trees and tried not to think any more about demons and the pit, so she thought of afterwards. They'd go to Dornan and sell the demon smoke there. Trade in smoke was illegal – anything to do with demons was illegal; even setting foot on demon territory was illegal – but that didn't mean there weren't a few people like her and Gravell who hunted them, and it certainly didn't stop people wanting to buy the demon smoke.

And once she had her share of the money she could buy her boots. Dornan was a week's walk away, but the journey was easy and they'd enjoy warmth, rest and good food before returning to the plateau. Tash asked Gravell once why he didn't collect more smoke and kill more demons, adding, 'Southgate said Banyon and Yoden catch twice what we do each year.' But Gravell replied, 'Demons is evil but so is greed. We've got enough.' And life was pretty good, as long as Tash kept running fast.

Eventually Gravell climbed back out of the pit, pulled the ladder up and put everything out of sight. Tash moved her pack to the trees. With that done, there was nothing left to prepare. Gravell circled the pit a final time, muttering to himself, 'Yep. Yep. Yep.'

He came over to Tash and said, 'Right then.'

'Right then.'

'Don't fuck up, missy.'

'Don't you neither.'

They knocked right fists together.

The words and fist bump were a ritual they had for good luck, though Tash didn't really believe in luck and was fairly sure Gravell didn't either, but she wasn't going to go through a demon hunt without all possible assistance on her side.

The sun was lower in the sky and soon would be below the level of the trees, the time when it was best to lure the demon out. Tash jogged north, through thin woodland, to the clearing that she and Gravell had found ten days earlier. Well, Gravell had found it. That was his real skill. Digging pits and lining them with guts anyone could do; his knack for killing demons with harpoons was due to his size and strength, but what made Gravell very special was his patience, his instinctive ability to find the places demons lived. Demons liked shallow hollows on flat ground, not too close to trees, where mist collected. They liked the cold. They liked snow. They didn't like people.

Tash used to ask Gravell all about demons but now she probably knew as much as anyone could about something from a different place. And what a place it was. *Not of this earth,* she thought, *or perhaps too much of this earth, of an ancient earth.* Tash had seen into it, the demon land: that was what she had to do. To lure the demon out, she had to venture in, where she was not allowed, where humans didn't go. And the demons would kill her for daring to see their world, a world that was bruised and brooding. Not so much dark as a different type of light; the light was red and the shadows redder. There were no trees or plants, just red rock. The air was warmer, thicker, and then there were the sounds.

Tash waited until the sun was halfway below the hill, the sky red and orange only in that small section. Mist was collecting in the gentle hollows. It was forming in her demon's hollow too. This hollow was slightly deeper than the other dips and undulations around it, but unlike the rest this had no snow in it, and at this time of evening the mist could be seen to have a tinge of red, which perhaps could be due to the sunset, but Tash knew otherwise.

Tash approached slowly and silently and knelt at the rim of the hollow. She reached back to clean the spikes on her boots with her fingers, pulling off a few small clumps of earth. She put her hands on the ground and spread her fingers, feeling the earth, which was not warm but was not frozen solid either – this was the edge of demon territory.

She dug in her toes and took a breath as if she was about to submerge, which in a way she was. Tash lowered her head, and with eyes open she pushed her head forward, her chest brushing the ground, as if she was nosing under a curtain into the hollow: into the demon's world.

Sometimes it took two or three attempts, but today she was in first time.

The demon land fell away before her, the hollow descending sharply to a tunnel, but that wasn't the only thing that was different from the human world. Here in the demon world, colours, sounds and temperatures were altered, as if she was looking through a coloured glass into an oven. Describing the colours was hard, but describing the sounds was impossible.

Tash looked across the red hollow to the opening of the tunnel, and there at the lowest point was something purple. A leg?

Then she made sense of it and saw that he – *it* – was sprawled on its stomach, one leg sticking out. Tash worked out its torso, an arm and its head. Human-shaped but not human. Skin smooth and finely muscled, purple and red and streaks of orange, narrow and long. It looked young. Like a gangly teenager. Its stomach was moving slowly with each of its breaths. It was sleeping.

Tash had been holding her own breath all this time and now she let out what air she had. Sometimes that's all she needed to do; just her breath, her smell, would get the demon's attention.

This demon didn't move.

Tash took a breath in, the air hot and dry in her mouth. She shouted her shout: 'I'm here, demon! I can see you!' But her voice did not sound the same here. Here, words were not words but a clanging of cymbals and gongs.

The demon's head lifted and slowly turned to face Tash. One leg moved, bending at the knee, the foot raising in the air, totally relaxed despite the intrusion. The demon's eyes were purple. It stared at Tash and then blinked. Its leg was still in the air and was totally still. Then it threw its head back, lowered its leg, opened its mouth and stretched its neck to howl.

A clanging noise hit Tash's ears as the demon sprang up and forward, purple mouth open, but already Tash was springing up too, pushing her spikes hard into the ground and twisting round in the air in a leap that took her out of the demon world and back on to the lip of the hollow, back into the human world.

And then she was running.

Catherine

BRIGANE, BRIGANT

There is no greater evil than that of a traitor. All traitors must be sought out, exposed and punished.
The Laws and Devices of Brigant

'Prince Boris has sent a guard to escort us there, Your Highness.' Jane, the new maid, looked and sounded terrified.

'Don't worry. You won't have to watch.' Princess Catherine smoothed her skirt and took a deep breath. She was ready.

They set off: the guard ahead, Catherine in the middle and Jane at the rear. The corridors were quiet and empty in the queen's part of the castle; even the guard's heavy footsteps were hushed on the thick rugs. But entering the central hall was like crossing into a different world: a world full of men, colour and noise. Catherine so rarely came into this world that she wanted to take it all in. There were no other women here. The lords were in breastplates, with swords and daggers, as though they didn't dare come to

12

court without appearing their strongest. Numerous servants stood around and everyone seemed to be talking, looking, manoeuvring. Catherine recognized no one, but the men recognized her and parted to allow her through, bowing as she passed, the noise quietening then building again behind her.

And then she was at another door, which the guard held open for her. 'Prince Boris asked that you wait for him in here, Your Highness.'

Catherine entered the antehall, indicating with a wave of her hand that Jane should wait at the door, which was already being closed.

It was quiet, but Catherine could hear her own heart beating fast. She took a deep breath and let it out slowly.

She told herself, *Stay calm. Stay dignified. Act like a princess.*

She straightened her back and took another deep breath. Then paced slowly to the far end of the room.

It'll be ugly. It'll be bloody. But I won't flinch. I won't faint. I certainly won't scream.

And back again.

I'll be controlled. I won't show any emotion. If it's really bad I'll think of something else. But what? Something beautiful? That would just be wrong.

And back again.

What do you think of when you watch someone having their head chopped off? And not just anyone but Amb–

Catherine turned and there was Noyes, somehow in the corner of the room, leaning against the wall.

Catherine rarely met Noyes but whenever she saw him she had to suppress a shudder. He was slim and athletic, probably the same age as her father. Today he was fashionably dressed in his leather and buckles, his shoulder-length, almost white hair tied back from his angular face in fine plaits and a simple knot. But, for all that, there was something unpleasant about him. Maybe it was just his reputation. Noyes, the master inquisitor, was in the business of seeking out and hunting down traitors. He didn't kill prisoners himself for the most part; that was the job of his torturers and executioners. In the seven years since the war with Calidor, Noyes and his like had flourished, unlike most Brigantine businesses. No one was safe from his scrutiny: from stable lad to lord, from maid to lady, and even to princess.

Noyes pushed off the wall with his shoulder, took a lazy step towards her, made a slow bow and said, 'Good morning, Your Highness. Isn't it a beautiful day?'

'For you, I'm sure.'

He smiled his half-smile and remained still, watching her.

Catherine asked, 'Are you waiting for Boris?'

'I'm merely waiting, Your Highness.'

They stood in silence. Catherine looked up at the high windows and the blue sky beyond. Noyes's eyes were on her and she felt like a sheep at a market ... no, more like an ugly bug that had crawled across his path. She had an urge to scream that he should show her some respect.

She turned abruptly away from him and told herself, *Stay calm. Stay calm*. She was good at hiding her emotions after nearly seventeen years of practice, but recently it had become harder. Recently her emotions kept threatening to get the better of her.

'Ah, you're here, sister,' Boris called as he barged through the doors, Prince Harold trailing in his wake. For once Catherine was relieved to see her brothers. She curtsied. Boris strode through the room, ignoring Noyes and not even bowing to Catherine. He didn't come to a standstill, but carried on, saying, 'Your maid stays here. You come with me.' He pushed open the double doors into the castle square, saying, 'Come on, Princess. Don't dilly-dally.'

Catherine hurried after Boris, the doors already swinging shut in her face. She pulled them open and was relieved that Boris had stopped; the scaffold ahead of them was almost blocking the way, as tall as the rose-garden wall.

Boris snorted a laugh. 'Father told them to make sure everyone gets a good view, but I swear they've cut down an acre of forest to build this.'

'Well, I don't know why *she* should get to see it. This isn't for girls,' Harold said, hands on hips, legs apart, staring at Catherine.

'And yet children are allowed to attend,' Catherine replied, imitating his stance.

'I'm fourteen, sister.'

Catherine walked past him, whispering, 'In two months, little brother. But I won't tell anyone.'

Harold grumbled, 'I'll soon be bigger than you,' before pushing past her and stomping off after Boris. He looked particularly small and slight as he followed behind Boris's broad frame. They were clearly brothers, their red-blond hair exactly the same shade, though Harold's was more intricately tied, and it struck Catherine that he must have had someone spend more time on his hair than her maids had spent on hers.

However, Harold's opinion about the propriety of Catherine's presence mattered as much as Catherine's own. She had been ordered to attend the execution by her father, on the advice of Noyes. Catherine had to prove herself to them. Prove her strength and loyalty, and most importantly that she was no traitor in heart, mind or deed.

Boris was already rounding the corner of the scaffold. Catherine hurried to catch up, lifting her long skirt so as not to trip. Although she couldn't yet see the crowd, she could hear its low buzz. It was strange how you could sense a crowd, sense a mood. The men in the hall had been polite on the surface but there was a barely concealed lust: for power, for . . . anything. Here, there was a large crowd and a surprisingly good mood. A couple of shouts of 'Boris' went up but they quickly died. This wasn't Boris's day.

Boris turned and stared at Catherine as she joined him. 'You want to show off your legs to the masses, sister?'

Catherine dropped her skirt and smoothed the fabric, saying in her most repulsed voice, 'The cobbles aren't clean. This silk will be ruined.'

'Better that than your reputation.' Boris held Catherine's gaze. 'I'm only thinking of you, sister.' He waved to his left, at the raised platform carpeted in royal red, and stated, 'This is for us.'

As if Catherine couldn't work it out for herself.

Boris led the way up the three steps. The royal enclosure was rather basic, with a single row of the wide, carved wooden stools Catherine recognized from the meeting hall. A thick red rope was strung loosely between short red-and-black posts that demarked the platform. The crowd was beyond the platform and it too was held back by rope (not red, but thick, coarse and brown) and a line of the Royal Guard (in red, black and gold, but also thick and coarse, Catherine assumed).

Boris pointed at the seat closest to the far edge of the platform. 'For you, sister.' He planted himself on the wide stool next to hers, his legs apart, a muscular thigh overlapping Catherine's seat. She sat down, carefully arranging her skirt so that it wouldn't crease and so that the pale pink silk fell over Boris's knee. He moved his leg away.

Harold remained standing by the seat on the other side of Boris. 'But Catherine gets the best view.'

'That's the point, squirt,' Boris replied.

'But I have precedence over Catherine and I want to sit there.'

'Well, I gave Catherine that seat. So you sit on this one here and stop your whining.'

Harold hesitated for a moment. He opened his mouth to complain again but caught Catherine's eye. She smiled and made an elegant sewing sign in front of her lips. Harold glanced at Boris and had to clamp his lips together with his teeth, but he did remain quiet.

Catherine surveyed the square. There was another platform opposite, on the other side of the scaffold, with some noblemen standing on it. She recognized Ambrose's long blond hair and quickly looked away, wondering if she was blushing. Why did just a glimpse of him make her feel hot and flustered? And today of all days! She had to think of something else. Sometimes her whole life seemed to involve thinking of something else.

The area before the scaffold was packed with common folk. Catherine stared at the crowd, forcing her focus on to them. There were scruffily dressed labourers, some slightly smarter traders, groups of young men, some boys, a few women. They were for the most part dressed drably, some almost in rags, their hair loose or tied back simply. Near her, people were talking about the weather. It was already hot, the hottest day of the year so far, the sky a pure pale blue. It was a day to be enjoyed and yet hundreds of people were here to see someone die.

'What makes these people come to watch this, do you suppose, brother?' Catherine asked, putting on her I'm-asking-a-genuine-question voice.

'You don't know?'

'Educate me a little. You are so much more experienced in these matters.'

Boris replied in an overly sincere voice, 'Well, sister. There's a holy trinity that drives the masses and draws them here. Boredom, curiosity and bloodlust. And the greatest of these is bloodlust.'

'And do you suppose this bloodlust is increased when it's a noble head that is going to be severed from a noble body?'

'They just want blood,' Boris replied. 'Anyone's.'

'And yet these people here seem more interested in discussing the weather than the finer points of chopping someone in two.'

'They don't need to discuss it. They need to see it. They'll stop talking about the weather soon enough. When the prisoner is brought out you'll see what I mean. The rabble want blood and they'll get it here today. And you'll get a lesson in what happens to someone who betrays the king. One you can't learn from books.'

Catherine turned her face from the contempt in Boris's voice. That was how she learnt about life – from books. Though it was hardly her fault that she wasn't allowed to meet people, to travel, to learn about the world from the world. But Catherine did like books and in the last few days she had scoured the library for anything relating to executions: she'd studied the law, the methods, the history and numerous examples. The illustrations, most of which showed executioners holding up severed heads, were bad enough, but to *choose* to witness it, to *choose* to be part of it, part of the crowd baying for blood, was something Catherine couldn't understand.

'I still don't see why Catherine needs to be here at all,' Harold complained.

'Didn't I tell you to shut up?' Boris didn't even turn to Harold as he spoke.

'But ladies don't normally come to watch.'

Boris now couldn't resist replying, 'No, not normally, but Catherine needs a lesson in loyalty. She needs to understand the consequences of not following our plans for her.' He turned to Catherine as he added, 'In every aspect. To the smallest degree.'

Harold frowned. 'What plans?'

Boris ignored him.

Harold rolled his eyes and leant towards Catherine to ask, 'Is this about your marriage?'

Catherine smiled thinly. 'This is an execution, so why you would link it to my marriage, I can't imagine.' Boris glared at her, and she added, 'What I mean is, I'm honoured to be marrying Prince Tzsayn of Pitoria and will ensure every aspect of the wedding goes to plan, whether or not I see someone having their head chopped off.'

Harold was quiet for a few moments before asking, 'But why wouldn't it go to plan?'

'It will,' Boris answered. 'Father won't let anything stop it.'

This was true, and Catherine's complete obedience to every detail of the plan was required, and *that* was why she was here. Catherine had made the mistake a week earlier of saying to her maid, Diana, that Diana could perhaps look forward to a marriage based on love. She'd asked Catherine whom she would marry if she could choose, and Catherine had joked, 'Someone I've spoken with at least once,' adding, 'Someone intelligent and thoughtful and considerate.' As she said it, she had thought of her last conversation with Ambrose as he escorted her on her ride. He had joked about the quality of food in the barracks, then had grown serious as he described the poverty in the backstreets of Brigane. Diana seemed to know her thoughts and had said, 'You spoke with Sir Ambrose at length this morning.'

The day following the conversation with Diana, Catherine was summoned to Boris and that was when she'd realized her maid was less her maid and more Noyes's spy. Catherine suffered lengthy lecturing and questioning from Boris, but it was Noyes who listened most closely to her answers, though he made a show of leaning against the wall and yawning occasionally. Noyes was not even a lord, hardly a gentleman, but the way his lips curled in a half-smile made Catherine's skin crawl and she feared him twice as much as her brother. Noyes was her father's presence, his spy, his eyes and ears. Boris was that too, of course, but Boris was always bludgeoningly obvious.

At the interview, Boris had repeated the usual lines about unquestioning loyalty and obedience and Catherine had been pleased with how cool she'd remained.

'I am merely nervous, as any bride-to-be is before their wedding. I have never even met Prince Tzsayn. Just as I try to be the best daughter I can be to Father, I hope to be a good wife to Tzsayn, and to be that I look forward to talking to him, getting to know him, finding out about his interests.'

'His *interests* are of no concern to you. What is of interest and concern to me is that you do not express an opinion that counters that of the king.'

'I've never expressed any opinion that doesn't agree with Father's.'

'You implied to your maid that your marriage could be improved upon and that you don't wish to marry Prince Tzsayn.'

'No, I merely said that Diana's marriage could be successful in a different way.'

'To disagree with the king's plans for you is unacceptable.'

'I'm disagreeing with you, not with the king's plans for me.'

'I often wonder,' Noyes interrupted, 'at what point a traitor is made. When precisely the line is crossed between loyalty and betrayal.'

Catherine straightened her back. 'I have crossed no line.'

And she hadn't: she had done nothing, except think of Ambrose.

'In my experience . . . and, Princess Catherine, I do consider my experience in this area to be considerable,' murmured Noyes. 'In my experience, a traitor in the heart and mind is soon a traitor in deed.'

And, the way he looked at her, it felt as if he truly could see inside Catherine's head. But she stared back at him, saying, 'I am no traitor. I will marry Prince Tzsayn.' Catherine knew this to be true. She would soon be married to a man she'd never even met, but she couldn't help her mind and her heart belonging elsewhere. Couldn't help that she thought of Ambrose constantly, loved her conversations with him, contrived to be close to him and, yes, had once touched his arm. Of course, if Ambrose touched her, he'd be executed, but she didn't see why she couldn't touch him. But were these thoughts and one touch really traitorous deeds?

'It's best to be clear where the line is, Princess Catherine,' Noyes said quietly.

'I'm clear, thank you, Noyes.'

'And also to be clear on the consequences.' He waved his hand casually, almost dismissively. 'And to that end you are required to attend the execution of the Norwend traitor, and witness what happens to those who betray the king.'

'A punishment, a warning and a lesson, all rolled neatly into one.' Catherine mimicked Noyes's hand wave.

Noyes's face was blank as he replied, 'It's the king's command, Your Highness.'

Sadly Diana had had a nasty trip down some stone stairs the day after Catherine's interview and had been unable to resume her duties because of a broken arm. Catherine's other maids, Sarah and Tanya, had been with Diana at the time but somehow had been unable to prevent the accident. 'We agree with Noyes, Your Highness,' Tanya had said with a smile. 'Traitors should be punished . . .'

Catherine was brought back to the present by shouts from the crowd: 'Bradwell! Bradwell!'

Two men had come up the steps on to the scaffold, both dressed in black. The older man held up his hand to the people. His young and surprisingly cherubic assistant carried the tools of their trade: a sword and simple black hood.

'It's Bradwell,' Harold said unnecessarily, leaning over Boris to Catherine. 'He's carried out over a hundred executions. A hundred and forty-one, I think it is. And he never takes more than one strike.'

'A hundred and forty-one,' Catherine echoed. She wondered how many of them Harold had witnessed.

Bradwell was walking across the scaffold, swinging his sword arm as if warming up his shoulder muscles, and flexing his head from side to side and then round. Harold rolled his eyes. 'Shits, he looks ridiculous. Gateacre should have been given the job.'

'I believe the Marquess of Norwend requested Bradwell and the king obliged,' Boris said. 'Norwend wanted it done cleanly and seemed to think Bradwell was best. But there are no guarantees on that score.'

'Gateacre has a clean cut too,' Harold said.

'I agree. He would have been my choice. Bradwell is looking rather past it. Still, it might add another level of interest if he botches the job.'

At the mention of the Marquess of Norwend, Catherine's gaze had moved to the opposite side of the scaffold to the other raised viewing platform. She had felt it too risky to discuss the people there unprompted, but now that Boris had brought the subject up she felt she could ask, 'Is that the Marquess of Norwend on the other platform, in the green jacket?'

'Indeed. And all the Norwend clan with him,' Boris replied. Though Catherine noted it was only the male members of the family. 'The traitor's kin must witness the execution; indeed, they must call for the traitor's death or they will lose their titles and all their lands.'

Catherine knew the law well enough. 'And what of their honour?'

Boris snorted. 'They're trying to cling on to that, but if they can't even control one of their own they'll struggle to maintain their position at court.'

'Honour and position at court being one and the same,' Catherine replied.

Boris looked at Catherine. 'As I said, they're barely clinging on to either.' He turned back to the opposite platform, adding, 'I see your guard is with them, though thankfully he's not in uniform.'

Catherine didn't dare comment. Was Ambrose not wearing the Royal Guard's uniform as a mark of respect for royalty or disrespect for them? She knew he had his own views on honour. He talked of doing the right thing, of wanting to defend Brigant and of helping make the country great again, not for self-gain but to help all in the country who were suffering in poverty.

She had noticed Ambrose when she'd taken her seat and had forced herself to turn away, but now Boris had mentioned him she could allow herself a slightly longer look. His hair, golden white in the sunlight, was loose and falling in soft waves around his face and shoulders. He was wearing a black jacket with leather straps and silver buckles, black trousers and boots. His face was solemn and pale. He was staring at the executioner and hadn't shifted his gaze towards Catherine since her arrival.

Catherine looked at Ambrose for as long as she would an ordinary man, then she made herself turn away, but still his image lingered in her head: his hair, his shoulders, his lips . . .

A flurry of courtiers appeared from behind the scaffold. From the way they were stepping back and bowing, it was obvious that her father was on his way. Catherine's heart beat erratically. She had lived a sheltered life in the queen's wing of the castle with her mother and maids, going weeks or months without seeing her father. For her, his one and only daughter, his presence was still an occasion.

The king appeared, walking quickly, his red-and-black jacket emphasizing his wide shoulders, his tall hat adding to his height. Catherine rose swiftly to her feet and demurely lowered her head as she sank into a deep curtsy. She was on a platform above the king but her head should be lower than his. Tall as her father was, it was still a contortion. Catherine held her stomach tight and thighs tense in a semi-crouch. Her corset dug sharply into her waist. She concentrated on the discomfort, knowing she'd outlast it. Out of the corner of her eye she could see the king. He leapt on to the royal platform, strode forward and the crowd, on seeing him clearly, cheered and a long, slow shout went up: 'Aloysius! Aloysius!'

Boris rose from his bow and Catherine waited the required two extra counts before lifting her head. The king was motionless, looking to the crowd, and he didn't acknowledge Catherine at all. Then he sat on the seat next to Harold, red cushions having appeared moments before to ease his royal rump. Catherine stood, feeling the relief in her stomach. Harold too had straightened from his bow and stood stiffly, hesitating before sitting, though Catherine was sure he'd be delighted to be next to the king. She waited for Boris to sit and then she straightened her skirt and retook her own place.

Things moved quickly now. The king wasn't noted for his patience, after all. More men ascended the scaffold. There were four men in black and four in guard uniforms and, barely seen among them, diminished, small and frail, was the prisoner.

The crowd jeered and shouted, 'Traitor!' Then, 'Whore!' and 'Bitch!' and worse, much worse.

There were words Catherine knew and had occasionally come across in reading but had never heard spoken, not even by Boris, and now they were flying through the air around her. They were more powerful than she'd known words could be, and they were not beautiful, poetic or clever, but base and vulgar, like a slap in the face.

Catherine caught a glimpse of Ambrose, still and stiff opposite her, his face contorted as the crowd jeered and insulted his sister. Catherine shut her eyes.

Boris hissed in her ear, 'You're not looking, princess. You're here to see what happens to traitors. It's for your own good. So, if you don't turn to face the scaffold, I'll pin your eyes open myself.'

Catherine didn't doubt Boris's sincerity. She opened her eyes and turned back to the scaffold.

Lady Anne Norwend was dressed in a gown of blue silk with silver lace. Her jewels sparkled in the sunlight and her blonde hair, pinned up, glowed gold. In normal times, Lady Anne was considered beautiful, but today was far from normal. Now she was painfully thin, her skin pale, and she was held upright by two guards. But most noticeable of all was her mouth: thick black lines of twine stretched from her top lip to her bottom where her mouth had been sewn up, and dried blood covered her chin and neck. Her tongue had already been cut out. Catherine wanted to look at Ambrose, but didn't dare turn to him, couldn't bear to see him again. What must he be thinking to see his sister like this? Catherine stared in the direction of Lady Anne and found the way to do it was to concentrate on the guard holding her up, and how fat his fingers were and how tight his grip was.

The king's speaker stepped forward to address the crowd, demanding silence. When the din subsided he began reading from a scroll, listing Lady Anne's crimes. 'Luring a married man into temptation' referred to her relationship with Sir Oswald Pence. 'Failing to attend on the king when requested' meant fleeing with Sir Oswald when Noyes and his men confronted them. 'Murder of the king's men' meant just that and, hard as it was to believe looking at Lady Anne now, she had herself stabbed one of the king's soldiers in the fight that left three dead including Sir Oswald. The murder was the key reason she was to be executed; murder of one of the king's men was tantamount to killing the king himself – it was high treason, and so, to round his speech off, the speaker said, 'And for being a traitor to Brigant and our glorious king.'

The crowd went wild.

'The traitor, murderer and whore is to be stripped of all possessions, which are forfeit to the king.'

One of the black-clothed men approached Lady Anne and began removing her jewels one by one. Each time he took an item – a brooch, a ring, a bracelet – there were cheers and shouts from the crowd. Each item was put into a casket held by another man. When the jewels were all removed, that man took a knife and cut the back of her dress, and a fresh cheer from the crowd rose as the gown was ripped from her shoulders. Lady Anne was almost dragged off her feet, but the guard pulled her upright and held her. The crowd bayed again like a pack of hounds and began a chant of 'Strip! Strip! Strip!'

Lady Anne was left in her underdress, clutching its thin fabric to her chest. Her hands were shaking and Catherine could see that her fingers were misshapen and broken. At first Catherine didn't understand why, but then she realized that it was part of the ritual of a traitor's execution. Those condemned for treason were not allowed to communicate with the king's loyal subjects and so had their tongues cut out, their lips sewn up. But, as all court ladies in Brigant used hand signs to speak to each other when they were not allowed to use words, Lady Anne had had her hands broken too.

One of the men loosened Lady Anne's hair, which was long and fine and the palest of yellows. He took a handful and cut it at the nape of her neck. He held the hair and that too went in the casket. Finally she was left near naked, shivering despite the summer sun, the tattered gown almost transparent and clinging to her legs where she had wet herself. It seemed even Lady Anne's dignity was forfeit to the king.

Turning from Lady Anne, the speaker called to the platform opposite, 'What do you say to this traitor?'

Her father, the marquess, a tall, grey-haired man, came forward. He straightened his back and cleared his throat.

27

'You have betrayed your country and your glorious king. You have betrayed my family and myself, all loyal subjects who have nurtured you and trusted you. You have betrayed my trust and my family's name. It would have been better if you had not been born. I denounce you and call for your execution as a traitor.'

Catherine looked for Lady Anne's reaction. She stared back at her father and seemed to stand more upright. In turn, five other male relatives – her two uncles and two cousins and her elder brother, Tarquin, who was close in looks to Ambrose, with the same blond hair – came forward and shouted their denouncements of a similar kind and called at the end for her execution. After each censure the crowd cheered and then went silent for the next person. And after each one Lady Anne seemed to grow in strength and stature. At first Catherine was surprised at this, but she too began to sit taller. The more they demeaned Lady Anne, the more she wanted to show them how strong she was.

The last to step forward was Ambrose. He opened his mouth but no words came out. His brother leant towards him and spoke. Catherine could read Tarquin's lips as he said, 'Please, Ambrose. You have to do it.'

Ambrose took a breath before saying in a voice that was clear but hardly raised, 'You are a traitor to Brigant and the king. I call for your execution.' His brother put his hand on Ambrose's shoulder. Ambrose continued staring at Lady Anne as tears rolled down his cheeks. The crowd didn't cheer.

Boris said, 'I do believe he's weeping. He's as weak as a woman.'

However, Lady Anne was not crying. Instead, she made a sign: her hand on her heart, the simple sign of love for Ambrose. Then she turned and her eyes met Catherine's. Lady Anne moved her right hand up as if to wipe a tear, as her left hand went to her chest. It was a movement so smooth, so disguised, it was hardly noticeable. But Catherine had been reading signs since childhood and this was one of the first she had learnt. It meant 'Watch me'. Then Lady Anne made the sign of a kiss with her right hand, while her left swept downwards and clenched into what looked like an attempt at a fist. Catherine frowned. A fist held before the groin was the sign of anger, hate, a threat. To pair it with a kiss was strange. Then another sign: 'boy'. Lady Anne turned to stare at the king and was making another sign, but the man holding her arm had moved in the way.

Catherine didn't know Lady Anne; she'd never spoken to her, had seen her in court only once. Catherine was confined to her quarters for so much of her life that seeing other women was hardly more common than seeing and talking to men. Had she imagined the signs?

Lady Anne was brought forward and forced to kneel on a low wooden block. She looked down, and then turned so her eyes met Catherine's again, and there was no mistaking their intensity. What was she trying to say, at the very moment of her death?

Bradwell, the executioner, was wearing his hood now but his mouth was still visible, and he said, 'Look ahead or I can't guarantee it'll be clean.'

Lady Anne turned to face the crowd.

Bradwell raised the sword above his head and the sunlight bounced off it into Catherine's eyes. The crowd hushed. Bradwell came a step forward and then to the side, perhaps to assess the angle of his cut, then he went behind Lady Anne, circled the sword in the air over his own head once, took a half step forward, swirled the sword over his head once more, and in a continuous movement made a sideways slice so fast that it appeared for a moment as though nothing had happened.

Lady Anne's head fell first, hitting the wooden floor with a thud, and then rolled to the edge of the scaffold. Behind it, blood fanned from the neck of the slowly toppling body. The crowd's cheer was like a physical blow and Catherine swayed back on her seat.

Bradwell moved forward, retrieved the head and held it up by the hair. A chant of 'Pike her' went up. Bradwell's assistant stepped forward with a pike and the crowd's frenzy increased further.

Somehow, across the scaffold and the roaring mob, Catherine's eyes met Ambrose's. She held his gaze, wanting to comfort him, to tell him she was sorry. She needed him to know that she was not like her father or her brother, that she didn't choose to be here, that despite the impossible distance between them she cared.

Boris hissed in her ear, 'You're not looking at Lady Anne, sister.'

Catherine turned. Lady Anne's head was being put on a pike, and there was Noyes standing at the foot of the scaffold, a half-smile on his lips as he turned his attention from her to Ambrose. And Catherine realized she'd been a fool: this wasn't a punishment, a warning or a lesson.

It was a trap.

Ambrose

BRIGANE, BRIGANT

'Couldn't you, for once, do as I command?'

It felt like the old days. When Ambrose used to live at home he had a regular summons to his father's study to be reprimanded about some disobedience or other, and now, two years after he'd left, Ambrose was back, standing before his father's desk. But things were different. The house his father had rented for his visit to the capital wasn't the usual smart mansion but a shabby villa. His father too seemed worn. His face was sagging slightly and there were more lines around his eyes, and for all his bluster and noise he seemed smaller. And of course there was another significant difference – his sister was now dead, her head on a pike on the city bridge.

'Can you have the decency to answer me, sir!'

'Which command in particular were you concerned about, Father?'

'You know what I'm talking about. I told you what had to be said in the denouncement and told you to sound like you meant it.'

'Well, as it turned out, no, I could not in this instance do as you commanded.'

'What is it with you, Ambrose?' His father pushed back from the desk, shaking his head.

'What is it that means I couldn't denounce my sister? I don't know, sir. Perhaps I believe her to be a good person. A good sister and a good daughter. The bigger question in my mind is how you could do it, and do it so well.'

Ambrose's father was still now. 'You are as impertinent as you are naive, Ambrose. You are my son and I expect more of you.'

'And Anne was your daughter. I expected more of you. You should have protected her with your life.'

'You, boy, do not tell me what I should do.' Ambrose's father lowered his voice. 'She killed one of the king's men. We're lucky it wasn't every one of us on the block. The king is looking for any chance to add to his income. We could have lost everything.'

Ambrose sneered. 'Well, I'm glad you know your priorities. It must be a relief to still have your lands even though you've no daughter.'

'You are pushing me too far this time, Ambrose. I warn you to stop now.'

But Ambrose couldn't stop. 'And I wouldn't worry about falling out of favour with the king. You denounced Anne beautifully. I'm sure the king, Noyes and all the court were impressed with your words, your manner, your loyalty. And, after all, what does it matter to you about your truth, your virtue or your honour?'

Ambrose's father shot to his feet. 'Get out! Get out of here before I have you whipped out.'

Ambrose was already leaving, slamming the door after him and striding down the corridor. Tarquin was running towards him.

'I could hear it all from across the courtyard.'

Ambrose strode past his brother. Outside and with nowhere to go he stopped and roared his frustration, hitting and kicking the wall.

Tarquin came to stand by him. He watched and winced. And waited for Ambrose to calm.

Eventually Ambrose stopped and rubbed the blood and broken skin from his knuckles. 'What is it with that man? A few words with him and I'm kicking walls and breaking my own fists.'

'He misses you and he cares about you. I admit he has a strange way of showing it. I suspect you miss him – and you have a strange way of showing it too.'

Ambrose gave a short laugh.

'It's good to see you smile.'

Ambrose leant his head against the stone of the wall. 'There've been few reasons to smile recently.'

'For any of us.' Tarquin put his hand on Ambrose's shoulder. 'You know Father loved Anne. Loves her still. This has hurt him deeply.'

'And yet he still denounced her.'

'What else could he do, Ambrose? She'd been found guilty. If he didn't denounce her, the king would take our lands. All the people in Norwend who depend on him would lose too. The king would win more. Father had to be convincing.'

Ambrose couldn't answer. He scraped his forehead against the rough stone.

'Anne would understand, Ambrose. She knew the law as well as anyone. She knew Father loved her. It's not right what happened, but don't blame him.'

'But what they did to her . . .'

Ambrose had thought many times of Noyes's men torturing his sister, the pain and the insults she must have endured, and yet she had stood tall at the end. He was so proud of her. Her intelligence and independence inspired him, though most lords wouldn't see those as good things. Anne had been extraordinary for a Brigantine woman – even for a man she would have been unusual. She had travelled widely, to Pitoria and beyond. She spoke several languages and had helped Ambrose and Tarquin to learn Pitorian. Ambrose remembered the lessons fondly as she encouraged him, saying, 'No, make it more guttural, from the back of the throat'; and to Tarquin, 'Don't stand so stiffly. Your hands and your body speak too.'

And her own hands, which had signed so swiftly and so well, at the end were broken, that quick tongue cut out, those smiling lips sewn shut forever. What must she have been thinking, as they did it to her? Would she have just wanted to die as quickly as possible? Probably. She'd been captive for three weeks before her execution. Every day they would have tormented her. She was so thin at the execution. And all he could do was watch – and denounce her too.

Ambrose felt Tarquin's embrace and only then realized he was crying again. He spoke quietly, still facing the wall. 'I don't believe she was guilty. I mean, I can believe she killed the soldier, but she would only do that to protect herself. But I don't believe she and Sir Oswald were lovers. They were friends since childhood; he encouraged her to learn. She admired him and valued him as a friend. And, anyway, since when is the king bothered who has a lover? Half the court would be in his dungeons if that was the case. Though what they were doing way over in the west, I don't know. That's never been explained properly. Something else was going on; I'm sure of that.'

Tarquin replied almost in a whisper. 'I don't believe we know the true story either, Ambrose, but I'm not foolish enough to say that to anyone but you.'

'I'm a fool, do you think?'

'You're honourable and true, Ambrose. And I admire you for your virtue.'

Ambrose smiled through his tears. 'I'll take that as a yes.'

Tarquin was serious, though. 'None of us really know what happened to Anne or Sir Oswald, but, whatever it was, it was against the king. I've just lost my sister; I don't want to lose my brother too. I know you found it almost impossible to denounce Anne, but it was obvious you didn't mean what you said. Small details like that can be enough to bring a man down when they're against the king. Loyalty is all he wants and expects. Total loyalty.'

'And loyalty to my sister? That counts for nothing?'

'Aloysius believes he comes first, you know that.'

'So you think I'm doomed?'

Tarquin shook his head. 'No, but I think it's dangerous for you here in Brigane now.'

'It's dangerous everywhere now.'

'That's not true. But we're not welcome here. At court hardly anyone meets Father's eye and even fewer talk with him. He's been invited to dine with no one since our arrival, and no one has accepted his invitations to call on us; they're all suddenly very busy with other engagements.'

'Father should count himself lucky. They're all two-faced rats. I wouldn't trust any of them.'

'Being ostracized isn't a positive thing, Ambrose. With no allies at court, we're weak. Back home, among our people, we'll be safer.' Tarquin took a deep breath. 'Father and I are returning north to Norwend tomorrow. Why don't you come with us? At home you'll be away from the Royal Guard, the court, and from the king.'

'My work is with the Royal Guard. I swore an oath to protect the princess. I'm not going to run away.'

Tarquin sighed. 'Your work is another thing that's dangerous, brother. I saw that look you shared with the princess at the execution. You show your feelings so plainly on your face, Ambrose. Noyes and Prince Boris will have noticed too. Noyes notices everything.'

'So now I can't even look at someone without them seeing a crime?'

And all he had done was look at Princess Catherine. He had to look at her. Her father and Boris appeared triumphant, but Catherine was different. She was so sad but calm too. Looking at her had helped him bear the sadness and pain.

Ambrose saw Catherine most days as he stood guard outside her chambers, rode with her, occasionally spoke with her. Ambrose loved the way she smiled and laughed. He loved how she answered Boris back, with wit and spirit and intelligence. He loved how she took on different personas, provoking Boris by being outrageous, but only with Ambrose would she be sweet and gentle and thoughtful. At least as far as he knew, only with him – and was it wrong that it irked him to think she might be sweet and gentle to other men? He loved the way she slid her slim foot into the stirrup and how she sat so strong and upright in the saddle and yet how, that hot day at the end of last summer, she'd ridden her horse into the sea with a look of such freedom and wildness, and jumped off, laughing, and swum around his own horse. He despaired when Boris heard of it and for two weeks she wasn't permitted to ride at all and had never swum again. He despaired that somehow they'd ruin Catherine as they'd ruined Anne. And yet somehow, so far, she wasn't ruined by them; she was as strong as them.

Tarquin nudged him. 'As I said, you show your feelings on your face, and I'd call that look "love".'

'Admiration, respect and, I admit, a certain level of fondness are what you see on my face.' Ambrose nudged Tarquin back, though he couldn't stop himself from smiling.

'Well, make sure that's all anyone sees. And make it a lower level of fondness too.'

'Take comfort, brother. This look of fondness will soon be replaced with a look of utter boredom: Princess Catherine leaves for Pitoria in a week to be married to a prince and I'll remain here, a lowly soldier and guard.'

'Still, you need to take care, Ambrose. Noyes was watching you closely.'

'Stop worrying! Even Noyes can't persecute me for a look.'

March

CALIA, CALIDOR

March stood still and silent by the drinks table. He was supposed to look straight ahead at the wall opposite but if he angled his head slightly to the right he could see as much as he needed.

Lord Regan sat with Prince Thelonius in the bay window at the far end of the room. The prince was leaning forward to Regan, almost looking up at him, almost asking rather than commanding. Regan rubbed his face with one hand and gave a short nod. The prince leant back and said loudly, 'Good. My thanks.' March had angled his head back to look at the wall as the prince called, 'Refreshments!'

March picked up the carafe of wine and the silver platter of grapes and moved towards the two men. He could feel the difference in mood. The prince was still looking tired; he'd aged ten years in the few weeks since his wife and young sons had died. However, his eyes now appeared not so empty; he was almost smiling. Prince Thelonius had seen few visitors and even Regan had been kept away since their tempestuous meeting after the funeral, but in the last few days things had changed. The prince had woken earlier, dressed, bathed, talked lucidly, and last night he had demanded Regan be sent for.

March poured the wine. Since his wife died, the prince had started drinking during the day. Not much, but every day, and that didn't look to be changing.

'Water for me,' Regan said.

March put the grapes down and walked deftly back to his position. He picked up the water pitcher and selected the wooden bowl of hazelnuts rather than the plate of dried apples, which looked unappetizing. He returned slowly, studying the two men again as he approached.

While the prince's demeanour had improved, Lord Regan's certainly had not. Regan, the trusted, closest, oldest friend of the prince, was typical of the lords of Calidor: attractive in the way of the rich, powerful, strong and healthy. He wore a frown now. It suited him no less than his smile. But then everything suited him. Today he wore a gold-coloured velvet jacket that glistened when it caught the sun and emphasized the breadth of his shoulders, as did the finely plaited brown leather straps that criss-crossed from his chest down to his hips, the straps holding his knives. Regan was the only man permitted to be armed in the presence of the prince; the only man able to frown while the prince smiled.

March put the bowl down carefully, moved the grape platter a little to the side, adjusted the bowl of nuts a final time.

'Your barbarian boy seems determined to be slow today,' Regan growled.

'Take your anger out on me not him, my friend,' the prince replied gently.

March poured the water slowly. He would have loved to throw it in Regan's face, but he concentrated on the slow and steady stream, letting Regan's words wash off him.

March was used to receiving the occasional slight, though it was rare for a lord to lower himself to comment on a servant. Mostly the insults March received were mild: 'jokes' about the prince having civilized him, or being referred to as 'the last of the Abasks'. Sometimes there was genuine interest, though that was mainly about his eyes, as people would stare into them and tell him their opinion, which was usually either 'amazing' or 'freak'. One young lord only the previous month had demanded March stand in the light so he could see them better, remarking, 'I'd heard that Abasks had ice eyes, but there's blue and silver in there with the white.' He'd ended by saying, 'Most unpleasant.' Sometimes people commented that they thought all the Abasks had been killed. March had used to think that too, until he met Holywell.

'I'm not angry,' Lord Regan said. 'Can't I disagree, though?' It seemed his anger was making him raise his voice, March noted as he made a snail-paced return to his post by the table.

'You're my friend. I need your help. I asked as a friend.' The prince's words were also raised enough for March to hear them now.

'And afterwards? What do you think will happen? You are respected, but this isn't like bringing in some Abask brat to wait on tables.'

March lost the prince's reply as he was thinking, *Fuck you! Fuck you!*

Regan was right, of course; Prince Thelonius was respected and March was nothing but a servant, a virtual slave. The prince represented all that was civilized and refined; March, all that was primitive and uncultured. The prince had a reputation for wisdom, honour and fairness; Abasks had a reputation for being mountain-dwelling trolls.

March had worked for the prince for eight years – half his life – and he'd learnt about his home country and his people from the Calidorians. There was no one else to learn from as Abask had been destroyed in the war between Calidor and Brigant. Prince Thelonius had been granted the princedom of Calidor by his father and had refused to hand it over to his brother, King Aloysius of Brigant, on their father's death. Then they had fought, as only brothers could, with hate more passionate because they shared the same blood, and as only rulers could – with armies.

It was an uneven fight. Brigant was bigger and stronger and Aloysius the more experienced leader, but Prince Thelonius had something Aloysius could never claim: the love of his people. He treated the citizens of Calidor well, taxed them fairly and ensured the laws were applied wisely. Aloysius ruled Brigant through terror and violence. The Calidorians feared Aloysius and loved Thelonius.

Abask, the beautiful, small mountainous region that was March's birthplace, lay on the border between the kingdoms but had always been considered part of Calidor. When Aloysius invaded, his armies burned their way across Abask, aiming for the Calidorian capital, Calia. Thelonius's army was almost overwhelmed. Pulling all his forces back into a defence of the city, Thelonius managed to hold Calia for over a year, before counter-attacking and driving Aloysius's army back across the border to Brigant, when, finally, a truce was declared.

Brigant was despairing, their treasury empty and their army depleted. Calidor was exhausted but jubilant at having thrown back the bigger invader in a glorious and honourable defence against greater odds. The bonds with the Savaants to the south improved further, trade grew in the following years, Calidorian farms and vineyards prospered, and the towns were rebuilt. Few Calidorians cared about what had happened to the mountain people of Abask. And there were few Abasks left to care either: the Abask fighters had been wiped out in the first battles of the war and Abask was overrun, its surviving people left to starve or taken as slaves by the Brigantines.

Only seven years old when the war began, March's own memories were vague. He remembered being told his father had been killed, and his mother and sisters died at some point but he wasn't sure when. Mainly he remembered his older brother, Julien, holding his hand as they went in search of food. He couldn't actually remember the feeling of being hungry, but he knew he must have been because he definitely did recall eating grass. But mainly he remembered holding Julien's hand and walking day after day until Julien collapsed, and some Calidorian soldiers returning from the border had prised him off his brother's dead body and carried him to the safety and warmth of the prince's camp.

March used to think of himself as lucky: lucky that he'd not starved; lucky that he'd been rescued by the Calidorians not the Brigantines; lucky that the prince had taken him in and trained him to be his personal servant; lucky to have enough food to eat every day.

He thought all that until he met Holywell.

March had been back to the land that had once been Abask, when he was travelling nearby with the prince. He'd slipped away from the royal entourage and climbed up into the rugged mountains. He'd hoped to remember places or recognize some feature of the landscape, but in honesty it all seemed strange: more rugged and inhospitable than he'd thought. After three days he returned to the prince, telling him some of the truth.

'I needed to see it, sire.'

'And what did you find?'

'The mountains remain, and a few ruins, but the bracken and woods have reclaimed the land. No one is living there.'

The prince had smiled sadly. 'It was always a tough existence, living in the mountains. Your people were strong and resourceful.'

And left by you to starve or to be taken into slavery, March wanted to shout in the prince's face.

'Well, I'm glad you returned to me, March. I was lost without you.'

And March had taken a breath and forced out his reply. 'It's right that I should come back to you, sire. After all you've done for me.'

Of course March didn't mention that he had met Holywell. They'd spotted each other from across the valley near his village ruins. Holywell had waved and approached, and March's heart had leapt when he'd seen Holywell's eyes were as pale and icy as his own.

Nor did March mention to the prince that he'd spent two days with Holywell, who had told him a different history of the war.

Holywell had known March's family and told him how March's father was killed in the first attack at the bridge at Riel; how his uncles died in the following battle at Teem, where the Abask troops were massacred as they led an attack that the Calidorians failed to support. How, after that battle, Aloysius occupied Abask and began to systematically destroy everything within it. How the Abask leaders sent a plea to Thelonius to come to their aid, but the prince, determined to protect his capital, refused. How the Abasks suffered for two long years, hiding in the mountains if they could, as Aloysius's army destroyed their homes, crops and animals and reduced their beautiful country to a wasteland of burnt-out villages and graves filled with the bodies of starved Abask children.

March had vague memories of his father and uncles, and Holywell spoke Abask like them, swore like them, even laughed as March thought he remembered his father had. Holywell had almost died in the war – he showed March the scars on his body, saying, 'The Brigantines cut me to shreds but I didn't die. I asked them to kill me and they laughed. Despite the hardships, I healed. I worked for them, a slave to start with, all the worst jobs, but with time I realized I didn't want to die any more; I wanted to get my revenge.' He smiled. 'And I will. The Brigantines killed my family and your family. But they were an honourable enemy and I work for them still. My real enemy is Prince Thelonius. He was sworn to protect our land. He said he was our brother. But he betrayed us. For that there is no forgiveness. For that there can only be revenge.'

Holywell had said all this in Abask and March thought it was the best speech he'd ever heard. It was the nearest thing to brotherhood that he had felt in years.

He also felt like a fool for believing the lies he'd been told. The prince was not the heroic winner of wars against all odds but a monster who'd sacrificed a whole people so that the fat merchants of Calia could continue to live in safety and he could still sit on the throne.

Holywell had shown him the truth – that no one in Calidor gave two fucks about Abask. Holywell spat on the Calidorians and their 'civilized' ways and now so did March. Holywell was Abask and proud of it, and so was March.

March asked, 'But how can we be Abask when Abask doesn't exist any more?'

Holywell jabbed March in his chest. 'In there is Abask. In there. In your soul, your spirit. Thelonius will destroy that too if you let him. He'll try to civilize you and turn you into one of them. Don't let him. Remember your father, your uncles, your brother. They were proud to be Abask, as should you be.'

Holywell encouraged March to return to his position with the prince and told him to stand patiently and wait and listen – and to keep Holywell informed of anything that might be useful to avenge the Abask people.

Now, out of the corner of his eye, March watched the prince slide from his finger the gold ring with his emblem on it: an eagle with a green emerald for an eye. Regan took the ring and put it inside his jacket, and March was certain that his days of patiently waiting and listening were nearing an end.

Tash

Tash was still running. She was pushing as hard as she could. And still she could hear the demon's breath behind her. This was all wrong. The demon was too close. Somehow she had to go faster.

A slope down to the right. It'd give her more speed.

But the pit was to the left.

The demon's breath was louder.

Shit! Tash veered to the right down the slope under some low branches. She heard them snap behind her but could no longer hear the demon's breath.

She'd increased the distance between them but she couldn't keep this pace up. And she'd gone off the direct route to the pit, gone to the right of one tree and then been forced further right by another. She needed to go left and that was up, but she had to get back to the pit.

There was a large tree ahead and to its left a large boulder. She could use them. She'd have to.

Tash ran towards the tree, driving hard at it, and at the last moment put her arms out, pushing off from the trunk, using her momentum to change direction, veering behind the boulder and up the slope. The branches were low here, perfect for her to scramble under, using her hands as well as her feet, up the slope, pushing hard. Behind her she heard the demon hiss and then a scream of frustration.

At the top of the slope she glanced behind but could only see branches, not the demon. No time to look harder. She had to keep going. It was downhill now and the ground was firmer. Tash let her stride widen out. Soon she'd be at the pit. She kept going, panting hard, nearly there, nearly there . . . and then she was in the clearing.

The pit was ahead, but she was at the wrong angle for leaping into the end of it. And where was the demon? She couldn't hear it. She glanced behind, slowing slightly. There was no demon there.

She slowed to a walk. Panting hard. Straining to hear the demon. She turned back to look.

Nothing.

She came to a stop and looked around her for a movement in the trees, for a hint of purple or red, for anything.

Nothing.

Shits. Where was it?

She looked over to Gravell, his face mostly hidden behind a tree. He didn't move.

She looked all around again and back the way she'd come.

No movement. No noise.

No demon.

Shits!

It wouldn't give up the chase, would it?

This had never happened before. What should she do? She didn't want to go back into the trees. That would be madness.

She looked over to Gravell and held out her arms as if to ask, *Now what?*

Gravell stepped to the side and made the same gesture.

They stared at each other for a moment, then Gravell glanced to Tash's left and swung back to her, roaring out, 'Run!'

Tash turned. The demon was coming towards her at full speed, already out of the trees. Its tall, slim human-like form was coming at her fast. On open ground it had the advantage. She couldn't outrun it now.

Gravell shouted, 'The pit! Get to the pit!'

The demon looked to Gravell and that gave Tash a moment to move. Her boots dug into the hard snow and she scrambled forward and leapt into the pit. The demon leapt too, landing at one end of the pit and sliding towards Tash, who had jolted hard on the ice in the bottom halfway along, catching her hands on the bloody wall. Her boots gripped on the ice and she turned and hurtled forward, grabbed for the rope and yanked it down. Her hands were tight on the rope as she began to rise. But then something wrapped round her ankle, and Tash's hands slid down the rope until they stopped at the knotted end.

The demon was holding her foot!

Tash screamed and clung on to the rope as she kicked out frantically, hitting something, and she kicked again and again, and then she was free and flying through the air, arms and legs flailing, not a lazy yawn but a floundering cartwheel, and she grabbed on to anything she could of the tree, still tangled in rope, and clung there. And clung there. And clung there.

The demon had touched her. She'd never been touched by a demon before.

Now the demon screamed and Tash clung tighter to the tree.

Another scream and Tash looked round. Gravell was throwing his second harpoon. Tash could just see over the edge of the pit. The first harpoon had pierced the demon's side; the second went through its stomach. Gravell held the third spear aloft. Waiting. The demon fell back against the walls of the pit and slid out of sight.

Gravell glanced up at Tash, then he jumped into the pit.

Tash didn't want to let go of her branch, but she forced herself to release her grip and slithered uncomfortably down the tree, hitting the ground hard and going over on her ankle, the snow cold on her foot. She only now realized that her boot was gone.

She limped over to the pit.

The demon was sprawled out in the bottom. Her spiked boot was in its hand.

Gravell was leaning over the demon, holding a glass bottle close to the demon's mouth.

Tash jumped down into the pit and yelped as her ankle buckled again. Gravell ignored her, his attention purely on the smoke. The demon was a deep purple with ruddy red patches and a few streaks of orange. It was naked. It had a handsome face, narrow shoulders, narrow waist, long arms. No wonder it had been hard to outrun; its legs were twice the length of Tash's. She looked at its private parts. She thought they were odd-looking, but from what she knew they were like any man's. She'd seen Gravell's private parts when he bathed in the lakes and streams, but she'd never been that close to Gravell and mostly what she'd seen of him was hair.

This demon, like all demons, had no hair. His skin was smooth. His eyes were half closed and Tash knelt to see the colour of the eyes. In the demon world they'd looked purple, but now here in the moonlight they were a softer colour, lilac. They were beautiful. His face was beautiful. He looked young, like a boy only a little older than her. Tash had to fight back that thought. He wasn't a *him*; he was an *it*, a demon.

The first curl of smoke rose out of the demon's mouth and Gravell held the bottle upside down, catching the tip of the curl. Demon smoke was their blood, but Tash thought it was also like their last breath, their spirit. The smoke left the demon's body and rose steadily into the bottle, nothing escaping. If the first wisp went in, the rest followed, almost as if the smoke wanted to stay together. It was a dark plummy red to start with but then the rest was purple, like the smoke from the other demon they'd had trouble catching.

The colour in the bottle was intense and darkening as still more smoke came and somehow it fitted into the bottle. Then the flow thinned, paled to lilac, and stopped. The bottle contained a swirling purple mass. Gravell took the cork from his mouth and still holding the bottle upside down he stoppered it. After doing that he kissed the bottle and said, 'Perfect,' as he always did. Then he turned to Tash. 'What the shitting shits were you doing?'

'Um . . .'

'He was almost on you. He *was* on you.'

'He was fast. Have you seen the length of his legs?'

'You came from the wrong direction!'

'He cut me off. I had to veer round. I told you he was fast.'

'So that'll explain why you stopped then?'

'I thought he'd given up.'

Gravell shook his head. 'Are you stupid? They don't give up. Ever.'

'Look, I got the demon here, didn't I? I jumped into the pit. The demon jumped in after me. You killed the demon. Sounds like it went well to me.'

Gravell swore under his breath. He stood up. 'If that's it going well . . .'

'And you've got the smoke.' Tash looked at the bottle and then at the dead demon. 'He seems younger than normal. Maybe that's why he acted a bit differently. Good job you bought me the spiked boots. Another pace closer and . . .'

'Another *half* pace and you wouldn't have got out of his grasp.'

'You worried for me?'

'Huh. More like I was worried that two kroners on boots was wasted.'

Tash smiled and tapped her finger on the bottle. 'Good smoke there. That should buy lots of boots.' She yanked her boot from the dead demon's grasp.

'Boots is all you think about. You should be thinking of the job in hand before you think of boots. And you forgot to bring the ladder. You're going to have to climb out.'

As she put on her boot, Tash looked at the walls of the pit, lined with blood and guts, and sighed.

'Give me a boost up then.'

Gravell bent down and made a cradle with his hands and she stepped on it, careful not to pierce his hand with her boot spikes. She needed to steady herself. The pit wall was covered with blood but at least it was dead; who knew what nasty things were crawling in Gravell's hair! She put one hand on the pit wall.

Gravell said, 'Up you go,' as he flung Tash up and she flew over the edge of the pit, rolled to the side and on to her feet. She limped to the bushes and collected the ladder, which she dropped over the edge of the pit for Gravell. She then retrieved her pack and sat down to put some snow round her swollen ankle. Gravell came over and held out the demon smoke. 'Just keep running next time.'

She took the bottle, which was warm round the top, and hot at the base. She'd use it to keep warm until Gravell got the fire going.

Gravell wandered away looking for firewood, all the time muttering and shaking his head. 'You just don't stop when a demon's running after you. You just don't. Who does that? Who?'

But Tash knew Gravell would calm down as he got back into his post-hunt routine. Tash would sit and Gravell would set up a fire, which on any other day was Tash's job. Then Gravell would make the stew, which was never Tash's job as Gravell made it the way he liked it and complained that Tash ruined it whenever she got involved. They had caught some rabbits and had some vegetables. It would be a good feast.

It was a dull night. The moon was full, but hidden by cloud. There was no colour anywhere except for the bright purple smoke moving slowly in the bottle. The glow seemed much stronger than from any smoke she'd seen before.

Tash looked at her swollen ankle. It would take a few days to heal but she'd survive. She prodded at the swelling and closed her eyes, trying to remember the touch of the demon again. He had been warm, not hot; not a hard grip but firm. The swelling was from going over on her ankle when she'd dropped out of the tree, not from the demon hurting her.

Gravell had always told Tash never to get caught by a demon, though he was rather vague on what would happen if she was, merely saying, 'Well, it won't be good, will it?'

She shivered. The night air was cold so she held the bottle to her stomach and the warmth from it spread through her. She liked the warmth of the smoke. She'd never inhale it, of course. Gravell had taught her that much. 'It ruins you, takes all your will and makes you a fool. A happy fool for a night, and that's what people pay for, but they're fools for all that.'

Tash set the bottle down between her feet to warm them and remembered the touch of the demon, remembered him running towards her. She'd never seen a demon run before, not properly. She'd seen demons sleep, wake, begin the chase, and she'd seen them get killed, but the most she'd seen of them running before today was a glimpse back through trees; she'd always been too busy running away from them. But the demon running towards her was . . . special. But that wasn't the right word; she couldn't think of the word that was right.

Gravell's singing came through the trees. He dropped the wood for the fire. 'Rabbit stew coming right up,' he said. 'Well, maybe by midnight.' And he laughed and did a little jig on the spot. 'We'll stay here tonight and head to Dornan tomorrow.'

'My boots are at Dornan.'

'You've only just got those boots. You don't need more boots.'

'I don't need them but I want them. They're the most beautiful things I ever saw. And they're going to be mine.'

With all this smoke she could afford the best boots in the world.

It was only after she'd eaten her stew that Tash remembered her twisted ankle and went to put some more snow on it. But as she slipped off her boot she found the swelling had gone. She circled her foot. It wasn't sore at all. She stood up and walked around. Her ankle felt strong. Obviously she hadn't hurt it that badly after all.

Catherine

BRIGANE, BRIGANT

Passage of Arms is a modern form of hastilude, which has grown popular since the war with Calidor, and is used as a proof of manly honour. A knight or knights take possession of an access point, such as a bridge, and challenge other men of rank who wish to pass. If the challenge is accepted, there follows a joust or duel to assess the stronger man, though honour is preserved for both combatants. If the challenge is refused, the gentleman challenged must give up his spurs, and his honour, to be allowed to pass. Passage of Arms duels usually end at the drawing of first blood but occasionally result in serious injury or death.

Chivalry in Modern Times, Crispin Hayrood

Catherine hadn't seen Ambrose since the execution of Lady Anne the day before. Fear for Ambrose had kept her awake all night.

They had only looked at each other, but she knew that wouldn't stop Boris or Noyes acting against her, or more probably against Ambrose. Mixed with her fear was the lingering shock of the execution. Catherine wanted to forget it but it was impossible. She also remembered the signs Lady Anne had made, and the more Catherine thought about it, the more convinced she was that she couldn't be mistaken. Lady Anne *had* been trying to communicate something to Catherine in her last moments of life: a kiss with her right hand and a fist with her left, then 'boy', then something else that she hadn't managed to see, accompanied by that look to her father. Did that mean it was all to do with the king?

When Catherine was dressing she asked Sarah if she knew the meaning of the kiss-and-fist sign. Sarah, always the most logical and practical of her maids, answered, 'Pairing a kiss with another sign changes the meaning, though a kiss is never normally paired with a fist. But if her hands were broken perhaps she couldn't make the sign properly.'

'But, even so, it could only mean she was trying to say "breath" or "air".'

'Perhaps she meant it as two messages,' Sarah suggested.

'Yes,' Tanya interjected. 'A kiss to Ambrose and Tarquin, and a fist in the groin to the rest of you. Sounds about right to me.'

It didn't sound right to Catherine at all. But she had no more time to think of it. She was desperate to see Ambrose. She hadn't dared send him a message for fear of interception, but she had to warn him about Noyes and Boris. Still, she had to act as normally as possible and go through her usual routine. She went to breakfast, ate sparsely and quickly, then walked to the stables, speeding up as she turned the corner, out of sight of the castle.

Sarah and Tanya were accompanying her, but if she could reach the stables ahead of them she'd have time to speak to Ambrose alone.

Catherine glanced back. Her maids hadn't yet turned the corner, and it occurred to her that they were being deliberately slow. They knew she admired Ambrose, though perhaps even they didn't know the extent of her addiction. That was how she thought of her feelings. It couldn't be love. She hardly knew him, even though he had been part of her guard for two years, but the brief times they had had together meant that all she wanted was more. Surely that was an addiction? She'd read of such things – some people felt the same about wine. But, whatever it was called – love, addiction, obsession – she couldn't stop thinking of Ambrose. And last night too she'd thought of him, remembered the tears on his face and thought how she'd love to gently kiss those tears away. Her maids definitely didn't know that.

Catherine entered the cobbled courtyard. Ambrose was standing alone beside her horse, Saffron, and he turned to her as she approached. He stared, almost frowned, before bowing. Why had he done that? Was it to do with her? The execution? Everything?

'Your Highness,' he murmured.

Ambrose took hold of the reins, patted Saffron's neck and bent to hold the stirrup steady for Catherine's foot. His hand on the stirrup was tanned and clean and smooth, though his knuckles were grazed and scabbed. She had purposely not worn her riding gloves, and now she gently lowered the fingertips of her left hand on to Ambrose's hand, gently touching the scabs and then the back of his hand where she pressed more firmly. Catherine's breath caught in her throat. Her skin was on Ambrose's skin. This was not allowed. Not seemly. Not done.

Ambrose had gone as still as stone, though his skin seemed almost to burn.

Catherine leant close to his bowed head and said, 'It's impossible for me to say how I feel about Lady Anne, Sir Ambrose, except that I am sorry for her suffering – and for yours. But I fear Noyes aims to bring you down next. And I would despair if you met the same fate as your sister.'

Ambrose looked up into Catherine's eyes.

'Thank you, Your Highness,' he replied in a low voice. 'I appreciate your kindness and concern. However, *my* concern is more about your brother than Noyes at this precise moment. Please put your foot in the stirrup and appear exceptionally keen to go riding. Prince Boris is here.'

Catherine quickly looked up to see Boris coming out of the stables, his eyes on her.

'You're alone with this man, sister?'

Catherine forced a smile. 'No, of course not. My maids are with me; they dawdle a little. See?'

To Catherine's immense relief, Sarah and Tanya appeared from round the corner at that moment.

'They need a whipping to waken them up.' Though they were now almost running to Catherine.

Catherine mounted Saffron and said, 'They're just not so keen on horse riding as I.'

'Well, I'll join you on your ride this morning. If you have no objection.' And Boris called for his horse to be brought out.

Catherine could think of numerous objections, but she said, 'I'm honoured to have my brother join me on my morning ride. Your company is the more precious to me knowing that once I'm married I'll be denied this pleasure.'

Boris laughed. 'Precious indeed.' And he swung himself on to his horse.

Peter, one of her other guards, led out horses for Sarah and Tanya.

'Your maids don't need to join us,' Boris said.

'But they always ride with me.'

'Not today. I'm here to accompany you. I and these two fine knights.' He gestured to Ambrose and Peter.

Being without her maids on a ride was unheard of, though if she was with her brother there could be no complaint of impropriety. Still, she was sure Boris was up to something. She said, 'My maids can amuse me when you tire of my company.'

'Tire of you, sister? That could never happen. You are endlessly fascinating. And I'm not waiting for them; as you say, they dawdle. Your men to guard the rear.' And Boris led the way out of the courtyard.

Catherine followed. Boris had caught her off guard, though thankfully it was only him; Noyes was nowhere to be seen. There was little she could do, but as she rode out of the courtyard she turned back and signed to Sarah and Tanya, *Follow me.*

They both signed *At once* in reply. Catherine smiled. Her maids gave her courage, but she had just made another slip in front of her brother. There had been so many recently: her unguarded remarks on marriage to Diana, looking too long at Ambrose at the execution, and now being found with Ambrose and without her maids. Still, perhaps the best form of defence was attack. She kicked Saffron on to ride alongside Boris.

'It's a delight to have your company this morning, brother. In all my years I've not seen so much of you as I have since my betrothal. It makes me wonder if your own thoughts have turned to marriage?'

Boris laughed and spat on the ground.

'Surely you'd like children?'

'I'd like a quiet ride.'

Catherine sighed. 'I warned you that you'd tire of me, and I was right – and we've hardly left the castle grounds. But, without my maids, I am your responsibility to amuse for the whole ride.'

'Oh, I plan to do that, sister.'

Catherine looked over at Boris. 'What do you mean?'

Boris ignored her and kicked his horse on.

Catherine kept up with him, saying, 'Well? Can you answer me?'

'All my activities for the last six months and indeed for today revolve around getting you wed to Prince Tzsayn, sister. That is the job Father has given me and I intend to make sure nothing prevents the wedding from happening. Soon you will have a husband.' Boris turned to her and smiled. 'Or, rather, he will have you. And my role is to ensure no one else has you first.'

Catherine stared at him. Had her brother really said something so coarse?

But then he continued as if he'd said nothing unusual. 'Just make sure you do as you are required before and during the wedding. After that you are your husband's problem.'

Catherine was still shocked at her brother's first comment and insisted, 'I don't intend to be anyone's problem.'

Boris snorted a laugh and shook his head. 'You're a woman. Women are always a problem. It's in your nature to disobey, it's in your nature to be tempted from honour, it's in your nature to lie about it.'

'I obey in all things.' Though Catherine knew she was tempted by Ambrose, but she also knew she'd never give way to temptation.

'And it's in your nature to argue.'

'Isn't it in every intelligent person's nature to argue against something that is wrong?'

'I'm not wrong.' Boris kicked on his horse, shouting, 'Now stop the chatter and ride.'

Catherine looked back. Her maids were not in sight and she had no choice but to keep up with Boris. They cantered down the track to the beach and across the sand to the shallow water, Boris riding slightly ahead. The beach was long and narrow and they rode fast to the far end, water and wet sand splashing up. It was years since she and Boris had ridden together. He was a better rider than her, as he always had been, but now he was so much a man that she could barely remember the boy he had been years ago.

Boris took the path through the dunes that led back to the castle through a patch of scrubby woodland and grass. Catherine, Ambrose and Peter followed it to a small stream and a rickety wooden bridge where, to Catherine's surprise, three riders waited on the far side. They wore the uniform of the Royal Guard so Catherine wasn't concerned for her safety, but something felt wrong; these men weren't here by chance.

'Who are these men?' Catherine asked Boris as they crossed, keeping her voice level.

Boris halted by them, saying, 'This is Viscount Lang. And this Dirk Hodgson, second son of the Duke of Vergen. The young man over there is Sir Evan Walcott.'

Catherine recognized their names but not their faces. There was something about them together that was overwhelmingly masculine and aggressive.

Boris said, 'You challenge him first, Lang. The bridge is ours. Keep it that way.'

'My pleasure, Your Highness.' Viscount Lang moved on to the bridge, blocking the path for Ambrose and Peter.

'What's happening?' Catherine asked.

'You asked earlier what this was about.' Boris turned to her. 'Respect for the king is what this is about. That Norwend scum stares at you as if you're his. At the execution you couldn't take your eyes off him. And today you left your maids behind, contriving a situation where you could be alone with him. You were warned. You won't be executed as a traitor – whatever happens, you will wed Prince Tzsayn – but this traitorous piece of shit is going to pay, and you are going to watch.'

Ambrose and Peter had halted ten paces from the bridge.

Lang pointed to Peter. 'If you wish to cross the bridge, sir, you may.' Pointing at Ambrose, he said, 'You, sir, may not cross without proving your honour.'

'No!' Catherine said. 'Ambrose is my guard.'

'Ambrose is not fit to be in your guard,' Boris snarled. 'He barely denounced his traitorous sister. He wept like a woman at her death. Noyes would like nothing more than to get his hands on Ambrose, but I am saving him the trouble. I deal with the cowards and traitors in the Royal Guard myself. Loyalty is not just in words and deeds but in spirit. And I see no loyalty to the king in him.'

'Do you intend to stay there and snivel like a coward, Norwend?' called Lang.

Ambrose squared his shoulders. 'I am here as bodyguard to Her Highness, to protect her, as is my sworn duty, and you should not hinder me.'

'Then you must cross the bridge to do your duty.'

'It's right that you should offer the alternative, Lang,' shouted Boris. 'He may hand over his spurs.'

'It would disgust me to touch them but I would accept them as an alternative, Your Highness.' Then Lang shouted to Ambrose, 'Surrender your spurs and you can ride over my bridge and back home to cry by your fire. I hear you weep like a woman.'

'I'll not hand over anything to you.'

'Then we fight.' And Lang drew his sword.

Catherine said, 'Boris, please stop this. There is nothing between Sir Ambrose and me.' No doubt, if he didn't fight, Ambrose would be taken by Noyes to some dungeon, but Boris would only choose the best of his fighters and Catherine had no idea how good Ambrose was with a sword.

However, Boris's eyes were fixed on Ambrose and he didn't reply.

At last Ambrose drew his sword and told Peter, 'Your duty is to protect Her Highness, not stay with me. Do your duty.'

'Ambrose, I –'

'Go.'

Reluctantly Peter kicked his horse on and crossed the bridge as Lang rode towards Ambrose.

Ambrose backed his horse away, glancing about nervously.

Lang charged.

With a cry, Ambrose kicked his horse hard and rode forward. They passed each other with a clashing of swords, turned and rode at each other again, but this time Ambrose's horse reared, hooves clawing at the air. Lang's horse backed up and instantly Ambrose was charging, slashing down with his sword. There was no contact between the swords, but Lang's horse screamed and reared. Its reins were cut on one side, as was its neck.

Lang dismounted easily, using his horse to shield him from Ambrose's sword until he could release the panicked beast as it was more of a danger than protection. The horse galloped away and Ambrose charged at Lang. Swords clashed and Lang staggered back.

'Dismount and fight honourably,' Lang shouted.

'It's not my fault you can't protect your horse or yourself,' Ambrose replied, and sliced at Lang as he rode past. Again the swords clashed, but Lang staggered and turned too slowly as Ambrose whipped round and cut him across the wrist, almost severing his hand from his arm. Lang screamed and dropped to his knees, blood splattering his face, his hand hanging loose and touching the sand. Lang stared at it.

Ambrose dismounted and walked over to Lang.

'Do you agree, sir, that I have proved my honour?'

Lang muttered something Catherine couldn't hear.

Ambrose shook his head. 'I have bested you. Say I have won and I'll let you live. You can learn to fight with your other hand.'

Lang raised his head and said, 'Fuck you. And your whore of a sister.'

Ambrose's hands were shaking as he walked round behind Lang and raised his sword.

'No!'

Catherine didn't know why she cried out. But at the sound of her voice Ambrose hesitated. Then he brought the hilt of his sword down on the back of Lang's head. Lang collapsed unconscious on the ground.

Boris said, 'I don't believe he has proved anything other than he fights like a villain. Dispatch him, Hodgson.'

'What! No, Boris! Ambrose has won.'

'Hodgson! Do it!'

'It's you who is the villain, Boris,' hissed Catherine. 'Ambrose defeated Lang. It's dishonourable to send in another man, giving him no time to recover.'

But no one was listening. Hodgson rode forward, slowly drawing his sword.

'Ride him into the ground!' yelled Boris.

Hodgson kicked his horse towards Ambrose, blade raised, but Ambrose dived and rolled forward before Hodgson had the chance to strike. The startled horse jumped over Ambrose, who rose to his feet as Hodgson struggled to control his mount. Ambrose cut across Hodgson's back. The knight cried out but turned his horse and kicked him forward. Once more, Ambrose ducked, then lunged to stab Hodgson's leg. As before, Hodgson grunted and slashed at Ambrose, who dropped flat to the ground and rolled under the horse.

Hodgson urged his horse to trample Ambrose, but the horse backed away. Ambrose got to his feet before Hodgson charged again, but this time the horse caught Ambrose and knocked him back to the ground.

Stubbornly Ambrose gathered himself and stood up. 'Your horse is the better fighter,' he snarled, but he looked shaken and tired.

'Is that so?' Hodgson replied. He dismounted and approached Ambrose, sword raised, and the difference between the men became more obvious to Catherine. Hodgson was taller, wider and more muscular. He was bleeding, though he seemed not to notice the wounds to his leg and back.

'Hodgson won my tournament last year,' said Boris. 'He's the best sword in my troop and as tough as they come.'

Ambrose backed away. Hodgson advanced. They circled. Hodgson thrust forward with a combination of hard, powerful lunges, each one deflected, but always Ambrose was moving backwards.

Catherine knew there was no hope for Ambrose. 'Stop this, Boris. Stop them.'

'All he has to do to stop it is give in and hand over his spurs.'

'Ambrose beat Lang and has first blood with Hodgson; it's Hodgson who should be handing over his spurs.'

'Seems to me that my man wants to carry on.'

And Hodgson moved forward, swinging his sword. Ambrose parried but his whole body seemed to shake with the force of Hodgson's blow. Again Hodgson advanced and Ambrose retreated, but this time he tripped on a clump of grass, staggering backwards, off balance, and Hodgson closed in on him, driving his sword down on Ambrose, who just managed to deflect the blow before falling sideways. Hodgson stepped forward, raising his sword to deliver the killing thrust.

'No!' Catherine knew Ambrose was lost.

But then Ambrose's sword was in Hodgson's chest.

Hodgson looked as shocked as Catherine. Then she realized it was all a ruse. The trip had been deliberate; Ambrose had feigned being off balance to move under Hodgson's guard, so his opponent's chest was unprotected and Ambrose could thrust his sword up, driving it through cloth and skin and bone.

Hodgson still tried to bring his own sword down, but Ambrose anticipated that too and rolled sideways, leaving his blade buried in Hodgson's chest. The big knight fell like a tree to lie face down in the mud. Ambrose picked up Hodgson's sword, glanced at Lang and finally turned towards Boris.

His chest was heaving and he shouted, 'The bridge is mine. Anyone can cross.' He pointed the sword at Boris and spoke in a voice that Catherine hardly recognized; it was so full of rage. 'Even you, Your Highness, are welcome to travel this way if you feel brave enough.'

Boris's face was twisted with fury, and for a moment Catherine thought he might charge at Ambrose. But at that instant Sarah and Tanya appeared, riding fast towards the bridge.

'Take your maids and return to the castle now,' growled Boris.

Catherine was sure that, if she did, Boris would attack Ambrose. To do so would be dishonourable and somehow even he couldn't do it with Catherine and her maids to witness it.

'I'm not leaving without my men.'

'Do as I say!'

'Not without my men!'

'Are you disobeying my instructions?'

'My instructions are always to stay with my guards. And your men, brother, have challenged mine and lost. Take the defeat like a man. Or you will lose all honour.'

'It's not my honour that's in question. What was I saying about contriving to be with that man?'

'It is you who have contrived all this, not me! Every day I ride safely here with my maids and my guard. Today, because of you, there is one man dead and another maimed.'

Boris pointed at Catherine. 'No, because of *you*. Stay with your maids then, and your lover. But Noyes will not be as merciful with him as I have been.'

And Boris kicked his horse and galloped off towards the castle, shouting, 'Evan, tend to Lang.'

Sarah and Tanya pulled up their horses, staring in horror at the men on the ground.

Catherine looked around. Peter was on horseback behind her. Sir Evan was running to assist Lang. Ambrose dropped to his knees, exhausted. And in the centre of them all was the body of Hodgson. But Catherine had to think: Boris had called Ambrose her lover. Whether there was proof or not was irrelevant; Noyes would come for him. If Ambrose was taken, he would be killed.

Catherine slid off her horse and ran to Ambrose. He looked up at her. His cheek and forehead were splattered with flecks of blood. He looked lost. 'I couldn't give them my spurs.'

'I understand, Ambrose. You've proved your honour and my brother has proved he has none, but Boris will send Noyes and his men now.' She held her hand out to Ambrose, intending to help him up, but instead he took her hand in his and bent forward to kiss it.

Skin on skin. His soft lips, his warm breath on her skin. So gentle, so strong and yet so vulnerable. Catherine wavered, wanting to kneel next to him, to hold him, but she was aware of Sir Peter's eyes on her. She forced herself upright and said, 'Please, Ambrose. This is impossible.'

Ambrose closed his eyes. 'Yes, Your Highness.'

And the way he spoke, with such emotion in those three words, Catherine had to bend to him again. 'Please, Ambrose. Noyes will be on his way here soon. You must leave.'

'I'm your guard, Your Highness. I can't run away.'

'I'm ordering you to go. It is not me who is in danger now. You are, and I'm ordering you to leave. Never to be caught. That is my order. Go!'

Ambrose gazed up at her and Catherine noticed how his eyes were hazel, blended with green and gold. She wanted to remember them, but still Ambrose didn't move.

'Please, Ambrose. If you stay you'll end up in one of Noyes's cells. I couldn't bear that. There is no dishonour in leaving now. I want you to go. I want you to evade Noyes. Frustrate him and Boris by remaining free. Don't be caught like your sister was.'

This final comment seemed to rouse Ambrose and he got to his feet. 'I'll go, but know that if you asked me to stay I would do that just as willingly.'

Tears were in Catherine's eyes now and one ran down her cheek. Ambrose brushed it gently away with his fingertips.

'You will be a great queen one day and I will do my best to live to hear of it, Your Highness.'

He took her hand again and kissed it. Another touch, but now the last time she would feel his breath and the warmth of his skin . . .

She closed her eyes to savour the feeling. Then his hand was gone; just the cool air remained. And he was on his horse, looking back at her, and then he rode off, quickly disappearing into the trees.

Sarah came to Catherine and asked if she needed water. Catherine waved her away. She didn't need water; she needed to know that Ambrose would be safe, but there was little she could do to help that. She went over to Lang, lying unconscious, and asked Evan, 'Will he live?'

Evan rose and bowed formally. 'Yes, Your Highness. I've stopped the blood. The prince will send a surgeon. I'll stay here until he arrives.'

And Catherine found herself saying, 'We'll return to the castle and ensure the surgeon is sent promptly.'

And perhaps somehow delay the pursuit of Ambrose . . .

Catherine walked back to Saffron, every step dreamlike and unreal. She knew she could never have a life with Ambrose, that she'd have to live with Tzsayn. What made her angry was that all this fighting was unnecessary. If her father or brother knew her at all, if they had any understanding of her, they'd know she would marry Tzsayn. Were they really concerned that Prince Tzsayn would be put off because a man had looked at her? Or was this another excuse to persecute the Norwend family?

Now Peter, not Ambrose, held the stirrup for her, and Catherine was on her horse, her mind still not caught up with her body. Sarah and Tanya rode close to her, though they hardly spoke. Catherine dreaded seeing Noyes and his men. They would hunt Ambrose down without mercy. But the more time he had to get away, the more chance he would have of survival.

As Catherine rode into the castle, her heart sank. Noyes and five of his men were already riding out. Catherine waved them to a stop, anything to delay their departure, even for a short time. Noyes approached and inclined his head in the smallest approximation of a bow.

Catherine didn't know what to say but asked, 'Where are you going, Noyes?'

'I can't reveal the king's business, Your Highness. But I'm confident that I'll soon catch the traitor I'm after. I always do. And I can assure you I'll deal with him in the harshest manner.'

You always do, Catherine thought.

March

March stood on the grass and watched the stream run by. Waiting again. But this time not for the prince but for Holywell.

Since the death of the prince's wife and sons, Holywell had insisted on seeing March once a week, and he always asked about the prince, who he met and when he would remarry. Everyone expected that: a new bride for the prince and nine months later a new heir. Only a few weeks after the funeral, March had heard the chief counsellor say to the prince, 'We all grieve for your terrible loss, sire, but it's never too soon to consider a new marriage. Without an heir, Calidor could fall back under Aloysius's rule. No one wants that. The lords are already beginning to wonder when this mourning will end.'

But March had heard the prince's reluctance in his voice as he replied, 'How can I not mourn? My wife is dead. My sons are dead. I want an heir too, but who's to say more of my children won't die?'

The prince had fought a war with his brother, but the loss of his own family had taken a bigger toll on him. He had lost three girls before his sons, all from different illnesses early in their lives. The two boys had been cared for as carefully as if they were precious jewels and still they had been struck with the fever, and this time his wife had been taken as well.

The prince had even blamed himself in a conversation with Lord Regan just a few days before.

'Is it my fault? Am I being punished?'

'It's not punishment. It's disease. The doctors are useless.'

'But *all* my family? Everyone dead except me. It has to be because of my blood, Regan.'

'The disease may attack the blood, but you are strong and you must stay strong, sire.'

'I'm not talking about disease, or doctors. I mean my *blood*.'

'You're tired. The doctors were –'

'Can't you listen? I'm not talking about that. I'm talking about my *true* blood. My s–'

'Out!' Regan had barked at March. 'Leave us!'

March had hesitated and looked to the prince.

'I said, get out! Now!'

Regan had dragged March to the door and pushed him out of the room, slamming the door behind him.

March had remained there, his thoughts tripping over themselves.

'My blood' meant family, real family, by birth not by marriage. So 'my *true* blood' had to mean another blood relative. 'True' because they were ... what? Honest? First? And, before Lord Regan had cut him off, surely the prince had been about to say 'my son'. Which meant ... Prince Thelonius, the noble leader of civilized Calidor, the man who had wept for days over his dead wife, had fathered another son. A bastard!

March couldn't stop smiling. No wonder Regan had wanted him out. Indeed, before he'd even had a chance to pass his suspicions on to Holywell, yesterday's meeting had all but confirmed them. The prince had given his ring to Lord Regan along with instructions that Regan didn't like. March had an idea what those were too: to find the prince's son and bring him home. The lawyers would do the rest, legitimize the bastard. The prince wouldn't have to remarry and father more children to die; the bastard would take the throne. The ring, the prince's seal, was a sign of the truth of the message.

Was it too far-fetched? Could it be true?

'Brother, it's good to see you. Though you need to keep a little more alert.' Holywell had arrived by his side while March was lost in thought. 'You have news for me?'

March tried to look serious and not too keen. 'I do,' he said. 'Much news.'

The telling took little time and at the end Holywell sat on the grass and thought for a few moments before saying, 'You've done well, March. Very well. Your theory seems sound. Even if there is no son, Regan is up to something important, news of which has a value to my master in Brigant. But where is Regan now?'

March smiled inwardly at his opportunity to again prove his worth. 'I followed Regan when he left the castle this morning. It was early, not even dawn. He went down to the docks. Alone. He boarded a ship bound for Pitoria.'

'Pitoria? You think that is where the prince's bastard is?'

'Prince Thelonius went there as a young man. He talked about it once.'

Holywell gave a gentle laugh of surprise. 'You know much, my friend. Did he mention fathering a child by any chance?' he added with a sly smile.

'No. He talked of the politics. He admired the country. Its wealth and tranquillity. He was disappointed that they didn't openly join in the fight against Aloysius but he said they supported Calidor by sending food by sea. He told me that the soldiers colour their hair to show which lord they are loyal to.'

'Ah yes, I've seen their coloured hair.'

'You've been to Pitoria?'

'And it seems I must go again.'

Holywell was already standing as if he was going to leave there and then.

'What will you do?'

'Find the prince's son, if I can. King Aloysius will pay handsomely for him. I will find him and –' Holywell smiled – 'use my talents to prevent Regan bringing him back here, and instead find a means to take him to my Brigantine master.'

March wasn't surprised by the answer. In fact, it was what he had been hoping to hear.

'I want to come with you.'

Holywell smiled and shook his head. 'I don't think so.'

'I want to help.'

'You *are* helping, my friend. You have unique access to the prince. You have given me priceless information.'

'It has a price, and that is me coming with you.'

Holywell shook his head again.

March bunched his fists. 'I can't stay here any longer. I'm going mad. You know what it's like to be a slave. Well, I'm no more than that, and a slave to a man I detest, my enemy, the man who caused the death of all my family and of my country.'

Holywell didn't laugh as March thought he might, but he put his hand on March's shoulder. 'March. To work best against your enemy, *our* enemy, you need to stay here. No one else could do what you've done.'

March shoved off Holywell's hand. 'And now I've done it. But I won't do more. Either I come with you or I'll go somewhere else. I'm not going back there to pour more fucking wine.'

'You get very Abask when you're angry.'

'Fuck you.'

Holywell chuckled. 'I imagine you pour wine beautifully.'

'I pour it fucking perfectly all the fucking time but I'm not doing it any more.'

'Working with me is a little harder than pouring wine and carrying a platter of fruit.'

March didn't know what else to say. 'I won't go back there. I'll follow you on my own if I have to.'

'March, brother. Calm yourself. I see you're serious about this, so perhaps we can agree on something. I'm not used to working with anyone, but I admit it does occur to me from time to time that I could use an assistant. Following and watching is tiring work. Two can do it better than one. But only if the second person is quiet and quick and doesn't talk too much.'

March looked at him and didn't dare say anything. He could do not talking.

Holywell laughed.

'I won't get in the way. I will help.'

Holywell now went quiet.

'I'll do anything that needs to be done. Anything that fucks them up.'

'That look in your eye is quite dangerous, March. And I have to say it intrigues me. I wouldn't work with any up-their-own-arse Calidorians or mad Brigantines, but you're Abask. You're Abask through to your bones. We are brothers.'

'So, I can come?'

'You can come. Though I warn you, March – you may be Abask, but I am too. I am not your master and I don't expect you to pour me my wine but, I tell you now, working with me will be hard, it will not be civilized. I will expect you to risk everything to help me, and I will do the same for you. As I said, we're brothers. And you may get hurt or you may get killed, but if you fuck up I'll kill you myself.'

Tash

NORTHERN PLATEAU,
PITORIA

'We'll be at Dornan while the fair's still on at this rate.'

Gravell was striding ahead, using two of his harpoons as walking sticks, the other three strapped to his back along with his huge pack of rope and skins. Tash followed behind.

They'd set off early the morning after the demon kill. Tash's ankle was strong and she was feeling good, very good. She kept thinking of the demon, though. He was beautiful, as an animal can be beautiful. He was fast too, but she'd outrun him. She, Tash, had outrun him, not just on a short dash but a long run through the forest. That was the fastest and furthest she'd ever run with a demon on her tail. She was an experienced demon hunter now and she felt faster and stronger than ever before. Perhaps she was growing at last. She was thirteen – at least that's what she thought she was – which was pretty much an adult, but everyone looked on her as a child. Some people in towns even treated her like a child. Just because she was small. One man in Dornan last time had even patted her head! She'd kicked him in the shins, punched him between the legs and now as she thought of it she muttered, 'He won't do that again.'

'What's that?' Gravell asked.

'Nothing . . . just thinking.'

'I've warned you about that before,' Gravell deadpanned, then added, 'Not about bloody boots, I hope.'

Tash hesitated to ask but had to. 'Do you think I've grown?'

'Grown?'

'Yes. Grown.'

'Taller, you mean?'

'Yes, taller. How else could I grow?'

Gravell's pack moved up and down in a shrug.

'I think I've grown,' Tash said.

Gravell turned to face her, walking backwards. 'Funnily enough, you know what struck me this morning when I looked at you? Your height. It really did. I noticed a change and –' he held his hand out as if surveying her like a building – 'yes, I'm certain of it. It's remarkable. Astounding. I'd say you've shrunk by a whole hand's width.'

'That's not even funny.'

'Your sense of humour is shrinking too,' Gravell replied, turning to face ahead.

'Piss off.'

'Your language ain't improving much neither.'

'Stop being in such a good mood. It doesn't suit you.'

'We tall people are known for our good moods.'

'Hmm, more like you're getting excited about drink and women.'

'Us tall men do attract the ladies, it has to be said.'

'Pah! I've never seen you with a *lady*.'

'Small person, small mind.'

'You're so annoying, probably because you're so tall. I've noticed that about tall people. Think they're above the rest of us.'

'That's cos I am above you.'

'And don't care about anyone but themselves.'

Gravell stopped and turned to Tash again.

'OK then, my little friend. Stand against this. Let me measure you.'

He planted the harpoon on the ground. Tash stood by it. Gravell put his hand on the top of her head, which was still well below his armpit. 'You come up to here. So, yes, you've grown.' Tash smiled. 'You were here when I bought you.' Gravell pointed to the middle of the harpoon.

'Well, I know I've grown since then! I mean, have I grown in the last few weeks?'

Gravell pulled her to him. She was *definitely* still well below his armpit. 'The honest truth? No. And don't take this the wrong way but your parents weren't exactly giants. I think you might have reached as high as you're ever going to get.'

Tash slumped inside. 'But I feel taller.'

'How can you feel taller? You seeing things from a great height now?'

Tash thought about it. 'Maybe I'm just feeling stronger. But much stronger. I feel so good today.'

Gravell smiled. 'Stronger is good. It's the food I give you. That stew last night was excellent, if I do say so myself. You need to be strong and fast. Don't want another demon grabbing you.'

'But I'd like to grow just a little bit.'

'Nah, I want those spiked shoes I bought you to last a few years.'

'That's a good point. The boots in Dornan were small. I need them to fit me.'

Gravell shook his head and set off again. 'Them boots is all you think about.'

'And what's wrong with that? They are the most beautiful boots in the whole world. And they're going to be mine. They were probably designed with a petite person in mind.'

'Petite? What's that?'

'Petite. It means delicate, small.'

'Short-arse, you mean.'

'I wish I hadn't brought this up.'

'So stop talking and get walking. You need to keep up, so we get to Dornan before your boots are sold. The fair will bring in plenty of customers. Short people will be flocking there. Dornan is known for being a magnet for short-arses.'

Catherine

BRIGANE, BRIGANT

It is commonly known that women cannot be trusted and are sly, secretive and vexatious. Whereas men form strong, honest relations with each other, women form weak, short-lived relations with men. Men who have strong relations with women are weaker for it. If your wife is disobedient in any way, immediate disciplinary procedures are required. Three to five strokes of a short cane to the palm of the hand will usually suffice. Dunking the head in a small barrel of cold water may also be helpful. For persistent disobedience, seclusion in small spaces is advised. Some women benefit from bricking up for a day, and the purchase of a coffin-sized box can have such strong deterrent effects that it may not have to be used at all. (If it is, ensure that there are vents for breathing.)

Marriage: A Guide for the Brigantine Gentleman,
James Daly

Catherine was sitting in the castle library staring out of the window and thinking about Ambrose. It was three days since he'd fled and she'd heard nothing. She told herself it was a good sign, a sign that he hadn't been caught, as she was sure Boris would have told her if he had. Boris would delight in telling her. Catherine shuddered.

'Are you well, Catherine? Don't catch a chill at the window.'

Catherine glanced over at her mother. 'I'm not cold. I was thinking about . . . Prince Tzsayn.'

Catherine had never met Tzsayn, never even seen him, never mind spoken to him, but in two weeks she would be married to him.

'Can you tell me more about him?'

Her mother smiled. 'He's the only son of King Arell of Pitoria. The queen died during the birth of his younger brother, who died shortly afterwards.'

'Yes, I know that.'

'Pitoria is wealthy and peaceful. A large country to manage, though the lords there, from what I can glean, are loyal. And through your marriage the difficult relations between our countries will be improved. During the war, Pitorian ships took provisions to Thelonius in Calia. It's taken your father many years and your forthcoming marriage to forgive that.'

Catherine had heard this all before. She knew that her father wouldn't even consider her marrying a Pitorian until last year. That he'd changed his mind (one would hardly dare use the word 'softened' with the king) to allow a Pitorian on to her list of suitors was surprising enough, but then there was the question of the groom's health. Everyone in Brigant knew that Prince Tzsayn was deformed: deaf in one ear and hideously scarred. Her father was never tolerant of any illness or disability, but, though there had been other eligible suitors, Prince Tzsayn had shot to the top of the list. And shortly after first hearing his name mentioned Catherine had been informed that they were betrothed.

'Yes, I've read about the country and I know about his family, but I'd like to hear more about Prince Tzsayn.'

'The man himself, you mean?'

'Yes, the man himself.'

'A man of rank is indistinguishable from his role. Tzsayn is of the highest rank. He is next in line to the throne of Pitoria.'

'Yes, I know that, but what about *him*?'

'I really can't think of anything else to tell you.'

Catherine was certain her mother was teasing her now and that she knew plenty more, but clearly she was going to make her work for it. It was almost a game between them. Catherine started with the most important point.

'How old is he?'

'Is that really relevant?'

'It's vital for childbearing and maturity in his role as heir.'

The queen suppressed a smile. 'I'm sure that's your only reason for asking. He's twenty-three.'

Which was not too old. He could have been ancient, as some of her other suitors had been.

The queen continued. 'Tzsayn was born in December, I believe. On a new moon. Some say that makes for a cold personality.'

'Was he cold when you met him?'

'He was not without charm or intelligence.'

'That sounds like a "yes".'

'Cool rather than cold. I sensed there was more to him than the chilly exterior, but, if there was, he had no inclination to show me.'

'Proud then.'

The queen shrugged. 'He's a man.'

'I've heard that he is deaf in one ear.'

'Perhaps you heard that wrong. I think he can hear quite as well as you or me, though he may pretend otherwise.'

'So he's deceitful.'

'I got the impression it was more that he was easily bored.'

This sounded worrying. Would he find Catherine boring?

'And his attitude to marriage? To me?'

'Attitude?'

'Do you think he will be gentle and kind? Considerate of my needs?'

'Is that what you want?'

'Better that than cruel.'

'Gentleness and kindness don't usually make for great rulers.'

'I want a husband for myself and a ruler for the kingdom.'

'Difficult to get both. But I believe he will suit you, my dear. The Pitorians are different from Brigantines. They're increasingly influenced from the east. They do have a more liberal view of women's roles for example.'

'Liberal?'

'Tzsayn told me he had travelled to Illast and was impressed that women there ran businesses and kept their own houses, owned property.'

Interesting, thought Catherine, *but irrelevant to me*. Her chances of running a business were exactly nought. She would live in the prince's castle, as much his property as any other object within it.

She handed her mother the pamphlet that recommended women be caned for disobedience. 'I've been reading this. I wonder if they agree with it in Pitoria.'

The queen looked through it. 'You shouldn't waste your time on this. No one should.' She dropped it on the table as if it was soiled. 'You need something new for a new country. Something inspiring. There's a biography of Queen Valeria of Illast you should read. She was an unusual woman and had an interesting life and marriage. I think that is what you need, my dear.'

'The book or the marriage?'

The queen smiled as she walked to the tall shelves. '*I'll* find the book. But *you* must shape your marriage.'

Catherine didn't dare say that what she *really* wanted was to not have a marriage like her mother's – cold, loveless and functional. And preferably not to Tzsayn. But that was what she would have. There was no other option. She would have to make the best of it.

But could there be love in her marriage? Would she love her husband? Could he love her? Did it matter? She'd had feelings for Ambrose, *strong* feelings, and while she'd denied it to herself before, now that she knew she'd never see him again, she could admit they had been feelings of love. But that's all she'd ever have, her feelings and her memories of him. And she had learnt from that too, though what she'd learnt she wasn't sure – mainly that not all men were like her father and brother. And she was determined not to forget Ambrose: his vulnerability and his strength, the way his hair would blow in the breeze, his way of standing, of walking, the incline of his head, the way he looked sideways, his shoulders, his thighs as he rode his horse. She'd once seen Ambrose training in the yard, the sweat on his neck, his shirt loose but clinging to the sweat of his back . . . But were those thoughts of love or desire? And could she love Tzsayn?

Her mother returned and handed Catherine a slender leather-bound volume: the book about Queen Valeria. 'Is there anything else you wanted to ask?'

'Umm. Yes. What about . . . love?' Catherine ventured, blushing as she said the word to her mother.

'Love?'

'I read that it may grow between two people.'

'Tzsayn may love you and you may love him. Show him kindness and gentleness, show him a little of your intelligence, develop your charm, and you will thrive in Pitoria.'

'I can't imagine thriving there at all. Or indeed anywhere. Where could any woman thrive?'

'Pitoria is not Brigant and Tzsayn is not Aloysius.' Her mother came to Catherine and stroked her cheek. 'And you are not me. Find your own way to make your life, Catherine. It will be a very different one to that you have here. I know you think my life is stifled, but I've made it the best I can to suit me. My advice is that from the start you make yours suit you. In Pitoria you will have many freedoms that you don't have here, that I can never have. You will be able to travel, to leave the castle, to mix with other people.'

'You're sure of that?'

'That is how Pitoria is.'

'Will I see you again, once I'm married?'

'You know your father will never let me leave the castle. It's taken all my power to get him to allow you to even ride out of the palace gates. My place is here, I accept that, and yours will be in Pitoria. I will miss you, Catherine.'

It was rare to hear emotion in the queen's voice but Catherine heard it then. Her mother kept her emotions as tightly controlled as Aloysius kept her life. Catherine yearned for freedom and wished her mother could experience it too. Wishing and yearning were one thing; doing was another.

'But how can I make my life suit me? I'll have a few maids and a few dresses and nothing more. No power. No influence.'

'You are a princess, daughter of Aloysius of Brigant, and you will be wife of the future king of Pitoria. That is much. True, you will have no money, no land, but Queen Valeria started with just as little. She used the one thing that she could influence. Possibly the most important thing.'

'Oh? Are you going to tell me what this thing is?'

'The people.'

Catherine felt a little deflated. She remembered the horror of the crowd at Lady Anne's execution, baying for blood and shouting Aloysius's name.

'Valeria won the people over. People loved her, sent her gifts, swore their loyalty. The people wanted to see her, wanted to bathe in her presence. They loved her.'

That certainly sounded much better than people shouting for an execution.

'Do you think I can do that?'

'You can achieve much, Catherine. It's how badly you want it. How hard you'll work for it.'

'I'd certainly prefer it to being locked up in a castle for the rest of my life.' Catherine immediately felt guilty for voicing her ideas too strongly, but her mother smiled.

'Then you should plan for it. And start as soon as you reach Pitoria. I'll do what I can to help you prepare.'

With a soft knock, a servant entered, bearing a scroll for the queen.

'From Prince Boris, Your Majesty.'

Catherine felt sick. Was this about Ambrose? Had he been caught? She couldn't stop herself from asking, 'Does it concern me?'

'It does.' The queen looked at her. 'You have your marching orders.'

'*Marching orders?*'

'Boris is planning your marriage like a military campaign. He's sent details of the travel arrangements.'

Catherine was relieved that it was something relatively minor, though Boris considered his role anything but that and was organizing her marriage with remarkable assiduity.

'Am I allowed to know what the plan is?'

The queen nodded. 'You are to leave here in six days' time and travel by sea to Pitoria, under the protection of your brother. Once in Pitoria you will travel to the royal castle in Tornia and be introduced to the key families. You are to act under the guidance of your brother at all times. And on the twenty-third of May, the day before your seventeenth birthday, you are to be married to Prince Tzsayn.'

The queen held the scroll out for Catherine, saying, 'Boris has been quite specific about the wedding festivities, naming all who are to attend the wedding, and to whom you are to be introduced. He's put effort into this.'

Catherine scanned the letter. Among numerous details were these words: 'Following tradition, the king requires that all the nobles of Pitoria be introduced to Catherine at her wedding and that she be given the respect that is her due as the daughter of King Aloysius and future queen of Pitoria.'

Catherine was surprised. All her life she'd been locked away in the castle, hardly allowed to see a soul, apart from certain courtiers and her guards. She'd never even been presented to any of her suitors.

But her father was ever practical. Locking Catherine away served the purpose of keeping her 'safe' until her marriage and, once married, her father needed her to fulfil a new role as the bridge between Brigant and Pitoria.

The king's aim was one her mother had taught her early: he wanted Calidor; he wanted to avenge his defeat and take his brother's kingdom, which he felt was his by right. And everything he did was driven by that aim, including the marriage of his daughter. And the best use of Catherine was marrying her to the prince of Pitoria so that relations and, most importantly, trade, could be improved and the black hole in the king's treasury could be filled in order for the war with Calidor to be resumed.

Catherine smiled at her mother. 'It certainly doesn't look like I'm going to be locked away before my wedding.'

'Make the most of that time, Catherine, and make of your marriage what you can.'

Catherine could make the most of it; she could help promote trade, promote other things, though she wasn't sure what they would be, but she could have a life where she wasn't shut away like her mother. She could help her father, his kingdom and herself. She knew she could never be with Ambrose – she had always known that – but perhaps he would continue to evade Noyes and she could find freedom of her own in Pitoria.

March

THE PITORIAN
SEA

The low faint green line of Pitoria was ahead on the horizon.
March was standing with Holywell at the bow of the ship,
enjoying the rise and fall and seeing the land before him take
shape, as if he was riding into his own future. This was a future
of his own making. His Abask life had been taken and he'd been
given a servant's life instead, but now he was on his way to
reclaiming his destiny and getting his revenge on Prince Thelonius.
Holywell's plan was simple: they would follow Regan to find
Thelonius's son and then kidnap the boy and take him to Brigant,
to King Aloysius himself.

'Have you met Aloysius?' March asked Holywell.

'A few times. You're not the only one familiar with royalty.'

'Is he as ruthless as they say?'

'Vicious is his nickname and it suits him well enough.'

'What will he do with Thelonius's son?'

'I don't know and I don't care. Apart from the fact that he'll
pay us well for him.'

'I'm not doing this for money.'

'Well, my young brother, I imagine Aloysius will take great pleasure in making sure the prince knows his son is not in the lap of luxury but in a Brigantine dungeon.' Holywell looked at March. 'He may kill him, though I doubt that; he's more valuable alive. Is a son's torture enough for you?'

March thought about it and in truth all he wanted was to imagine the prince's face when he discovered that not only had he lost a son, his blood, the first and last of his children, but that he had lost him because of March, because of how he had treated the Abask people and how he had betrayed them.

'I want him to know it's because of what he did to us all.'

'Well, my angry young friend, you will have to tell him.'

March wasn't sure how he'd do that, but he liked the thought of it.

'Maybe I will one day.'

'Have confidence,' Holywell said. 'You'll be surprised what we Abask nobodies can achieve.' He slapped March on the arm.

And March did have confidence, because Holywell had confidence. Holywell knew so much, more than March had expected. He spoke four languages, knew how the sails worked to move the ship and how it was steered, and he explained these things with surprising patience to March. Holywell spoke in Pitorian to March, teaching him and testing him. Holywell also taught him card tricks and dice and sometimes joined in the games with the sailors, but only enough to make a few friends and lose enough money to keep them. Just being with Holywell was enough to make him think that anything was possible.

March looked back towards Calidor. It had disappeared from sight on the afternoon of the first day, but March enjoyed knowing that the prince and his drinks table were still there, small and insignificant and far, far behind him.

March said to Holywell, 'I went back to the castle before we left.'

Holywell raised his eyebrows. 'When?'

'Early, before our ship sailed. I wanted to tell the prince that I was leaving.' He'd lain awake all night imagining what he'd say, the swear words he would use as he told the prince how he hated him, how he despised his supposedly civilized ways. How Thelonius's fine manners and clothes couldn't hide what he really was: a man who betrayed his promises, broke his oaths, a man no one should trust, and that he, March, could see the prince for the traitor he really was.

'And did you tell him?'

'He'd gone out riding at dawn. One of his old habits, but he'd stopped going since his wife's death.'

'It seems the prince is recovering. So what did you do?'

'I poured myself a glass of wine – poured it beautifully, you'll be pleased to hear – and sat in the prince's chair in the bay window and looked out across the castle to the walls and city and sea beyond.'

'A pleasant breakfast.'

March shook his head. 'I thought of my brother. Of when we were so hungry we had to eat grass and worms. I spat the wine out.'

'You'll get your revenge soon, brother.' Holywell clamped his hand on March's shoulder. 'And afterwards you'll find wine tastes much sweeter.'

Ambrose

FIELDING,
BRIGANT

Ambrose was sleeping at the edge of a clearing when he was attacked. The soldier ran at him from the trees beyond the clearing, sword aloft and footsteps thundering across the hard ground, shaking him awake. Ambrose now slept holding his sword and he rolled to his side and rose to his feet as his assailant reached him and, in a smooth move, his sword entered the soldier's chest just as easily as it had Hodgson's. Then Ambrose realized the soldier *was* Hodgson. The dying man cursed him, blood pouring from his chest, as he brought his sword swooping down in an arc that Ambrose knew would slice his head off. He had to move, to parry, but he couldn't. He was frozen. That's when he woke.

Eyes wide open, Ambrose sat up, sweat on his back. He was breathing hard and grasping his neck where the sword would have struck him. The woodland around him was still. There were no attackers. There was no one here but himself. The only sound was his panicked breathing.

He swore and calmed his breath. Then he listened: he had dreamed the attack but that didn't mean Noyes's men weren't nearby.

The air was still and silent.

Ambrose got up and walked around the clearing, telling himself, *You can never be too careful*, but knowing as well that it was because he was afraid.

Hodgson had attacked him every night since Ambrose had fled Brigane, and every time it filled Ambrose with the same paralysing terror.

From a young age, Ambrose had imagined fighting in battles and killing the enemy; that was what all Brigantine boys were brought up to hope for. Ambrose had visualized many times thrusting his sword into a Calidorian soldier, a Calidorian lord even. But Hodgson was a Brigantine. A member of the Royal Guard. A brother in arms. Ambrose told himself that he'd done nothing wrong. He'd been challenged and he'd defended himself. Hodgson was overconfident and had fallen for his feint, and Ambrose had been lucky, because otherwise it would have been him with the sword in his chest.

Ambrose sipped water from his flask and lay down again. He needed to sleep. He'd been riding hard for three days, with little food and less rest. He closed his eyes, trying to empty his mind, and eventually drifted back to sleep. He dreamed of lying in bed with Catherine, the drapes dark red around them as he pulled her gown from her shoulders and kissed her neck. She took his hand and touched the back of it gently with her fingertips, the touch that he loved so much. But as she looked up at him she turned into his father and said, 'This hand killed a Brigantine soldier. This is the hand of a traitor.'

Ambrose woke with a start. It was getting light. He was covered in sweat again and he went to the stream to wash, hacking at the undergrowth with his sword as he went, saying to himself, *I'm no traitor. Catherine knows that. So does my father. It was them or me. Them or me.*

He wanted to act with honour. That was all he'd wanted his whole life. To fight well, to act properly, to uphold his family name, and he had done all that and yet it had all gone disastrously wrong. Because of Boris, because of Noyes ... because of the king. Because in Brigant now there was no honour. They had killed Anne and now they wanted to kill him.

And had Boris really challenged him because of one look he'd given Catherine?

He wasn't sure.

But was he acting honourably with her?

Catherine was not even his to think of, and yet he couldn't stop thinking of her. She was all he wanted to think of. She was betrothed to another man and yet he dreamed of her in his bed, sleeping with him, loving him. But that was not his future; it never had been and it never could be. His future should have been the army but that was now out of the question. He needed to find a different future for himself but first he wanted to understand the past. He wanted to understand what had happened to his sister.

He was heading north-west to escape Noyes and his men in this quiet part of Brigant, but his aim was to go to Fielding, the place on the remote west coast where Anne had been captured and Sir Oswald had been killed. Ambrose didn't know why his sister had gone to Fielding, but he suspected that it held a clue to why she had really been executed. His sister had been accused of having an affair with Sir Oswald, but Ambrose didn't believe it for a moment. He knew they'd had a brief dalliance years ago but it had come to nothing and they had remained what they both preferred, which was close friends and fellow travellers. They had been to many places together, staying away for long periods, always returning with stories of exotic foreign lands. So why had they been in a small village on the west coast of Brigant? What could possibly have interested his sister there? Ambrose wanted to see Fielding and find out. Even if he didn't find an answer, he wanted to say he had tried, that he had not simply accepted the lies about his sister.

He went back to his meagre camp and pulled out the last of the cheese and ham he'd bought at a farm the day before. He counted the money he had left. Eight shillings. It wasn't much. Still, he wasn't without resources. He had his most valuable possessions: his horse, saddle, sword and knives. He'd bought an old jacket from a man in one of the villages he'd passed through. The leather was worn and split, but it was better than nothing. He'd kept his guard's uniform, which was merely a cloak and jerkin, to wear at night to keep warm. He didn't sleep at inns, partly because of the risk of Noyes hearing about him, partly because he needed the money for food, not a bed.

He ate the last of the cheese, saddled his horse and set off.

By noon, he was out of the woods and into rolling grassland given over to sheep. He passed through a small hamlet and bought some milk, ham and more cheese and got directions to Fielding. The roads were narrow, stony and potholed, but by mid-afternoon he reached the coast. There was no sign of a town or village, and the only indication that there was a farm somewhere was the presence of some thin, bedraggled sheep. However, it was a beautiful place. The sea was vast and blue-grey and the beach wide and sandy. And far away on the beach Ambrose saw a figure. Ambrose rode across the sand, and the old man, who had been bent over digging for whelks, stood upright and watched him approach.

'Good afternoon to you,' Ambrose said.

The man stared at him and gave a nod in reply.

'I'm looking for the village of Fielding.'

The old man gave a wheezy laugh. 'You're a bit old, ain't you?'

'Old? For what?'

The man shook his head and then gestured to his left. 'That way. North. The camp's in the dunes. There's bugger all in the village; it was abandoned years ago.'

Ambrose wasn't sure what to say to that but, regardless, the man had picked up his bucket of whelks and was walking away.

Ambrose rode north along the coast. The tense feeling in his stomach had returned. It was unlikely Noyes or his men would be here. But something was. Something to do with Anne. Something that had led to her death.

It was late in the day when he saw the sand dunes ahead. They were high and wide, like small hills, and he could see a few figures in the far distance on the beach. He cut inland to avoid being seen, then turned back north to ride through sandy fields where a few sheep nibbled at the poor grass. It was getting dark as he made his way through some thin trees, towards where he thought he'd seen the figures on the beach. He led his horse on a path through the dunes. Ahead, he could hear a few shouts and a laugh. Ambrose recognized the familiar and welcoming sounds of an army camp.

On a wide expanse of flat scrubby ground in the dunes were numerous tents and a few small fires. It looked like a typical army camp, except for one thing: all the soldiers were boys. Some seemed to be fifteen or sixteen, but others looked much younger, no more than twelve or thirteen.

Ambrose knew that many young men became soldiers as a way out of poverty, but none were allowed to swear loyalty to a lord until they had come of age, as Ambrose himself had done. As a young boy he'd wanted to fight for Brigant. He'd played war games with Tarquin, tracking and setting up ambushes, camping out for days on end, training in combat and horsemanship. His army training, the comradeship with his fellow guardsmen – those were days that he recalled with feelings of true happiness. But to gain those skills you needed to learn from older soldiers. Here there seemed to be only children.

This had to be what his sister had seen and it was certainly unusual, but it seemed of minor importance: boys training to be soldiers wasn't news in Brigant. So why would the king have persecuted Anne for coming here?

Ambrose edged closer in the darkness. By the nearest fire was a group of boys, all wearing jerkins, which seemed to be their uniform. The two boys in the centre were wielding wooden practice swords and those around them were watching, giving occasional whoops of admiration and encouragement. The sword-wielders were impressive for their small stature, moving fast on their feet, their swords crashing hard into each other. And they kept at it. Ambrose knew only too well how tiring swordwork was.

'Seen enough?' Ambrose felt a sharp poke in his back.

There were two of them, about thirteen or fourteen, wiry and muscular, wearing army jerkins, though where there would normally be a badge to identify their lord was a square of red cloth. Both were carrying wooden practice spears.

Ambrose glanced around. Two boys would be easy to deal with, but he wanted to know what was going on. Better to try talking first.

'Who's your commanding officer, boy?'

'Who's yours?'

Ambrose smiled. 'Prince Boris. I'm with the Royal Guard. Who are you with?'

The boy swung his fist to the red patch on his jerkin. 'The Reds. Strongest and best.' But he quickly looked uncertain. 'You're not in uniform, sir. You coming to see the captain?'

'Of course.' Ambrose didn't want to see any captain, as the captain would know he hadn't been sent here by Boris.

'Oy, Rashford. We've got a visitor.'

The two boys with the wooden swords came over and, as they approached, it occurred to Ambrose that these two would not be so easy to beat in a fight. And their cockiness as they walked over seemed to indicate that they knew it too. One of them shouted, 'What've you got, Frank? More spies?'

'Says he's with the Royal Guard. Says he's here to see the captain.'

Ambrose got to his feet, dusting sand off his thighs and saying in as casual and friendly a tone as possible, 'I'm no spy, though I admit I wanted to watch you without you knowing I was here. I wanted to see how good you were. I saw you two practising with swords. That was impressive. You're Rashford, are you?'

'Yes, leader of the Reds.'

Ambrose now had an idea of how to get away. 'How are you with spears, Rashford?'

The boy smiled. 'Not bad.'

'It's my weakest weapon,' said Ambrose with a rueful grin. 'I've never mastered the throw. Care to show me your technique?'

'Give me your spear, Frank. And give our visitor yours, Luke.' Frank twirled the spear in one hand, then tossed it sideways to Rashford, who caught it and twirled it round in his hands before spiking it into the ground. Luke tossed his spear to Ambrose. It was well balanced and the wooden point sharp. It might have been a training weapon, but it could do serious damage.

Rashford said, 'You throw first, sir. I'll see if I can match your distance.'

Ambrose weighed the spear in his hand and flexed his shoulder. Then he took a few paces forward and threw the spear.

'Not so bad, sir. Nice style.'

'You're very generous.'

'Well, I didn't comment on the distance, which, if I'm honest, sir, is pretty dismal.'

Ambrose had to stifle a laugh. 'Let's see how you do then.'

Rashford raised his spear to his shoulder. He was small and wiry, with narrow shoulders – not the right build for a spearman at all. He took a few paces forward, threw – and Ambrose turned and ran.

He reached his horse in a few strides and swung himself into the saddle. As his horse wheeled round, Ambrose saw Rashford's spear had gone almost twice the distance of his own. It was a huge distance for a slim boy, and for a moment he was frozen with surprise. But then he gathered the reins and kicked his horse into motion.

The boys were running after him, shouting for him to stop. They were quick too, keeping pace with him and grabbing for his legs, but then he kicked the horse harder and galloped away.

The thud to his head knocked Ambrose sideways and forward across his horse's shoulders. He lost a stirrup and before he knew it he was half under his horse's body and being dragged along the ground. A hoof caught his back, knocking him free, and he rolled forward through the sand and tried to get up, but everything was swaying and then it went black.

Catherine

BRIGANE, BRIGANT

People dismiss, belittle or ignore women. But when I
represent my country I am not a woman: I am a land
and a people and a queen.

Queen Valeria of Illast

It was less than a week before Catherine's departure for Pitoria and
the arrangements were coming to dominate her every waking
moment. She thought of Ambrose still, every day, but she was also
having to think of Tzsayn, her marriage, her journey and now her
clothes. Her mother had ordered for her numerous dresses in the
Pitorian style, and they had finally arrived. The day dresses were each
a different colour of the Pitorian flag: green, red and black. Her
mother had said, 'You must show the Pitorians that you are one of
them. Show them you are proud to be Pitorian and they will be too,
and they'll thank you for reminding them that they should be.'

Still, Catherine had snorted when she saw the gowns laid out next to each other in her dressing room. They were ridiculously bold. Even the black ones had shiny ribbons and feathers woven round the bodice, sleeves and hem.

'They look complicated.' Catherine picked one sleeve up in her fingers. 'What there is of them.'

'Pitorian women are more comfortable exposing skin,' agreed her mother. 'Believe it or not, these are quite conservative.'

Catherine tried one of the red ones on, but it didn't seem to hang correctly and she felt exposed; the left side of the gown was open from armpit to hip.

'I look like I'm in rags . . . bloodstained rags.'

'Hmm . . . Can't you do something with your arms?'

'Such as?' Catherine put her hands on her hips, elbows poking through the slashes in her sleeves.

'No, don't do that! Hold them straight.' Her mother winced when Catherine did so. 'Oh dear, that doesn't look right either. Perhaps carry something. A prop. Yes, that would be useful. Something to help tell your story.'

'A hint of despair?'

Her mother frowned. 'Never show that, Catherine. Remember Queen Valeria. She won her people over to her. But to win people over they need to see you as a winner. You don't want them to link you to despair, but to hope. To a brighter future. To success.'

Catherine couldn't think of anything that could link her to success. She'd never felt she'd had any success or even the opportunity for it. As for hope, in these clothes she could only hope people didn't laugh at her.

At that moment there was a knock on the door to her chambers and then Sarah almost ran into the dressing room, bobbed a curtsy to the queen and turned to Catherine.

'Your Highness,' she said breathlessly. 'A messenger has come from the king. His Majesty commands you to appear before him.'

Catherine felt her heart race. She had never been summoned by the king before. Was it about her marriage? Possibly. Probably. But there was also a chance it had something to do with Ambrose . . .

The queen rose, a picture of calm.

'Tell the messenger the princess is dressing. She will attend on the king as soon as she has finished.'

When Sarah had gone the queen said, 'You've gone pale, Catherine. Do you know what this is about?'

'Perhaps the wedding arrangements?' Catherine replied.

'Is there anything else it could be?'

Catherine knew her mother must have heard something of the fight between Ambrose and Boris's men, but she hadn't been able to bring herself to talk about it. Now it seemed she had no choice.

'There was . . . an incident a few days ago, when I was riding at the beach.'

'A trial of honour, I believe. I heard that Boris lost a man. And the traitor fled.'

'He's not a traitor. And he didn't flee.'

'You show your emotions too clearly, Catherine.'

'But it's true. Sir Ambrose is no traitor; he's a loyal guard.'

'Sir Ambrose Norwend? The one with the hair?'

'They all have hair.'

'You know what I mean. The blond hair. Attractive.'

'He's intelligent and considerate. He's –'

'Trouble. Trouble you cannot afford. I understand why Boris is concerned.'

'Understand! A man is dead. Ambrose did nothing but defend himself.'

'You talk of this man as if you care about him. As if he's important to you. Do you expect your future husband to accept that?'

'You said he was more liberal.'

'I expect he'll be a lot less liberal when he hears about Sir Ambrose and how intelligent and considerate he is. You've a lot to learn about men, Catherine. Prince Tzsayn expects his bride to be a virgin and for there to be no doubt about it.'

Catherine blushed hard. She had never heard her mother even say that word before.

'Tzsayn may be different to your father but no man likes to be made to look a fool.'

Whereas we women love it, Catherine thought and at the same time glanced at herself in the mirror in the absurd red dress. She said, 'I will ensure at all times that my devotion to Prince Tzsayn is made clear,' she said coldly. 'But perhaps it doesn't matter. Noyes has probably caught Ambrose, and the king has summoned me to require that I attend another execution.'

The queen took Catherine by surprise, moving quickly to her side and kissing her on the cheek.

'I've not heard that he's been caught. Calm yourself. Go to the king like the princess you are. But be mindful of your own honour, Catherine. Make sure there can be no doubt of it, as without it you are lost.'

Catherine looked down at her slashed red dress.

'I can't go like this.'

'Of course you can. There's no time to change now; we've already kept the king waiting. And, besides, the dress is stunning. It's the perfect royal red. Just hold your shoulders back and have confidence.'

Catherine was sure her mother wouldn't say that unless she meant it, and it did help. She walked through her outer chambers and followed the Royal Guard towards the Throne Room. Could this just be about her wedding or was her mother mistaken? Was Ambrose dead or lying in the castle dungeons below, his tongue cut out, his soft lips sewn up? Well, whatever it was, she was going to handle it. She pulled her shoulders back, telling herself, *I won't flinch. I won't faint. I certainly won't scream.*

Catherine had only been inside the Throne Room on a handful of official occasions – royal proclamations or visits from an ambassador or some such infrequent occasion when the king wanted to impress or intimidate some lord. Each time she'd been part of a great crowd. Today she was alone.

Catherine arrived as the doors were swinging open. The king, her father, was sitting on his throne at the far end of the long, elaborately decorated room. Boris stood to his right, Noyes behind him to his left. A few other courtiers and soldiers lined the walls. Ambrose was not there.

Catherine wasn't sure if she was supposed to wait to be announced or go in. Her mother's voice seemed to whisper in her ear, *A princess doesn't wait. And neither does a queen.*

Catherine straightened. 'I am not afraid,' she murmured to herself, and discovered, to her surprise, that it was true. Still, as she advanced into that great chamber, she felt as conspicuous as a red ant on a grey paving slab.

She came forward – slowly, slowly – and kept coming, past the chancellor and the steward and the castellan, until she reached the bottom of the dais and stopped directly in front of her father. His hair was grey at the temples, but he looked as strong as ever. He sat upright in the wide, heavy throne, and Catherine thought how he never seemed right sitting down – striding around suited him better. His grey eyes were on her and met her gaze, which she instantly dropped, and she curtsied as low as her dress would allow.

'Your Majesty.'

'Straighten up. Let's see you.'

'We can't *not* see her,' Boris said loudly, and there was a short laugh from one of the courtiers. Noyes had his head on one side but no half-smile on his lips.

Catherine stood as tall as she could.

'You're off soon. To be married.'

'Yes, Your Majesty.'

The king tapped the arm of the throne with a nail that was bruised black.

'It's a fine match that I've arranged with King Arell for you.'

Could that really be all this summons was for? A conversation about her marriage?

'Yes, thank you, Father. But much as I look forward to my marriage it grieves me more than I can express to leave my home and my family. I am thankful you have asked to see me before I go.'

'I summoned you to give you instructions, not for an emotional farewell.'

Catherine watched the king's finger tap-tapping on the throne and then it went still.

'You ordered one of my Royal Guards to leave Brigane.'

There was nothing to be gained by denying it.

'Yes, Father. Boris's companion, Viscount Lang, challenged one of my bodyguards, Sir Ambrose Norwend, to a trial of honour. Sir Ambrose beat him, though generously allowed him to live. Then Boris ordered Dirk Hodgson to challenge him too. He was killed. I thought it best that Sir Ambrose should leave before any more nobles came to harm.'

Catherine glanced meaningfully at Boris and there was a short laugh from one of the onlookers that was quickly stifled.

Boris flushed angrily. 'He fought like the villain he is.'

'You are the villain in this, brother.'

'Silence!' The king tapped his throne.

Catherine stayed still. She'd forgotten herself.

'Do you think Tzsayn will put up with this behaviour?' grunted the king.

'I'm sorry, Your Majesty. I don't understand. What behaviour might he object to?'

'You failed to follow your brother's instructions to return with him to the castle. And even now you disagree with him.'

'I followed your own instructions, Your Majesty. Those that I have always been told are vital to my safety: that I stay always with my maids and my bodyguards. Boris's men followed his orders and as a result one lost a hand, the other his life. I wasn't certain that Boris's instructions were sound.'

'It's not your place to judge them but to *obey* them,' Boris hissed.

'I disagree. Where my safety and honour are concerned, I must choose who I obey. And I chose not to obey you in that instance.'

The king sat back an inch in his throne and regarded Catherine as if he'd never seen her before. Catherine wasn't sure if she'd gone too far, but knew she should go no further.

'You are my daughter, and a royal princess. But you are a woman and must obey the men who are there to protect you. Let me be clear: from this moment until the moment Tzsayn puts his ring on your finger, you will follow Boris's instructions in every detail. You will not bring dishonour to me or to Brigant. You will not bring my name into disrepute. You will do nothing to endanger your marriage. Is that clear?'

'Yes, Your Majesty.'

'Tzsayn may tolerate your behaviour. He may even find it curious and charming – after all, he is a foreigner and has strange ideas – but if I were him I'd whip it out of you once and for all.'

Catherine swallowed. 'I will try to be a good wife to Tzsayn, and I am and always will be your loyal daughter.'

'See that you are. Now, Noyes has some news for you.'

Catherine felt dread creep over her. She took a breath and looked at Noyes. He held her gaze for what seemed like forever before saying, 'We caught the traitor yesterday.'

Catherine felt dizzy. 'Caught?'

'My men found him riding north. It seems *they* were more than a match for Sir Ambrose. But sadly we won't have the pleasure of a second Norwend execution this week. The traitor died of his wounds in the cells last night.'

The half-smile was back on Noyes's face and Catherine wanted to run at him and rip it off.

'You look pale, sister,' Boris said.

Catherine had no tears, at least not yet. She remembered Lady Anne, and stood straighter and forced out some words, though she wasn't even sure of what she was saying.

'It saddens me to hear of another death. Perhaps I'll find a more peaceful life in Pitoria.'

Boris actually snorted a laugh then cut it short.

'If you want a peaceful life,' grunted the king, 'make sure you follow my instructions. Now, get out.'

March

WESTMOUTH, PITORIA

March and Holywell had landed in the bustling port of Westmouth and immediately begun to enquire about Lord Regan. He hadn't been hard to trace. The ship on which Regan had travelled was still in port and the captain provided information for a small fee. The stable where Regan had bought a horse wasn't hard to find either, but neither the ship's captain nor the stable boy knew which direction he was travelling in.

'When did he leave?' asked March in shaky Pitorian.

The stable boy replied, 'Two days ago, in the morning.'

March said to Holywell, 'So Regan spent a night here. Maybe he told the innkeeper where he was going.'

Holywell shook his head impatiently. 'Regan is clever and cautious. He won't have given such information away. We'll get horses from that stable and take the road south. If we find no news, then we try the east road and then the north.'

March considered this a poor plan – they were already two days behind Regan – but he didn't have a better one. He didn't know how many roads there were or how they might lead to other roads. He asked Holywell, 'Do you have a map of Pitoria?' And then, saying that, a new idea emerged. 'Does *Regan* have a map of Pitoria?'

Holywell smiled. 'Clever, brother. Find the nearest mapmaker.'

Soon they were in a small shop in a narrow cobbled lane just off the harbour.

'Yes, the gentleman you describe was here,' said the shopkeeper. 'But he didn't want a map. He was after something else.'

It took the purchase of a map before the man revealed what Regan had wanted.

'Ah yes, the gentleman took the schedule of the summer trade fairs. A full schedule costs two kroners. They are pieces of art, really.'

'They're bloody expensive,' muttered March, but Holywell just smiled at the mapmaker and said, 'I'm sure they are.'

'Did our friend say where he was going?' asked March.

'No, but if you look at the schedule you can see where the fair is at present.'

'Can I see the schedule?'

'Can I see two kroners?'

Holywell slammed the money on the counter.

The schedule was simple. From April to September the fair moved every three weeks to a new town in northern Pitoria. It was now at Dornan and would remain there for another two weeks.

Holywell and March set off back to the stables.

'Now we know where our man is bound. We'll have to ride hard, but we can catch him.' Holywell glanced at March. 'How *is* your riding?'

Like all the people of Abask, March had been brought up riding small, stocky mountain ponies. But that was a long time ago.

'Servants don't get to do much riding.'

'Much or any?'

'Don't worry. If I fall off, I'll get back on.'

'Oh, of that I'm sure, my determined friend. But our future together doesn't just depend on being able to climb back on to a horse. You need to be able to learn quickly and act decisively.' Holywell grinned. 'Time to try out your training.'

'My Pitorian?' March asked. He had been spending every spare moment going over words and phrases he'd learnt, and was always asking Holywell about new ones. 'I managed well enough with the stable boy. And I followed most of what you said to the mapmaker.'

'No, not that. I showed you how to take a purse, didn't I?'

Holywell had been teaching March to pick pockets because 'it's a useful skill to be able to deprive someone of something they value'. It was a lot harder than learning a language.

'You know I'm not good enough,' March objected. 'Why waste time on this now? If I get caught, we'll be delayed and Regan will get to the prince's son before we do.'

'If you get caught, *you'll* get more than delayed: *you'll* be lashed and *you'll* be imprisoned. And *I'll* follow Regan alone.' Holywell was serious now. 'We need the money, brother. I paid for passage for two of us on the ship, and those maps were hardly cheap. I like you, March, but you wanted to come with me. Now I need you to contribute your share.'

'But you can pick pockets better than me.'

'True. And I will if I need to. But I also need to know you will if you need to. You're sharp enough, I've seen that, but I need to know your will. We've come to Pitoria to take a man. To do that, you need determination. You're not going to serve wine and spy on other people's conversations; you're going to exert your will on others. And I need to know you can do this, otherwise you're wasting my time, and my money.'

And March knew Holywell really would leave him there and carry on alone if he didn't prove himself.

'Fuck it then. I'll exert my will.' March surveyed the market-place, looking for a likely target. 'On that man there.'

'What, the old fella? His heart will give out when he finds his money is gone. We don't want an old man's death on our conscience.'

March frowned and said, 'Well, him then,' nodding to a fat gentleman in a green woollen cape.

'No,' Holywell replied. 'Pick on someone your own size. Him.'

The young man Holywell indicated was probably a few years older than March. Tall, strong. And wearing a dagger.

'Hardly anyone in this country is armed and you pick the man with a knife!' March spluttered. 'I thought you didn't want a death on your hands?'

'The man in the cape was armed too. His dagger was hidden.'

March was irritated now. He said, 'Fine. The young man with the dagger.'

Without another word to Holywell, he set off, following his target through the market. March moved close and saw where the man's coin purse sat inside his jacket. He would have to brush into him or distract him as he slid his hand inside the jacket. But there were too many people here; he knew he'd fail. March felt his chest tighten. *How can I do it without getting caught?*

The young man left the market square, so March set off down a backstreet, hoping to come around ahead of him. He was just speeding up when, to his surprise, the man appeared before him, taking a shortcut, no doubt.

March seized his chance, rushing into the young man and pushing him against the wall. In his broken Pitorian he managed, 'I want your money.'

'What?'

'Give me your money. Now!'

March slid his hand into the young man's jacket, but his victim grabbed that hand with his left, while his right hand went to his knife.

But the knife stayed in the scabbard.

March smiled at the man. 'Why don't you take it out?'

He wasn't sure he said it correctly, but the young man looked terrified, his hand gripping the knife yet seeming to push it further into the scabbard. And the thrill of it was wonderful. For once March felt like he had some power.

March hissed at the young man, 'Give me your money. Now. Or I . . . cut . . .' March's Pitorian ran out, so he gestured a slit across his throat. He wasn't armed but the man didn't know that. The man had only to take the dagger from his scabbard, to run March through, but he seemed frozen still.

'You want to die?' March jolted the man against the wall.

The young man shook his head.

'Give me your money. Now.'

'Take it,' the man croaked, and he reached into his jacket and handed over his purse.

It wasn't heavy.

'Now run,' March barked, and he pushed the young man away. His victim ran, stumbling past Holywell, who was walking towards them.

Holywell beamed and clapped his hands slowly. 'Not exactly the technique I taught you, but we each have our own methods.'

That he said in Calidorian but the rest he spoke in Abask. 'You are quite special, March. You do know that, don't you?'

March stared back at Holywell. He felt exhilarated. It had been good to exert his will, to have someone do *his* bidding for a change.

'You look like you will kill; there is no doubting it. That gleam in your eye.' Holywell squeezed March's shoulder. 'A fine asset, that look. But don't be killing anyone just yet. There's plenty of time for that, brother.'

Edyon

DORNAN,
PITORIA

Edyon entered the dimly lit tent and took a moment to let his eyes adjust. Across the small wooden octagonal table sat Madame Eruth. Her body was covered – *dressed* seemed the wrong word – in faded patterned scarves that blended so well with the rugs it was always a challenge to know where the tent ended and she began.

'You've brought the bones this time.'

Madame Eruth spoke with certainty, as she did all things. Her comment wasn't a prediction but a statement of the obvious.

Edyon put a kroner and the bones on the table.

'Tell me my future.'

The kroner and the request were the same as Edyon gave every time he and Madame Eruth met, which was at least three times a year, but the bones were a new development in Edyon's search for knowledge. Madame Eruth had a crystal ball, which she preferred. However, with Edyon she'd also used tea leaves, palm reading and cards. Edyon had had his future told and retold based on these devices for many years, but the last time they met, at the fair at Gorgant in the autumn, Madame Eruth had said he should kill an animal and bring the bones with him next time.

And as luck would have it, at least for Edyon, a chicken had come into his possession a few days earlier. He'd managed to kill it, though he hadn't wrung its neck properly and the wretched creature had squawked and flapped and clawed until Edyon had cut its head off, apologizing at the same time. Once it was dead he'd boiled the body until the meat fell off the bones then he left them to dry in the sun. He'd scattered the meat in the woods for the foxes to find, hoping some gift to nature might help with the prediction. He didn't really believe in the power of nature and spent half his time telling himself Madame Eruth was a fraud, and yet he always came back. There was something here in the tent, with her, away from books and learning and logic, something deeper that he hoped would help him.

Madame Eruth swayed forward and a wrinkled hand extended from the scarves to prod the chicken bones.

'Move the table. Cast the bones on the floor,' she said.

Her hand and Edyon's coin were already back in her scarves.

Edyon set the table to one side and Madame Eruth widened her legs. The scarves parted a little and Edyon glimpsed the inside of her thigh, pale, blue-veined and hairless and reminding him of chicken skin. He picked up the bones and, holding them in his cupped hands, right hand over left, shook them, feeling their lightness, hearing their soft clatter. He swapped his hands over and shook them the same number of times with left hand over right. All the while he was thinking to himself, *My future . . . My future . . .*

'You don't need to think of anything,' Madame Eruth said. 'Best not to think.'

Edyon carried on shaking the bones. Madame Eruth was beginning to sound like his mother with all her instructions. And he really didn't want to think of his mother at this moment; he wanted to think of the future. *His* future. Not his mother's plans and ambitions for him. Not the failure of his law studies – or, rather, the success of those studies but the refusal of two universities to grant him a place. Not the lack of friends. Not the rejection of Xavier of Ruen, whom he'd met at the midwinter fair and approached with all the courtesy and poetry of the best of legitimate lovers, only to be spurned at the first of the spring fairs and called in public a 'common bastard'. All things that, one way or the other, Madame Eruth had predicted, though in truth anyone with common sense could have foretold, anyone except his mother, who insisted he was talented enough to do whatever he wanted, or indeed what *she* wanted. But while she had money enough to pay for his tutoring, and he had the brains to get the highest marks, his mother had forgotten to marry Edyon's father, and all her money and clever talking could make no difference to the fact that being illegitimate meant being ineligible for university. So he might work as a lawyer's scribe, slaving away for someone he could out-argue and out-think, but he'd always be a lackey, scribbling notes and running errands and –

'However, you do need to throw the bones,' Madame Eruth reminded Edyon.

He gave them a final shake and threw them.

Edyon waited. He knew not to ask questions, never to interrupt. However, after a long silence he looked up from the bones to Madame Eruth.

Madame Eruth had her eyes closed, but she pointed to Edyon.

'You are not honest but the bones are true. They don't lie. They don't steal.'

Edyon clenched his jaw. If he'd wanted another lecture, he would have stayed for breakfast with his mother.

He looked down at the bones, willing them to reveal something hopeful, something different.

Madame Eruth swept her hand above them, saying, 'Speak to me. Tell me. Show me.'

Edyon found himself thinking, *Tell me. Show me.*

Madame Eruth went still and opened her eyes. She pointed at a bone with her crooked finger. 'Your future . . . has many paths. You must make a choice. And –' she laughed a little – 'thievery is not always the wrong one.' She looked up at Edyon. 'But you must be honest.'

Edyon nodded earnestly, already feeling he'd wasted his money. This was even vaguer than usual. And who in the whole country was truly honest?

'With the new moon, a new man enters your life.'

Edyon had been expecting this. There was always a new man entering his life.

'A foreign man. Handsome.'

Madame Eruth's new men were always handsome, though not often foreign, but this was hardly a dramatic revelation.

Madame Eruth turned her gaze back to the bones, swooping her head low as if smelling them. She closed her eyes, her head still moving in a circle over the bones, round once . . . twice . . . then she sat up and shuddered. 'This is not like anything I've seen before. Did you kill the bird yourself? You didn't find it dead somewhere?'

'I killed it. And prepared the bones.'

'You're not lying?'

'I would never lie to you.'

Madame Eruth frowned but turned to the bones once more and leaned over them.

After a long silence she looked at Edyon and said, 'There is a new influence on you. One I've not sensed with you before.'

Edyon couldn't stop himself from asking, 'A good influence?'

'His presence has changed everything.'

And somehow Edyon knew what she was going to say.

'Your father.'

Madame Eruth had always told Edyon that she could only sense his mother's presence, never his father's.

'My father's presence? Is he . . .? Do I meet him?'

Madame Eruth didn't reply.

'So . . . his influence? Does he want to help me? With university?'

'There is no university.'

'Then what?'

Madame Eruth turned from him and passed her hands over the bones again, and a spasm of something like fear crossed her wrinkled face. 'The foreign man is in pain. I cannot see if he lives or dies.' Madame Eruth caught Edyon's eye, frowning as if this was his fault. 'You might help him. But beware: he lies too.' She pointed to the wishbone. 'This is the crossroads. Your future divides here. This is where you must choose a path. There is a journey, a difficult one to far lands and riches or –' and here she pointed to the cracked thigh bone – 'to . . . pain, suffering and death.'

Edyon had to ask. 'My death?'

Madame Eruth shook her head.

'I see death all around you now.'

March

DORNAN, PITORIA

Lord Regan had ridden north-east towards Dornan, following the main road and staying at inns along the way. March and Holywell picked up his trail simply by enquiring after a foreign lord. If anyone asked why they were looking for him, Holywell had a simple response: 'He's an acquaintance. The sort who owes us money.'

March was surprised how most people quickly took their side just from this comment. Holywell laughed and said, 'Regan looks rich. People don't trust the rich; they want to believe the worst of them and hope they get a good kicking from time to time, whether they really deserve it or not.'

The journey to Dornan had taken Regan five days, though March and Holywell did it in half that, so it seemed Regan was not in a desperate rush to hand over the prince's seal. Pitoria was greener than Calidor and cooler, but also bigger. The roads seemed wider, the rivers deeper, the towns larger and more prosperous. Holywell may have said that people resented the rich, but here everyone seemed well fed and well satisfied.

They arrived in Dornan in the early evening. March had thought Westmouth busy but really no more so than Calia on market days. However, here the streets of Dornan were so crowded with stalls it was hard to move. The pavements thronged with men with coloured hair – some bright red (they were the sheriff's men) and many teal, showing they were with the local lord.

March and Holywell were directed to a field and temporary stable, where they were charged more to stable their horses than they'd paid for a night in a roadside inn. There was no alternative though and this was the end of their journey. Soon they would find Regan. Holywell asked for the best inn in town and they went there, March listening in to the conversations, practising his new language in his head.

At the inn, Holywell said he was looking for a friend from Calidor, just arrived today.

'You from Calidor too?' the innkeeper asked, staring at Holywell's eyes and then at March's.

'Indeed,' Holywell replied, adding, 'but our friend has brown eyes.'

'Whatever colour they are, they ain't here. We're full and been full for the last week. In fact, we're more than full. Some rooms have four or five in 'em. And I can't see any other inn being different.'

Holywell led the way to the next inn. However, after two more it was obvious that the inns really were full and it didn't matter how rich or noble Regan was – there wasn't a room to be had. They learnt that there were beds available in private houses or in tented accommodation on the outskirts of town.

'Hard to find him if he's staying in someone's home,' said Holywell.

'He won't do that,' replied March. 'The great Lord Regan bedding down in the house of some common man? Never. We should try the tents.'

The sleeping tents were large marquees with rows of narrow camp beds, partitioned by curtains and with a heavy metal chest at the foot of each bed to store clothes and possessions.

Holywell eyed them doubtfully. 'Poor lodgings for a lord.'

March shook his head. 'Regan is a soldier. He'll fancy himself as being back on campaign. Look – there!'

March had spotted Regan emerging from one of the compartments further down the tent. He lowered his head and turned as casually as he could, diverting himself and Holywell out of Regan's path. Regan might not have recognized March's face but his eyes were too distinctive. Regan strode past without a glance in their direction and Holywell and March followed in the crowd.

Regan walked around the fair, as if assessing the whole place. He had a meal in a food tent but didn't meet anyone or seem in a hurry to find his man, and when it was dark he returned to his sleeping marquee. Holywell took a bed in the same tent, but March didn't want to risk Regan spotting him so he told Holywell, 'I'll find somewhere else.'

'Don't go far. Our man may be up early. If the prince's boy is here, we must be prepared to act quickly. We can't let him go with Regan.'

'I understand.' March felt he should be more assertive, so he added, 'I'll do what needs to be done.'

'And if what needs to be done involves the removal of someone? Regan, for example? Your conscience will not suddenly rise up and stop you?'

March felt a tightening in his stomach. He'd half known this was going to be part of Holywell's plan. Lord Regan might not be enthusiastic about the task he had been given, but he would do it and he would kill all those who tried to stop him. He was a lord of Calidor, friend to Prince Thelonius and an honoured soldier. He was a formidable opponent and March and Holywell would have to use force to stop him.

'Regan supported Prince Thelonius when Thelonius sacrificed Abask and all our people were killed. My conscience will be clear. My conscience says, *Why have you waited so long to get your revenge?*'

Holywell smiled. 'You'll have your revenge, brother.'

March left Holywell and wandered through the fair, excitement growing within him that he was finally going to *do* something, finally going to act rather than wait. Holywell would kill Regan, and he, March, would assist him. And it was the right thing to do. He was a fighter, an Abask. Why shouldn't he punish those who had betrayed his countrymen? Regan deserved no favours from him. He'd had a long and privileged life. March's brother, Julien, had not.

March watched other men talk and laugh. Holywell was now his friend, his only friend. It helped to remember that Lord Regan was a close friend of Prince Thelonius. Regan's death would hit the prince hard. That, coupled with the loss of his son, would be a double blow. March tried to remember the friends he'd had growing up in Abask. It was getting harder to remember their faces, but he went through their names: Delit, Hedge, Anara, Amark, Granus, Tarin, Wanar. All dead. For them and for all Abasks, Regan would pay.

March looked at the excellent pies, meats and cheeses on offer but he wasn't hungry. He watched stilt-walkers and acrobats, and slipped into a tent devoted to men dancing, but he found nothing that could distract him from his thoughts until he passed a barber's tent, where a group of men were having their hair dyed scarlet. He stopped and had his own hair cut in the Pitorian style, longer on top and shaved round the neck. The result made him feel less conspicuous. Then he went to the woods to the north of the fair and laid his bedroll down and again thought of his brother and his family and all the friends he'd known in Abask, and told himself, *This is right. This is for them.*

But, still, sleep was a long time coming.

March woke at dawn and went straight to the sleeping marquee, waiting at a distance from the entrance. When Holywell appeared, he came straight to March and pulled March's hood off. March thought he'd laugh at him, but Holywell just said, 'You almost pass for a Pitorian.' They bought porridge at a nearby stall and ate while the fair began to slowly wake up.

'What do we do?' March asked.

'We keep an eye on Regan and see where he goes.' Holywell grinned. 'And here he comes now. Let the fun begin.'

Regan came out of the marquee, ignoring the food stalls and walking quickly towards a part of the fair March hadn't visited the night before. It had a different atmosphere. Here the tents were big and beautiful, bright with flags and pennants. Some even had gold and silver decoration, while others were trimmed with crystals. Wind chimes chimed and guards stood around. The clientele here was different too: older and definitely richer. It was also much quieter, making it more difficult for March and Holywell to remain unseen. They kept well back, and watched Regan go up to a small food stall. He ate a pie and then stayed standing there.

'Is he waiting for someone?' March asked Holywell.

Holywell shook his head. 'He's watching that tent, the one with the red and gold pennants. How about you go and make some enquiries about who owns it?'

March went over to another food stall and bought his own pie.

'Good morning, sir.' The pie seller stared at him. 'You're from Abask, is it, with those eyes?'

March nodded.

'Haven't seen eyes like that for many years. And let me guess: it's your first time at the fair here in Dornan?'

'Yes and it's amazing. Excuse my Pitorian – I'm still learning. I was just looking at that tent over there. It's the most beautiful I've ever seen.'

'Impressive, isn't it? Belongs to a woman too.'

'A woman! Who is she?'

'A trader. Too old for you, though, my friend.'

'Ah, you never know!'

'Well, Erin does have a reputation for taking men in and spitting them out.' The man looked March up and down. 'You wouldn't last a day.'

March laughed, though he wasn't totally sure he understood what the man had said. 'What does she trade?'

'Furniture – fine furniture from the south, from abroad. Travelling there to buy; coming here to sell.'

'She does this on her own? With no husband?'

'She has a son, but he's no use. Spoilt. Soft as butter. Wants to be a lawyer but no one'll have him.'

'He's not clever then?'

'Oh, he's bright enough. But born on the wrong side of the sheets.'

'He's a bastard, you mean? His mother never married his father?'

'That is indeed what I mean, sir. A shame for young Edyon; it means he has no future.'

'His father won't help? Do you know who he is?'

The man shrugged. 'Ain't me, mate. That's all I know.'

March wandered back to join Holywell just as a well-dressed youth came out of the red-and-gold tent. He was wearing fine boots and tight trousers and a figure-hugging soft leather jacket. His light brown hair blew into his face and he tucked it behind his ears.

March almost laughed. 'It's him,' he said to Holywell. 'Like a younger version of the prince. The same hair, the same build. He's like Thelonius must have looked twenty years ago. He's the right age and the man at the food stall told me he's illegitimate.'

Holywell looked over to Regan, whose eyes were fixed on the young man. 'Seems like Regan knows it too.'

And indeed Regan was following Edyon through the fair.

'Come on,' said Holywell urgently. 'We can't let them speak.'

They hurried through the next field of tents, closing in on Regan, but the Calidorian lord didn't seem in a hurry to talk to the young man, instead keeping his distance. Finally the young man disappeared inside a tent with the sign of a fortune teller hanging above it. Regan paused for a moment and then set off back the way he had come.

Ducking aside, Holywell said, 'I'll follow Regan; you stay with the young prince.'

'What? Why?'

'I need to see what Regan is up to. Perhaps he has friends here. Friends we don't want surprising us later.' Holywell's eyes gleamed. 'We have found our prize, brother. Now we make sure we don't lose it.'

Edyon

DORNAN,
PITORIA

Edyon stamped across the worn grass towards his mother's caravan. He had gone back to Madame Eruth's tent to demand more explanation of yesterday's ominous foretelling from the bones, only to be denied entry by her assistant.

'She won't see you. She says you have death around you. She won't see you ever again.'

'Nonsense,' Edyon muttered as he walked away. 'She's the thief, not me. Taking people's money and trying to scare them. Telling them stories then refusing to explain their meanings.' Edyon stopped. 'She's a fraud. A liar.'

A passing merchant shrugged. 'Typical woman then, mate.'

Edyon ignored him and carried on walking. 'I should insist on my money back, and damn her *I sense your father's presence, death is all around you* bollocks.'

He stopped, ready to turn and retrace his steps, but something caught his eye. To his right were the caravans that the merchants used to transport their wares between towns.

Edyon felt a smile pulling at the corners of his mouth.

The nearest caravan belonged to Stone, another trader, a rival of Edyon's mother. Like all travelling merchants, Stone journeyed between towns in a highly decorated personal caravan: luxurious, comfortable, with plenty of cushions and silk. But the valuable merchandise – artwork, precious rugs and ornaments – was kept in these larger, heavier transport caravans. And these caravans were always guarded. In fact, all the caravans, from the simple kitchen transports to the luxury personal ones, were guarded, because at the fairs there were always people willing to take an opportunity to steal food, a cooking pot or a precious casket.

Edyon knew this because, in his time, he'd stolen all those things.

Stone's was a typical transport caravan, wooden and plain, with sides that could fold down for large items to be put on or taken off. At the rear was a small wooden door, which was locked at all times to ensure the contents were secure. Except the door to Stone's caravan wasn't locked. It wasn't even shut properly. Edyon could almost see inside. He *could* see inside, but only a sliver of the dark red carpet, rich with silk and wool and luxuriously soft – the fabric of far lands.

You must make a choice. And thievery is not always the wrong one . . .

To leave an open caravan unguarded was a dismissible offence. But perhaps there was a guard inside. Edyon's brow furrowed. He ought to check. He strolled forward to the caravan, peered in to see if there was someone inside – there was no one – and before he could think about it he'd stepped up through the door, pulling it closed behind him.

As easy as that.

It was warm and gloomy inside the caravan. The roof was slatted, with canvas drawn tightly across the wooden beams so that the glow of sunlight threw barred shadows across everything. The noises of the fair were muffled, like sounds from another world, and Edyon took a few moments to enjoy being there, surrounded by possibilities. Then he began looking. He was never sure what he was looking for, but he would know it when he saw it.

Edyon was methodical, swift and careful in his search. He'd been brought up around these objects, able to unwrap and rewrap a statue in no time. He could tell the value with little more than a glance, but he wasn't interested in that. The right thing would speak to him when he held it, and then it would be impossible for him to put it back. It would be something he needed, something he *had* to take, though the need never lasted and after a few days it would lose its charm; once it was his, he no longer wanted it, was even disgusted by it, and by himself. He always got rid of the things he stole: gave some away, dropped others in alleys or woods. He'd only ever sold two things that he'd stolen, which had made him feel sick and guilty, and though he'd given the money to a beggar it hadn't made him feel better. Once he even put a picture back in the home he'd stolen it from, though it had made him shake with fear at the thought of being caught. Strange, as he was never afraid when he was stealing, but always buzzing, as now. But, even so, he wasn't sure he stole for the thrill of it; it was just something he had to do. Some men were drinkers, others womanizers; he was a thief.

Edyon worked his way through the caravan, opening and closing boxes, unwrapping and rewrapping objects, and he had got over halfway round before he found it.

A tiny silver ship.

It sat on his hand as if about to set to sea. The sail was a fine silver sheet and the cargo hatch opened to reveal . . . well, nothing, but perhaps it was intended to hold coins or – yes! – a small candle: the sides of the ship and the stern were dotted with tiny portholes through which the light would make a pattern. It was fine work but worth little, a silly ornament, yet Edyon was instantly in love with it. He kissed the prow of the boat and whispered, 'You're mine.'

'And you, matey, are mine.'

Edyon turned to find a burly guard behind him and another burlier guard looking through the doorway.

Edyon froze. The ship floated on the palm of his hand, its prow pointing away from the door and the guards blocking it. Trying to run seemed like a bad option, but there weren't many good ones.

'Neither of you gentlemen are foreign, are you?'

'You what?'

'That's a relief.' Edyon needed an excuse quickly and found himself saying, 'I'm looking for Stone. I thought I saw him come in.'

'Bollocks.'

'We're acquaintances, Stone and me.'

'And what's that in your hand then?'

Edyon's eyes widened innocently. 'This? Oh, this delightful trinket had fallen out of its packaging. I was just putting it back. It's quite charming. From Abask I'd expect, judging from the workmanship. Probably fifty years old.'

'Double bollocks.'

'You think it's older? Or perhaps from Savaant?' Edyon scrutinized the ship closely. 'You may be right.' He stepped forward and handed it to the first guard, saying, 'Well, as Stone isn't here, I should be on my way.'

The guard grabbed a fistful of Edyon's jacket, crushing the silver ship painfully against his chest. 'You need to come to see Mister Stone. Now.' And he threw Edyon out of the caravan.

Edyon landed on the grass face first, mud in his mouth.

'Get up.'

The order was unnecessary as the second guard was already pulling him to his feet. People were staring as Edyon was dragged past them; one boy pointed and laughed. Edyon gained momentum in his legs and managed to make them walk. He spat out the mud and was relieved to find his jaw wasn't broken.

They arrived at Stone's tent and Edyon was told to wipe his boots before going inside. While he felt that in this instance thievery had been the wrong choice, and he was perhaps not on the path to riches, being asked to wipe his boots felt not at all like the sort of thing that would come before pain, suffering and death, and so he was more than happy to cooperate. He'd hardly finished when he was shoved into the tent and pushed down on to his knees, from where he looked up as beseechingly as possible.

Stone, the pudgy-faced ass, was sitting on one of a pair of very fine mahogany and velvet folding chairs.

Edyon knew silence was often more powerful than speech.

The silver ship, bent out of shape from being shoved against Edyon's chest, was in Stone's sausage-like fingers.

'Edyon, Edyon, Edyon.'

Still best not to speak. Wait to hear the accusation.

'What will your mother think of this?'

'This?'

'Stealing . . . again.'

'*Stealing?* No. I think your men have misled you. This is a silly misunderstanding. I thought I saw someone entering your caravan.

The door was open, there were no guards around – a gross dereliction of duty – and I followed, in order to investigate. There was no one there, but I happened to notice that charming silver ornament had fallen from its wrapping.'

Stone sighed heavily. 'Please don't, Edyon. It's embarrassing.'

'I'm not sure I'm with you.'

'As I said before, what will your mother make of it?'

'She'll understand I was only trying to help.'

'Help yourself to my property, you mean?' Stone frowned. 'Lying, on top of stealing, Edyon. It's not good.'

'Your door was open. Your guards were gone. Anyone could have entered that caravan. Fortunately it was only me, Edyon, who picked up the ship to save it from being crushed.'

Stone put the silver ornament on the table beside him. It fell over.

'The reason it is crushed is because I have suffered rough treatment from your guards. My face. My jaw. The ship too. All without cause.'

'Today, a silver boat. Last month, a gold ring. The month before, a picture frame, and before that an Illastian prayer rug. All items missing from my inventory. They were all you, weren't they, Edyon?'

'No! Absolutely not.'

Though, in honesty, Edyon wasn't totally sure. He couldn't remember ever taking a picture frame; admittedly there was the gold ring, but as for a prayer rug, not recently, though perhaps . . .

'The next man you try to steal from won't be so kind and forgiving as me, Edyon.'

Forgiving? Edyon's head came up, half smiling, half hoping.

Stone gave another heavy sigh. 'I will not tell your mother. You know I am fond of Erin. Genuinely fond.'

Edyon nodded and waited.

'I will not tell her, because that is what *you* will do. Tell your mother that you have been stealing from me. That is your punishment.'

Edyon couldn't believe he'd got off that lightly. There was clearly going to be a catch.

'Well, of course I'll tell her what happened today.'

'Oh – and, Edyon, you had better also tell her that the cost of the missing items is fifty kroners. I have not added interest and I use a conservative estimate for what I could have got for the gold ring. You will have her pay me the money by the end of the fair, or I will do to you again, only worse, what is about to happen to you.'

'What?'

Stone nodded to the guards. 'No permanent damage. This time.'

'*Stone!*'

'Take him.'

Edyon turned, rose and then ducked as the guard swung at him with some sort of wooden mallet, so close that Edyon felt the weapon whistle past his cheek. He scrambled towards Stone, thinking to use his table as a shield. But it was too late: the guards were on him and although he cowered back to protect himself all this achieved was ensuring the mallet struck his jaw and not his eye.

He tasted blood and was vaguely aware of the guards hauling him up, and then he saw the field of caravans and then they were in the trees and the ground was coming up to meet him again. Then he felt a boot in his balls and he doubled up. The men laughed.

Edyon spat out blood. Was it better to curse them or be quiet? It didn't matter – he couldn't form words, though his balls were screaming for him. He took a kick in his back and then another in his stomach, and on his arm and shoulder.

Edyon waited for another, but it didn't come.

He could hear that the men were still there, but at least they'd stopped the kicking. He had a loose tooth and blood in his mouth again, but it wasn't too bad. His balls were still intact. If they'd just leave him here, he'd be all right.

'Oi, mate. We've got something for you.'

Edyon looked up. The men had opened their trouser flaps and laughed as they pissed on him.

March

DORNAN, PITORIA

March followed the prince's bastard from the fortune teller's tent to a field where rows of plain wooden caravans were lined up. The young man climbed into the back of a caravan and March was considering going closer to investigate when two large men beat him to it. They emerged from behind the caravan, went inside, pulled the young man out and threw him to the ground, then dragged him off to a tent so close to his mother's that March ended up standing twenty paces from Holywell, who came over.

'We'll need to act soon,' Holywell said. 'Regan is with the mother.'

'She's called Erin. The son's name is Edyon.'

'Well, with Regan visiting, I think we both know what daddy's name is. And right now Regan is in there telling her that he wants to take her son back to see Thelonius.'

'So what do we do?'

'We talk to Edyon and tell him our version of events before Regan gets him to believe his.'

'And what is our version of events?'

'That it's we who have been sent by Prince Thelonius to find his long-lost son. That we will take him back to his father for a joyous reunion in Calidor. And that he should come with us right now.'

'And we take him where?'

'North, by land, to Brigant.'

'Not exactly the direct route to Calidor.'

'No. But we can tell him we have a ship in Rossarb. Once there, we'll have to make him our prisoner, but the further we get on the journey before having to tie him up, the easier it will be for us all.'

'We might convince Edyon, but what about his mother? What if Regan was here with Thelonius eighteen years ago? If she knows him, she'll believe him, not us.'

'That's why we need to keep Edyon away from his mother, and away from Regan. That's your job, March. Can you do that?'

'Yes,' March said, though he wasn't sure how.

'And we need to remove Regan from the game, and get hold of the prince's ring. If we have that, Edyon will believe we're sent by the prince. Oh, fuck.' Holywell nodded towards the tents. Edyon was being dragged away by the two guards. 'They'd better not kill him or no one will be getting anything,' Holywell muttered. 'Follow them. I'll watch for Regan.'

The guards took Edyon into the woods just beyond the tents and March followed as casually as he could. It seemed unlikely they were going to hurt him too badly as they made no attempt to hide the fact they were taking him, but once they were alone they let go of Edyon and he collapsed like a sack of grain. Then they started to kick him.

March wondered if he should step in, but the kicking wasn't that bad and March wasn't inclined to rescue a prince's son. So he watched as the men cursed Edyon, calling him a thief, a bastard thief, in fact, and Edyon responded by curling up in a ball, which seemed to irritate them. March couldn't help but smile as the guards laughed, then unhitched their front flaps and pissed on him. When they were finished, they turned and ambled back to the fair.

March waited until the guards were out of sight and checked no one else was around, but the woods were deserted. Then he walked over. Edyon didn't move. There was some blood on his jacket along with a lot of piss. His face was dirty with mud, but March was struck by how similar Edyon was to his father: the same light brown wavy hair, the same mouth, and the jaw, that same strong jaw. Their build was similar, though Edyon was not heavy with muscle – in fact, he seemed to have no muscle at all – but he was tall, with long legs, and hands like the prince's, with long, slim fingers.

Edyon groaned.

'Oh, thank goodness you're alive!' March tried to sound relieved.

Edyon continued to groan as he moved his hands from his groin to his jaw. Blood dribbled from his mouth. His eyes fluttered open – the same pale brown eyes as his father's.

Finally Edyon stopped groaning and began to sit up, and March caught a glimpse of a thick gold chain round his neck through a rip in his shirt.

'Here, drink,' said March, holding out his water bottle, at the same instant realizing that he was once again serving water to a prince. He shuddered and took a sip himself before offering it again to Edyon, who drank, spat and then said, 'Thanks.'

'Did they rob you?' March asked.

Edyon looked blank.

'Your attackers,' March repeated. 'Did they rob you?'

'No,' Edyon replied, but he still patted his jacket, presumably for his purse, and also the middle of his chest. March suppressed a smile; whatever was hanging at the end of the gold chain was precious to Edyon. He made a mental note to tell Holywell.

'So, if they weren't after your money, can I ask – and I apologize, I don't speak your language so well – why did they beat you up and piss on you?'

'It's an old Pitorian custom.'

March smiled.

'You're from Calidor?' Edyon asked, speaking in Calidorian.

'What makes you think that?' March replied, also in Calidorian, which was so much easier.

'Your accent.' Edyon looked at March properly now and his eyes widened. '*A new man enters your life,*' he murmured, almost too quietly to be heard. '*A foreign man. Handsome.*'

'What?' Had Edyon just called him handsome?

'The words of my fortune teller,' said Edyon. 'She didn't mention amazing eyes, though.'

It was always the eyes. 'I'm from Abask. It's a small region between Calidor and Brigant.'

'I know,' Edyon said. 'They make good carpets and fine silverwork.'

'Used to,' March corrected.

'Of course. The war.' Edyon paused for a moment and March braced himself for an insensitive question, but then Edyon asked, 'Are you here to trade in carpets and fine silverwork?' His eyes twinkled with a spark of mischief.

March shook his head. 'I'm here to travel and to learn.'

Edyon tried to smile, but winced and felt his jaw again. 'Excellent pursuits. I'm a student myself. What have you learnt so far?'

'That Pitoria is a pleasant enough country.'

'If you're not being kicked almost to death.'

March couldn't help smiling. 'You're not anywhere near death.'

'You've seen people closer to death than this?' Edyon indicated his filthy body.

'Yes, but they've not smelt any worse, even when they were dead.'

Edyon chuckled and held his gaze until March swallowed and looked away. Edyon got to his feet unsteadily.

'That we can agree on, my friend. Right now, I'm going to the bathhouse, but if you meet me for a drink afterwards, when I'm smelling of rose blossom, I can repay you for your water and you can tell me your name.'

March realized that in the joking he'd forgotten about the plan to keep Edyon away from Regan. If he was going to the bathhouse now, that was probably safe, but if he went home after that there was a chance Regan might be waiting. Better to keep him out drinking. He hesitated and then said, 'Yes, that would be good. My name's March.'

'Edyon,' Edyon said, and then he bowed. He added, 'Bowing is what we do in Pitoria on meeting a gentleman. What's the custom in Abask?'

'New acquaintances bow, friends shake hands, close friends and family embrace.'

'Well, I can tell you're relieved that we are still only at the bowing stage,' said Edyon with a wink. 'Now, please don't think I'm rude, or that I don't want to talk to you more because I absolutely do and I will be furious if you don't meet me later, but I really need to get out of these stinking clothes.'

'Where shall we meet?'

'The Duck. It has the best wine and the best food. I'll come straight from the bathhouse.' Edyon leant forward and stared at March again. 'Do you get tired of people telling you your eyes are amazing?'

March wasn't sure what to say. He shrugged.

Edyon started to limp away, but he turned to look back at March. 'I hope you come. I'll transform myself for you; you won't recognize me.'

'I'll be there,' March called, and added to himself, 'and I'd recognize you anywhere.'

Catherine

BRIGANE, BRIGANT

Catherine, daughter of Aloysius II of Brigant and Isabella Birkbeck, was born on Sunday 24th May at 2 a.m. The child was healthy. The mother was tired after the birth, which had continued through the night.
The Family Record of the Royal Household

Catherine was in the castle library, making her farewells to the books – things she was more familiar with and felt more fond of than most of the people in Brigane. She had wept and cursed her frustration on hearing that Ambrose was killed. Part of her knew that it could be a lie, but she would never know for sure, would always wonder; only they would know the truth. And the way Noyes had smiled let her know he knew this. He knew that she would never be certain, could never know for sure if Ambrose was dead in a ditch or had escaped to freedom. That was Noyes's power and he abused it as he abused everything else.

Men and power. They loved it and were addicted to it more than she could understand. And her love for Ambrose, her addiction to him, well, it was still there. She had him in her head, in her memory, and there he would stay, alive in her memory.

She ran a fingertip over the words that marked her birth, words that were as old as she was, and even in those scant lines she could feel the influence of the king. He was everywhere; it even felt like he was watching her now, though that was ridiculous, but still she looked around.

She suspected her birth was the first and last time she had been allowed to keep her father waiting, and that he probably wouldn't have waited so patiently, probably wouldn't have endured the wait at all, if he'd known that a girl was going to appear at the end of it.

The births of Boris and Harold were recorded in the book too, in greater detail – the joy of the king was described over several sentences! – but that was understandable: Boris was first in line to the throne, Harold second. Catherine, in theory, was third, though the king so much detested the idea of a woman ruling his kingdom that her mother had once told her it would be a close-run thing as to whether he would prefer Brigant be ruled by the sons of his hated brother Thelonius than by her. Thelonius's boys had recently died, however; their deaths were also recorded in the *Family Record*, along with the observation that, following the young princes' demise, 'Calidor was one step nearer to being returned to the rule of its true king, Aloysius'.

It was strange to think that the future of nations depended as much on the health of royal children as on success in war. The deaths of Prince Thelonius's sons proved how quickly fortunes could change. After defeating his brother's invasion, Thelonius seemed to have secured his dynasty forever, but now the future of Calidor was uncertain. Equally, an illness for Harold and an accident for Boris, and Catherine would be the rightful heir to both Brigant and Calidor.

Of course her marriage to Prince Tzsayn would make that inheritance much less likely. Once she was married she would no longer be considered a Brigantine. Her loyalty would be to her husband and Pitoria. It seemed impossible that the lords of Brigant or Calidor would ever accept a foreigner as their ruler. Perhaps that was another reason her father was so keen on this marriage – because it was a way of removing her potential, tiny though it was, to ever challenge for the Brigantine throne?

Her mother had told Catherine many times that her father was a king but also a man. He didn't understand women and thought of them as quite different from himself. 'He believes women are weak, lesser. Don't ever appear to be stupid – you are his daughter after all – but you must never seem to know more than him, or your brothers, or know better than them.'

Advice Catherine had disregarded in their last audience, she thought ruefully, letting the pages of the *Family Record* fall back into place. They had made her suffer for it, and yet . . . she had survived.

She carried the book back to its shelf and took down an equally large tome: *The Accounts of the Royal Household*. Again her mother's voice echoed in Catherine's head: 'It is one of the duties of a queen to know the incomings and outgoings of the court.'

Catherine had mostly found bookkeeping extraordinarily dull, but there was one section marked for the recording of the costs involved in arranging her marriage – and Catherine had been drawn to this since she'd first found it. There she could see in pounds, shillings and pence, the price at which her father valued her. And it was not an inconsiderable sum.

Over the last year there had been many payments for visits, deputations and gifts. The first gift to Prince Tzsayn from her father – *A stallion, black, fifteen hands, four years old, excellent gait* – had cost him little, as it had been bred in the royal stables, but he'd valued it as a reduction in stock value of thirty pounds. Catherine wondered if she, also bred in the king's household, would be recorded similarly. *A girl, mousy, small, nearly seventeen years old, prone to wilfulness. Reduction in stock value: fifty pounds and ten shillings.*

But the horse was a mere trifle compared to the costs for the visits of her father's representatives to Pitoria 'to assess the suitability of a match' – hundreds of pounds spent on chartering ships and preparing gifts for Pitorian nobles. Then visitors were invited back to Brigant and hundreds more had been spent on lavish entertainment, food and wine. Her father had been exceptionally busy and extravagant, especially given how dire Brigant's finances were.

Catherine flicked back to the income and expenses section. It was grim reading. The monthly income from taxes was consistent but small, while the returns from the gold mines had dwindled to almost nothing. After the war had emptied his coffers, her father had increased the mining in the north and there had been some extra income initially, but now the gold too was depleted. Meanwhile, the expenses covered pages and pages: wages of staff, the never-ending food bills, items from *Cloths: 6 pence* to *2 barrels red wine: 5 pounds and 7 shillings.*

Catherine closed the book, letting the pages riffle through her fingers. As she did so, she glimpsed another page of writing.

It was at the back, a few pages on from the wedding costs section. It was entitled 'Fielding'. Where had she heard that name before?

There were only three entries, the first dated from the previous autumn:

Wexman – Uniforms: 60 pounds
Wright – Tents, tools: 32 pounds
Southgate – Smoke: 200 pounds

Catherine stared at the entries. The cost of uniforms and tents were nothing unusual, but two hundred pounds for smoke was both a huge sum and a very strange item. Could it mean demon smoke?

When Catherine had been reading about Pitoria, trying to prepare herself for her marriage, one of her books had mentioned demon smoke, which was rarely seen in Brigant. The book claimed it was the blood of strange creatures that supposedly inhabited the barren plateau north of Pitoria. In Tornia, the capital, she had read, there were illegal smoke dens, where people went to inhale the smoke and lose days of their lives to 'the pleasure of the demon breath'. But why her father would want smoke she didn't know. He hated even wine and beer, saying they made men weak and stupid. She couldn't see smoke appealing to him any more than drink. How much smoke did you get for two hundred pounds? It was a vast sum. Surely it couldn't really be the blood of some magical creature?

And now Catherine remembered. Fielding was the place where Sir Oswald Pence had been killed and where Lady Anne had been captured. She had read that in the account of the arrest when she'd been trying to learn about executions.

So Lady Anne and Sir Oswald had been to this place. Had they seen the tents, the uniforms and the smoke?

That's when Catherine remembered something else. She got up in excitement and rushed deeper into the shelves of the library. She knew the book she needed: an old favourite that had first introduced her to the language of signs. She found the book and flicked through it quickly.

The sign that Lady Anne had made at her execution was a kiss with her right hand paired with a fist in her left, though it was a poor fist, her first two fingers extended because of her broken fingers. Well, Catherine had *assumed* it was because her hands were broken. But what if that wasn't it? What if she had been saying something else?

Catherine found the page:

Kiss
A commonly used sign, now made with either left or right hand.
Strictly, however, made with the left hand, it means 'kiss', while made with the right it means 'breath'.

When 'breath' is paired with a horizontal flat palm it means 'life', and with a vertical flat palm it means 'air'. When paired with a closed fist it means 'smoke'. Paired with a closed fist with fingers one and two held straight it means 'demon smoke'.

Ambrose

FIELDING,
BRIGANT

Ambrose woke to the sound of arguing.

'We can't kill him. We just have to wait for the captain. He'll know what to do.'

'He'll tell us to kill him.'

'We're supposed to be showing the captain that we can organize ourselves and be disciplined. For all we know, this is a test. It'd be just like him to send someone in.'

At that the others went quiet. Then one said, 'Probably one of his best men.'

Another boy laughed. 'It would be funny if we did kill him then.'

'Hilarious, Frank. Hilarious.'

'So what do we do with him?'

'Tie him up. Guard him. Wait till the captain's back in the morning.'

Ambrose was dragged through the sand. He pretended to be unconscious as they tied his wrists and ankles. They were on the outskirts of a bigger circle of boys sitting round a fire. Ambrose recognized the voice of Rashford telling the story of his capture.

'He was riding fast. Good control of his horse, like the captain says the enemy will have. But, fuck me, Kellen was on to him, spotted him running for it, flipped his sword round to hold it by the sharp end ... though as Fitz constantly points out –' and here everyone chimed in – *'it's wood; we can't splinter them to death!'*

There was much laughter and when it died down Rashford took up his story again. 'So, as I was saying, Kellen braved the splinters and threw his sword, and ... it was poetry in motion ... The soldier rode away, the sword whirled up, over and down, ending with a precise coming-together ... a perfect smack on the back of his head. Bang! Our friend over there rolled off his horse like he'd fallen asleep.'

There was much cheering and laughter.

'Lucky you had Kellen with you. Most of you Reds can't throw for shit.'

Ambrose opened his eyes a sliver to see that another boy, probably about fifteen or sixteen, had come into the circle round the fire.

'Stop your whinging, Gaskett. We won the last trials fair and square.'

'You cheated, Rashford, like you Reds always do.'

Rashford rose and marched over to Gaskett. Ambrose couldn't hear what was said, but it ended with Gaskett pushing Rashford backwards. Rashford shook his head and said, 'You need to relax. After the invasion we'll all have plenty.'

Gaskett shoved Rashford again, muttered something to him and turned and walked away.

Rashford stuck a finger up at his retreating figure. 'And fuck all of you Blues too. Dickhead.'

Ambrose tried to make sense of their words, but his head was throbbing and for now all he knew was that he had to get away before the captain returned. He closed his eyes and concentrated on loosening the rope round his wrists. Fortunately the boys weren't as good at tying knots as they were at throwing wooden swords, and by the time most of them had fallen asleep he had worked his hands free of the ropes and untied his feet.

The last boys awake were paying him no attention. He slipped into the bushes and crept away. He had his weapons but no horse. Skirting the camp, he saw that it was tethered with some others, but the boys guarding the horses were awake and talking to each other. It was too risky: he didn't want another sword to the back of the head. Ambrose turned away. He'd have to walk.

Tash

DORNAN, PITORIA

The suede boots that Tash had seen a month earlier were, according to the cobbler, 'sold to a charming young lady weeks ago'. Tash's disappointment lasted only a moment as the cobbler said, 'But I have these. Only just finished them yesterday.' And he lifted from the highest shelf a pair of delicate boots, pale grey, almost silver, suede, similar to the other boots but with finer ties, which ended in fur tassels, and instead of the top rims having an embroidered edge these were trimmed in fur.

Tash gasped. They were the most beautiful boots she'd ever seen.

The cobbler held the grey suede boots on the palm of his hand, stroking them like two baby rabbits. Tash stretched out her own hand to touch them. The cobbler half turned, holding the boots to his chest, saying, 'Not with those.'

Tash looked at her hands. She had washed them that morning, but now she saw they perhaps weren't *perfectly* clean. She'd wanted to try the boots on but she wasn't sure about the state of her stockings or feet either.

'How much are they?' she asked instead.

'Four kroners.'

'What? The others were three!'

And that was already an absurd sum for a pair of boots when most cost no more than two.

'There's more work and more fur in these. They're lined with fur too. Four kroners is the price. They'll sell soon enough with all these people here for the fair. But I understand if you can't afford them.'

'I can afford them. I just haven't got the money with me. Can you keep them for me? I'll be back later.'

'Keep them? As in, not sell them until you come back to try them on, cover them with your grubby fingermarks and then say you don't like them? Or more likely you won't come back at all.'

'But I will be back. I love them!'

'Well, I'll see you later then, when you have the money.'

Tash and Gravell had only arrived in Dornan the night before, but Gravell had already let it be known to his contacts that he had some good smoke: it wouldn't be long before he struck a deal.

Tash folded her arms. 'I'll get paid today or tomorrow and when I do come back I'll expect a good price.'

'You can expect a clip round the ear. You'll pay the right price, the fair price – that's the good price. Do you know how much work went into making these? I don't think so. You youngsters have everything so easy. So easy. No idea about craftsmanship or hard work.' The cobbler put the boots back into the display case, high out of Tash's reach, and turned back to face her, folding his arms. 'Anything else?'

Tash wanted to tell the cobbler where to shove his boots, but words always failed her when she was angry and now, just when they weren't wanted, tears of frustration filled her eyes. She walked out, letting the door slam behind her, and marched back to find Gravell and demand her pay.

The roads through Dornan were dusty and dry and everywhere was noise and people and smells. It was all the sort of thing Tash normally enjoyed: seeing people come together to sell, play, laugh, drink, eat and party. It was fun to watch and Tash always felt pleasantly inconspicuous. Wherever she travelled with Gravell, people always stared. Gravell was so huge and hairy that he seemed like a giant, while people were always asking Tash if they could touch her dreadlocks. Here at the fair, where folk from all corners of Pitoria and even beyond came together, she didn't stand out.

Gravell had made good use of his size yesterday, though, and of the smoke. He'd taken a room at the best inn, a small amount of smoke decanted into the innkeeper's bottle, ensuring that miraculously a room had become available by the time she and Gravell had eaten their evening meal.

It was still early. Gravell wouldn't have traded the smoke yet. But even so he must have some money and surely he could give her a bit of what he owed her. Money was key. The cobbler wouldn't care that she was young and dirty if she had money. If she'd had money he'd have been nice as pie. She should have asked Gravell for a loan for the boots and he could have taken it out of her cut for the demon smoke. Well, she'd ask him now.

Tash ran up the stairs of the inn and unlocked the door to their room. Gravell's large pack and furs were there, as were his harpoons and Tash's small bundle of furs and clothes. Gravell was not. Tash frowned. Gravell would not leave money or the demon smoke here unattended. He would keep it close by him at all times.

Tash asked the maid, 'You seen Gravell? Tall guy. Big. Black hair. Beard . . . Big.' Tash held her arms up to indicate Gravell's height but the woman shook her head.

'Never mind,' Tash said, and she walked out and up the road. 'He can't be far. And he's easy to spot after all.' She smiled at her own joke and began her search.

The fair was set up just on the edge of the town, with caravans and tents in ordered rows. The tents were mostly coloured, though often sun-faded, and the caravans painted and decked with flags and banners. Tash wasn't that good at reading but knew which banners meant what products were for sale – food, drink, jewellery, pottery, ironwork, silverware and more. Tash knew Gravell would be eating, very probably drinking, and hopefully negotiating a sale too.

Tash worked her way around the fair. It was one of the largest she'd ever been to and Dornan had been transformed to ten times its normal size. It was getting to lunchtime and delicious smells eventually made her give in and eat a pastry with a flaky crust and spicy meat and potatoes inside. She asked the vendor if he'd seen Gravell. He hadn't but another customer said, 'The big bloke? He was in Milton's bar in the centre of town earlier.'

Tash stomped back to the town and found the bar. It was gloomy and the smoke hung low from the ceiling, though not low enough to affect Tash, who was tiny compared to most of the clientele. She checked all the corners for Gravell but he couldn't be seen, so she asked the landlady, who said he'd left earlier. 'Said he was going to the bathhouse.'

Tash went back to where she'd started – the bathhouse was close behind the cobbler's shop. She walked past the window and saw that the grey boots – her boots – were still high on their shelf.

Round the back of the shop and down an alley, with fields behind, was the bathhouse.

She'd been here before and knew the layout. It was a small building that had started out as a barn but now had three large wooden baths in it. Each bath was like a huge wine barrel with steps up to it. The water was heated by a fire in the yard and carried to the baths in large pitchers by two scrawny boys employed for their height and long arms.

At the front of the barn was a separate area where four barber's chairs stood. Last time Tash was here, she'd been with Gravell and he'd been the only customer, but now it was busy. The chairs were all currently occupied and more men waited on a row of stools nearby. Hair was being cut and dyed, beards were being trimmed and boots shined at the same time. She asked one of the barbers if he'd seen Gravell. The man glanced at her dreadlocks and said, 'You could do with a good trim, luv.' He snapped his scissors at her and laughed. Another of the barbers joined in, saying, 'We could get rid of all that. It'd cost you, though.' Everyone was looking at her now.

Tash stood her ground. 'Have you seen Gravell? The big bloke. Big enough to kick the shit out of you both in one go.'

The men only laughed and Tash was trying to think of another comment when she saw the man who ran the bathhouse so strode over and asked him if Gravell was in the bath.

'He's a friend. My boss. It's important.'

'Privacy is our watchword.'

Tash rolled her eyes and said, 'Bollocks is your watchword, more like,' and she was pleased with how confident she sounded, even if the words didn't make much sense.

She walked round behind the barn, hoping to find a way in. There was a small door that the boys used to carry the hot water in to the baths, and Tash waited until one of them carried a pitcher into the barn and slipped in behind him. There was a series of three curtains partitioning the left side of the barn and she knew that behind each was a bath. But which one was Gravell's? Only one way to find out . . .

Tash sidled into the first curtained-off area.

There was a pair of boots behind the bath. Fine dark brown leather with green stitching. Very nice. And definitely not belonging to Gravell. There was a splash from the bath as its occupant ducked underwater and Tash took the chance to dash behind the tub, but blocking her way was a ladder from which hung numerous towels. She had to squeeze behind it and, just as she did so, her back to the wall, her eyes fixed on the rim of the bath, a youth rose out of the water. He had his back to her as he swept the water from his shoulder-length brown hair and stood, revealing shoulders, waist, hips and buttocks. Then he turned round, to reach for a towel.

He stopped, arm out, staring at Tash.

Tash stared back. The young man was naked.

Tash's eyes rose and she realized the man wasn't totally naked. He was wearing a gold chain with a strange pendant. At first she thought the man's skin was red and blotchy from the heat of the water, but then she realized that he was covered in bruises.

'Seen enough?'

Tash turned her head away, shielding her eyes.

'Sorry, wrong bath!'

And she slid between the ladder rack and the wall and on to the next bath, feeling the eyes of the young man on her all the time. She peered round the partition. The half-barrel bath was huge but Gravell still managed to make it seem small.

She slid round the curtain and smiled at him winningly.

Gravell said, 'If this is about those bloody boots you can leave now.'

Edyon

DORNAN, PITORIA

The bathwater was no longer hot and Edyon's aches hadn't eased by much. He'd paid the lads at the bathhouse to wash his piss-stinking clothes, giving them six kopeks each, promising the same again if the clothes were dry by the time he was.

Edyon gently soaped his body, going over the events of the morning as he went over each lump and bruise: Madame Eruth's refusal to see him; Stone's trap (stupid, stupid!); the beating; and then, most surprisingly and pleasantly, the young man called March with the beautiful eyes. March had improved his day immeasurably and certainly fitted the handsome-foreign-man prediction. He'd drink with him tonight, eat with him, perhaps more.

Edyon floated on his back, thinking of March's face, his lips on the water bottle. Nice lips. Not too fat, not too thin, just right. Yes, he'd see March tonight, but he really needed to see his mother too. The money for Stone was a big problem. Fifty kroners was a lot of money. His mother had it, but she wouldn't just give it to him. Edyon would have to explain why he wanted it. And he suspected that if he lied to his mother, Stone would somehow find out and hold it over him forever. The only way to avoid that was to tell his mother what had happened. The truth. A full confession. That was the way forward.

You must be honest . . .

And yet, fretted Edyon, sometimes his mother was not good at understanding the truth. She loved him, he knew that, but she lacked an appreciation of what real life was like, at least for Edyon. When he'd told her that the university rules said that a father must put his son forward for a place, she'd said, 'You're too negative, Edyon. Rules are meant to be broken.'

At first he'd believed her, working hard with his tutors, first in languages, then in law. The people he knew in the fairs didn't care if he had no father, that his name was his mother's. And so he'd gone to the university at Garya and stood in front of the professor, explained his interest in law, and the professor seemed delighted . . . until the question of family came up, at which point the professor had politely, sadly even, but firmly pointed out that it was impossible. The professor at Tornia had been even clearer: he'd looked at Edyon as if he was a dog turd and said, 'We only teach gentlemen.'

Since then Erin had suggested he try working as a clerk in court, which seemed even more laughable to Edyon. If a university treated him like shit, a court certainly wouldn't be any better.

Erin was unusual in being a successful businesswoman, and being an unmarried mother wasn't unique, but her disdain for convention was the problem. She had affairs with men and made no effort to hide them or pretend that she was interested in marriage. She'd once said that if she met a man who was attractive, loving and intelligent, she might marry him – but that she doubted such a combination existed. And that made Edyon wonder what she really thought of him. At the core of it, Edyon thought that his mother didn't actually like men very much, and the older Edyon got – the more like a man and less like a boy he became – the less she liked him too.

And so, now that he had to confess his crimes to her, he wasn't totally sure his mother would be sympathetic. She hated thieves above all else. She was ruthless with those who stole from her, taking them to the local courts, demanding the harshest of punishments. Any servant who took even a crust from the stores without permission was punished.

Still, what choice did he have? He would have to confess: tell the truth and swear that he'd never steal again.

And of that he *was* certain. He would never steal again.

This was the crossroads. This was his choice.

No more.

Edyon submerged himself, as if cleansing himself completely of his old ways. Then he stood and turned to get a towel, and that was when he saw the girl.

She was scrawny and small, like many of the urchins who followed the fairs. But this girl was different. Her hair, for a start. She had long blonde dreadlocks, tied back in an unruly bunch. Her skin was brown, the colour of dark honey from the south, but her eyes were blue, a sea-sparkling blue. He knew who she was, of course. Edyon had seen her at the fairs at Goldminster and Cheamster. She went around with the huge man, Gravell, who was rumoured to be a demon hunter.

'Seen enough?' he enquired, and the girl hid her eyes, mumbled an apology and dashed through the curtain.

With a wry smile, Edyon wrapped the coarse towel round himself and gingerly stepped out of the barrel. He felt a little better, but no more than that. He couldn't face even patting his body dry and so just stood still and tried to relax. As he rolled his shoulders it became impossible to ignore the conversation on the other side of the curtain. The deep voice had to belong to the demon hunter, Gravell.

Gravell: I told you, I'm in negotiations.

The girl: It doesn't look like it.

Gravell: You can't rush these things. I'm sussing out the interest. I was hoping that Southgate would be here but he's in Tornia. Flaxman's around but I hate his guts and I'd rather starve than sell it to him.

The girl: How long will it take?

Gravell: It takes what it takes. Can't I have my bath in peace?

The girl: How long?

Gravell: A couple more pitchers of hot water, a bit more soaking, then I'm going for dinner and then –

The girl: No, not how long will you stay in the bath! How long until you've negotiated?

Gravell: You're turning into a nag.

Silence.

The girl (*quietly*): Fine, well, I wouldn't want to nag. To stop my nagging I just need a small loan.

Gravell: What for? Not those boots, is it?

The girl (*wheedling*): Gravell, honestly, he has an even better pair, with fur and tassels. When you see them you'll realize they are the most beautiful boots in the whole world.

Sound of splashing.

The girl: So? Can you loan me four kroners?

Gravell: FOUR KRONERS!

Sounds of more splashing.

The girl: It's not so much.

Gravell: FOUR KRONERS? FOR BOOTS?

The girl: It's my money. How I spend it is up to me. You spend that on gambling and women.

Gravell: Exactly, not on boots!

The girl: I just need the loan. In fact, really it's not so much a loan as an advance.

Gravell: I don't do loans. And I don't do advances.

The girl: But . . . if he sells the boots they're gone for good.

Gravell: And you'll have saved four kroners.

The girl: And I'll hate you forever.

Gravell: There's a couple of cobblers here at the fair. You can get different boots. Nice boots. At a sensible price.

The girl: But I want the grey suede boots.

Gravell: And on what occasion will you be wearing these boots with fur and tassels?

The girl: Any occasion I please, if they're mine.

Gravell: Then you'll have to buy them with your money when you get it.

The girl: But I've done the work. I've risked my life. It's just up to you to sell the stuff. If you did your part of the job as efficiently as I did mine, I wouldn't even be asking for a loan or an advance. You owe me the money.

Gravell: I told you, no.

The girl: You're . . . you're . . . I hate you!

This was followed by a clatter and a splash, a growl from Gravell, a scream from the girl, and then by Gravell swearing and shouting, 'Bring my boots back!'

'You can have these when I get mine.'

This was followed by more splashing and cursing and threats of the direst kind, then the sound of the curtain swishing and Gravell shouting again. Edyon peered out of his own compartment to see Gravell naked, huge, hairy, wet and furious in the middle of the barn. The boys who worked there were watching and grinning. Gravell shouted to them, 'Ten kopeks each if you get her!'

The girl replied, 'He doesn't pay! He'll make you wait for what he owes you!'

This infuriated Gravell more than ever. 'You! Besmirching my name!' And he growled and ran after the girl. The boys seemed keen on earning some money if they could, so one of them shut the small door to the back of the barn and stood in front of it with his arms crossed. The other advanced on the girl. She was startlingly fast, though. She ducked round the approaching boy and went close to Gravell, shaking his boots at him.

Edyon wondered briefly how she and Gravell caught demons. The danger of it. The adventure. He wanted to help the girl. She should have her boots. Surely Gravell would keep his purse near his bath . . . so Edyon slipped round the curtain on to Gravell's side as the shouts and curses carried on beyond.

Gravell's clothes were in a pile on the floor. Edyon quickly rummaged through them and felt something warm. He snatched his hand away. Was there an animal in there? The pile of clothes didn't move – but they glowed faintly, purple. Edyon parted the clothes and saw beneath them a large bottle with a braid round its neck. The bottle was clear thick glass but inside was a swirling mass of purple smoke.

Edyon had seen demon smoke before but only in the tiny quantities they sold in smoke dens. The first time he'd visited one, at the fair in Cheamster, he'd inhaled it all at once, copying a man who seemed experienced in the matter. Edyon had passed out and woken up the next morning in a back alley, without his purse. That's how he learnt that copying the smoke addicts wasn't the wisest idea. The second time, he knew to take just a small amount, sniffing it into his nose and down to his lungs, holding it in for as long as possible and then releasing. The sensation was extraordinary, the most perfect relaxation in his life. That smoke had been pale and sluggish, barely moving in its tiny vial. The smoke in this bottle was intense and fast moving. And there was so much of it, enough for a hundred inhalations or more.

Edyon's hand reached out and, as he touched the bottle, the smoke seemed to gather round his fingers, as if it was alive to his presence. Edyon had to have it. The bottle was in his hands now, heavy, as if full of sand, not smoke. Edyon gazed into the swirling cloud of purple. It was almost hypnotic, but he was quickly brought back to the present by a screamed warning from Gravell: 'Watch her kick. Her kick! No! Don't let her get past you!'

Edyon slipped back to his side of the curtain and wrapped a towel round the bottle, but the purple glow could still be seen. The chase was coming his way. As his curtain was whipped aside, Edyon dropped the towel-wrapped bottle into his bath, and the girl carrying Gravell's boots ducked behind the towel ladder, pulling it over one of the boys in hot pursuit.

'Yes, you should run!' shouted Gravell, and there was a laughing answer from the girl.

'Well, at least I *can* run, old man.'

Edyon put the towel ladder back in place and straightened the curtains. The purple glow in his bath couldn't be seen. It all looked normal.

The sound of Gravell's shouting came from outside, getting louder as he returned, grumbling about the girl and how slow the boys were.

Edyon took a step up to the bath but stopped at the sound of Gravell's roar, so loud that the curtain seemed to quiver.

'The little thief! I'll kill her! I'll tear her legs off!'

Then there was the sound of Gravell dressing and cursing and muttering to himself.

'So, steal my smoke will you, missy? Well, I'll get you, and when I do I'll teach you what happens to smoke thieves. You'll be begging to be put in the stocks . . .'

Edyon was still standing by his bath as Gravell stomped away. All was quiet again. He shivered. He heard the boys come in and check Gravell's bath area, and the boss of the bathhouse giving them orders to tidy everything up.

Edyon climbed back into his bath.

The water was hotter than he remembered, and he sank into it with a smile. He felt around for the bottle and found that it had sunk to the bottom. He held on to it and lay back and his aches began to ease away.

Catherine

THE PITORIAN SEA

The seed-stolen slow rot of nutshells,
open coffins on the forest floor.
'Life's Journey', Queen Isabella of Brigant

The sea crossing to Pitoria took three days. Catherine's farewells in Brigant had been brief. The most surprising was the one with her father, who had come to her room for the first time ever on the morning of her departure. He had demanded to see her jewellery, taken away the smaller and cheaper pieces, and given her a heavy gold-and-diamond necklace in their place.

'It was your grandmother's,' he grunted when Sarah put it round Catherine's neck, then added, 'You're my daughter. Now at least you look like it.'

And that was that. He had appeared on the quay as she boarded her ship but hadn't spoken to her, reserving his conversation for Boris.

Catherine's goodbye from her mother was longer but hardly an outpouring of emotion. She kissed Catherine on the cheek and handed her a thin volume of poems and a new book on Queen Valeria.

'What have you decided about your new life, Catherine?'

'To do what I can with it. Valeria is an inspiration, though I'm not sure I have her force of personality.'

'Don't expect everything to come to you overnight. Learn as you go. You will make mistakes, but don't make the same one twice. No one has all the answers from the beginning. Even Valeria took time to win the people to her.'

'I'll do my best.'

'Good. Then I'm sure you'll succeed. Also, listen to Sir Rowland, the Brigantine ambassador. Trust him. I know him well. He'll help you.'

Something in the queen's tone set Catherine wondering how her mother knew Sir Rowland, but she was prevented from wondering for long. As the ship hit the first waves outside the harbour, she was overcome by a feeling of nausea. One of Boris's soldiers was already being sick over the side.

'Are you a woman, Webb?' Boris berated him. 'Weak at the knees at the first sign of a wave?'

Deciding the comment was directed at her as much as at poor Webb, and determined not to show weakness in front of her brother, Catherine descended to her cabin as quickly as her dignity allowed – and proceeded to throw up into a bucket for the rest of the day.

For the first two days of the voyage, Catherine stayed prone on her tiny bed feeling miserable. She slept at odd times and couldn't face conversation with her maids, though she heard them talking of the soldiers on the boat, how handsome they were and how strict Boris was. On the second day, she looked through the first book that the queen had given her and realized that her mother had written the poems herself. Many were about loneliness, lovelessness and womanhood. Catherine was surprised at the emotion they contained, but rather than depress her they made her more determined. She didn't want to have the life her mother had. She didn't want to end up writing a book of sad poems. She turned instead to the book about Queen Valeria, wishing that someone might one day write such a book about her.

On the second night, Catherine improved and found herself desperate for some fresh air. Her maids were sound asleep, and Catherine was in no mood for corsets or fiddling with her hair, so she dressed herself. As she crept up the steps, she remembered that there would be men on watch and perhaps sailors. Sails still needed to be tended at night, she assumed. She cautiously raised her head above deck, but as the breeze hit her face she realized that no matter who was there she wasn't going to go back below; the fresh air felt wonderful.

The deck was empty and she moved quietly to the ship's rail. The sea was black and calm, the stars out in their thousands. Catherine filled her lungs with the cool, salty air and felt the last twinges of seasickness fall away.

By now her eyes were accustomed to the darkness and she saw there were men in the rigging. Eight – no, more, perhaps ten or twelve – were moving silently and quickly, astoundingly quickly. Dressed in black, they descended rapidly, sliding down dark ropes. Catherine was hidden from their view by some wooden containers that were lashed to the deck. Hidden until one of the men slid to the deck right in front of her. Not only was the man dressed in black but he was wearing a close-fitting black mask. He stared at her and seemed as surprised as she was.

Catherine forced herself to speak. 'Good evening, sir. May I ask what you're doing?'

The man didn't reply and didn't move. She was about to ask her question again when a horribly familiar voice spoke from behind her.

'You're feeling better, Your Highness.'

Catherine turned. 'I . . . I didn't know you were coming to Pitoria, Noyes.'

Noyes just gave his usual half-smile, then said, 'I wouldn't miss your marriage for the world.'

Catherine wanted nothing more than to get away from Noyes and back into her cabin but she forced herself to meet his eye.

'Are those your men? What are they doing up there?'

'I train my men for many circumstances, Your Highness, even the sailing of ships.'

Catherine did not believe that was what he was doing for a moment and she stood waiting for him to leave, but of course all he did was look at her and she felt her skin crawl with it, so without another word she returned to her cabin.

In the morning Boris came to see her, bending his head to avoid hitting it on the beams.

'You were on deck last night.'

'Yes. I had been feeling unwell but I am much better now. Thank you for your concern, brother.'

'I am concerned but not for your health. You were alone. Again. None of your maids were present. You weren't even dressed properly.'

'I needed air.'

'What you need is discipline. Don't you care what people will say? You're about to be married.'

'The seasickness has caused me to empty my stomach, not my memory.'

'You should learn to behave with dignity. Until you do, you stay in your cabin. Your maids too. I don't want any of you on deck for the rest of the voyage. And if I see you gadding about I'll have you in leg irons.'

Boris left and Catherine screamed with frustration. Here on the ship, a Brigantine ship crewed by Brigantine men, Catherine knew she had no choice but to do what Boris demanded. However, she was determined that the moment she stepped on Pitorian soil things would change.

Early in the afternoon of the third day, the ship manoeuvred into the dock in Charron. As soon as the ropes were made fast, Catherine went up on the deck and scanned the crowd. Boris came to stand by her and commented, 'You're out of your cabin quickly, sister.'

'I've been cooped up in that box for three days. I'm keen to see my new country.'

'And your new husband.'

'Indeed.' Catherine looked at all the figures on shore. There were many young men, all well dressed. Some dark-skinned, some light. One very tall. One huge fat man. 'Which one is he?'

Boris's eyes flicked about. 'I can't see him or his pennants.'

'But I thought he was supposed to meet me here,' Catherine couldn't resist replying. 'It's so hard organizing a wedding, isn't it, brother? So much to remember, so easy to forget things . . . like the husband.'

Boris leant close to her and snarled, 'I didn't forget anything, nor will I.'

But, while it was entertaining to goad her brother, Catherine was surprised to find that she felt disappointed her future husband wasn't there to greet her.

A walkway had been set up to the shore and the ship's captain and two of his officers saluted smartly as a man dressed in Brigantine style stepped aboard and bowed deeply.

'Sir Rowland Hooper, Your Highness. His Majesty's ambassador to Pitoria.' He smiled at Catherine. 'I hope you have had a good journey.'

'I'm afraid I'm not suited to sea travel.'

'Well, I don't suppose you'll need to make another such journey again. Pitoria is your home now.'

'Indeed.' Catherine didn't bother to smile.

'Where's Prince Tzsayn?' interrupted Boris. 'He's supposed to be here.'

'Prince Tzsayn asked me to send his apologies. He is slightly unwell and has decided to remain in Tornia, to ensure he is fully recovered for the wedding ceremony.'

'Slightly unwell!' Boris snarled. 'Couldn't be bothered to ride for a few days to meet his wife, more like.'

Catherine's face tightened. Did he really care so little for her? It hardly boded well for their future life together.

Sir Rowland smiled apologetically. 'Instead, Prince Tzsayn has arranged for Princess Catherine to make a progress to Tornia that takes in the key towns along the route. With the prince unwell, it seemed the best option.'

Boris seethed. 'This is not what we agreed. We *agreed* to go straight to the castle. We *agreed* he would have all the lords of Pitoria there.'

'And that will happen, Your Highness,' said Sir Rowland soothingly. 'The lords will all be there when we arrive. I can assure you no one will be missing that day or the wedding itself. There is much excitement about it. But first there are dignitaries on shore to whom I should introduce you, and then we will begin our progress to the capital, through the most beautiful country-side. It's almost a match for Brigant.'

Catherine straightened her back. Whatever the real reason for Prince Tzsayn's absence, she would have to take this as an opportunity. Boris couldn't lock her in her cabin any more. This was her chance to make an impression. Before her own wedding, Queen Valeria had made a progress through Illast, which drew the crowds and the people to her. Catherine was going to make sure she was seen and make sure people talked about her.

'It will be a wonderful opportunity to see the country. We should have festivities organized for each evening,' Catherine said.

Sir Rowland turned to her. 'An excellent suggestion, Your Highness. The Pitorians love a party. They will be glad to celebrate your arrival.' Sir Rowland looked to the shore. 'Oh. The dancing has already begun. It's a demonstration for your entertainment.'

Catherine could see a group of men leaping around, more like acrobats than dancers. She smiled. 'I've heard that the men of Pitoria love to dance. Such a refreshing change from hunting or jousting.'

'They use dance to show their athleticism and power. It is remarkably skilful. I can arrange for your men to have lessons, if they desire.'

Catherine beamed. 'What a delightful suggestion! I would love my brother to experience that.'

Boris was making a strange face. 'That won't be necessary.'

'You're an accomplished dancer already, Your Highness?' Sir Rowland asked.

'As accomplished as a man needs to be, which is to say not accomplished at all, sir.'

Sir Rowland bowed his head, but Catherine could see he was smiling. When he looked up again, though, his face was blank. 'So. We should be getting on with it.' He gestured towards the dancers. 'Shall we brave them?'

Catherine felt a small smile creep to her lips. She hadn't ever imagined enjoying her arrival in Pitoria, but now she began to realize it might even be fun. She followed the ambassador and Boris ashore, Noyes and her maids following behind. Catherine was alarmed to find that stepping ashore felt like walking across a swaying bridge. She wobbled and Sarah took her arm, but Catherine freed herself gently. Noyes saw every little weakness and she was determined to show him none.

Catherine was introduced to a series of people in a flurry of smiling, bowing and curtsying. What struck her was how different everyone seemed. Everyone in Brigant was pale-skinned and light-haired, but here skin colours ranged from black, brown and gold tan to white, and hair was quite literally all the colours of the rainbow.

She was able to put faces to many of the names she had learnt before her journey: Lord Quarl, one of King Arell's counsellors, Lord Serrensen, a distant cousin of the king, and Lord Farrow, the local magnate, who guided her into a carriage, with Sir Rowland and Sarah, for the next leg of her journey. Boris, Noyes and their men were already mounted, their horses having travelled ahead. Catherine had to admit Boris's men looked impressive, their armour shining brightly in the sun.

Ahead of her carriage rode ten other men on horseback, each carrying a long spear with a gleaming silver head and a green pennant below it. Most remarkably the green of the pennant matched the green of each man's hair, which was cut short at the back and sides but left long on top. Catherine had read that men showed allegiance to their leaders through their hair colour, but knowing it and seeing it were two very different things. The green exactly matched the badge Lord Farrow wore on his jacket.

'You've spotted Lord Farrow's green,' Sir Rowland commented.

'It's very noticeable, sir. I had heard of the hair colouring, but it's rather more dramatic than I imagined.'

'You know the origin of the tradition?' asked Sir Rowland. 'The dye is to ensure the men don't switch sides mid-battle, which happened in the wars with Illast over a century ago. Of course no one is going into battle now.'

'Though Brigantine soldiers on our land is hardly a reassuring sight,' said Lord Farrow shortly.

Catherine shifted in her seat. It seemed Sir Rowland had been exaggerating when he said everyone was delighted to see her . . .

Noting her embarrassment, the ambassador tried to smooth things by saying, 'The green of Lord Farrow is much admired. Though I'm sure that's not the only reason men wish to join your ranks, my lord.'

'My ranks are always full and my men are the best,' Farrow replied, looking at Catherine.

'Better even than Prince Tzsayn's?' Catherine asked pleasantly.

Lord Farrow's face turned sour. 'The prince, of course, has excellent troops.'

'His blue is admired by all,' purred Sir Rowland.

Thankfully the clatter of the horses' hooves along the cobbled streets was loud enough to halt the conversation, allowing Catherine to put aside Lord Farrow's barbs for a while and take in her surroundings.

The buildings were taller and narrower than in Brigant, and the people dressed more brightly. It looked to be a clean and well-cared-for place. As the parade of soldiers and carriages passed, people came out of buildings and even hung out of windows to see what was happening. Many waved and smiled, but a few merely stood and stared at the Brigantine soldiers.

The town soon gave way to countryside, where there were fewer people as they passed through green fields and past orchards full of blossom. The carriage ride lasted until the late afternoon. At Lord Farrow's vast home, Catherine was treated politely enough, given beautiful rooms, a bath and privacy but little time to enjoy them, as that evening there was a reception at which she was guest of honour.

As Sarah laid out her Pitorian dresses, Catherine realized she disliked them as much as ever; they were unstructured and revealing. She much preferred her corseted Brigantine evening gown, a silver-grey dress with embroidery and pearls at the cuffs and neck. She tried the necklace her father had given her, though it didn't sit properly over her dress, so she didn't keep it on. She had her maids pin up her hair, curled in the simple style she was used to.

Jane smiled at the result. 'Very dignified, Your Highness.'

Tanya frowned though. 'It's dignified, but I've seen some of the other guests arriving, Your Highness. They're amazing. One lady has feathers in her hair that almost scrape the ceiling. I think one of the Pitorian dresses might be more in keeping.'

'Perhaps tomorrow. It's been a long day and I'm more comfortable in this.'

But as soon as Catherine entered the hall she realized her mistake. Every woman, indeed every man, was dressed more extravagantly than she was. The women had their hair piled high on their heads, woven through with ribbons, pearls, flowers, feathers and even bells. Not only were the hairstyles more elaborate and stylish, they added to the ladies' height. Catherine was supremely conscious of her lack of it as she stood at the hall, unable to see above the shoulders of most of the guests. In the distance she spotted Noyes, staring at her as always. Thankfully Sir Rowland appeared at her side.

'Your Highness, apologies for keeping you waiting. Let me introduce you.'

And so it began. Small talk and false laughter during which Catherine was aware of being assessed and equally aware of how small and young she appeared, but mostly aware that she was irritated and tired. Eventually they were all guided to another room for the banquet, where Catherine was seated between Lord Farrow and Boris. Conversation was in short supply.

As the meal came to an end, Farrow made a brief and remarkably unwelcoming welcome speech dwelling on the bloodthirsty history of Brigant and the unexpected absence of Prince Tzsayn.

'And so we must accept that this small invasion of Brigantine troops is not here to conquer Pitoria,' Farrow concluded, 'but to ensure that our two kingdoms will indeed be joined by marriage. It may be that the soldiers are necessary after all, as it seems that even the brave Prince Tzsayn quaked at the thought of his imminent wedlock.'

A low ripple of amusement passed round the table. Catherine was mortified. Boris looked furious. He was supposed to make a reply on Catherine's behalf, but he didn't stand, his jaw clenched with rage. Sir Rowland glanced at Catherine and began to rise, and Catherine knew she should allow him to smooth over the situation, but she was irritated – by Lord Farrow's tactless humour and by the patronizing glances of the guests.

Before she had time to think, she was on her feet. People were talking and, while some stopped to look at her, many did not. She was determined that her voice would be firm and not wobbly, but as she looked at the sea of faces – all older, all wiser, mostly male, mostly from Pitoria – she felt like what she was: a sixteen-year-old foreign girl. Worst of all, she could feel Noyes's eyes on her again. She immediately regretted standing, but it was too late now.

'It would be normal in Brigant for my brother, Prince Boris, to reply on my behalf. But I'm now entering a new country, a new life and a new marriage – with the assistance of my brother's troops, if necessary, though I'm hoping we won't have to resort to that.' She paused as the audience laughed politely. 'With these great changes to my life in prospect, it is time I spoke for myself. I am, of course, delighted to be in beautiful Pitoria, though sad at the parting from my parents and my beloved Brigant.'

Catherine looked around the room and could see that the guests were curious rather than interested. Was it just the spectacle of a woman standing and speaking for herself? But now Catherine couldn't even do that – her mind had gone blank. A couple at the back leant together and whispered. Catherine needed to hold their attention, get people on her side.

That was it, the way to win them round – the people.

'I am come to you as a young woman, a woman of just sixteen years. And I also come as a princess, the daughter of King Aloysius of Brigant.' And now she was surprised to realize that she spoke with true pride. 'But I have the honour of marrying your prince, and I have today had the pleasure of seeing the kingdom of Pitoria for the first time, and it is truly a beautiful place. But a kingdom is more than a land and a king. Imagine a country as beautiful as Pitoria yet empty of all people. Put a man in this country. Now call that man king. Still this land is nothing special. There is no kingdom, merely a land and a man called a king. But now fill the country with people who love their country and their king and you have a true kingdom. I understand that the people of Pitoria love their king, and also love Prince Tzsayn. I have seen a few of these people on my journey here today and I intend to meet as many more as I can. Pitoria is my new home. The Pitorians are my new people. I left Brigant as a child of that country, but I continue on my journey as a Pitorian who loves her new country. I look forward to my life here. So my toast is to Pitoria and to all its people.'

Catherine raised her glass. There was a moment's silence, and then, at the far end of the table, a man stood, and then another, and another, until the guests were all standing to drink the toast and applause rang through the room.

Catherine sat and Boris turned to her. 'A pretty speech, sister. Though I don't remember suggesting you make it.'

'I thought of it all by myself,' replied Catherine lightly. 'And do stop scowling, brother. There seems to be an element of hostility in Pitoria – in this room even – to my marriage. My words will do more than your frowns to ensure these people warm to me. We wouldn't want anything to prevent the wedding, would we?'

With a tight smile, Boris got up and left. As he swept out, Sir Rowland came to Catherine to escort her to the hall for the dancing.

'My compliments on your speech, Your Highness.'

'Boris was not so pleased with my words.'

'I suspect he's less pleased with Lord Farrow's. Boris is a soldier, Your Highness, and Lord Farrow is no diplomat.'

'While you are definitely the latter, Sir Rowland. My mother mentioned you to me. She said I could rely on you.'

Sir Rowland hesitated for the first time. 'I had the honour of spending time at court in Brigant while the king was absent during the war with Calidor. I met Her Majesty the Queen then. She would be proud of you today.'

A friendship at court! The ambassador must truly be a careful operator, Catherine mused. Had anyone suspected any impropriety between him and her mother, Sir Rowland wouldn't have such a good position now. Had her father suspected, Sir Rowland wouldn't have his head.

'Regarding my speech, I would like to improve on it next time. I'd appreciate your advice.'

'Certainly, Your Highness. That would be an honour.'

'Good. In the morning then. Is there a quiet place we can meet?'

'The library is a lovely room. I'm sure it will be quiet before breakfast.'

'Perfect.'

'But now, I'm afraid, there's more work to be done here. Many people are keen to be introduced to you. May I escort you?'

'Please do, Sir Rowland.'

Much, much later Catherine fell into bed, exhausted, but she realized she was smiling. She felt that she'd achieved something. She'd stood up to Boris, made a speech, and won her audience's applause. And she'd done it all wearing the wrong dress.

Tomorrow the latter would be corrected.

Ambrose

NORWEND,
NORTHERN BRIGANT

It was two days after his escape from the boys at Fielding and Ambrose was almost home. The distant snow-topped mountain peaks rose behind the jagged hills of Norwend, the sun so bright that Ambrose had to squint. A cold northerly breeze seemed to find a way through the seams of his jacket and he shivered. The lump on the back of his head was still tender, and yet Ambrose found himself smiling. It was two years since he had left Castle Tarasenth and until now he hadn't realized how much he missed it. It felt good to see home.

He approached from the west, which allowed the best view of Tarasenth from a distance, found a sheltered spot and sat down to watch. He could see no signs of Noyes's men or soldiers, but that didn't mean that they weren't there. Noyes was no fool; he knew that the first place a fugitive looks for help is his family home. Ambrose could only hope the king's spymaster had credited him with more intelligence than to come here.

When it was dark and the moon hidden by cloud, Ambrose crept silently down the slope. He made his way over the kitchen garden wall, climbed the pear tree on to the pantry roof and across to the window of the room above it. The window was barred but one bar had been lost to rust long ago and Ambrose could still, just, squeeze through the gap.

He was in the nursery and across the corridor was his bedroom. He took his boots off and carefully made his way across the old squeaky floorboards, the familiar smell of his house filling his nostrils.

He pushed open the door to Tarquin's bedroom. There was a shape in the bed and Ambrose had a sudden fear that it was a trap, that it was one of Noyes's men. He drew his dagger and approached the bed.

But as he stepped closer he relaxed. The long blond hair on the pillow was unmistakable. And then Tarquin opened his eyes, saw Ambrose and rose soundlessly from the bed, signalling that Ambrose should be silent before crushing him into an embrace.

'It's good to see you,' Tarquin said, his voice barely audible.

'Are we whispering because we don't want to wake the servants or for a more serious reason?'

'Noyes has two men here in Tarasenth. They arrived three days ago. Father had no alternative but to allow them in. But they don't seem to expect you. Since they searched the place they've just been sitting around looking bored. It's just another way for the king to show his power, how he can send men into our home whenever he likes.'

Tarquin was clearly trying to make light of this news, but Ambrose knew the men would not be too slack if they worked for Noyes.

'I knew it was a risk to come here, but I had to see you.'

Tarquin put a hand gently on Ambrose's arm. 'And I'm glad you've come. I've heard so many rumours. Some said you'd been killed, others that you were captured. And all because you challenged one of Boris's men.'

'They challenged me.' And he quickly related the story, telling all – except the depth of his feelings for Princess Catherine and how he'd been sick and scared after killing Hodgson.

Tarquin shook his head. 'Noyes came to question us. But of course he wouldn't say exactly what had happened. And the little he told us was lies, it seems. He said you'd killed a royal guard. You're now wanted for treason.'

'Treason! I was challenged! I defended myself.' It was no worse than Ambrose had expected and yet his anger surfaced again. 'How can I ever prove myself innocent? It's impossible. The king, Boris, Noyes, they make it impossible.'

'Calm yourself.' Tarquin laid his hand again on Ambrose's arm. 'Those of us who know you need no proof.'

'And if you support me or help me you'll be treated as a traitor too. You and Father.'

'Only if they find out,' Tarquin corrected. 'And they won't. The evening you left, Noyes and four of his men came to the house we rented in Brigane. Noyes turned the place over, taking Father's papers, questioning everyone, including all the servants, leaving Father and me till last. But you know Father's at his best when he's cornered. He told Noyes how you were a born rebel; how he'd tried to tame you and failed; how you'd left Norwend two years ago to take a position with the Royal Guard against his wishes – I particularly loved the truth of that. He said that he'd confronted you only the day before for failing to denounce Anne, and you had criticized him for denouncing her so clearly. He finished by disowning you entirely and offering his own men to help hunt you down, knowing Noyes wouldn't accept.'

So Noyes would have no leverage against his father, but Ambrose was still concerned about Tarquin.

'And what did they ask you?'

'To all their questions I, too, told the truth, brother: that I cared for you deeply, that I hadn't seen you since the day after Anne's execution, and that I think you're a bloody fool.'

Ambrose smiled. 'I'm a little hurt.' He was sure the questioning would have been a lot more difficult than Tarquin was indicating.

'You're not a fool, Ambrose. You're brave and honourable and true. But, if they get their hands on you, they will have no mercy. You have to get away from Brigant, away from Noyes.'

'I plan to. I'm going to Pitoria and then . . . Don't look at me like that.'

'Like what?'

'I know you're thinking that I'll search out Princess Catherine.'

'Who insisted on you escaping. Who said she cared for you. For a princess to say that is . . . well . . . it's not very princess-like.'

'She's going to be married in two weeks. And one day she will be queen of Pitoria. I'm a wanted man on the run. She won't want me near her. My plan is to go to Pitoria first, then on to Illast. And who knows where after that. I want to do it for myself but also for Anne. She always said I should travel and not be stuck in the army, marching round the walls of castles.'

Tarquin smiled. 'I remember her saying just that. She called it "saluting for a living".'

Ambrose smiled too, but the memory faded quickly. 'Talking of Anne, I need to tell you what I saw in Fielding. The place where Anne was caught. There's something strange going on there.'

'*What?* You've been there?'

'I had to go. Neither of us believed the story about her and Sir Oswald being lovers. I still don't, but something is going on in Fielding. There are boy soldiers there. A few hundred of them. I've no idea why, but Aloysius is up to something, and I think Anne found out what. That's why he had her killed.'

Tarquin held up his hand. 'Quiet, brother. This is wild talk.'

Ambrose clutched Tarquin's hand fiercely. 'Promise me. Promise me you'll look into it! I would, but I've done all I can here in Brigant for now. Promise me you'll do it for Anne.'

Tarquin squeezed Ambrose's hand back. 'I promise.'

Ambrose nodded, a lump in his throat. 'I need to leave soon, but I should speak to Father before I go.'

'Wait here. I'll fetch him.'

Before Ambrose could say anything more, Tarquin had darted out of the room.

Ambrose went to the door to listen and then to the window, checking all was clear. The door opened and Ambrose whipped round as Tarquin re-entered.

'He's coming.' Tarquin came to stand by Ambrose and put a hand on his shoulder. 'I've never seen you so jumpy before.'

'In honesty, brother . . . I'm terrified. For me and for you. I can bear what has happened only because you and Father are safe. If they catch me here, you and Father will be dragged down with me. My life isn't exactly looking rosy; however, if I get to Pitoria I'll survive, but if I bring more trouble on to your heads, that would be more than I could bear.'

'We'll survive, Ambrose. And, if things get bad for us, it won't be your doing.' Tarquin sighed. He turned back and looked at the room. 'Do you remember when we shared this room? I told you there were monsters under your bed. I made up the most frightening stories I could but you just laughed. I so wanted to frighten you then, but I never managed it.'

'Monsters never frightened me. I relished the idea of fighting them. I was so desperate to prove myself.' Ambrose smiled at the memory. 'I remember how you were tall enough to see out of this window and watch the horses in the field. I wasn't big enough. I was so jealous of you.' The sill of the window didn't even reach his waist now. 'How old was I? Five or six? It feels like yesterday.'

At that moment the door opened. Ambrose whirled round; it wasn't Noyes's men who entered. Ambrose was struck by how old his father looked: smaller, weathered and wrinkled, not the vibrant, strong man Ambrose remembered from just a few months earlier. The death of one child and the exile of another might do that to a man, he supposed.

Ambrose bowed. 'Father.'

His father entered the room, closing the door silently behind him. 'It's many years since I've sneaked around these halls at night, but I can still do it.' He approached Ambrose. 'So, it takes the king and Noyes's men to bring you back to Tarasenth.'

'No, Father. My behaviour last time we met brought me here. I wanted to apologize for what I said in Brigane. It was foolish and cruel, and I'm sorry. And I'm sorry to have brought danger to you and Tarquin and anyone in Norwend.'

'Foolish indeed. I tried to warn you, but you wouldn't listen. Your recent troubles are a consequence of your behaviour at Anne's . . . the execution.'

'And as a consequence of having a tyrant as king.'

Norwend bristled. 'With an attitude like that . . .' His face softened. 'But let's not go down that road again. Your brother tells me you're bound for Pitoria. Perhaps your idealism will fare better there.'

'Perhaps. At least, I hope no one will try to kill me for it.'

The silence stretched. Ambrose didn't know what else to say. Perhaps there was nothing more *to* say.

'I must go. The longer I stay, the more danger I bring.'

His father frowned. 'You're a good soldier, Ambrose, and you'll be a fine man one day. Remember, the world does change. Perhaps one day you will be able to return here to Tarasenth. This is your home and, whatever happens, you are my son.'

And to Ambrose's surprise his father opened his arms to be embraced. Ambrose went to him and held him. 'Farewell. Remember, your brother and I care much for you.'

Ambrose turned to Tarquin and hugged him hard, but Tarquin smiled and pushed him off, saying, 'You don't need to say goodbye to me yet. I'm coming with you.'

Tash

DORNAN,
PITORIA

Tash entered the Black Bat Inn and made her way to the corner table where Gravell sat alone, eating an enormous steak. A tankard of beer stood close by. Tash stopped at a safe distance to assess his reaction. Gravell's eyes roamed the room as he chewed and then his chewing stopped. His eyes were on her as he stabbed the steak with his fork, then cut at it as if he was sawing off a limb.

Tash thought this looked pretty promising: he hadn't shouted or thrown the knife at her.

She'd been lurking around the edge of the fair, giving Gravell time to calm down, but she'd quickly become bored and also realized that the chances of her getting her beautiful grey boots were precisely nil unless she made up with Gravell. So she'd gone to retrieve his boots and managed to recover the one she'd hurled into a particularly stinking outhouse. The other one, which she'd thrown into the road, had disappeared.

Tash moved closer to the table slowly, as one might approach an injured bear. Gravell did look like a bear, but not so much injured as angry. She stood opposite him, keeping the table and a reasonable distance between them, and a clear route out of the inn directly behind her. Gravell stared at her, clutching his knife in his fist, the blade pointing up from the table.

Tash held up the item she'd retrieved from the outhouse and said, 'Your boot.'

Gravell's face twitched.

'I looked for the other one, but I couldn't find it.'

'Fuck my boots. Where's my bottle?'

Gravell's hand slammed on the table and his plate and steak jumped.

'What?'

'Don't play the innocent with me.'

'But . . . you mean . . . the bottle of smoke?'

'Don't shout it out to the world! What do you think I mean, a bottle of pruka?'

'It's gone?'

Gravell shook his head. 'I trusted you, I did. Thought we were partners. Didn't think you'd steal off me.'

'But I didn't. I wouldn't steal from you.'

'Didn't have you down as a liar or a thief.'

'I'm not either! I haven't got your . . . bottle – our bottle. I took your boots.'

'So it seems you *are* a thief then.'

'Well . . . that's not . . . Look, I took the boots cos you were being unfair, but I'd never take the smoke, I mean *bottle*. You know me, Gravell. I wouldn't do that.'

'I *thought* I knew you.'

Tash edged closer to Gravell. 'Did it disappear while you were in the bathhouse chasing me?'

Gravell didn't say yes, didn't say no; he just looked mean. Tash continued, 'Well, I think I know what's happened. When you stepped out of the compartment after me, someone went in there and took the smoke.'

'Or you took it and you're too scared to admit it.'

'Honestly, Gravell, I wouldn't.'

'Honesty doesn't seem to be one of your strengths, missy.'

'Look, you wait here. I'll go to the bathhouse and ask if they saw anyone looking suspicious.'

Gravell snorted. 'Why don't you go and ask the sheriff for help while you're at it?'

'Well, if anyone tries to sell it, then everyone knows we're the only demon hunters around here so . . .'

'So all the people who buy smoke are such honest, law-abiding people they're bound to come and tell me about it.' Gravell glared at her.

'Well, they know not to cross you.'

'Someone stole off me! They crossed me! I don't know who, but when I get my hands on him – or her – I'll . . .' He hacked again at his steak.

'Look, I'll ask around. Someone must know something. But you do believe I didn't take it, don't you?'

'Yes, I believe you,' growled Gravell. 'But that bottle's gone because of *your* antics, missy. Get me the name of the person who took it and I'll think about forgiving you.' Gravell pointed his knife at Tash. 'You'd better sort this out, or our partnership is off for good.'

Edyon

DORNAN,
PITORIA

Edyon relaxed in the bath after Gravell left, dozing in the warm water that never seemed to cool. He felt not just clean but reinvigorated. His tooth was still a little sore, and definitely loose, but his body no longer ached. He could believe that was due to the warmth of the water, but his lumps and bruises had completely gone, and his skin was glowing and smooth as a newborn baby's. *Warm water alone can't do that*, he mused.

Edyon dressed in his clean, dry clothes, wrapped the smoke bottle in a fresh towel and then covered it with his leather jacket. Tucking that under his arm and checking the purple glow from the smoke couldn't be seen, he left the bathhouse. If the sheriff's men caught him with demon smoke, he'd be in serious trouble. Demon smoke was illegal as well as expensive; possession of it alone would mean twenty lashes and a year's hard labour.

Edyon worried at his loose tooth as he walked. He'd told himself he'd never steal again. But stealing wasn't a decision; it was a . . . a compulsion. The need to take the bottle, to possess it, had seized him as simply and as strongly as it always did. He couldn't explain it any more than he could have explained his need to take a picture frame or a silver ship. And, while his body felt good, his mind now followed the path it always did after he had stolen – a troubled one.

Edyon liked the girl and didn't want her to be blamed for his actions. He didn't want to get caught by the sheriff's men and he particularly didn't want to get caught by the huge monster of a man that was Gravell. It wouldn't be long before Gravell worked out that the girl hadn't taken the smoke, and therefore it wouldn't be too long before Gravell would work out who was responsible for its disappearance.

He knew he should get rid of it. He'd like to give the bottle to the girl. If he saw her now, he'd just hand it over, or perhaps drop it on the ground so she'd see it as she walked along . . . But she wasn't here and he knew the idea was just a silly fantasy. He briefly played through another: the idea of selling the smoke to get the money to pay off Stone. The smoke had to be worth fifty kroners. But it was illegal goods and the buyers would be the worst sort of people to deal with. They'd probably know it was stolen from the giant Gravell. They'd sell him out for sure.

And now Edyon's other worries came to mind. He'd promised himself he would tell his mother about his stealing. But how could he? What would she think of him? He'd thought about showing her what Stone had done to him. Stone had ordered him beaten. That was not the way civilized men behaved, and pissing on people certainly wasn't. Stone and his men were barbarians; his mother would understand that and sympathize. Except now he didn't have any bruises. He wasn't even sure himself how they had vanished, unless it was something to do with the demon smoke, and how could he explain that? 'Yes, Mother, Stone's men did beat me to a pulp, but I think this highly illegal bottle of demon smoke might have cured me. Oh, and by the way I stole it.'

No, he couldn't face Erin now. He'd think of a way to tell her later. Besides, he had an appointment with March, a far more promising companion. Edyon was smelling and looking better than ever; he didn't want to waste that. He deserved some pleasant company after the day he'd had. Tomorrow he'd deal with his mother and Stone.

He needed to go to the Duck and find March, but first he'd have to stash the smoke somewhere safe. Not in his tent, where the servants or his mother would find it. Somewhere quiet . . . He headed towards the woods.

The woods were silent, the noise from the fair not reaching into the trees. Edyon kept walking, past the place where he'd been beaten, and on to a stream, which he flopped down beside. He unwrapped the bottle and stared in fascination at the swirling smoke.

Perhaps he should try some? It had been months since his last visit to a smoke den, and he could do with the relaxation. What was the point in having all the risk of owning a whole bottle of smoke and none of the pleasure of inhaling it? He'd have one smoke, hide the bottle and then go and see March. A perfect plan.

He eased the cork off the bottle and let a wisp of smoke escape. It curled up through the trees, glowing purple, and vanished among the leaves. He let another wisp escape, but this time he leant forward and sniffed it into his nose. It was hot and dry, and weaved its own way down his throat and into his lungs and then back into his mouth, where it seemed to swirl over his tongue and round the loose tooth and through the roof of his mouth, then it seeped warm and purple into his brain.

Edyon laughed and the smoke burst out of his mouth in a purple cloud. He lay back and floated above the ground, as if he was smoke too, as the cloud floated up and away, glowing in the darkness below the canopy.

The trees were beautiful. The leaves waved at him from above. He smiled at them and waved back. Everything was beautiful.

March

DORNAN,
PITORIA

While March waited outside the bathhouse for Edyon to reappear, he had plenty of time to think. He'd been foolish earlier, bantering with the prince's son, letting him compliment him about his eyes when he had a job to do. Next time March would remember his task. He had to talk to Edyon before he got to his mother and definitely before he got to Regan. He had to tell Edyon his story convincingly and to do that the story had to be mainly true. By the time Edyon appeared March knew what he had to say.

The prince's son emerged from the bathhouse, walking fast, with his jacket under his arm. March cut through a side street, hoping to come out ahead of him with a 'surprised but delighted to see you' face on and persuade Edyon to go with him somewhere quiet. But Edyon didn't appear in the road that led back to the fair. March ran back the way he'd come and just caught sight of Edyon heading out of town in the direction of the woods. Edyon seemed in less of a hurry now and March followed at a distance. The woods might be a good place for them to talk quietly and unobserved. Deeper and deeper Edyon went, past the place where he'd been beaten and pissed on, past the place March had spent the night, and on to a stream where he stopped and sat on the ground and took out from his jacket a bottle that glowed purple.

March had never seen anything like it. Edyon cradled the bottle and looked at it and then held it upside down and took out the cork. A wisp of purple smoke climbed through the trees; it didn't disperse but remained strong and bright until it disappeared above the canopy. Edyon released more of the smoke, but this time he inhaled it, laughed and then flopped back on the ground.

For a long time, he didn't move. Finally March stepped forward. 'Edyon.'

Edyon didn't respond. He seemed to be sound asleep.

'Well, at least you're not with Regan,' March said. He sat down next to Edyon and stared at his face, so like that of his father, the prince, and yet different too. Softer somehow.

Eventually, in the early evening, Edyon stirred, stretched and sat up. He was smiling. Then he saw March and his smile widened.

'Hello, my handsome foreign man. What a delightful surprise to see you here. Madame Eruth didn't say anything about me waking up next to you. But perhaps she knew I would misinterpret her.'

March felt flustered again. 'You look better,' he managed.

'Thank you. Though, as when you saw me last I was beaten up and covered in piss, I'm not sure "better" quite conveys the level of improvement.'

'You, er, smell better too.'

Edyon laughed. 'Hmm, I suspect compliments are not your strong point. But that's fine. Do you know that your eyes look even more amazing in this twilight?'

'Um, no.'

'Taking compliments is a struggle too, it seems. I'm afraid you might have to get used to that this evening. I intend to drench you in them. How long have you been here?'

'Since you arrived. I was watching out for you.'

'Watching out for me? Now that sounds promising.'

March shifted awkwardly. He had to get the conversation on to the subject of Regan. He said, 'I have to be honest with you. I'm concerned for your safety.'

'Well, that's rather wonderful of you, my new handsome foreign man. But you needn't worry – Stone's thugs won't beat me up again. At least, not until the end of the week.'

'I don't mean them. I'm talking about someone much more dangerous.'

Edyon gave a sour grin. 'Don't fret – I know about him.'

'You do?' Had Edyon somehow got a message from Regan or his mother while he was in the bathhouse?

'Of course. I figured he would work out it was me, though I thought it would take a little longer. But, if he's put the word out already, I'll probably be dead by morning.'

Edyon didn't seem that concerned about being killed. In fact, he looked totally relaxed. He was clearly still suffering from the effects of whatever was in the bottle.

'Well, he knows it's you . . . you're you. But he won't tell anyone else: he's here to kill you himself.'

'Here?' Edyon looked around, slightly more alert now.

'Here at the fair, I mean. That is why I've come, to warn you. But how did you know about him?'

'I stole the smoke from him; so of course I know about him.'

'Smoke?' March pointed at the bottle. 'That?'

'Yes, that.' Now Edyon looked confused. He squinted at March. 'Are we talking about the same person? Big. Hairy. Demon hunter.'

'No, Edyon.' This wasn't going to plan at all. March shuffled closer to Edyon so he could speak more quietly. 'There's a man from Calidor: Lord Regan. He's here at the fair and he's here to kill you.'

Edyon gave a sharp laugh. 'Well, he'll have to join the queue.'

'This is serious, Edyon.'

'Well, I see *you're* serious.' Edyon flopped back on the ground and turned his head to March. 'I don't feel at all serious. This smoke is amazing. *Much* better than last time. My body's been floating among the treetops and . . . how can I tell you? . . . My body feels happy. I mean every muscle and every bone is smiling. Does that make sense?'

March shook his head. 'First you're covered in piss, now you're drugged.' But what could you expect from the son of a prince?

'I'm merely happy and relaxed, my friend. Very, very wonderfully relaxed.' Edyon put his hand on March's knee. 'And you are just as handsome as I remember. I do hope I'm looking better too. The betterest of betters. I feel incredibly better. My bruises have gone, and even my wobbly tooth seems to have stopped wobbling.'

March looked down at Edyon's hand on his knee. He needed to stop this, to tell his story. He did it the only way he knew how, by becoming the servant. He stood and bowed.

'My name is March, sir. I'm here to bring you a message.'

Edyon raised his head to look, then let it fall back, saying, 'A message, hurrah!'

'Sir. Edyon.' March kept his servant voice together. 'This is serious. The message is secret and to give it to you I need to be sure of your identity. Can I ask about your parents . . .?'

Edyon sat up again. 'You *are* real, aren't you, March? Absurd, handsome, foreign . . . but real? Not a smoke dream?'

'Please, sir!'

Edyon frowned but said, 'You want to know about my parents? Well, my mother is a trader. Erin Foss. She buys things and sells them a short while later. Generally for a lot more than she bought them.'

'She's always done that? And you've always been with her?'

'Since the womb. That answer applies to both your questions.'

'And your father?'

Even in his sleepy state, Edyon seemed to tense at the word.

'It's no secret that my mother was never married. She says she loved my father for a while, but he left. Since then she's never found a man that meets her standards. I'm the man in her life now, though I sometimes think she'd prefer me to be an ivory-inlaid walnut chest of drawers. So, anyway, I have no father, at least none who'll own up to it.' Edyon shrugged and added, 'I assume he's dead.'

'Dead? Why?'

'Because my mother said that he was noble and good. And anyone good and noble would not ignore his blood.'

'That is what I believe too, but sometimes there are . . . circumstances, difficulties –'

'As far as I'm concerned, the only acceptable difficulty is death. So that is what I choose to believe.'

'So you don't know your father's identity?'

'Look, March, I've answered your questions. Now tell me the message or change the subject to something more interesting.'

'Your father is not dead, sir. He wants to meet you.'

Edyon gave a short laugh but he looked nervous. 'My father's presence? You haven't been sent by Madame Eruth to torment me, have you?'

'I've been sent by your father, sir.'

Edyon looked March in the eye and the gleam of hope that March saw there struck him dumb for a moment.

Eventually Edyon said, 'This is the strangest of days. And you really do have the most amazing eyes. Say that again.'

'Your father is alive. I've been sent by him. He wants to see you, and I am to take you to him. If you wish to go.'

Edyon blinked, the smoke fog seeming to clear from his brain. 'You're being serious, aren't you?'

'Yes.' March said this as gently as he could, and was surprised how tender it sounded. And he began to tell his story.

'I am a servant to the prince of Calidor, Prince Thelonius. I've been his servant for eight years, since I was a boy. I think perhaps because I was young he talked to me more as a boy than as a servant, and he still talks to me as he talks to no one else except his closest family.' March paused. 'But recently I have been the only one he could talk to. You may have heard that his wife and two sons died not long ago?'

Edyon didn't say anything, so March pressed on. 'As a prince, he must have an heir. The prince is under pressure from his ministers to marry again, to have more children, but he cannot face that. He loved his wife and children dearly. He doesn't want another wife. But he does want another child ... his long-lost, illegitimate son. You.'

Edyon stared at March and then shook his head. 'This has to be the smoke.'

March carried on. 'The prince asked me to find you. He trusts me like no other, because I'm only a servant, no threat to him. This information is important and dangerous. There are those in Calidor who would see you dead before they bow to you as the prince's heir.'

'*I see death all around you,*' murmured Edyon.

March could see that Edyon's breathing was fast and shallow.

'You are very like the prince. Your hair, your stature, your skin colour. You are like a younger version of him. Do you know nothing at all about your father?'

'My mother told me that he was a nobleman from another country. They met at one of the fairs and were happy together for a few months one summer. Then he was called home. She realized she was pregnant after he left and didn't tell my father about me until after I was born.' Edyon shook his head. 'By then he was married to another woman. He wrote back to her only once, to send a gift for me.'

That gold chain about your neck, thought March.

'And your mother never indicated who this nobleman was?'

'Never. She said it didn't matter, that I was hers.'

'You are the prince's too. That is the truth. I can see it just by looking at you.'

Edyon laughed nervously and looked at his hands. 'I'm shaking. I don't think it's the smoke.'

'The prince wants you to come to Calidor.'

'And what about my mother?'

'The prince talked only of you.'

Edyon ran his fingers through his hair. 'Is he . . . what sort of man is he?'

A lying traitor, were the words on March's lips, but he swallowed them and said, 'He's respected by his people.'

'That doesn't answer the question.'

'He knows his duty. He left you alone because of his duty. But he also believed it was best for you to find your own life here in

Pitoria. Now he is older, though, and he has lost all those he loved, he wants to meet you.'

'And we should all do as he wants?'

'He's a prince.' March shrugged. 'That is his way.'

'And I'm the son of a prince, so you say. But why should I believe any of this? Why didn't you tell me when we met before?'

'I judged the time wasn't right. It is momentous news and –' March extended his hands, palms open – 'I didn't think you should hear it while you were lying in a pool of piss.'

'You know, that might actually have been more appropriate. My life is . . . a bit of a mess at the moment.'

'You have a new life to think of now. This *is* momentous news for you, sir, but not just for you: for all of Calidor. As I said, some in the prince's court think he should remarry and have more children. Others see his sons' deaths as an opportunity to take more power for themselves. Lord Regan is one of them. He has been a loyal friend to the prince, but on this matter, the matter of an illegitimate son being made heir, he is not happy. While the king remains without a son, Regan will have an opportunity to seize the throne. Lord Regan is here at the fair to prevent you going to Calidor.'

'*Pain, suffering and death.*'

March nodded gravely. 'Death is his aim.'

'And what's yours?'

'I have been instructed to guide you safely and secretly to your father.'

'And if I don't want to go?'

'Then I will have failed, and I must tell the prince. But Regan is here. Even if you somehow avoid him, others who are against the prince's plans will come. Once your identity is known, and it will be known soon enough, then your life can never be the same again.'

'So you're saying I have no choice but to come with you?'

'You have choices. If you choose to let me guide you to the prince, we should leave this place soon. Tonight. Regan was at the fair this morning and he was watching your tent.'

'Our tent? What about my mother? Is she safe?'

'She's safe. She is no threat to the Calidorian lords. It's you who is in danger. Your mother will be safer if you leave.'

'I need to speak to her. To tell her what is happening.'

'It's not safe to go to your tent now. Regan may still be watching it.'

Edyon bit his lip. 'How do I know this isn't some joke? You've given me no proof.'

'My partner, Holywell, has the proof. And I think it marries up with that chain round your neck.'

Edyon put his hand to his chest. 'I didn't know you had a partner.'

'He's watching Regan. Listen, I have an idea. I'll go to Holywell and see if it's possible to get you to your mother. But you must wait here until I return.' March had no intention of letting Edyon see his mother, but it was clear that the young man needed proof – which meant March needed the gold ring Regan was carrying. With that he was sure he could convince Edyon to go with him. 'Will you do that? Please, sir, it's for your own safety.'

Edyon looked uncertain. 'I don't know what to do. I'm still not sure this isn't some strange effect of the smoke.'

'This is all real, sir. Your safety is my responsibility. The prince has charged me to look after you.'

Still Edyon looked uncertain. 'So much of what Madame Eruth said seems to be true . . . I'll wait here for you. But I need to see my mother and your proof before I decide what to do.'

'Thank you, sir,' March said. 'I'll be as quick as I can.'

March walked back towards the tents. It was almost done. Edyon wanted to believe him, March could see that. It would only take one final thing to convince him, but it was the hardest thing of all: Thelonius's ring. And there was only one way to get it: Lord Regan would have to die.

Tash

DORNAN,
PITORIA

Tash walked thoughtfully back to the bathhouse. *Someone* there had to know something about the stolen smoke, though of course it would be a delicate matter asking about it. She made a mental list of who could have taken the bottle.

One: the boys who carried the water.

This seemed unlikely as they had been busy chasing her, but possibly one of them could have snatched the bottle at some point.

Two: another person who worked at the bathhouse.

Three: a customer.

There were two customers she had seen – the young man with the bruises and the gold chain in the first compartment, and a thin old man with a sunken chest and grey hair in the third compartment. But the big question was who would dare take it? Tash was sure the employees at the bathhouse knew Gravell wasn't a man to cross, so that left the two customers. She went straight to the boys to ask them if they knew who the other customers were.

The older boy, his face a mass of spots, laughed at her question. 'The old man . . . didn't you recognize him without his gown? He's the mayor. Why do you want to know anyway?'

Tash cringed. She wondered how much the mayor had heard or understood of her conversation with Gravell about the smoke. He could have called the sheriff's men. Hopefully he was deaf . . .

'What about the other man? The young one. He had a gold necklace.'

The spotty boy grinned. 'Sure, we know his name. We'll tell you for ten kopeks.'

'Each,' the other boy added.

Tash handed over the coins, saying, 'If I find you've lied to me, I'll be back for my money.'

The boys didn't seem at all intimidated. 'He's called Edyon. His mother trades in furniture.'

Tash left the bathhouse and went to the fine arts end of the fair. She rarely came to this part, the posh end. The people here were wealthy, well dressed and old. Tash felt very out of place. It was quieter too. The tents were beautiful, but there were a lot of guards; each of the large tents seemed to have one or two. She asked one if he knew someone called Edyon whose mother dealt in furniture. The man shrugged. 'Ask at the food stall over there. Ged knows everyone.'

And, indeed, Ged did know an Edyon.

'About eighteen?' Tash asked.

'Yep, that's the one I'm thinking of. He's the son of Erin Foss. She deals in fine furniture or, as she puts it, "the finest and most exclusive of all furniture".'

'Which is her tent?'

'The finest and most exclusive of all tents, of course. The red and gold.'

Tash found the place easily. It was huge, with a large main section and two small circular tents attached at the back. The big area was where business was carried out; the two smaller ones would be the sleeping and private quarters. There was a guard at the front and no sign of Edyon.

Tash frowned. She could wait for Edyon, but what could she do when he arrived? She was almost certain he was the thief, but to get the smoke back she'd need more muscle . . .

Back at the inn, Gravell was seated where she'd left him, though now he had a woman next to him. Tash sat opposite them as Gravell turned to face her, saying, 'Ah, my young assistant returns. No doubt to tell me she's found the thief and got my goods back?'

Gravell's voice was slurred. The woman leant over and kissed his ear.

'How much have you had to drink?' Tash asked.

'Not enough.' And Gravell drank heavily from his tankard.

'I've found the thief. Well, I've not found him exactly but I've found out who he is and where he lives.'

Gravell listened as Tash described her detective work. 'Edyon's young; quick and agile enough to take it. He must have heard our conversation and guessed you had some . . . goods.'

'And intends to sell it or use it himself, the villain,' Gravell said. 'So, you're certain it's him?'

'I'm sure.'

'Good. I'm in the mood for some action. Been sitting down all afternoon.' He rose, swayed, then sat down again. 'Not sure how much I've had to drink.'

And then he fell forward in a faint, his face squished on the table.

The woman sighed and looked at Tash. 'He owes me a kroner.'

'He owes me more,' Tash responded.

She picked up the tankard and took a sip of the beer for herself, staring levelly at the woman. Tash had seen plenty of women getting money out of Gravell over the years. All the work he did and risks he took, and then he frittered his money away on these women. Tash didn't understand it at all.

The woman didn't go and so Tash said, 'Can I help you with something?'

'My kroner.'

'Ask Gravell when he wakes up. That'll probably be around breakfast time, knowing him.'

The woman started to pat Gravell's jacket, searching for his purse. Gravell didn't move. He was like a mountain with his head resting on the table, his jacket stretched tight over the muscles of his back.

Tash said, 'If you take anything of his, I'll slice your hand off with my skinning knife.'

Tash's knife was in her pack in their room and she had no intention of chopping anyone's hand off with it, but it was gratifying to see the woman jerk her hands back. She was twice Tash's weight and a lot taller.

'Probably don't have the money anyway,' the woman muttered. 'You and him are the same – barely civilized.' She slipped out of the seat and left.

Tash took another sip of the beer and pulled a face; it was warm and flat and not very good. She tipped the rest over Gravell's head, hoping it might wake him, but he didn't even stir.

Ambrose

NORWEND,
NORTHERN BRIGANT

Ambrose tried to dissuade his brother from coming with him, but Tarquin was immovable.

'It's only as far as the border. I want to see you safely out of the kingdom, little brother. Consider it my duty as a loyal subject of the king,' he added with a grin.

They left the house the way Ambrose had arrived. Tarquin took horses from the field, and brought food and money. Once they were riding, Tarquin questioned him about Fielding.

Tarquin listened carefully to Ambrose's story, but he, like Ambrose, couldn't make sense of it.

'The king's army does recruit some boys.'

'Yes, but only as squires to the older knights. This was a whole unit of boys; no men at all. In fact, it was at least two units, more than three hundred boys, all in training. They seemed to think I was part of a test set by their commanding officer.'

'Good job they didn't know who you really were.'

Ambrose winced. 'I think they'll work that out easily enough. I had to leave my horse. The saddle has my unit and initials on it.'

'Well, soon you'll be over the border and it won't matter. Did you find anything that might explain why Anne went there?'

'Nothing I could make sense of. But they did say something about an invasion.'

'Of Calidor? Another war!'

'That's what the king has always wanted.'

'But to send boys into battle is desperate. They're no match for trained men.'

'They managed to capture me. And I know this sounds strange, but one of them threw his sword fifty paces to hit me squarely on the head as I rode away. Another threw a spear twice the distance I can. They're strong and fast.'

Ambrose tried to remember the other things the boys had said, something about the blue unit having lost and not having something that they'd get after the invasion. He went over it all with Tarquin but it still made no sense.

The narrow road was quiet, apart from a few ramshackle carts coming back from Pitoria, having traded goods over the border, but the grass to each side was worn and there were signs that many horses had passed that way, travelling north. The brothers slept by the road the first night and next morning were surprised to see the road ahead blocked by a slow-moving stream of soldiers, perhaps five hundred of them, some on horseback and some on foot.

'What are they doing here?' Ambrose asked.

'Could be training,' Tarquin said. 'But those things are organized months in advance and I've not heard of anything. Perhaps a jousting tournament at Tallerford?'

'No, this is no tourney. The numbers are too large.'

Ambrose could see the pennants of the king's men and the southern lords – Wender, Thornlee. However, none of the royal pennants were visible, indicating that the king and prince were not themselves there.

'Wherever they're going, we can't pass them. We're too recognizable,' Ambrose concluded.

There was no option but to travel behind at a distance. That night the troops stopped and camped by the road but didn't break camp the next morning.

'What are they waiting for?' muttered Tarquin after they had been hanging around most of the morning, waiting for the men to move off.

Ambrose looked back the way they had come and cursed. On the horizon, more banners fluttered. 'They're waiting for them.'

'Into the woods, quick!' Tarquin said, urging his horse off the road. They barely had time to take cover before the first of the soldiers from the south marched into view.

'That's Lord Gunnar's colour . . . and behind them the Earl of Karrane.'

Tarquin frowned. 'Your boy soldiers talked about an invasion. But did they actually mention Calidor? Because this looks a lot like an army and it's heading towards Pitoria.'

'But we can't be invading Pitoria. Catherine's on her way there now to marry the prince.' Ambrose looked at Tarquin, hoping for reassurance but getting none. And everything he knew seemed to be pointing to this impossible idea. 'The boy soldiers knew of an invasion. Do you think Anne knew too? Is this all linked to what she found out?'

'You're making assumptions again, Ambrose. We don't know what she knew. We don't know if this is an invasion.'

'I know Father should have heard of any tournament or army manoeuvres. He's not been told, so I can't think why else this army is here.' Ambrose's voice was rising.

'They can't be invading Pitoria. That would be madness. And, anyway, I know little about war stratagems, but invading a remote, poor northern part of a country, leagues from the seat of power, doesn't seem the right way to go about it, even to me.'

'Nor me.' Ambrose continued, 'But something important is happening. I've got to find out what ... If we could see what orders the commanders have been given, then we'd know for certain.'

'Ambrose, no . . . that's impossible.'

'Difficult, but not impossible. I can go into their camp tonight and see what I can find.'

'What? That's the craziest idea I've ever heard. You're a wanted man and that is a military camp. You won't make it past the first perimeter defence.'

'I have to find out, Tarquin. There's something strange going on and I'm sure it's related to Anne's death somehow.'

Tarquin let out a long breath. 'Then I'll go in and ask the commanding officer what they are doing.'

'*Ask them?* That's a worse idea than mine! They won't tell you a thing.'

'We're still on Father's land. I have a right to know,' said Tarquin hotly.

'Do you really think they'll tell you? No. You mustn't be involved. I'm already a condemned traitor. I've nothing to lose. The plans will be with the most senior of the lords, Lord Thornlee.

I'll get into the camp wearing my Royal Guard uniform without trouble, then I just need to get into Thornlee's tent.'

Tarquin shook his head and sighed. 'I can't believe I'm saying this but you'll need a diversion.'

Ambrose smiled. 'And you can provide one?'

'Will a fire by the horses be good enough?'

'If the panicked horses get loose in the camp I think that would be reasonably disruptive.'

'I'll need to be in the uniform of the Thornlee men,' said Tarquin.

'For that we need to borrow a man's clothes. Is it too much to hope that some of them are washing in the river?'

Tarquin grinned. 'Let's see.'

It almost felt like a child's game, stealing the clothes. The day was already hot and there were about twenty men in the river, washing and swimming. Ambrose stripped off, entered the water downstream from the men, then swam up to the nearest pile of clothes in the Thornlee colours of red and green. He picked them up and walked to the bushes where Tarquin was waiting with Ambrose's own clothes.

Tarquin put on the Thornlee trews and tunic. The trews were a little short in the leg but good enough with boots on. He pulled his hair up and into the hat while Ambrose smudged some mud on his face.

'Not bad,' Ambrose said. 'I don't think I'd recognize you.'

Ambrose put on his Royal Guard uniform. That ought to be enough to get him access to the camp. He just had to hope that no one recognized him as a wanted man.

Ambrose watched as Tarquin skirted the Thornlee camp to the horses. The king's men, Wender's and Boris's, were all in distinct sections. Ambrose hung well back in the trees. Soon he saw smoke rising from the far side of the camp and then there were shouts and the sound of the first horse running. Ambrose grinned. The panicked horses were stampeding into the camp of the king's men – a double embarrassment for Thornlee. As the noise spread, Lord Thornlee himself emerged from his pavilion and stalked off to investigate.

As confidently as he could, Ambrose marched forward, past the rows of tents and men hurrying to fight the fire Tarquin had started. Ambrose got a few stares, but no one challenged him. He strode on towards Lord Thornlee's tent, which was guarded by a single soldier.

Ambrose went up to him and said, 'I need to see Lord Thornlee.'

'He's just left, sir.'

Ambrose sighed. 'I'll wait.' And he walked past the guard into the tent.

'But . . . you can't wait in here, sir.'

'Well, I'm not going to hang around outside. His horses have run amok in the camp. Get Thornlee now.'

'But he's just left to sort it out, sir.'

'Then get him back, you idiot.'

'Yes, sir.'

As the flustered guard left, Ambrose moved quickly round the table in the centre of the tent. A pile of letters lay on the polished wood. Ambrose flicked through them until he found one with the royal seal.

'Who did this man say he was?' barked a voice from just beyond the side of the tent.

Thornlee!

Tucking the letter into his belt, Ambrose drew his dagger, cut a slit in the back of the tent and stepped out. His heart hammered as he forced himself to walk calmly towards the trees, expecting with every step someone to shout 'Stop!' But no one did, and as soon as he was under the cover of the trees he broke into a run, not stopping until he had reached the meeting point he had arranged with Tarquin.

'Success?' asked his brother.

Ambrose held out the letter, trying to catch his breath.

Tarquin took it and unfolded the heavy paper. He scanned the contents quickly.

'Well, it seems our illustrious king knows something of war strategy that we don't, because this army is going to invade the most remote northern part of Pitoria.'

Catherine

LEYDALE, PITORIA

Queen Valeria is famously quoted as saying: 'The people love their queen and the queen loves her people.' These words would never, could never, be said by a king.
        A History of Brigant, Thomlyn Thraxton

It was all very well talking about being one of the Pitorian people, but Catherine didn't look like them or feel like them; they seemed elegant, elaborate and exotic, and for her plan to work she needed to look like them, only better.

She rose at dawn on her first morning in Pitoria and had her maids set out her Pitorian dresses. When Catherine had first seen them, back in Brigant, she thought they were dangerously exposing, but the ladies the night before had been even more daring. Indeed, most of the men last night had been more elaborately dressed than Catherine. She needed some of that daring, but not too much – something that suggested Pitoria but was also uniquely her.

Her wedding dress was not laid out so she asked Sarah to bring it. It was white and gold, with crystal work covering the bodice and more crystals scattered over the wide skirt. It covered her from ankle to throat, but with slashes in the shoulder and bodice that didn't expose bare skin as a fine transparent gauze lay beneath. This was a dress that said 'Pitoria' and 'Princess' perfectly.

'Put this green one on, Jane,' she said.

Jane approached Catherine and started to lift her nightdress.

'No, not on me. I want you to wear it.'

Jane stopped and stared.

'Tanya, you wear one of the red ones.' Tanya curtsied and grabbed the red dress that Catherine had worn in front of her father. 'Sarah, you're in the black. Today I'm going to ride rather than sit in the carriage. You'll ride with me. Get dressed.'

Sarah, Jane and Tanya glanced at each other with a mix of excitement and nervousness but willingly stripped off their beige maids' dresses and, with help from one another, were quickly transformed into Pitorian ladies. The dresses fitted well enough with a few quick stitches. Standing together, they looked like the stripes of the Pitorian flag and they looked stunning.

'Will you wear the dress from yesterday, Your Highness?' Jane asked.

'I'll be wearing the white dress,' Catherine replied.

'But ...' Jane said meekly, 'that's for your wedding, Your Highness.'

'I intend to get another for that occasion. I want to wear this one now.'

They helped her into it. It was heavy and tight on the chest and neck. Riding in it in the hot sun would not be particularly pleasant.

Sarah started to pack the train away, folding it carefully.

'No. I want the train too. Sew it to the bodice.'

'But it's so long!' Tanya said.

'Yes. It's perfect.'

Sarah quickly unravelled the train, which was sprinkled with crystals. She sewed it to the bodice at the shoulders and clapped with delight as Catherine walked across the room to see how it fell.

'Should I wear my necklace or not?' Catherine mused.

The maids looked uncertain.

'No, you're right – we must show some Brigantine restraint. The dress is enough.'

Just then there was a knock on the door, a servant with a message that a gentleman was waiting in the library. Catherine hadn't realized how long dressing had taken but now she was ready to test the effect of her outfit on Sir Rowland.

When they were organized, Catherine said, 'Sarah, you lead the way. I would like you to assess the look on Sir Rowland's face when I enter.'

'You look stunning, Your Highness,' Tanya said.

Catherine smiled. 'Good. Nothing less will do.'

She followed Sarah downstairs to the library, Jane and Tanya a step behind, ensuring her train didn't catch on anything. Sarah opened the doors and Catherine entered. She had intended to surprise Sir Rowland but it was she who was surprised.

'Noyes!'

The eyes of the king's spymaster went wide as he saw her and he took two quick steps backwards. Catherine wasn't sure if that was a good effect or not, but she certainly liked to see Noyes in retreat. She could feel Tanya twitching at her train, but couldn't tell if she was straightening it or indicating Catherine should hold back.

'I was expecting to meet Sir Rowland.' Catherine immediately regretted telling Noyes what she was doing. 'Did you wish to talk with me?'

'I wanted to compliment you on your handling of the situation yesterday evening, Your Highness.'

'A compliment from you. A rare thing indeed.' Catherine braced herself for the catch.

'Lord Farrow's speech was clumsy and unwelcoming. Your own rescued the situation as well as could be expected for a young woman making what was clearly her first public speech. It was an interesting novelty, I'm sure, for much of the audience. However, I know that your father would not approve and would require you not to repeat it.'

Catherine pursed her lips. 'I had several compliments yesterday evening and certainly got the impression that the guests appreciated hearing my views. I intend to ensure they see us Brigantines as friends and not as threats, which is surely what my father intends.'

'The anti-Brigant feelings held by Lord Farrow and his like will not be swayed by a pretty speech, Your Highness, and you risk ... well, you risk making a mistake, risk making a public spectacle of yourself.'

Noyes, you're becoming predictable, Catherine thought, *playing on my insecurities*. He knew her fear of failure, of being laughed at, but what Noyes didn't know was how she was changing. Free from the shadow of her father, the reward of success now outweighed that fear of failure, and Catherine was finding she was more of a gambler than she had realized.

'Thank you for your advice, Noyes. You'll be pleased to hear that I don't intend to make a speech today. Or, rather, I'm going to let my dress do the talking. I'm hoping the crowds will like it.'

Noyes smiled. 'Alas, I fear most won't be able to see it from the carriage.'

'An excellent point, Noyes. That's why I've decided to ride.'

For the second time that morning Catherine had the pleasure of seeing Noyes wrong-footed.

'Ride! In that?'

'Yes. The dress will look splendid on horseback.' How it would feel was another matter; Catherine wasn't sure if she could even sit down in it yet. She turned, swishing her dress so that the jewels jangled. 'Was there anything else, Noyes?'

Noyes didn't reply.

'In that case, you may go.'

Noyes hesitated, then bowed hastily and stalked out of the room. As he left, Sir Rowland entered. He beamed at Catherine and held out his arms.

'You look magnificent, Your Highness. And your speech last night was a great success. Already I've heard people discussing you on their morning rides.'

'Discussing me?'

'Being talked about is always a good thing in Pitoria. And soon they will *all* be talking about that dress.'

'Good. But I need your help on other things too, Sir Rowland. Firstly I need a horse to ride today, and horses for my maids too. They must be the most well-groomed and well-behaved animals in the parade.'

'Wonderful. Wonderful! Yes. Yes. Yes. I'll see to it at once.'

Catherine laughed. She was so used to being told why she couldn't do things that Sir Rowland's quick and positive response warmed her heart.

'Secondly I want to make our progress more of an event. Some musicians or acrobats perhaps.'

'Excellent suggestion. Fewer soldiers, more entertainers. Music that people can be drawn to. That is easily arranged. And dancers, of course.'

'And finally I need a symbol. Something to carry that will link me to Pitoria. Some flowers might do it.'

'A wissun, perhaps? It's a white flower that grows all over Pitoria. Fragrant and beautiful. Loved by everyone.'

'I like that. I knew you'd be a good adviser.'

'Then white will be your colour.' Sir Rowland hesitated, then said, 'If you don't mind me saying, Your Highness, it's good to see you embracing Pitoria in this way. There were some who thought the marriage was a ploy of your father's. It's well known he has held a grudge against King Arell since the war between Calidor and Brigant. Your actions will help dispel those concerns. I think Prince Tzsayn will be pleased to hear of your enthusiasm too.'

'Really?' For a moment, Catherine had almost forgotten that her wedding was the end point of this journey. 'I hope so. I want to find a position for myself in this country, Sir Rowland. I don't want to be locked away in a tower. I want to do something with my life. The people of Pitoria think we're bloodthirsty warmongers. I want to prove them wrong. I want to conquer the people not as my father would, with swords and spears, but with a dress and a flower. Do you think that's possible?'

Sir Rowland bowed. 'I think you have the power to conquer anyone, Your Highness, as you have already done me. Today, I myself shall be wearing a wissun and I'm sure many of the crowds will soon do likewise.'

March

DORNAN,
PITORIA

March ran through the woods back to the fair, hoping that he could find Holywell. He went to Erin's red-and-gold tent and was relieved to see that Holywell was still there. March walked up to him as casually as he could.

'Edyon is in the woods. I've told him about his father and that we're here to take him back to Calidor.'

'And he believes it?'

'Yes, but he wants proof. We need the ring the prince gave to Regan.'

Holywell sucked his teeth thoughtfully. 'Regan is still in there with Edyon's mother.'

'So she must know what he's here for.'

'Which means we must keep Edyon away from her and get rid of Regan. The plan hasn't changed, brother,' Holywell said, and he nodded over to Regan, who had appeared from the tent, 'and the time is right. We need to get him alone, somewhere quiet. There's a place beyond the caravans, a little dip by the stream. I'll be waiting there. Your job is to bring him to me.'

March nodded. 'I'll tell him the prince has sent an urgent message.'

Holywell slapped March on the arm. 'Good. Be ready to assist me. Regan will be no pushover.' And, before March could reply, Holywell strode off towards the stream.

March had no time to think as he hurried after Regan, getting back into a servant frame of mind; becoming a servant was as easy as slipping on a coat for March. He broke into a run and, full of urgency, called out, 'Sir! Sir!' and finally, 'Lord Regan!'

Regan turned round.

'Lord Regan.' March bowed low. 'Excuse me, sir. I've been sent with a message.' March raised his head so Regan could see his face. 'I'm March, sir. Servant to Prince Thelonius.'

'And you were told to shout my name out in the streets?'

'My apologies, sir.' March bowed again. He knew not to make excuses but to wait and hope that the lord would forgive and in this case believe that his own master had sent a message.

'Stand up straight, boy. Let us go somewhere quiet.'

'Yes, sir. My associate is this way. He has the message, sir.' And March set off, trying to lead the way from behind, which was always the difficulty with noblemen. 'The prince sent us with the utmost urgency. I've been searching the fair for you.'

'Who is your associate?'

'Brown, sir.' March chose the name of another of Prince Thelonius's servants whom he was sure Regan wouldn't know by sight.

'And when did your master send you?'

'The prince said that you had been gone three days, sir.'

'You've done well to catch me up.'

'That was the prince's order, sir. And we had favourable winds for our crossing.'

'How did you find me?'

Was that suspicion in Regan's voice?

'Brown, sir. He worked out where you would be.'

'Did he now? How did he do that?'

So many questions. Too many questions . . .

'I'm not sure, sir. He can tell you himself. He's just ahead, sir. Beyond the tents, by the stream.'

'And did the prince send anything else?'

March felt sweat breaking out on his brow. Something was wrong. Perhaps a real messenger would have been given a password or token to confirm their identity. Regan was certainly suspicious about something.

'Brown has everything, sir. I was honoured that the prince trusted me with this task, but he still considers me too young and inexperienced to travel alone. Brown has been to Pitoria before and speaks the language.'

They rounded the last tent, and the open field was ahead. It felt exposed, but March realized it was a good place for an ambush. The slope of the ground down to the stream would hide them from view from the tents and yet the spot wasn't so isolated as to feel like a trap.

Holywell was there, standing with his back to March and throwing small stones into the stream. March stopped a pace behind Regan, ever the polite servant.

'Brown?' Regan asked.

Holywell turned and bowed low, keeping his head down so Regan couldn't see his eyes.

'My Lord Regan.'

'You have a message for me.'

'Yes, my lord.' Holywell rose and stepped forward, putting his hand into his jacket as if to draw out a paper. He took another step, frowning as if he couldn't find it, and then another step and he drew out his hand, blade gleaming, and charged at Regan.

'Treason!' shouted Regan, instinctively stepping sideways, grabbing Holywell in a headlock and forcing the arm holding the dagger behind his back. They staggered around like a wild beast, Regan grunting and wrenching at Holywell's head as the dagger fell to the ground.

March had to do something to help Holywell. Heart racing, he picked up the fallen dagger, but Regan was watching him. The lord released Holywell, pushing him away, and drew one of his own daggers, slashing at March. March leapt back, and Holywell threw himself at Regan, grappling him round the waist, propelling them both down the slope past March, and they tumbled headlong into the stream.

March ran after them. Holywell was lying on his side, purple-faced and panting, blood pouring from a wound in his neck. Regan was face down in the water, not moving. Upstream, March could see a woman and child looking their way. He turned from them as casually as he could, walked slowly out of their view and then plunged into the water. He had to get the ring and get Holywell away as quickly as possible. March splashed over to Regan and heaved at his body. On the second attempt, March managed to turn him over. Blood was colouring the water around Regan from a stab wound in his chest and he didn't seem to be breathing. Hands shaking with the cold water and fear, March unbuttoned Regan's jacket, his years of practice at dressing and undressing others finally proving its worth. He quickly found the ring, put it in his own jacket and grabbed Holywell, who was still purple and gasping.

'We need to go. Now.'

March pulled Holywell to his feet and supported him as they walked towards the trees. He looked back, but the woman and child he had noticed earlier had gone. How much had they seen? Well, it was too late to worry about that now.

Holywell weighed more than he looked and, as soon as they were under cover, March collapsed with him on to the ground.

'So, that went well,' Holywell rasped. He was a mess. Wet and panting, the wound in his neck bleeding steadily. 'Tell me you've got the ring.'

March pulled it out. It gleamed back at him in the light of the setting sun. The prince's true seal: the gold eagle with an emerald eye.

Edyon

DORNAN,
PITORIA

Could Madame Eruth be right? Was Edyon's father exerting an influence on his life? Certainly, life had seemed so dull and hopeless yesterday and now . . . now he was the son of a prince. And not just any prince: Prince Thelonius, hero of Calidor! A small country, yes, but rich for its size. Civilized. Home to many musicians, painters and sculptors. The architecture was supposed to be simple but of good quality, the clothing less ornate than the Pitorians', their furniture was well crafted, favouring oak and ash or fruit woods. They didn't dance, which was a good thing as far as Edyon was concerned, since he hated dancing, though they were renowned as good fighters, but he hated fighting too. They were most famous for holding out in the war against Brigant, brother against brother, and Thelonius was respected, intelligent and honourable.

That honour would be tarnished when Edyon appeared. He thought about what March had said about the unhappy lords, and it seemed entirely plausible that some of the prince's courtiers wouldn't want a bastard on the scene. But it was gratifying to think that his father had finally realized that he, Edyon, was important, and was willing to risk his reputation to see him. Edyon had imagined many fathers, from king to vagabond, but somehow the reality seemed too preposterous and he couldn't take it in.

And then there was March. Edyon had fancied they'd be lovers when he first saw him – he was sure the handsome Abask felt the same spark between them, even if March seemed embarrassed to admit it. But now March behaved like a servant. In his years of travel through Pitoria in his mother's caravan, Edyon had met many people from different lands and cultures, but in all that time he hadn't met anyone from Abask, had never seen anyone with such remarkable eyes. Edyon could easily imagine a prince wanting such a servant. Perhaps Edyon could have him as a servant and a lover too.

It was getting dark now and March hadn't returned. But Edyon's doubts had. Had it all been his imagination? He'd had a lot of strong smoke. But he'd met March *before* the smoke. Could the whole thing be a prank? There had been, after all, just words so far. He would need proof before he could go with March to Calidor.

It sounded unbelievable. Going to Calidor to meet his father.

He was now truly at a crossroads; his old path of thievery had run its course and he had to choose a new way forward. Madame Eruth had been right about the new man entering his life, but was March showing him the way to far lands and riches, or pain, suffering and death? No, staying put would lead to that, through either Stone or Gravell or this new threat, Regan. The path to his father had to be the right choice. But, then again, hadn't Madame Eruth said something about the foreign man lying too? Was this all a lie? A joke?

And *still* March hadn't returned.

Edyon paced anxiously. The glow of the smoke bottle seemed to get brighter and brighter, as if signalling his presence. He walked along the riverbank until he found a recess into which he pushed the bottle so that none of its light could be seen.

Edyon crept closer to the edge of the wood, hoping to catch sight of March. The tents were only a field away, and he could see people coming and going. But there was no sign of March. Had he been lying about it all?

Suddenly Edyon knew that he had to speak to his mother. Her word was the only real proof. He had given up asking years ago, but now he had a name. She'd have to confirm or deny it.

Now she'd have to tell him the truth.

Erin stood as he entered the tent.

'Edyon. At last. I've had Mal out looking for you. I need to speak to you.'

'That's good, because I want to speak with you too.' Edyon moved closer to his mother. 'Today has been rather eventful. Shall I tell you what I've done?'

'First I need to tell you about a visitor I've had –'

'I've been to see Madame Eruth, stolen a silver ship from Stone, been beaten up by Stone's men and pissed on by them as well, met a beautiful boy from Abask, had a bath, taken some demon smoke and discovered my father is a prince.'

Edyon stared at his mother. Erin's face was a mask. 'Shall I repeat the last bit? Someone told me that my father is Prince Thelonius of Calidor.'

'Who . . . who told you that?'

'Well, it certainly wasn't you.'

'You're angry.'

'You're surprised?'

'Did you see Regan? Did he tell you?'

'What does that matter?' Edyon's voice cracked with frustration. 'I wanted *you* to tell me.'

His mother was silent but not for long. 'You know I've always done what I thought was best.'

Edyon rolled his eyes. 'I've heard that before. Heard it for long enough. Just tell me: is it true? I need to hear it from you.'

Again she was silent. The mistress of silence, as she always had been. Then she spoke.

'Prince Thelonius is your father.'

She sat down. Edyon sat too.

It was true.

His father wasn't dead.

His father was a prince.

He was a prince.

'How?'

And so his mother told her story. The same one she'd always told him, except now his father had a name. She had met Thelonius when he was still a young man, before he was granted the rule of Calidor. They fell in love, had a brief but wonderful affair, and he left not knowing she was pregnant.

'Would you have married? If he had known?'

Erin shrugged. 'Probably not. He was a prince and I was a trader from Pitoria.'

'You should have told me.'

'I did what I thought was best.'

'It wasn't best. I needed to know. It doesn't matter that I couldn't have done anything about it. I needed to know.'

'I'm not sure about that.'

Edyon ground his teeth. 'Even now you won't admit you got it wrong!'

'I didn't do this to hurt you, Edyon. You need to be your own man. The prince, your father, didn't want to know you. Now he does. Now he needs you. Now his legitimate children are dead. He'll use you, Edyon, pull you on a string.'

'He's my father. I want to meet him at least.'

Erin sighed. 'Yes. Of course. I do understand, Edyon. Did you meet Lord Regan?'

'No. I heard from one of the prince's servants who was sent here to find me and to . . .' Should he tell his mother that Regan was here to kill him? She'd worry, but Regan might be a danger to her as well.

'To what?'

'To warn me. Regan doesn't want me to go back to Calidor, Mother. March says he's here to kill me.'

'But that's impossible! He was here this afternoon, talking with me, waiting to see you. I said I'd send for him when you returned.'

'And why do you say it's impossible?'

'Regan is a close friend of your father. His oldest friend. I met him once, years ago, when they were here. He was aloof, maybe, but always polite and courteous.'

'I admit I don't know many killers but I imagine some are capable of being polite and courteous.'

'You know what I mean. He's an honourable man.'

'You knew him that well? And, if you did, do you know him now, seventeen, eighteen years later?'

Erin looked at Edyon, doubt in her face for the first time.

'And I can imagine that plenty of his fellow lords don't like the idea of a bastard like me turning up.'

'Love child, not bastard.'

Edyon rolled his eyes again.

'Love child,' she repeated insistently. 'That is what you are.'

'Not to them.'

Erin rubbed her face. She looked tired.

'So?' Edyon asked. 'What do you think I should do?'

'Do you want to meet your father?'

'Yes, I do.'

'Then go to him.' Erin sounded petulant.

They sat staring at each other.

In a slightly softer voice Erin said, 'I thought Regan could be trusted but perhaps I'm wrong and this servant is right, but who knows.'

'March, the servant, could have killed me this afternoon and didn't. I trust him that much.'

'There will be some people, many perhaps, who are against you. The best way, the safest way, is to trust no one.'

'And will you be safe, Mother?'

She gave a bitter laugh. 'I am merely the mother. No one's interested in me.'

'Would you want to come to Calidor?'

'What would I do there? Here I have my own life, my own business. If you stay there, I'll visit you.' She forced a smile. 'Maybe I'll find some new customers.'

Edyon thought of going to her and hugging her, but it didn't feel right. They rarely touched. Never hugged. He couldn't now, but maybe later, before he left.

Erin said, 'Whatever happens, I would like to think you won't forget me. You'll write often, I'm sure.' She sounded hurt. Formal. Businesslike.

'I'll write often,' Edyon assured her.

They were silent again. Edyon wasn't sure what to do. Just packing a bag and walking out felt heartless, but that's all that was left to be done.

'What was all that about stealing things and being pissed on?'

And suddenly it didn't seem so hard to tell her after all.

'I steal things. I always have. This time Stone caught me. His guards beat me up and pissed on me, so I went to the bathhouse to clean up and stole some demon smoke from there.'

'What?'

'As I say, it's been a busy day.'

'People who trade in demon smoke are dangerous, Edyon.'

'Perhaps it is a good time to leave then. I've hidden the smoke. Stone wants paying, though. Fifty kroners. I'm sorry to ask, but . . . could you pay him? I'll pay you back.'

'Of course, Edyon. The money's not a problem. Though stealing is.'

'Yes, I'm sorry. It's not something I'm proud of. But don't worry about the demon hunters. They don't know I took the smoke. And, even if they find out, it's me they'll look for and . . . well, if I leave soon . . . tonight . . . I wouldn't worry about them.'

'You'll go tonight?'

'Yes. Regan could come back at any moment. Him, I *am* worried about. I'll go as soon as I can. Make my way to the coast with March. I should be there in a few days. We can get a boat easily enough. I'll be with Father in a week.' Edyon was just saying things as they came to him, but that final phrase hit him. He'd see his father in a week. It sounded like a dream or a fantasy. It sounded unreal.

Erin rose. 'I'll get Mal to prepare some food for your journey. Are you hungry now? He can bring you something.'

'Yes. Thanks. I'll just go and pack a few things.'

Edyon hesitated, thinking he should hug his mother now, but she was already going to call for Mal and so he went to his sleeping tent, sat down on the rug and stared at nothing. Mal brought him a bowl of stew and some bread and a glass of wine. Though Edyon didn't think he'd manage to eat it, he devoured the lot. He knew he should start thinking about what to take on his journey, but he wasn't sure what he needed. What did you need to meet your father? To meet a prince?

He put on his most comfortable clothes and put his best boots, jacket, trousers and his two best shirts in a bag. It wasn't that heavy, so he added another warmer jacket. Was it cold in Calidor? Could he take more? Would March carry his bag? He had no idea.

His mother said he should trust no one, but he did trust March. He liked him. He seemed honest. So far, it seemed he hadn't lied at all. And certainly if he'd wanted to kill Edyon he could have done it when he'd been lying in a pool of piss or when he was sleeping off the demon smoke. Edyon could make his way to Calidor by himself easily enough, but wouldn't it be more pleasurable to spend time with the handsome March? And March could tell him about the prince, how to behave at court, who his enemies might be. Yes, March would be valuable to him.

Edyon was full of energy now. He had made a choice. He was the son of a prince. And he was on his way to meet his father. He picked up his bag and went to say goodbye to his mother.

They did hug, though a little uncomfortably. He kissed her on her cheek and accepted the bag of food and the money she offered him. He took a step towards the front of the tent, but his mother said, 'Not that way. Just in case someone is watching. Go out the back.' She came to him again and this time hugged him hard, saying, 'Take care, Edyon.'

And Edyon kissed her again, taking in the smell of her perfume.

'Thank you, Mother. I will see you again, but now I need to see my father.'

And he went to the hidden flap at the back of the tent that Mal held open for him and he was out into the cool night air.

Tash

Tash had given up on Gravell and gone back to Edyon's tent.

She was almost certain he had taken the smoke, but there was one way to be sure. If she could get into the tent, she could search for the stolen bottle. It was risky, but getting the smoke back was the main objective. Edyon could wait – Gravell would find him soon enough.

Tash sauntered casually past the guard at the front of the tent before ducking down the side and picking her way through the web of guy ropes to the rear. But just as she arrived another figure stepped out through a low flap. He immediately tripped over a guy rope, cursed, stumbled, leapt high over another rope, laughed and ran off towards the woods.

Tash had quickly moved back out of sight but even in the dim light she recognized the boy as the one she'd seen in the bathhouse.

Edyon.

He had a bag over his shoulder and certainly looked guilty, slipping furtively out the back of the tent. Was he afraid Gravell was already after him? Tash hurried in pursuit.

Edyon went towards the woods, speeding up when he was clear of the tents. He continued into the trees, then stopped by a stream and seemed to be waiting for someone, looking around constantly.

Tash wasn't sure what to do. Was he meeting a buyer? If he had the smoke it must be in his bag, but she couldn't snatch it from him as it looked too heavy for her to run with. But if someone else turned up she'd have even less of a chance to get the smoke back. There was only one thing for it.

She stepped forward and said, 'Hey.'

Edyon jumped like a scalded cat, but he turned and gave a very casual wave of his hand. 'Hey.'

'I saw you in the bathhouse,' Tash said.

'I remember. What a coincidence seeing you here too!'

Now he was looking around him with more concern.

'Something went missing from the bathhouse while Gravell and me were . . . when Gravell stepped out of his compartment. I know it was you who took it. I can shout him over – he's just back there at the tents – but it'd be much easier if you gave it back to me.'

Edyon looked a little more relaxed. He wasn't afraid of her, just of Gravell. He said, 'It?'

'The bottle of smoke. Hand it over. Or shall I call Gravell and you can go through all this with him?'

'Look, I know you're not going to believe this but I'm actually glad you're here. Really. I admit I took the smoke, but I don't want it. I'm leaving and I wasn't going to take the smoke with me. I hid it in the riverbank.'

Tash smiled. 'Sure you weren't. And sure you did. And when I go down there to look you'll hit me on the back of the head with a rock and run off.'

'I wouldn't hit anyone, and definitely not with a rock.'

'So hand it over then.'

'But how do I know that, after I give it back to you, you won't still send Gravell after me?'

'All you need to know is that, if you *don't* give it back to me, I'll call Gravell and he'll be much less patient than me.'

Edyon smiled. 'Why isn't he with you now? I'm guessing you saw me come out of my tent and followed me here, and he doesn't know you followed me or he'd be here by now.'

'I can run and get him easily.'

'Go on then. I'll wait.'

Tash wanted to stamp her foot. If Gravell were here, Edyon would be cowering and whimpering, but instead he was all cocky smiles and clever talk.

'Look. You said you want to give it me. And yet you haven't. Gravell blames me for the loss of our stuff. He'll beat me if I don't get it back.'

Edyon looked doubtful. 'Somehow I can imagine him taking pleasure in knocking my teeth out but not in doing it to you.'

'Shall I show you my back where he whips me?'

As soon as she said it she knew she'd made a mistake.

Edyon put his hands on his hips and grinned. 'I think the answer to that has got to be yes.'

Tash felt like screaming. This was so unfair! Why did her conversations always go wrong?

'Just give me the smoke and we can forget it.'

'He's not here at all, is he?'

Tash hesitated but decided to plead to his good nature. If he had one.

'Fine, fine. I admit he's not here. Satisfied? He's back at the inn, if you must know. But he really will hunt you down if you don't give the smoke back. And he'll do more than knock your teeth out.'

Edyon spread his arms. 'Why didn't you say so in the first place?'

He slipped down the riverbank. Tash ran forward to see what he was doing. There was a faint purple glow as Edyon pulled a bottle out of a hidden niche. The demon smoke!

Tash hurried down the bank and held out her hand for the bottle.

'Please tell Gravell I'm sorry for the –'

Edyon stopped. The sound of heavy footsteps was unmistakable. Edyon looked up, his eyes wide and panicked. Tash raised her head to peer over the top of the bank. For a moment she thought that maybe Gravell had woken from his drunken stupor after all and followed her.

But it was much worse than that.

The man was big, almost as big as Gravell, but this man had scarlet hair. He was carrying a spear and a small lantern. And he was marching quickly towards them. Tash ducked down again while Edyon stuffed the bottle under his jacket to hide the glow, but the violet light seemed even brighter than ever – and it was far too late anyway.

'Come out from there. I've seen you and I know what you've got.'

Tash cringed but slowly looked up. The sheriff's man was standing on the lip of the bank only a few paces away, his spear pointing at Edyon.

'And don't even think about running.'

But Tash was definitely thinking of running. Being caught, being arrested, being convicted of having demon smoke meant prison for a long time. Running meant the possibility of a spear in the back, but the man only had one spear and Edyon had the smoke, not her. She hesitated, though, hoping for a better chance.

'You're both under arrest for possessing demon smoke.'

'I don't have any demon smoke,' Tash said, thinking that if Edyon had just given it to her when she'd asked and not argued so much they'd both have been away from there. In all her years of demon hunting she'd never had any difficulties with the sheriff's men. This Edyon was just constant trouble.

'Put the bottle by my feet and step back.'

The sheriff's man flicked his spear at Edyon to show he was talking to him.

Edyon said, 'There's been a terrible misunderstanding here.'

'Shut up and do as you're told.'

Moving as slowly as possible, Edyon laid the bottle on the bank, close to Tash. It was so tempting to snatch it up and run. So tempting, but so very, very risky.

'Now step back, both of you, and get on your knees.'

'I can explain all this,' pleaded Edyon.

'Explain it on your knees.'

Edyon moved back.

'That goes for you too, girl,' the sheriff's man said, and he jabbed his spear at her face so that she stepped quickly back to stand next to Edyon and they both dropped to their knees.

'Please, sir,' Edyon said. 'My friend and I were taking a walk in the woods when I noticed a faint glow coming from the river. A purple glow that was most unusual and certainly like nothing I'd seen before. We had just come down to investigate. It never occurred to me that it might be demon smoke. I've heard tell of demon smoke of course, in bars and such like, but I thought it was red. So when I saw purple, well . . .'

Edyon carried on spinning his story with such conviction he almost made Tash believe it. He certainly sounded like *he* believed it. But she doubted the sheriff's man would. She would have to run for it. She could cope with the loss of the smoke if it meant escaping prison. She could cover the ground to the first bend in the river in twenty paces. She could do twenty paces before the sheriff's man could throw the spear. Probably. Almost definitely. The ground was cold and damp. Tash dug her toes in and got ready to push off.

'Hello, there. Is there any trouble?'

The voice was deep and the accent foreign. Tash strained her neck to see who it was, but the riverbank blocked her view.

'No trouble that concerns you, sir.'

There was the sound of a horse walking forward. The rider came into view, middle-aged, with greying hair and a bandage round his neck, and close behind him another much younger rider, about the same age as Edyon.

'Hey, what's that light?'

The older man jumped down from his horse and came towards them.

'Demon smoke, sir. Please step back.'

'Demon smoke! But surely that's forbidden?'

Tash had a bad feeling about this man. He seemed relaxed and friendly but he carried himself like a fighter. She'd seen people like him dealing in smoke and wouldn't trust any of them as far as she could throw them.

The sheriff's man said, 'They'll get twenty lashes and a year's hard labour – and you'll get a spear in your guts if you come any closer.' He turned to face the stranger.

Tash took her chance. She pushed off and ran as hard and fast as she ever had done, splashing through the shallow water. She was half expecting a spear to pierce her back, but all she heard was a shout of 'Come back here!'

As if that was going to happen.

She made it round the bend in the river, slid to a stop, scrambled halfway up the bank and pressed herself against it to see what was happening.

The newcomer had his hands raised, but he was arguing with the sheriff's man. Edyon was climbing up the bank. The younger man had dismounted and was holding three horses, so it looked like they had brought a horse for Edyon. These must have been the people he was waiting to meet.

The sheriff's man shook his spear at the older man but seemed to lose his grip on his lantern, which fell to the ground and went out. The only light was the purple glow from the smoke and it was hard to see what was going on. The younger man stepped forward, but the sheriff's man jabbed his spear at him and the young man cried out in pain. With an angry shout, Edyon charged into the sheriff's man with so much force that the huge man spun round and then all the figures seemed to come together in a big tussle.

When they separated, there was one man – Edyon – holding the spear, another holding the horses' reins and clutching his shoulder, and a third with a knife in each hand. The fourth man was on the ground.

No one was moving. Even the horses were still.

Tash muttered, 'Shitting shits! Shitting shits!' And she slipped a little lower and pressed more into the bank so that she could only just see.

The older man bent down and wiped his knives on the body on the ground and slid them back out of sight in his jacket. Then he picked up the bottle of smoke, saying, 'We need to leave here. Now.'

Edyon said, 'But . . . the sheriff's man . . . he's . . .'

'Dead. Yes. Thanks to you.'

'But, but . . . I was only trying to stop him hurting March. I didn't want . . .'

'March'll live. The wound's not too bad. But we need to get moving.'

March said, 'Edyon, sir. There's nothing we can do here. This is my friend Holywell, another servant of the prince. He can keep you safe.'

Edyon was still standing with the spear and staring at the sheriff's man.

The man called Holywell looked towards Tash and she sank out of sight.

'Who was the girl? Can we trust her to be quiet?'

'She's . . . she's a demon hunter,' replied Edyon. 'She won't be running to the sheriff.'

Holywell said in a loud voice, 'If she does, she'll have her guts cut open.' And Tash knew the message was meant for her to hear.

She risked one more peek over the bank. Edyon still seemed to be in a daze as Holywell took the spear from him and dropped it to the ground. Holywell virtually pushed Edyon on to a horse, saying, 'Come on, Your Highness. Let's get going.'

Tash watched them ride off and then stayed where she was for a few moments, ensuring everything was quiet. Nothing moved. She crept back along the river towards the sheriff's man. She'd seen dead demons before but never a dead man. The sheriff's man was not so beautiful, but there was something about him that was the same as a dead demon: he was just a shell, the life gone out of him.

Tash ran. She needed to get away from that place. Running helped. Running took her mind off things. She ran as fast as she could, following Edyon and the others, but really she just wanted to go back to Gravell, to rewind everything to before she'd seen Gravell in the bathhouse and before she'd seen those stupid grey boots.

Ambrose

THE BRIGANTINE–PITORIAN BORDER

'This is madness!' exclaimed Ambrose. 'It makes no sense. Why invade Pitoria? It's Calidor that Aloysius wants – it's always been Calidor.'

'Perhaps he learnt his lesson after the last war and is looking for easier pickings,' Tarquin replied.

'But relations with Pitoria have been improving, Catherine is about to marry the heir to the throne!'

'Which means every lord in the kingdom will be in Tornia for the wedding. Perhaps Aloysius's plan is not so ludicrous. What better time to invade? Get a foothold in the north, then move south. The marriage is a wonderful diversion.'

'But . . . they'll think Catherine is part of the plot.'

'Are you sure she isn't?'

Ambrose had to remind himself that Tarquin didn't know Catherine at all. 'She's not. I'm sure of it. She'll be imprisoned – or executed! I have to warn her!'

'Careful, brother. Communicating war plans to a foreign power is treason against Brigant.'

'I've no intention of communicating plans to a foreign power, only to Catherine. I swore an oath to protect her and that remains my duty and . . . and . . .'

'And you love her,' finished Tarquin simply.

There was no point denying it.

'I do.'

'Then you must go. Find her. Warn her. The invasion is set for the day before the wedding. That's only a week away. You have to reach Tornia before then. Take the letter to show her.'

Ambrose nodded. 'What about you? Noyes's men will have noticed your absence from Tarasenth.'

'I'm carrying on my normal duties, making a tour of our villages,' said Tarquin, shrugging. 'I'll do so briefly, then return home and warn Father.'

'They'll have a description of the man who stole the orders. I don't think it will take much for them to realize it was me. That will lead them to you.'

'Stop worrying about me. I can handle their questions. But, Ambrose, whatever happens, even if you warn the princess, a war *is* coming. Aloysius will invade. I hope at the end of this you'll be able to come home, but for now we must part and I fear it will be a long time before we see each other again.' Tarquin embraced Ambrose. 'Be careful, little brother.'

This parting was so sudden. Even if Ambrose succeeded in warning Catherine, he was fleeing his native country as a proclaimed traitor. It seemed unlikely he'd see Tarquin again, and at the thought of that he pulled his brother tighter. 'You're the best of brothers. The best. I will make you proud.'

He felt Tarquin kiss his forehead and then release him, saying, 'Remember us. Remember Anne too.'

Ambrose nodded. He couldn't speak.

Tarquin swung himself into his saddle. 'I'll miss you more than you realize. I know you'll act with honour.' And he wheeled his horse round and rode away.

Ambrose cut east towards the coast and soon the Bay of Rossarb lay huge before him and, across the water, Pitoria. The narrow road hugged the coast as it rolled towards the Brigantine castle of Nort, an ugly square stone building set back from the beach and following the steep slopes of the mountain foot. Beyond it, a small river bridge marked the actual border; on the other side of it lay a small Pitorian fort. In the far distance was the town of Rossarb and, behind it, the strange flat mountains of the Northern Plateau. It was a desolate place, still and silent, marked by a few straggly shrubs and stunted trees, and Ambrose struggled to imagine how, in just a few days' time, thousands of men would be marching through it to invade Pitoria.

His hands tightened into fists on his reins. An invasion without warning by a king bereft of honour. A man who, to gain a tactical advantage, thought nothing of sacrificing his only daughter, a woman with more of the prized qualities of kingship – intelligence, compassion, justice – than her father would ever possess. She was alone in a foreign land, unaware of the danger that closed in around her.

Despite his impatience to keep moving, Ambrose had to wait for nightfall before striking out for the border. Nort Castle straddled the road. On the landward side, a steep, bare hillside sloped down to the castle, impossible to navigate on horseback.

That left the shore. With the tide out, an expanse of sand offered the only clear way to the border.

His heart in his mouth, Ambrose rode out of the sandy grassland and on to the beach in full view of the castle. The night was dark, the moon obscured by clouds, but he still felt horribly exposed. Surely the castle would be on high alert with the invasion so close. With every moment he expected a shout of challenge or an arrow to come flying out of the darkness.

He was within bowshot of the castle, certainly, when the gates began to open. One rider came out, then another and another. Four in total, trotting towards him. Their horses would be fresh. His was not. Still, there was no going back, that was certain.

The soldiers drew themselves up in a line as Ambrose approached, smiling and shouting a cheery 'Good evening, sirs!' But he was close enough now to see Boris's badge on their tunics and he knew he couldn't bluff his way through. There was only one thing to do. He kicked hard and rode at a gallop directly at the men. The soldiers shouted for him to stop, but Ambrose drew his sword, his wild slashes forcing them apart. And then he was past them, his body bent forward, his eyes on the Pitorian fort in the distance, knowing that his horse hadn't the strength to go far at speed.

'Come on!' he urged, as his horse skirted the castle and returned to the road on the far side. Ahead lay the bridge and the border, but his horse was tiring fast. He glanced back. The four soldiers were close, but not as close as he'd feared. Spurring his horse again, Ambrose forced a final burst of speed from the creature's legs and clattered on to the bridge. Ahead, he could see a mounted soldier, roused by the disturbance, making his way out of the Pitorian fort.

Two of the pursuing soldiers had pulled up before the bridge, perhaps reluctant to cross the border, but the others were close behind him. If they were as good at throwing their swords as the boy at Fielding, Ambrose was a dead man. But no blade hit him and he rode hard, shouting, 'Help! Help!'

The Pitorian soldier was riding fast towards him now, close enough for Ambrose to see his purple hair and, as Ambrose's horse finally staggered to a halt, the soldier asked, 'Trouble, sir?'

'Just a little,' gasped Ambrose. 'I bring news for King Arell, but my friends here don't seem to want me to deliver it.'

Ambrose could hear the Brigantines riding up and he turned his horse as one of the soldiers, a captain, shouted, 'Sir Ambrose Norwend, you are to return with us. You're wanted in Brigane.'

'I'm not returning with you anywhere.'

The captain rode forward, saying, 'You're a traitor. You're coming with us.'

The purple-haired man rode slowly forward too. '*If* this man is a traitor, he's a traitor to Brigant.' He stopped his horse and flicked his hand at the soldiers as if shooing off a child. 'You're on *Pitorian* soil. You have no authority here. If this man doesn't wish to go with you, you can't make him.' Then his face hardened. 'So I suggest you piss off back to your side of the border.'

The two Brigantines stared at him, clearly itching to fight and weighing the odds: two against two, and Ambrose exhausted. But, just as their hands were creeping towards their swords, a shout came from the Pitorian fort and more soldiers began walking towards them.

The captain spat on the ground and said, 'Fuck you. Fuck Pitoria.'

But he turned and rode slowly back over the bridge.

Edyon

DORNAN,
PITORIA

Edyon was riding fast but his mind was whirling faster. He had killed a sheriff's man. Blood had spurted from the man's neck, just as it had when he had killed the chicken for Madame Eruth, but to see it spurt from another human being, to hear it splatter on the ground, to feel it splash on his face . . . Edyon was riding close behind Holywell with March to his side. He could hear the horses' hooves and smell their sweat and yet all he could see was the sheriff's man lying on the ground. Dead.

I see death all around you now . . .

Edyon's stomach heaved. He slowed his horse to a stop just as his stew-and-wine supper erupted from his mouth, down his leg and on to the ground. He stared at it, waiting for more to come, and it did with another heave of his stomach. He spat. The taste of vomit filled his mouth, throat and nose. The ground was shiny with his sick as it had been shiny with the sheriff's man's blood. Edyon shuddered, spat again and wiped his lips with the back of his hand.

March and Holywell had pulled up and were watching him. Their faces said more than words could and they certainly didn't communicate sympathy. Holywell looked amused. March looked disgusted, but then his face changed, and Edyon thought perhaps he had been mistaken. March's shoulder was covered in blood.

Edyon's stomach twisted again and he leant over and waited, but nothing more came up. The worst had passed and he took a breath and sat up. Holywell and March were no longer looking at him. Holywell was inspecting March's wound instead and talking to him in a language Edyon didn't understand.

How had this happened? How was he fleeing into the night with these two men he didn't even know? How was it that he was involved in a murder? All Edyon had been doing was trying to help March. When the sheriff's man had attacked March with his spear, Edyon had lunged forward to stop him, but he was huge, bigger than Stone's guards, and Edyon had expected to be flicked away like a fly . . . Instead, he had spun the sheriff's man round easily and pushed him back into Holywell, who had raised his knife at the same time, catching the man in the neck.

Holywell had been quick. Had he meant to kill the man? It didn't matter. Holywell might have been holding the blade but Edyon had pushed the sheriff's man on to it with his strange newfound strength. And he, Edyon, had been the one the sheriff's man was trying to arrest. A man was dead and it was his fault.

I see death all around you now . . . And, if he had been at a crossroads as Madame Eruth had foretold, there was no going back. He had thought his future lay in moving towards far lands and riches, but pain, suffering and death seemed to be the truth of it after all.

Holywell produced some bandages from his pack and began binding March's shoulder. March stared straight ahead, face pale, his jaw clenched.

'That'll have to do for now,' Holywell said to March. He turned to Edyon, saying, 'When you're ready, Your Highness, we need to keep going.'

Edyon nodded then muttered, 'Yes. Of course. Is March . . . Will he be . . .'

'March is fine, Your Highness. A flesh wound. It looks worse than it is. Are you ready to go on?'

'Yes, but where are we going?'

'North. As far as we can, as fast as we can.'

'North? But Calidor is west of here.'

'It is, Your Highness, but first we need to get away from Dornan and any of the sheriff's men who may be after us, and then we'll find the best route to Calidor.'

'But can't we do that by going west?'

'That would mean doubling back. Too late for that now.'

'They won't be searching for us yet, surely?'

Holywell replied, 'Perhaps not, but we can't risk it. They may have caught the girl and wrung the truth from her already.'

Edyon hoped the girl had fled safely. She'd had no part in the killing.

'Besides –' Holywell indicated a bandage round his own neck – 'March and I are both already wounded. I don't know how well we could protect Your Highness if we're caught. The more ground we cover now, the better.'

'He's right,' March said. 'We should go. Holywell will get us all to safety, Your Highness, but we need to keep moving.'

Edyon nodded. If March could ride with a wounded shoulder, then he wouldn't be the one to slow them down. March, who had come to help him and been hurt and was now implicated in a murder too. It was all Edyon's fault.

They set off again and as Edyon rode he went over the way he'd grabbed the sheriff's man and shoved him on to Holywell's knife. The huge man had felt as easy to control as a child. It must have been panic, the fear and shock of seeing him stab March. But Edyon would give anything now to undo it. If only he hadn't got involved. But then he'd have been arrested. If only he hadn't been there with the girl. But she was chasing her smoke. If only he hadn't stolen the smoke in the first place. If only, if only, if only . . . What a fool he was.

The sky was a pale grey-blue with dawn when Holywell finally stopped. They were in woodland and all was quiet and still. Edyon didn't feel tired though; he was strangely alert and strong. His body seemed to want to do more.

Holywell said, 'We rest here for the morning. I'll move the horses near the stream and have a check around. March, you stay here and guard His Highness.' Holywell took a small bundle from his pack and threw it down at March's feet. 'There's bandages there and some bread and cheese. Leave some for me – food and bandages. And cover up that bottle. It's like a beacon.'

Holywell led the horses away.

'How was Holywell hurt?' Edyon looked at March.

'We had a coming-together with Regan.'

'A coming-together?'

'Regan attacked us. He's dead too.'

'Oh shits.'

Indeed, Madame Eruth's foretelling was true. Death was all around him all right. And here was March, the handsome foreign man she'd promised. But what else had she said about him? *Beware: he lies too . . .*

'You said you had proof,' he blurted. 'About being sent from the prince.'

March nodded and reached into his jacket, saying, 'This is for you, from your father.'

It was a ring, glowing gold in the low morning light, an emerald sparkling from the head of an eagle. The craftsmanship was exceptional.

'Prince Thelonius's seal. He wore it every day I knew him, until the day he entrusted us with the mission of passing it to you, his son, to show how much he wants you to return to him.'

Edyon took the chain from inside his shirt. From it hung a swirl of gold, like brambles, round a central flat medallion. The ring slid through the brambles and latched on to the medallion underneath.

A perfect fit.

Edyon looked at the ring. 'Two men have already died because my father sent me this. I hope no one else will suffer the same fate.' He looked up at March. 'But I have a bad feeling.'

Pain, suffering and death . . .

March had a strange look on his face but he turned away and began to take off his jacket and shirt. The bandage at his shoulder was bloody and grimy. March started to undo the dressing but winced.

Edyon said, 'Let me help.'

'I can do it, Your Highness.' But the movement had caused the wound to reopen and fresh blood was already trickling down March's chest.

'That's clearly not true. Lie back and stay still. Don't make it worse.'

'There's a blanket in my pack,' March said.

Edyon bent down and pulled it out, wishing he had packed one himself.

Then he stopped. 'Oh shits!'

'What is it?' March asked. 'Are you going to be sick again?'

'No . . . I . . . I think I've done something stupid. I had a bag of things with me. I forgot about it in the . . . the rush to leave the woods. It probably won't be too hard for whoever finds it to work out it's mine.'

That was an understatement. The bag had his best shirt in it, the one embroidered with his initials. If he'd wanted to leave a clue to who had killed the sheriff's man, he couldn't have done better. He really was a fool.

March smiled gently at Edyon and said, 'We all make mistakes, Your Highness.' But Edyon had a feeling that March wouldn't have made such a basic one. Well, there was nothing to be done about it now.

Edyon threw the blanket on the dewy ground and March hesitated, then lay down, wincing. Edyon carefully lifted March's shirt away from his chest and cleaned around the wound with a fresh bandage and water from March's flask.

'Is it bleeding at the back? It hurts there too.'

Edyon gently raised March's shoulder. 'There's no cut at the back but it's swollen and bruised.' He touched the bruise and March yelped in pain. 'The cut looks deep. It must have hit the bone.'

Edyon took his time to clean gently around the wound. March stared up at Edyon, who felt his stomach flutter as their gazes met, but then March closed his eyes. Edyon didn't mind. It gave him the chance to study his new friend, his handsome face and smooth, muscular chest. But the cut to his shoulder was deep. Holywell had said it wasn't so bad, but perhaps riding had made it worse, or perhaps Holywell had lied so that they could escape.

March's breath was deep and even now. He was sleeping. Edyon ran his fingers along March's strong jaw and settled his head against the blanket. As he turned away, he saw the bottle of smoke lying on the ground next to March's pack. Was it really only yesterday he had taken it? Already it felt unreal, as if it hadn't really happened, and yet that was what had led him to this mess. But no, in fact it was before that, the stealing of the silver ship, which had been the start of it. That's what had got him beaten up and pissed on. Left bruised and battered and stinking so he'd had to go to the bathhouse, where he found the smoke.

He probed his mouth with his tongue, feeling for the loose tooth he remembered, but found no wobble, no swelling, no soreness. He vaguely recalled waking up after his smoke dream to find that his tooth was better. And it had been his bath in the smoke-warmed water that had soothed away the pain of his beating . . .

Had the smoke healed his bruises and his tooth?

It seemed ridiculous. He'd been to smoke dens and the smoke never healed; it just made you feel good. And now he was no longer feeling good. He might be the son of a prince, with a prince's gold ring, but he was still a bastard and a thief (a pretty useless one at that). And a killer responsible for a murder – two murders: Regan's and the sheriff's man's. Responsible for March's wound as well.

Pain, suffering and death. Death all around him.

And Edyon couldn't help thinking that there would be more to come.

Tash

DORNAN,
PITORIA

Tash had followed Edyon, Holywell and the other man for a good part of the night. They were on horseback, but she was fast. She'd half thought of waiting until they made camp, then running in, snatching the smoke and running off. But they only stopped briefly for Edyon to be sick. Of course they'd want to put as much distance as possible between themselves and the sheriff's men. And when they did stop they'd be on their guard, so sneaking into their camp would be dangerous and the man with the knives wasn't to be messed with. So, as it began to get light, she turned back for Dornan.

It was mid-morning when she got back and there was much activity around the woods. The sheriff's men had obviously found the body and were out in force, though she'd not seen any sign that they'd followed Edyon's trail.

She walked into Gravell's room. It smelt stale and sour with sweat. There was a Gravell-shaped mound on the bed. Tash went over and shook it.

'Wake up. I've got news.'

Nothing. Not even a snore.

Tash leant into him, pushing and rocking rather than shaking him.

Gravell farted.

She moved round to the head of the bed.

'Wake up, Gravell!'

Gravell groaned, then belched a belch so stinky that Tash had to step back. But this wasn't the first time she'd experienced Gravell's smells, and his hangovers, and she knew how to deal with both. She took the washbowl, filled it with water, went back to the bed and threw the water in his face.

'Wake up! I need to talk to you.'

Gravell licked around his mouth.

'I know where the smoke is! I've seen a man get killed!'

Gravell grunted and turned over.

With a sigh, Tash sat down on the chair and listened as Gravell started to snore.

Catherine

THE ROAD TO TORNIA,
PITORIA

Hair whitened. 50 kopeks. Guaranteed pure white.
Noticeboard of a travelling barber

Catherine was exhausted. Exhausted but relieved and a little exhilarated. Things had gone well for her and her dress. She had worn it every day, hour after tiring hour in the saddle. But it had been worth it – the crowds, it seemed, could not get enough of her.

The weather had been in her favour too, warm but not hot, with no rain. Progress had been slow and steady to accommodate her growing band of followers. The horse she rode was large, handsome and quiet, selected by Sir Rowland from Lord Farrow's stable. The trumpeters were well chosen too, loud but not jarring, and again Sir Rowland had been personally involved, selecting them for their appearance as much as their playing ability; they were all young and handsome. They walked well ahead of the procession, so that by the time Catherine arrived crowds had gathered. There were dancers too, of course, and once more Sir Rowland had managed to find the most handsome band. When Catherine commented on their looks, Sir Rowland replied with a smile, 'Why have ugly things when you can have them beautiful?'

And there had been large crowds. The people of Pitoria liked to party: that Catherine had learnt quickly. Every night there was a feast and every day the road was lined with people celebrating her arrival; young and old ran, stared, pointed and waved, and children literally jumped up and down with excitement.

As the cavalcade arrived in the town of Woodville that morning, a little girl on the front step of a baker's shop had shouted, 'I love you!' then she blushed and hid her head in her hands. Catherine was carrying a sprig of the pretty and delicate wissun, with its many tiny white flowers that made a round head. She pulled up her horse and passed Tanya the flower, saying, 'Give it to the girl,' remembering to add, 'and speak in Pitorian.'

Catherine watched as Tanya manoeuvred her horse over to the girl and held out the wissun to her, saying, 'With thanks from Princess Catherine.'

The story quickly spread and soon more girls and some boys were also shouting, 'We love you!'

Catherine smiled gracefully and gave out more flowers. They rode slowly onwards and Sir Rowland handed Catherine another blossom of wissun.

'It's fortunate indeed that it grows wild all the way to Tornia,' he remarked. 'But I begin to fear that there will be no wissun left in all of Pitoria by your wedding day.'

Catherine laughed. 'Indeed I would not wish that.'

'You are doing well, Your Highness. Though I'm not sure your brother appreciates your efforts.'

Catherine glanced towards Boris. 'Well, at least he looks smart.'

Boris's horses, men and weapons were all handsome and gleaming in the sunlight. Her brother rode at the front of Catherine's entourage, with Noyes, as always, at his shoulder, keeping his watchful eye on things. Boris ensured that the cavalcade kept moving. He was determined they shouldn't be delayed from reaching the capital and complained bitterly that Catherine was deliberately slowing their progress. He was right, but for once Boris's power was limited. He could get his men to keep the roads clear and he insisted on an early start in the mornings, but he could not control the crowds nor their determination to see their new princess.

'I must thank you once more for your assistance, Sir Rowland,' Catherine said. 'It is through you that all this has been possible. But I've been thinking of something else that I'd like to do, and again I need your advice.'

'I'm all ears, Your Highness.'

'My colour is white. Is it possible to arrange for my own men to have their hair dyed white? I don't mean the soldiers, but the entertainers, dancers and musicians.'

Sir Rowland clapped his hands. 'An excellent suggestion, Your Highness. It would add hugely to your prestige. Only the most powerful of lords display their colours in this way and, I have to say, no other women do.'

Catherine was delighted but cautious. 'There's no reason I shouldn't do it, is there? It wouldn't offend the prince or the king?'

'The reason is purely financial, Your Highness. Supplying the dyes can be costly when you have many men and their hair does keep growing.'

'I can find the money,' said Catherine thoughtfully. 'But can hair even be dyed white?'

'I believe so. We will transform the dancers' hair this evening and judge the effect. You really are changing the fashions, Your Highness. Reports from Tornia say that your dress is already being copied. Few wore white before you arrived as it was considered too simple a colour.'

Catherine smiled. 'It seems we are all learning.'

The next morning Boris came to Catherine's bedchamber as she was dressing.

'Can you never be ready on time?' Boris complained.

'I've been busy.'

Catherine had been working out her debts. She needed money. Since arriving in Pitoria she had been showered with gifts – a horse, shoes, cushions, lace, fans, feathers, wine and even some books, but what she needed was money.

'Busy deciding which dress to wear?' Boris mocked. 'Or dyeing your hair?'

'It's my men who dye their hair, not me.'

'I've seen them prancing around this morning. They look ridiculous.'

'I think they look wonderful. Though I feel the white is a little too yellow at the moment, but perhaps that was just the firelight last night. If we can get it with a hint of blue, they will match much better with Prince Tzsayn's men.'

'What do you think you're achieving with this performance, sister? Other than appearing ridiculous?'

'Happiness. Pleasure. Joy. The things you never appreciate.'

Boris curled his lip and turned to leave. 'I'll be happy, pleased and joyful if you depart on time for once.'

'Before you go, Boris, there's one more thing we need to discuss. I need money to buy dresses.'

Boris turned back. 'You have dresses.'

'It appears I need more.'

'Not to me. You're clothed, aren't you?' And he leant forward and picked at the slash in her dress. 'Though barely. You like to reveal your body, don't you, sister?'

Catherine drew a calming breath. 'I am following the Pitorian fashion. Fitting in. Becoming like them, as I said I would do. It reflects badly on Father for me to wear the same dress every day. It looks as if he's poor, as if Brigant is penniless. At the very least I need a new wedding dress and new garments for my maids. I hear Tzsayn is extremely discerning about fashion.'

'Then he can buy you a dress.'

'Sir Rowland tells me that Prince Tzsayn listens to daily reports of our progress. I would hate for the prince to be disappointed to hear that I'm wearing the same gown each day. What a shame it would be if the lack of a few dresses were to prevent my marriage.'

Boris hesitated before muttering, 'Have your dresses then. But you'd better make sure they're good. If Tzsayn refuses you because the cut of your sleeve is wrong, you'll . . .'

'Yes?'

'You'll have to explain it to Father.'

Catherine forced a smile. 'Well then, I will ensure that the dresses are the best. That means they will be more expensive, of course.'

Boris's mouth was a thin, hard line. 'Of course.'

He turned and stalked out.

Catherine let out a shaky breath.

'Has the prince really been asking about our progress?' asked Sarah.

'I have no idea,' replied Catherine. 'I would in his place, but I don't presume to know his mind.'

She didn't add that she was starting to worry that the prince hadn't sent her *any* sort of communication – not a letter or even a token. Was he ill or just not interested? She knew so little about him still and yet in four days' time she'd be married to him and her life would change again. But she was determined to do all she could to shape her future the way she wanted it.

Edyon

SOMEWHERE NORTH OF DORNAN, PITORIA

It was the end of the third day after fleeing Dornan, and they had been riding slowly north all day. March's shoulder was causing him agony if his horse moved above walking pace. Now they were around the fire, Edyon asked, 'Shouldn't we head west to the coast tomorrow? March can't go on like this.'

Holywell shook his head. 'Since we can only go slowly we'll have to stick to the quieter routes, Your Highness. We can't outrun any pursuers so we have to avoid them, and the ports will be the first place the sheriff's men will be looking for you.'

'If they're looking for me,' Edyon said.

'They'll have found your bag near the body of the sheriff's man. While I'm sure they're not the world's greatest minds, I think it's safe to assume they'll manage to piece those few clues together.'

Edyon wished he hadn't told March about leaving his bag, or, rather, he wished March hadn't told Holywell.

'Are you handy with a sword, Your Highness?'

For a moment Edyon thought he detected a mocking note in Holywell's voice, but, when he looked, the man's face was sincere. Edyon laughed bitterly.

'I'm sure you've noticed that I don't have a sword and, just so that you fully understand the situation, as a general rule in fights I get beaten to a pulp and pissed on.'

Holywell tilted his head. 'You handled the sheriff's man well enough.'

Edyon couldn't reply. He wasn't proud of what he'd done. What would happen now to the man's family? His wife? His fatherless children? Their misery was his doing.

'Will you take first watch, Your Highness?' Holywell said. 'Then March and I can relieve you and you can sleep through till dawn.'

Edyon nodded and Holywell lay down and closed his eyes.

Edyon wasn't sure what he was supposed to be watching for. The first night he'd just sat and listened to the noise of the woods and Holywell's snoring, staring at March's face in the thin light of the new moon. But even that wasn't a pleasure any longer. March's face was glistening with the sweat of a fever.

As if he could hear Edyon's thoughts, March turned to him from his bedroll, his eyes even paler than usual in the moonlight.

'How are you feeling?' Edyon asked, smiling gently.

March turned his face away and said, 'I'll be fine, Your Highness.'

The foreign man is in pain. I cannot see if he lives or dies . . .

Edyon shook his head. Madame Eruth had been right about everything so far, but even she didn't have all the answers. Edyon was determined March wouldn't die if he had anything to do with it.

Edyon went over and said, 'Let me see your wound. I'll clean it again. Some cold water from the stream may ease it a little.'

March didn't answer and his lack of disagreement was, Edyon now knew, the closest he would come to admitting he was suffering. Edyon carefully unpeeled the bandage. March's skin was hot and swollen and there was dried blood and some yellow pus on the dressing and in the wound. It looked bad and had definitely got worse since he'd last seen it.

Edyon cleaned the wound but he had to do something more. He was sure the smoke had somehow helped him heal after his beating by Stone's men. His bruises were gone and the tooth that had come close to falling out was now solid as a rock.

If the smoke had healed him, he had to try it on March.

But how? He'd inhaled it. March had a cut deep in his shoulder. Edyon brought the bottle of smoke over and laid it gently on the wound, causing March to cry out.

'What are you doing?' he said.

Edyon felt ridiculous even saying it. 'I think it might help.'

'Help how?'

'Help heal you. I had a bath with the bottle of smoke and my bruises disappeared. Stone's guards nearly knocked one of my teeth out and that was healed too.'

He remembered how the smoke in his mouth had seemed to search out the loose tooth. Perhaps it would seek out March's wound, but how would he stop it escaping? He needed a container, but the only things they had were tin bowls from March's pack and they were too big.

There was one other thing he could use. He could suck some of the smoke into his mouth and then put his mouth on March's shoulder. Not the worst job in the world. But what if he inhaled it and passed out? He'd have to concentrate, hold it just in his mouth.

'I have an idea. If you're willing to let me try.'

March turned his head. His eyes were like moonlight. He blinked and said, 'Try.'

Edyon took up the bottle of smoke. It glowed bright in the darkness, almost seeming to pulse with life. He held it upside down, easing the cork free to let out a wisp of smoke, which he sucked into his mouth. He then lowered himself over March. Their eyes met and he froze for a moment, the intensity of March's gaze fixing him in place. Then slowly, so slowly, Edyon lowered his head until his lips brushed March's skin.

March gasped, his hands grasping Edyon's shoulders, and Edyon couldn't tell if it was in pleasure or pain. Then Edyon parted his lips and the smoke was in his mouth and on March's wound. He held his breath, trying not to take the smoke down into his lungs, but he could feel a light-headedness, as if his body was floating. He couldn't help but smile, because it felt so good, and the smoke escaped out of one side of his mouth and he watched it climb into the sky. He looked down at March.

'Did you feel anything?'

'It's warm,' March replied, closing his eyes.

Edyon inspected March's wound. Was it the effects of the smoke or did it seem less angry? He let out more smoke from the bottle, sucked it in and lowered his lips on to March's skin again. He could feel the smoke in his mouth, its heat and its movement, faster it seemed than in the bottle. Edyon held his breath and stayed still as long as he could before releasing the smoke. He looked down at March to share the moment with him but March's eyes were closed.

There was no doubting it now. The swelling had gone and the cut had healed over and a scar was forming. But Edyon's head was spinning. He was so tired he couldn't keep his eyes open. Taking the demon-smoke bottle, he curled up next to March and slept.

March

When he was sure Edyon was asleep, March stopped pretending and sat up. He rolled his shoulder, then prodded it with his finger. There was no pain. The warm and slight stinging sensation he had felt when Edyon had applied the smoke had gone. He looked down at Edyon, curled round the bottle of purple smoke, which roiled and seethed in slow, endless movement.

Edyon's idea had worked.

Perhaps he wasn't such a fool as he claimed. Or, if he was, he was a gentle one, a kind one. March remembered the kiss of Edyon's lips on his skin with a shiver. The son of the prince touching him. No one touched him, ever.

'You're looking better.'

Holywell was staring at him from his bedroll. March found himself suddenly flustered. He wondered how much Holywell had seen.

Holywell's eyes narrowed and he spoke in Abask, a sign that he didn't want Edyon to know what he was saying. 'You like the feel of his mouth on you, eh? That infection should have killed you. Now the wound looks like it's been healing for weeks. What happened?'

'Edyon . . . used the smoke to heal me.'

Holywell shook his head. 'You've no idea what that smoke really is or what it might do.'

'I know it worked. My arm feels as strong as before.' March showed the scar to Holywell, who held out his hand to touch it, then seemed to think better of it. 'Do you want to try it on your neck?'

'I'm not having that stuff near me. I'll heal the normal way.'

'Well, the normal way wasn't working for me.'

Holywell sneered. 'Do I detect a tone of gratitude to the young prince?'

'He's not a prince.'

'No, he's not; he's a soft, spoilt fool and he's going to be Aloysius's prisoner. So don't be getting too grateful to him – it's not natural.'

And March felt sure Holywell meant more than just the smoke. He flushed red.

'I'm not. I agree he's an idiot. Another spoilt idiot son. I see them in court all the time. I was just telling you about the smoke.'

'Well, you can take the watch now you're feeling so much better. Then we head north. We keep telling the fool we're being pursued – for all we know it's true. Edyon will get what's coming to him soon enough. Him and the prince of Calidor.'

Tash

DORNAN,
PITORIA

On the second morning after the smoke had been taken, Gravell woke, rose, walked doubled-over to the pisspot, puked in it before pissing in it, and then staggered back to sit on the side of the bed, groaning. This was an improvement on the previous day, which he had spent curled in a ball.

'You've only yourself to blame,' said Tash, clinking together the money she had earned making deliveries for a local pie seller, which she'd started doing out of desperation for money. So far she'd been given one particularly large tip for her speed and discovered that pie delivery was a lot safer than running from demons.

'Can you keep the noise down?'

Tash rattled her coins even louder.

'I've never felt this bad before.'

'Actually, there was that time in Hepdene. You were ill for four days and swore you'd never drink again.'

'That woman spiked my drink; that's the only explanation. She was after my money.'

'Or perhaps you had more than one drink and they weren't spiked. And, by the way, she still wants a kroner for her wonderful company.'

'Don't pay her.'

'I don't intend to.' Tash stopped playing with the coins. 'Gravell, do you have any money left at all?'

Gravell didn't reply.

'The innkeeper has asked me twice when you're going to pay the bill. I suppose I *could* loan you this money to help out, but then again I could use it to buy my new boots.'

Gravell glared at her, then went over to the washbowl and threw up again. He looked worse than when he'd been killing demons.

'You need fresh air. Water.'

He shuddered. 'My head feels so bad.'

Tash rolled her eyes. 'You're such a wimp.'

Gravell went back to sit on the bed and put his head in his hands.

'Are you ready to hear the latest news?'

'So long as I can hear it quietly.'

'Shall I go over what happened the other night first? When I followed Edyon and the sheriff's man got killed? I wasn't sure you were taking it all in.'

'I took it in well enough. I'm not stupid,' said Gravell.

'And drinking half a barrel of ale is not at all a stupid thing to do,' Tash said.

'There are times you remind me of my mother.'

She moved to sit by Gravell. 'Well, let me tell you a story, young man. The sleepy little town of Dornan has been transformed. There hasn't been a murder here for as long as anyone can remember. The sheriff's men are up in arms.'

'They're always up in arms – they're sheriff's men.'

'I mean they're angry and marching around asking lots of questions. The good news for us is that they don't know I was there and they don't know why the sheriff's man was killed, but they do seem to suspect Edyon was involved. And he's run away, so it looks particularly bad for him. Though I don't know why he'd want to go with those two. The older man, Holywell, was really mean. But Edyon obviously planned to; he'd packed his bag and everything.'

But now Tash remembered Holywell pushing Edyon on to his horse and Edyon definitely didn't have anything in his hands then. She slapped her palm against her forehead. '*That's* how they know Edyon was there. He left his bag.'

'The boy's stupider than I thought.'

But Tash felt stupid for not remembering the bag sooner. If she'd hidden it, or taken it, the sheriff's men wouldn't have any idea who killed their comrade. She said, 'Anyway, I followed them. They went north.'

'Then we go north.'

'It was Holywell who took the smoke with them. Edyon was going to give it back to me before the trouble started.'

'You believe that?' Gravell shook his head. 'He's a thief and a friend to killers. He'll sell it or smoke it himself.'

Tash did believe it, though. And she really couldn't see why Edyon would go with Holywell. Edyon seemed so naive, whereas Holywell certainly wasn't. And it didn't really tie in with her other news.

'I should tell you something else I've heard about Edyon. It's from a very good source – my contact at the pie stall.'

'You like it at the fancy end of the fair, missy? Selling pies to the posh folk?'

Tash shrugged. 'It's clean. People pay you well – and on time.' She looked pointedly at Gravell but he didn't react. 'Erin, Edyon's mother, has her own business. A proper business.'

'I have a proper business.'

'Yes, but hers isn't illegal.'

'She'll sell you a chair for thirty kroners, saying it belonged to some sultan from the east, and sleep at night happy. That should be illegal!'

'Anyway, the news from the pie seller, who got it from one of the servants who works for Erin, is that a nobleman from Calidor called Lord Regan was with Erin before Edyon left. They had spent all afternoon together, as if they were old friends, and . . . I'm glad you're sitting down for this bit . . .'

'Get on with it!'

'Apparently Lord Regan was here to take Edyon to Calidor, because Edyon is the son of Prince Thelonius.'

Gravell stared at Tash and then started laughing. He laughed and laughed, until he rolled back on the bed and kicked his legs in the air.

'Our thief is the son of a prince?'

'Yep. Illegitimate son. But son.'

'A bastard in every way then.' Gravell sat up and scowled. 'Should have known it. It's in the blood. Royalty – they're all bastards.'

'So I have this theory of what Edyon's going to do.'

'A theory, eh?'

'Yes. He's going north with the two men. They weren't Pitorian. I think they were from Calidor too. So I think they're going to go back to Calidor with Edyon, which means they need a ship. But now they're wanted men so they'll have to be very careful.'

'If Lord Regan was here to take Edyon back with him, why did he go off with this Holywell instead?'

'Well,' said Tash, 'I heard he was attacked, robbed and left for dead, so maybe Holywell works for Regan or something. But that doesn't feel right somehow.'

'Your contact in the pie business can't tell you? I thought he knew everything.'

'Point is, they'll probably head north to Pravont and then along the river to Rossarb. From Rossarb they'll get a boat to Calidor.'

Tash knew Gravell loved Pravont. It was quiet and beautiful and had cheap beer.

'Pravont.' Gravell stirred, rolling his head on his shoulders. 'Nice place, Pravont. Right on the edge of demon territory.'

'So? Do you think I'm right, about him heading there?'

Gravell stretched. 'I think that if you are then we're in luck. We could go up the coast road, cut across to the river road and catch them at Pravont. It's like demon hunting, only easier.'

'I'm not so sure about that. Holywell, the man with the knives, is dangerous.'

'We'll be careful. They won't be expecting us. I'm not letting people think they can steal from me and get away with it.' Gravell shook his head. 'That'll be the end of me.'

Tash looked at Gravell. While he'd been passed out, she'd half wondered about staying with the fair. She could probably get some good work with the pie seller or even some of the furniture traders. But deep down she knew she couldn't bear to be parted from Gravell. The thought of him travelling alone, or, worse, getting another girl as demon bait, was horrible.

'And even if we don't get the smoke back we'll be in the perfect place for the next hunt.'

'Oh, we'll get the smoke back. I know that territory like the back of my hand.' Gravell was standing now. 'I'm feeling better already.'

Catherine

TORNIA,
PITORIA

*Zalyan Castle stands on a hill in the centre of Tornia.
It was rebuilt over thirty years during the reign of King
Jolyon. The five pentagonal turrets are linked by a high
wall of stone and within lie the main buildings, which
are arranged about an elegant central tower and
decorated with white tiles that shine brilliantly,
changing with the position of the sun. It is sometimes
referred to as 'the height of beauty'.*

Pitoria: The Modern Era, Staryon Hove

The final two days of the progress saw the cavalcade grow even
more. On the last morning Catherine's party stopped at a country
house a short distance from Tornia to have lunch and to make the
final preparations for her entrance into the city. Catherine's room
was decked out in white: freshly decorated, just for her. Her
adoption of a colour had clearly been a success.

Catherine was so nervous she could hardly eat, and her maids were anxious about her.

'Have you seen the play, Your Highness?' asked Tanya. 'The actors have been rehearsing it all week. Perhaps it might take your mind off things.'

'What play?'

'Your play, Your Highness. It's the story of your marriage.'

'Really? Well, I suppose I should see it then,' said Catherine, forcing herself to smile. 'I should very much like to know how it ends!'

Seats were quickly set up in the garden and the play began. There were no words, only dancing. One actor, a young boy dressed in a dazzling white gown, was accompanied by three other boys dressed in red and black and green. Opposite them stood two men, one older in purple, one younger in blue, clearly meant to be King Arell and Prince Tzsayn. The two men danced, the younger one copying the older one, but eventually doing everything with a higher leap or more turns, until finally the lady in white leapt in the air with joy, to be caught by the prince and lie in his arms in a faint.

Boris sneered. 'Only Pitorians would expect a woman to be overcome by dancing.'

'Whereas Brigantines just expect a woman to be overcome,' Catherine replied sharply.

Sir Rowland applauded. 'In Brigant, men joust to prove their worth. In Pitoria, they dance. Both pastimes are skilful and athletic and, alas –' he leant to Catherine – 'both favour the younger man.'

'Dancing proves nothing manly in my eyes,' growled Boris. And he left them.

'But if you could, Sir Rowland, which would you choose? Having lived away from Brigant so long, do you only dance?'

'Well, I was never much of a fighter.'

'Or only with words.'

'You can't fight with words alone, Your Highness. Words without actions are like dancing – pretty but ineffectual.'

'But both my words and actions have irritated Boris and you are assisting me rather than holding me back. I think, once I am married, you may be recalled to Brigant.'

Sir Rowland nodded. 'I had surmised as much. I'm wise enough to know that my use must always outweigh my cost. I've worked hard for Brigant all these years, but I'm under no illusions – the future is never certain when working for your father. But I do feel that we – if I may say "we" – have achieved something in just these few days, Your Highness, and the attitude of the Pitorian people towards Brigant is more positive.'

Catherine had never imagined working, but now she felt like she had a role. In Brigant she was just a princess who did nothing, who was required to do nothing. The thought of going back to such an existence was depressing. She loved making plans and carrying them out, but much of the fun was doing it with someone else. 'You've helped me so much, Sir Rowland. Both in what I've achieved and in taking my mind off other troubles.'

'You've left most of your troubles behind, I hope, Your Highness.'

Clearly Sir Rowland thought she meant her family, though she was thinking of Ambrose.

'Alas, not all of them. But you are helping me recover. And, if my father does recall you, please don't go. I would welcome you as my permanent adviser.'

Sir Rowland bowed and Catherine thought his eyes seemed moist. 'Thank you, Your Highness.'

The conversation had reminded Catherine not only of Ambrose but that she had thought little of the 'message' that Lady Anne had tried to communicate to her. She felt that she'd been too absorbed in her dresses and procession, and was suddenly ashamed. In her last moments of life Lady Anne had been trying to communicate with Catherine, so she, Catherine, had a duty to do her best to understand that message. She asked Sir Rowland, 'What can you tell me of demon smoke?'

Sir Rowland looked surprised. 'Well, it's an expensive way to bring some relaxation. And an illegal way.' He leant towards Catherine, saying, 'No one will admit to using it but I'm sure half the court have tried it at least once.'

Catherine hesitated, then said, 'I need to confide in you, Sir Rowland.' And she told him about Lady Anne's execution. When she had finished she asked, 'Have you any idea why Lady Anne would be warning me about demon smoke?'

Sir Rowland shook his head. 'I wish I could help. But as far as I know the smoke is no more than a pleasure drug. It sounds like she was implying your father had it.'

'He does have it. I know he's bought at least two hundred pounds' worth of it. But he would never use it himself.'

'No. I can't imagine your father seeking pleasure that way.'

'But Lady Anne made the signs on the scaffold. She was in pain, about to die. She wouldn't use that moment to tell me something trivial. The smoke must be important.'

'Let me make some enquiries.' Sir Rowland paused before saying, 'While we're discussing your father, I hope you take no offence when I say that he will use all ways and means to achieve his chief aim.'

'That being the retaking of Calidor?'

'Precisely. And ... your marriage is a way for him to ensure Pitoria doesn't aid Calidor in any future war.'

'And increase his trading revenues to fight that war,' Catherine added.

Sir Rowland smiled. 'I see you are fully aware of the situation. But the demon smoke seems to add another dimension. As I said, let me make some enquiries.'

The final journey to the outskirts of Tornia was especially slow. The procession had grown so large that the trumpeters at the front were out of sight for Catherine, though she could hear them clearly enough. Ahead of them were the actors and musicians, who drew the crowds but who were not part of the official parade. Next came a guard from Pitoria of twenty men on black horses. Each man carried a long spear and wore a breastplate and cloak but no helmet so that everyone could see their short purple hair, the king's colour.

Catherine rode her white mare, with a sprig of wissun pinned to her dazzling new white dress. She had been told it would be hard to have her new gowns made in time, but Catherine had found that if she spent Boris's money liberally enough most difficulties could be overcome. This dress had even more crystals than her previous one, and was high-throated and slashed to reveal hints of glittering silver and gold cloth beneath. There was no doubt as to who was the star of the procession.

Tanya, Jane and Sarah came next, also in new, more elaborate dresses, and behind them was Boris and his fifty guards. And, while the men didn't have coloured hair, their shining metal helmets had red plumes that matched the grandeur of the occasion.

Behind them, at a much further distance, were the caravans and horses of the numerous servants and camp followers who had attached themselves to the procession since Charron. It was almost a travelling village. Some of them had adopted white hair despite not having any official role to play, merely wanting to identify themselves as part of the princess's entourage.

Ahead, the greens of meadows gave way to browns of timber-framed buildings cloaking the gentle hillside. And at the summit of the hill, above the houses and the grey stone wall of Tornia, was Zalyan Castle with its five famous turrets, each almost impossibly tall and elegant, surrounding the central pentagonal tower that seemed to shine like a beacon in the sunlight.

Even to Catherine, raised a princess of a powerful kingdom, it was a breathtaking sight, and she felt a mix of admiration and apprehension sweep over her.

As the procession approached, even the road seemed to smarten itself up, becoming straighter, wider and pale grey like the colour of the castle beyond. A bridge spanning the River Char was also of grey stone and strong, with three wide arches and a low wall along each side. People were standing here, cheering and shouting greetings of welcome. Hundreds of people – thousands!

The procession continued through the outskirts of Tornia, past homes and shops, the buildings becoming smaller and closer together, even though the road remained wide, clean and straight. The trumpeters blew loudly and shouts and cheers came from all around. Catherine couldn't help but smile and wave to the people hanging out of windows and calling greetings to her.

The road became a little steeper and then bent to the right, up a slope towards the castle walls and a huge open gate from which bright flags hung. More people were crammed along the road up to this point but beyond the gates the crowd changed. An immense courtyard, so large that Catherine's father's whole castle might have sat within it, opened up around her. It was filled with an equally immense crowd of Pitorians. There seemed to be three groups: purple-haired foot soldiers standing to attention; an impressive array of mounted cavalry with blue hair; and, in the middle, a throng of men in tight trousers and jackets. At last the procession came to a halt, with Sir Rowland saying, 'We must wait here, Your Highness. There is to be an official welcome.'

Catherine felt her breath coming fast and shallow. The noise and the heat were overwhelming. She swayed for a moment in the saddle, and caught herself thinking how it would look if she fainted.

Pull yourself together. Sit straight.

And then the dancing began. Only in Pitoria would the official welcome open with a dance. But these dancers were clearly of a standard Catherine had not seen on her travels. The first pair vaulted impossibly high, passing each other and twisting in the air, even bouncing off each other. Others joined them until there were ten men, a dozen, whirling in a blinding dance. The speed was intense. The sun beat down and the ground seemed to throb with footsteps as still more men joined in until the whole courtyard seemed to be a mass of leaping men. It ended in a synchronized twirling bow to each other. Then they turned as one and, their faces serious, they bowed to Catherine. As they rose, she noticed one man was smiling. Catherine smiled back and said to Sir Rowland, 'Wonderful as always.'

'Yes, Vario is one of the prince's best dancers. It's a great honour for him to lead the welcome.'

'Of course,' said Catherine, though she was irritated with herself for forgetting that such intricate formal dances were led by a single man. She might have made an impression on its people, but she still had much to learn of this country.

'We will now meet the king and Prince Tzsayn. I will go first with Prince Boris, and you must follow with your ladies, Your Highness.'

Boris dismounted stiffly and as Sir Rowland made his way to the doors of the great keep Catherine turned to her maids and signed, *Look happy. Dazzle!*

She set off slowly, purposely dropping further behind the men. She was confident that King Arell would not be as impatient as her father, but she was also sure that a little waiting wouldn't do him any harm. She may just be a pawn in this game but a pawn still had some power.

The sun was low in the sky behind her now and Catherine's dress shone golden in its light. She moved more and more slowly, letting Sir Rowland and Boris disappear inside, passing the men who had danced in her honour and who now lined the route. Catherine concentrated on keeping her back straight and swaying her dress so that the crystals caught the light and sparkled. She reached the doorway and stopped, aware that anyone looking out from within the keep would see her as a shining light.

Dazzle, she told herself. *Dazzle.*

Catherine took a breath and stepped into a huge marbled hall. Again she paused, letting her eyes adjust to the darkness. The room was lined with nobles, mostly men but many women too. At the far end was a dais and standing on it were two men. Sir Rowland and Boris stood to their right, their introductions seemingly over. Catherine was pleased she had taken her time. Now all eyes were on her.

She walked on slowly, resisting the urge to look around and focusing ahead. King Arell wasn't as old as she'd expected, or, rather, he was thin and wiry but stood strong and upright. He wore a purple velvet hat with a fur trim rather than a crown. Beside him . . .

The prince was of a similar build to his father, his skin a dark golden-brown colour on the right side of his face, but his left, even from this distance, seemed strange. He stood gracefully, one hand on his hip, staring directly at her. His eyes seemed dark, almost black, but there was no expression there.

Finally Catherine arrived at the foot of the dais, where she stopped and looked up at the king. This was the man who'd negotiated with her father for her to be delivered up to a man she barely knew. Her amusement at the dancing had left her and she was reminded again that she was here to marry a man she'd never spoken to.

Sir Rowland said, 'Your Majesty, Your Royal Highness, may I introduce Her Royal Highness Princess Catherine of Brigant.'

Slowly, deliberately, Catherine took a step back from the dais and sank into the Brigantine deep curtsy, her head below the knee of the king, as low as she could go, reminding all those present of where she stood in the hierarchy. She might have her fine dress and her own white-haired followers, but she was being given to a prince by a king, and she wanted these men – and everyone watching – to see it for what it was. It wasn't a celebration of love; it was a deal. At best, the forging of an alliance; at worst, a sale.

As she stood, Catherine met the king's eyes for a moment and only then dared to look into the face of the man who was going to be her husband.

Prince Tzsayn was not ugly; indeed, he might have been handsome if not for his strange complexion. The left side of his face was a lighter brown colour than the right, and smooth, as if all lines and wrinkles had been melted away. He wore a fur-trimmed hat, below which his black wavy hair curled, and a high-necked jacket with sleeves so long they brushed his fingertips.

'It's a pleasure to meet you at last, Princess Catherine. I hope your journey to us has been pleasant.' King Arell's voice was surprisingly gentle.

'Thank you, Your Majesty. My journey was interesting and enjoyable. Pitoria is beautiful and its people have been most welcoming.'

King Arell smiled. 'I hear that you are winning them over.'

'I think they have won me over, Your Majesty.'

'Then I hope my son and I can do the same.'

Catherine was so surprised she didn't reply. The words were so unlike anything her father might have said that she didn't know how to react.

She glanced quickly at Tzsayn but he still wore the same formal expression as he had on her first approach.

King Arell continued, 'I must now make my welcome speech, but let us talk more this evening.'

Catherine was escorted to the side of the dais by Sir Rowland. From there she had a good view of Prince Tzsayn's unscarred side. He was striking from this angle, with high cheekbones, dark brown eyes and black hair curling to his jawline. This was to be her husband. He seemed cool, as her mother had said he was. Cold even. But what could she really tell just from looking at him? She wanted to talk to him but King Arell was still speaking, and as soon as his father's speech was over Tzsayn turned, bowed to her and walked slowly from the hall.

'This way, Your Highness,' murmured Sir Rowland. 'I will show you to your rooms. You must be tired.'

Catherine allowed him to guide her down from the dais and through a pair of elaborately carved wooden doors, though she was desperate to look back and see more of her future husband.

That evening Catherine was escorted by Boris to a banquet in her honour. She had not thought she would tire so quickly of such things. As she entered the great hall, Prince Tzsayn was standing across the room talking to two elderly lords. The prince was dressed immaculately and elaborately in fine pale blue leather trousers and a silk jacket that seemed to be made of plaited ribbon and decorated with tiny silver beads. The material of the right side of his jacket was slashed, exposing Tzsayn's skin, which was painted a deeper blue. Catherine had thought her new dress with its short sleeves and low-cut bodice was daring, but she felt conventional in comparison to Tzsayn. The prince noticed her staring and turned and bowed to her. Catherine froze, then curtsied, blushing. She felt ridiculous, as if she'd been trying to attract his attention and charm him in some way, which she definitely was not trying to do.

Boris muttered, 'Hopefully they won't keep us waiting long, so we can eat and get out of here.' He glanced around, saying, 'Each woman is more ludicrously dressed than the last, but I have to say your future husband excels in the attention he pays to his appearance. As if that's going to fool anyone.'

'Fool anyone?'

'His scars cover his whole left side. We had a full description of his wounds – Father demanded it.'

So that was why he wore his sleeves long and his collar high – to hide his skin.

'I heard it was a childhood accident,' Catherine commented.

'Running through the kitchens, and a cauldron of hot oil spilled on him. I assume the kitchen staff were boiled in oil themselves for that.'

'And his illnesses?'

'Oh, he's a typical weakling. The thought of a hot day probably fills him with fear.' Boris chuckled. 'Perhaps it reminds him too much of his skin being on fire. I suspect that's why he didn't come to meet us. Too soft, too used to having his every whim for silk and blue bloody body paint pandered to.'

Before Catherine could ask more, they were guided to the table for the banquet.

Catherine was seated to the left of King Arell. Prince Tzsayn was seated to the king's right, with Boris on his other side. Catherine glanced at Tzsayn as he spoke with her brother, his voice too low for her to make out the words. From this position, she saw his scarred side. She glimpsed his ear, which was small, as if most of it had shrivelled away in the heat of the fire. His eye drooped and looked tired, though the prince's upright posture showed no signs of fatigue.

'The prince is slightly unwell,' Sir Rowland had said upon her arrival in Charron. He certainly didn't look it now. Perhaps Boris was nearer the truth of it and Tzsayn simply couldn't be bothered to make the ride to meet her. Catherine felt a stab of anger that even though she was to be Tzsayn's future wife she was considered unimportant. However, she soon forgot those feelings and relaxed a little. King Arell was a good host, telling stories about his court and the history of Pitoria, but never dominating the conversation as her father would have done. Catherine responded with anecdotes from her books on Queen Valeria and comparisons of the fashions of Brigant and Pitoria.

'And what are you hoping for, Catherine, from this match that your father and I have cooked up?'

Catherine was shocked that the king would ask her opinion at this late stage, and replied formally.

'My concern is to ensure I represent Brigant well.'

'You do that, princess. Everyone is quite charmed by you.'

Catherine smiled and glanced over at Prince Tzsayn, who hadn't seemed to look her way all evening. Now he was describing something to Boris in great detail and with much florid hand-waving. Catherine strained to hear the conversation and caught enough to learn that he was describing the process of making the silk for his jacket. Boris's face seemed a mix of revulsion and boredom and Catherine smiled but then wondered if her own expression would be similar when she was married to the prince.

The evening continued as had all the evenings before, with speeches and dancing. The prince did not dance, and Catherine had to stifle a yawn as nobleman after nobleman dedicated their dance to her. After that, Catherine was introduced to many more lords and ladies, smiling through the same conversations about her travels and Brigant and how lovely Pitoria was.

Finally the king took his leave, which meant that she could go too. Tanya and Sarah led her back to her chambers, so tired she could barely stand. Before the door to her sitting room waited a servant holding a silver plate with a small envelope on it. Inside was a note.

You might find the gardens more interesting than the dancing.

Tomorrow morning, nine o'clock, on the terrace?

'Who sent this?'

'Prince Tzsayn, Your Highness. He asked for a reply.'

Catherine hesitated. She wasn't supposed to meet him alone before the marriage and she definitely didn't want a lecture on the manufacture of silk. On the other hand, Boris and Noyes certainly wouldn't approve. That decided her.

'Tell Prince Tzsayn . . . yes.'

Tash

NORTHERN PITORIA

Tash lay dozing in the back of the wagon, warm in the sun. Gravell was up front, sitting by the driver, who was returning to his farm having sold his load of vegetables at the Dornan fair. It would have been quicker to travel on horseback, or even by the daily coach service that was put on for the fair, but they didn't have enough money, so they'd agreed with the wagon driver on ten kopeks each to take them as far as he was going north. From there, they'd walk.

The wagon was slow but the farmer travelled from dawn to dusk. They had passed through several roadblocks that had been set up to stop the murderer, but as they were manned by unpaid locals Tash didn't think they would be very effective. The old men and boys were more interested in taking bribes than catching fugitives. Sheriff's men were highly visible in each town, warning the populace against harbouring the villain, Edyon Foss, though that seemed unlikely, given that the general view was that he was a fearsome killer.

Towards nightfall, as they stopped at the latest roadblock, Tash and Gravell got down from the wagon. The farmer was almost home and could take them no further. Pasted clumsily to the pole that barred the road was a poster.

Gravell scanned it.

'*Wanted. For murder. Edyon Foss. Seventeen years old, tall, slim, brown hair. Reward: twenty-five kroners.*' He moved to the side so Tash could see and said, 'Nice picture too. Is it a good likeness?'

Tash nodded. The picture of Edyon was totally accurate.

'He's worth half a bottle of smoke, which seems generous to me. Though the reward *and* my smoke back would suit me nicely.'

'But you wouldn't hand him in to the sheriff, would you? I told you, he didn't kill the sheriff's man; Holywell did. If Edyon's arrested, they'll hang him.'

'No, you're right. He's only a thief who hangs about with murderers. He shouldn't lose his life, just his hand, and maybe some other parts of his anatomy too.'

Tash smiled at Gravell. 'You're joking, right? I mean, we just want the smoke back.'

But Gravell had wandered away, muttering, 'They'll all think they can steal from me if this idiot gets away without punishment. They'll all be at it.'

Edyon

They travelled faster once March was healed, but keeping to the quieter roads meant slow progress and the villages were often so small there wasn't even an inn. They studied the map every morning and evening to work out roughly where they were. Holywell said they were heading towards Pravont to catch a barge downriver to Rossarb and from there they'd get a ship to Calidor. But to get that far they needed to eat. Edyon was tired and hungry. And now as they crested the hill they saw a small roadside inn beside a stream in meadowland surrounded by wooded hills. There were chickens pecking around the back, goats in a pen and a few pigs too. Fresh eggs, bread and milk would all be there. It was beautiful.

'I'll go,' Holywell said.

Holywell or March always went. And only one of them, as if they didn't trust Edyon to be left alone. Holywell said that one person at an inn was less conspicuous, but Edyon thought that one person buying enough food for three was more noteworthy.

He was tired of the whole charade. Holywell was paranoid – they were miles from Dornan and perfectly safe. And Edyon wanted a warm pie straight from the oven.

'Actually, I think I should go.'

'How do you figure that?' Holywell asked. 'Your Highness.'

'You're a foreigner. Your accent gives you away and your eyes are ... distinctive. We're in the remote north of the country. What reason will you give for being here?'

'It's none of their business.'

'Maybe not, but that doesn't mean they won't be interested. They won't get many customers. What else are they going to talk about?'

'And what reason will you give for being here?' Holywell asked.

Edyon didn't hesitate. 'I'm going north to join my uncle's law business. He specializes in trade contracts, though really my interest is criminal law, but I'm young and have to start somewhere.'

'I suggest you avoid any mention of criminals or where you're going.'

'You think I need a better story? I could be . . . going to buy the special wool they make in the north for my lover, a great dancer, who dances at court in Tornia.' He waved his arm dramatically. 'He'll look so wonderful in woollen trousers.'

Holywell seemed, for once, stunned into silence. March was almost smiling, though, which was at least a little gratifying.

'You lie well,' said Holywell, giving him an appraising look that made Edyon feel uncomfortable. 'Stick with the lawyer story. Get a couple of those chickens if you can. And eggs. Ham. Cheese. Stuff that'll last. Find out if the sheriff's men have been by. We'll ride round and meet you in the trees at the far side. Don't dally. The longer you're there, the more likely it is others will turn up. Possibly sheriff's men.'

The chances of the sheriff's men having followed them there seemed tiny. Edyon was sure Holywell was trying to frighten him. And he'd completely forgotten about addressing Edyon as 'Your Highness', not that that really bothered him. The words sounded strange in his ears, particularly when they fell from March's lips.

'I'll be as swift as an arrow, Holywell.'

'And leave the smoke with us. Don't want you getting into trouble over that stuff again.'

Edyon set off, quickly forgetting about Holywell and thinking instead about bread, cheese and – if he was lucky – hot pies.

A boy ran out as he rode up, offering to take care of the horse for a kopek. Edyon dismounted, gave him the coin and brushed the mud stains from his trousers as he walked to the door of the inn, realizing too late that most of the marks were actually blood.

He was the only customer. He exchanged greetings with the woman behind the crude bar – little more than a trestle table, really – and ordered a pie for his lunch. While he waited, he went to sit outside in the sun. That's when he noticed the poster pinned to the wall.

WANTED. FOR MURDER.

His blood seemed to freeze in his veins.

EDYON FOSS

And below his name was an awful picture of him.

His life should have improved once he knew his father was a prince. Instead it had got worse, much, much worse. But was it about to get worse still? Had the innkeeper recognized him from the poster? Had she gone for help?

Just then she appeared and set his pie down on a table by the door, just below the poster.

'Actually, I've had enough sun on the road. I'll eat inside.'

The woman sighed. 'Yes, sir.'

But as soon as he was indoors Edyon regretted moving. If she *had* recognized him and called for help, now he was trapped inside.

Edyon ate the pie as fast as he could. He was starving, but he also felt sick with anxiety. He wanted to leave, but he knew he had to get food for March and Holywell.

Then a man appeared. 'Ah, sir, my wife said we had a customer. Nice to see you on this lovely day. You've had a long journey from the looks of you?'

Edyon coughed on the last crust of his pie. Was this a ruse to delay him or was the man just being friendly?

'A long journey and a difficult one.' He held his arms out to show rather than hide his sorry condition. 'I got lost, dropped my bag crossing a river, and spent the night in the open. I'm not used to this sort of travelling.'

'Well, I can give you a room for the night, a bath and dinner. All at a good rate.'

'Alas, your offer is tempting but I've lost too much time already. I have a new legal position awaiting me with my uncle.'

'Where's that, sir?'

'Pravont.'

The word was out before he could stop it and Edyon could have kicked himself. Still, it was too late now and he could at least ask directions. 'Can you confirm my best route? And perhaps sell me some bread and cheese to sustain me on my way?'

'To be honest, I didn't even know they had lawyers in Pravont.'

'How so?'

'Well, it's so small.'

Another mistake! But a short time later Edyon had a bag of food, a well-fed and groomed horse and a full if slightly nervous stomach as well as clear directions to Pravont. He rode swiftly away and waiting under the trees out of sight of the inn were Holywell and March.

'All go well?' Holywell asked.

'Yes. Fine.' He hesitated. 'There was a poster there. A wanted poster. For me.'

Holywell swore.

'You weren't recognized, though?' asked March anxiously.

'No.' Edyon shrugged casually. 'No one ever looks at those things. I knew I'd be fine.'

He handed over the sack to Holywell. 'Bread, cheese and eggs. And a pie.'

Holywell's eyes gleamed 'Well done, Your Highness. Given the poster, though, we're best being on our way.'

'Yes, but at least now I'm sure of the way. I got directions.'

Holywell looked up. His voice was dangerously expressionless as he asked, 'How did you do that? Your Highness.'

'Well, I mentioned that we were going to . . . to Pravont.'

'We?'

'I mean, *I* was going there. Of course I didn't say "we". I said "I".'

'So they have a poster of you. And you told them where you were going.'

'He didn't recognize me,' insisted Edyon. 'I would have known.'

'Yes, but next time he walks past that poster I'll bet he has a little think, and then he mentions the remarkable likeness to one of his customers – who was on his way to Pravont – to the next sheriff's man that comes in.' Holywell shook his head. 'We need to move faster.'

Edyon's face burned. 'I'm sorry. I realize I made a mistake.'

'Do you, Your Highness? I'm so gratified.'

Holywell mounted his horse and set off.

Just to make things perfect, it started to rain.

The midges were thick in the air. March, Edyon and Holywell were sitting round their campfire with cloths wrapped round their faces and necks, and their jackets tightly secured. The rain had been bad, but the midges, which had been attacking them from the instant the rain stopped, were worse.

March was picking at the last of the pie with his long, delicate fingers, while Holywell had his map out and was working out a route to Pravont that was not the way the innkeeper had told Edyon.

March said, 'We could try cutting west, but I think there'll be more sheriff's men on this westerly road.'

Holywell shook his head. 'We keep going to Pravont. We can't risk getting a boat now – they'll be watching the river – but we can cross there and go west to Rossarb. And from there it's a ship to Calidor.'

'There's nothing north of the Ross except the Northern Plateau,' Edyon said.

'Is that a problem for you, Your Highness?' Holywell asked with what Edyon thought was exaggerated patience.

'It's forbidden. No one goes there.'

Holywell smiled. 'I like the sound of it already.'

'It's forbidden because it's demon territory.'

If Holywell heard him, he ignored it.

'We'll get more provisions in Pravont. And another horse to carry them.'

Holywell seemed determined and Edyon didn't have the will to argue with him. And after all, which was worse? The sheriff's men or demons?

'Well, I'm sure we're safe with you, Holywell, right, March?' He smiled at March, who turned his face away. 'I'm sorry if I've made a mess of things.'

March glanced back at Holywell but didn't say anything.

They sat in silence.

Edyon scratched his midge bites and then he had an idea. He took the bottle of demon smoke, uncorked it, holding his lips close to the top, breathed in a small wisp of smoke and then put his mouth over the bites on his wrist. He looked at March, who was watching him closely and for once didn't look away or pretend he wasn't interested.

Edyon relaxed his lips, the smoke curling from his mouth, and he sucked it back in, showing off a little, and this time he took March's wrist and put his mouth over the welts and held it there. Edyon half expected March to resist or snatch his hand away, but instead he let Edyon hold him and he kept totally still. Edyon could feel March's pulse, slow and steady, as he held his mouth over March's cool skin, but the smoke didn't seem to move around the welts as it had done with his shoulder wound. Edyon breathed the smoke out and watched it float up and away, aware that Holywell was staring at him.

'I wanted to see if the smoke works on midge bites,' Edyon said.

'You're not going to try it on mine, Your Highness?' Holywell asked.

The thought of touching Holywell with his hands, never mind his lips, made Edyon's skin crawl, but he said, 'You could try a little on yourself?'

Edyon offered the bottle. 'It relaxes you too. You might get a double benefit.' And he laughed at the thought of it.

'Seems the drug is affecting your brain but not the bites,' Holywell said, staring at Edyon's wrist.

Holywell was right: the welts on Edyon's and March's wrists hadn't improved.

Holywell snorted and lay down to sleep, saying, 'March, you're on first watch. Don't you go getting drugged either.'

But a short time later, when Holywell's snores became regular, March took out his knife and told Edyon, 'I'm going to try something.'

Before Edyon could reply, March cut the flesh of his palm and took the bottle of smoke.

He mastered the technique first time, sucking a wisp in and then holding his lips over the cut. March breathed the smoke out and then raised his hand in front of his face.

The cut had healed.

'So it works on cuts but not bites,' Edyon said. 'Though I've not really had a cut. I had bruises and a wobbly tooth. Will you try it on me?'

March hesitated. Then said, 'If you wish, Your Highness.'

'Please don't call me that,' Edyon said. 'It sounds all wrong.'

Edyon held his hand out and March grasped his wrist and, before Edyon could change his mind, March had cut the pad of his thumb with the tip of his knife.

March sucked in some smoke and put his lips on Edyon's hand. Edyon closed his eyes. He could feel the smoke twining round his thumb, seeking out the wound, but he was mainly aware of March's lips against his skin.

'Do you feel light-headed?' Edyon asked, his voice barely a whisper.

March grinned, which was a first. 'A little. Sleepy too.'

'Sleep then,' said Edyon softly. 'I'll watch.'

And March lay down and covered his face against the midges while Edyon sat, gently stroking his thumb against his lips.

Ambrose

TORNIA, PITORIA

Ambrose had ridden hard for three days from the northernmost part of Pitoria to the capital in the south. It was evening when he arrived in the city of Tornia. He was dirty, sweaty and exhausted and he was almost too late. The advance on the border by Aloysius's troops would begin in less than a day, and the invasion of Pitoria would happen the day after that: the day of Catherine's wedding.

As he entered the city, he stopped at a public well to drink and wash and heard people talking of Catherine's procession to the capital.

'Well, I certainly never expected a Brigantine girl to be beautiful,' said one old man.

'And her dress!' said a woman. 'And all the followers with white hair. So elegant. I might get mine done . . .'

Ambrose felt a twinge of jealousy, that these people had seen Catherine more recently than he, but also a strange pride. She had clearly made a success of her progress to the city and an impression on its citizens, but that made it all the more galling that it was for nothing – her wedding no more than a distraction from the imminent invasion in the north. Even if Catherine had succeeded in winning the people over, that very success would soon be interpreted as her complicity in her father's aims. Ambrose had to find a way to see her.

After darkness fell, and with the worst of the filth of the road sponged from his Royal Guard tunic, Ambrose rode through the streets of Tornia to the castle gates, where his path was blocked by a purple-haired soldier.

'Well met, sir. I'm Sir Ambrose Norwend. I'm with Princess Catherine.'

'Not at the moment you're not.'

Ambrose smiled tightly. 'I was delayed. Are you going to delay me more?'

The guard looked undecided for a moment, but then stepped to the side, allowing Ambrose through. He rode on, feeling hopeful, but that lasted only until the next gate, where the guard was less accommodating.

'Your name's not on the list of the princess's party. Do you have a pass?'

'A pass?'

'A sealed letter giving you admittance.'

'No, but I don't need to get in. I need to get a message to Princess Catherine.'

'Uh-huh.'

'It's urgent.'

'It always is.'

Ambrose spoke through gritted teeth. 'How can I get a message to her?'

'In the morning the stewards make a list of those wishing to present themselves. Gifts and messages can also be left.'

'How can I get a message to her now?'

'You present your pass and go through.'

'I've told you, I don't have a pass.'

'And I've told you, you need one.'

'But the message is vital. I've ridden hard to get here.'

'My heart bleeds for you. Come back in the morning.'

'I'll wait.'

'Fine by me.'

Ambrose slid off his horse, sat on the ground, his back against the wall, and waited.

Until dawn Ambrose dozed, worn out by his long ride. The guard changed, and he made a new attempt to talk his way in, with as little success as the first time. But now the castle was waking up. Servants and officials were entering and leaving, and Ambrose saw a group of boys with white hair approaching the gate.

'Are you with Princess Catherine?' he asked.

'We're her dancers,' one of the boys replied.

'Will you be seeing her today?'

'We're performing at the luncheon.'

'I need to get a message to her. Can you take it to her now, or to one of her maids?'

The boy nodded.

'Tell her that Ambrose is here. I'm by this gate and waiting to see her.'

'The princess?'

'Or Jane or Tanya. Any of them.' Then he had an idea. He took his knife and cut off a long lock of his own hair and handed it to the boy, saying, 'That's to prove it's me.'

The boy pulled a face. 'That's to prove you hardly wash.'

'It was a hard ride to get here. My message is urgent.' Ambrose gave the boy a kroner. 'There's another for you after you bring the maid here.'

The boy sighed theatrically. 'You Brigantines are so lacking in style.' Then he produced a beautifully embroidered handkerchief from his pocket, laid the lock of hair in it and wrapped it up.

'Just get it to them urgently.'

'You can rely on me. What was your name again?'

And the boy grinned and disappeared through the gates without waiting for a reply, leaving Ambrose only four-fifths sure he was joking.

Catherine

TORNIA, PITORIA

*A gentleman and lady must never be alone together.
When talking or walking they should remain at a
distance so that if they were each to stretch out their
arms, their fingertips would not quite touch.*
  Modern Manners and Behaviour, Percy Bex-Down

It was Catherine's first morning in Tornia and another fine day, the sun bright in the clear blue sky. Catherine had risen early to prepare for her meeting with Prince Tzsayn, changed her hair twice and her dress three times, and now she was almost late. As she hurriedly pulled on a fourth option, pushing down a rising sense of panic, she asked Tanya, 'What do you think?'

'I think he'll be just as nervous as you are. And as for the dress, Your Highness, the first is the most flattering to your figure.'

Catherine put the first one back on. It was a new one, a very pale silver, more simple than the others, with the slashes in the fabric revealing not skin beneath but pure white silk.

Exactly as the bell struck nine, Catherine stepped on to the terrace with Tanya.

The prince wasn't there.

Catherine's face tightened. This was ungallant. The man should be waiting well in advance to avoid this sort of embarrassment, even if the man was a prince and the meeting was . . . of questionable propriety. Especially then!

Catherine smoothed her dress and waited.

The gardens were neat and well tended, though she could see no gardeners anywhere, no sign of anyone.

'Are you sure this is the right place?'

'I believe so, Your Highness. Shall I check?'

Catherine sighed. 'Yes.'

Prince Tzsayn certainly didn't seem keen to meet her. He'd left her waiting on the dock in Charron and now couldn't even be bothered to come to a meeting he'd arranged himself.

As Tanya went back inside, Catherine strolled over to look at the roses. Only a few weeks ago she had been walking in her mother's rose garden, discussing Queen Valeria and her imminent departure. So much had happened since then and yet the situation was the same: tomorrow she was to marry a man she cared nothing for and still hadn't even spoken to.

Damn him, where was he?

Then she heard footsteps and turned to see the prince walking slowly towards her along the path between the roses.

He bowed. She curtsied. They stood awkwardly, neither willing to break the silence.

Catherine looked at his face, half scarred and half handsome, and wondered how that changed a person.

'So, we meet again,' said Tzsayn, his voice low and level.

'Isn't that what rival warriors say to each other?' *Why had she said that?*

Tzsayn raised his eyebrows, or at least the one on his unscarred side. 'I can see already where your Brigantine expertise lies.'

'And what is *your* expertise, Your Highness? Is it dancing? Or fashion perhaps?'

The words were out before Catherine could check them and she saw Tzsayn's face twitch.

What are you doing, *Catherine?*

She'd waited to talk to him for so long, played out this conversation in her head a thousand times, and now she was insulting him.

'Oh, I have no expertise. I'm quite useless.' The prince wandered a few steps away, saying, 'Shall we look at some flowers?'

Catherine knew she should wait for Tanya but Tzsayn had already set off. Catherine caught him up and he walked along, pointing out plants, saying, 'Rose ... bush ... another rose ... You see, Your Highness, though not quite an expert, I know my plants.'

'Yes,' Catherine said. 'Though I think I recognize those myself.'

Was he joking? Was this the Pitorian sense of humour? Catherine glanced over her shoulder, desperate for Tanya to come to her aid, but there was no sign of her. Catherine took a breath and told herself to relax and be herself.

He'll be just as nervous as you are. Of course he will ...

'Did you enjoy the reception yesterday evening, Your Highness?'

'Oh, it was delightful.' Tzsayn's voice was flat. 'And how did you find it, Your Highness?'

'Everyone was quite charming.'

'Indeed, "delightful" and "charming" sum up the evening perfectly.'

Catherine took the plunge. 'I do detect that you're not being totally sincere.'

Tzsayn stopped. 'Is that what you detect?'

'It is,' replied Catherine. 'Are you still unwell?'

'I am perfectly well, thank you.'

'Then might I ask what is the matter?'

'Call me a spoilt prince – and I warn you that my father has many times used just those words – but I'm not used to having things forced on me. Particularly princesses. I realize it's not your fault. You are in the same situation as me, after all, but still . . . it grates.' He resumed his stroll.

Catherine was almost too stunned by the prince's openness to feel the sting of the implied insult. *It grates, indeed!*

'We must all do as our fathers bid,' she said politely. 'And I am delighted to be joining our two countries –'

Tzsayn laughed. 'I'm sure you're always delighted. Delighted and *charmed*.'

Catherine felt her blood burn. Was this all a joke to him?

'Well,' she snapped, 'I will always be delighted and charmed to do as you bid me. As I must when we're married.'

Tzsayn glanced at her and, to his credit, his laughter died as he saw her expression of barely suppressed fury. 'You do have the Brigantine fighting spirit, I think. But I assure you, Catherine, that while I'm very keen on people doing as I bid them, when we have children –' her step faltered and he stopped – 'the idea of which seems to be a shock to you but is, I think, rather the whole point of this marriage. That's what my father wants . . . and yours presumably wants it too. The family line must continue.'

'I'm seldom sure of my father's objectives concerning anything, least of all myself,' Catherine replied coolly.

Tzsayn studied her for a moment before he continued. 'Anyway, if we do have children, I won't force them to go through this absurd arranged-marriage nonsense.'

Catherine was silent. Was he serious?

'Am I too blunt for you, Your Highness?' he asked.

'I appreciate your candour, Prince Tzsayn, but I wonder what other option you would propose.'

'I think I'd stay out of it.'

Catherine gave a bark of astonished laughter. 'Even if your daughter wanted to marry the son of your worst enemy?'

Tzsayn smiled, and this time there was just a flicker of warmth in the expression. 'We're in Pitoria, Your Highness. We have no enemies here.'

Cautiously Catherine returned the smile. 'I'm glad to hear that.'

'Do you wish to see the water garden? It's just beyond that hedge.'

'That would be *delightful*.'

Catherine's tour of the garden with Tzsayn took half the morning. Tanya, having eventually found them, shadowed them at a respectable distance. They stopped in an arbour for elderflower water and some fruit before strolling to the walls to look out over the city and the land beyond. After their rocky start, Catherine was pleased to find Tzsayn both intelligent and courteous, and the conversation ranged over their education, touched on his travels to Illast, her journey to Pitoria, and the inevitable comparison of food and clothing. By the time they returned to the castle, Catherine felt almost at ease with her husband-to-be. Of course that didn't mean she particularly wanted to marry him but, she reflected, it could be a lot worse. He could be like Boris. At that thought, she said, 'You seemed deep in conversation with my brother yesterday evening.'

Tzsayn smiled. 'I thought Prince Boris would be interested in how we manufacture the silk for my clothes. With the first course I began with the silkworms and by the end of our eighth course it only remained to detail the process of making the dyes. I'll have to complete my explanation next time I have the pleasure of his company at dinner.'

Catherine nodded, again feeling unsure how serious Tzsayn was being.

'I should add,' the prince explained, 'that when I met Prince Boris on my visit to Brigant, he and his delightful and charming friends spent a full evening telling me of their hunting exploits in incredible detail and with a certain amount of repetition, specifying their weapons, the best types of spear, the best type of horse, the best saddle, boots, leg protection and so, so much more. I thought it must be the Brigantine way to pick a topic and go over and over it.'

Catherine smiled. 'Actually, that is the way of many Brigantine men.'

At that they arrived back at the terrace and Catherine was surprised to see Sarah, pacing up and down in some agitation. When she spotted Catherine her hands flew into a blur of signs.

Slow down, Catherine signed back. *What is it?*

Sarah returned just two words.

Ambrose. Here.

Catherine felt the ground shift beneath her. Noyes had said he'd been caught, been killed. Of course it was a lie! She couldn't get her breath. Tears filled her eyes. Ambrose was alive!

'Catherine?' Tzsayn's voice was concerned.

With a supreme effort, Catherine controlled her emotions. 'Excuse me, Your Highness. I fear I've had a little too much sun.'

'Come, Your Highness,' said Tanya soothingly. 'Too much sun before your wedding will not do.' She curtsied to Tzsayn and, taking Catherine's arm, led her inside.

Ambrose

TORNIA,
PITORIA

Ambrose waited by the gate as more and more people came and went. He wondered if the boy had just thrown his hair away and forgotten about him. He started at the appearance of each new person, his heart lifting, hoping it would be someone he recognized. He noticed one woman who was coming towards him staring at him, and it took him a few moments to recognize her. It was Sarah, Catherine's maid, but she looked completely different. She was wearing a pale green dress in the Pitorian style. She looked stunning.

She came to him and curtsied. 'Sir Ambrose.'

'Sarah!' beamed Ambrose. 'It's wonderful to see you.'

She returned his smile. 'It's good to see you too, sir, though more than a little surprising. Catherine was told that you had been killed by Noyes's men.'

Ambrose shook his head. 'As you can see, I'm alive and well, though in urgent need of seeing the princess.'

Sarah's smile faded. 'That's not possible. The princess is with Prince Tzsayn at the moment. Their wedding is tomorrow. Nothing must stop that.'

Ambrose felt the familiar tightening of his chest at the thought of Catherine marrying another, and for the first time it was accompanied by a twinge of doubt. Would his news be rejected as the invention of a love-struck fool?

'I've not come to stop it. But I have urgent news. It's not about me, or the marriage. It's . . . much more important.'

'The marriage is the most important thing. Perhaps after the wedding . . .'

Ambrose shook his head. 'That's too late. Listen, you know she'll want to see me.'

'But that doesn't mean it's a good idea. Boris is in the castle with fifty men. If he sees you, you're a dead man, and the princess will not thank me for that: to find that you are alive and then bring about your death! Never mind the trouble she'll be in.'

'I understand you want to protect her, and I have no wish to bring her trouble. You know I would never wish her any harm. But this news cannot wait.'

Sarah looked torn.

'Please,' he begged. 'She'll want to hear it. Once I have spoken to her, I'll go.'

'You'll have to,' Sarah agreed, then she turned to the guard. 'You know whom I serve? I am taking this messenger to the princess. He is safe with me.'

'As you wish, my lady,' said the guard, bowing.

Ambrose followed Sarah through the castle. She walked quickly, saying, 'I'll take you the quiet way but everywhere is busy. There are so many people here.'

The place was indeed bustling, though once they passed the shining walls of the Great Tower it became quieter. Still, Ambrose's nerves were stretched to breaking point. Noyes could be round any corner. And if he was taken now Catherine would never know.

'Nearly there,' Sarah said.

'Nearly where?'

'The morning room. Actually, there are about twenty morning rooms but this one is relatively private.'

But, as they went along the side of a small courtyard, Ambrose turned to see two purple-haired Pitorian soldiers talking with another man whose hair wasn't dyed and who was wearing the uniform of the Brigantine Royal Guard.

'Damn!' Ambrose swung away and moved behind a pillar. But he knew he'd been seen. And from the way the man had stared at him he'd been recognized as well.

'Please, we must hurry,' he told Sarah. He only needed a moment to tell the princess his news and give her the letter he'd stolen from Lord Thornlee. Even if he was caught, it would be worth it; as long as he delivered the message there was a chance the princess could escape.

Sarah hurried up a flight of stairs and along one more corridor. 'Inside, quick. I'll bring the princess.' And then she was gone.

Ambrose paced the room. He had dreamed of seeing Catherine again, but not like this. He looked down at his boots, thick with dust and dirt. What would she think of him? Well, that didn't matter; the point was to warn her, the point was to make her believe him. But then what? They were still trapped, hundreds of leagues from home in a foreign country, enmeshed in a plot he still didn't fully understand. After all, Boris was in Tornia too. Had Aloysius betrayed his son as well? That made no sense. If

Boris knew about the coming invasion, he must be planning an escape. Possibly with Catherine. Ambrose had been going over all these things for the last three days and still wasn't sure what to make of it. Then there was the sound of footsteps approaching, the door opened and Sarah entered, followed by Catherine, and all thoughts flew from his mind.

Catherine was wearing a figure-hugging silver dress slashed with white silk. Her hair seemed blonder than before and was piled on her head, pinned with white flowers. Her face was pale with shock. And then her eyes filled with tears.

'Ambrose . . .' Catherine breathed. 'I thought . . . They told me you were killed.' And now the tears fell down her cheeks.

Ambrose wanted to brush the tears away. Tears shed for him. He stepped closer. It always amazed him how she looked at him. So fiercely and so lovingly. He carefully reached out and as gently as he could he wiped the tears away with his fingertips. Catherine took his hand and kissed it.

Kissed him.

He held her hand and pulled it to his lips. 'I never thought I'd see you again. And seeing you is both wonderful and painful. I have a message of great importance but I must be brief; one of Boris's men saw me on my way here.'

'What! Then you must *go*!' Catherine looked back at the door, where Sarah had stationed herself. 'This is madness. I wanted to see you but not at the risk of your life.'

'I'll go soon, but I have to tell you my message first. Your father is planning an invasion. He has thousands on men on the border at this moment ready to invade Pitoria.'

'*What?* No, you must be mistaken – my marriage is supposed to bring our countries closer together.'

'Your marriage is a diversion. I've seen their orders.' Ambrose held out the letter to Catherine. 'Today they are advancing on the border and they invade tomorrow at first light.'

Catherine scanned the letter, her eyes wide, and it pained Ambrose to see her so shocked and confused.

'You believe it?' she gasped.

'Your father's seal is on the orders.'

'But . . . why? Why the invasion at all? And why this sham of a marriage? It makes no sense. I'm here, and Boris and Noyes too. An invasion would put us all in danger.'

'That's why I had to see you. To warn you. I believe Boris must be party to it. Who arranged for all the lords of Pitoria to be at your wedding? Who *insisted* on it?'

'He's my brother . . . he wouldn't,' breathed Catherine.

'The lords away from their castles, the whole country distracted by celebrations. It's the perfect opportunity for an invasion.'

Catherine shook her head. 'But . . . why invade at all?'

'That I don't know, Your Highness. But whatever your father's reason, it's happening.'

From the corridor came the sound of running and shouting.

'Boris is here!' Sarah cried.

Ambrose took Catherine's hand. 'Don't let him know what I've told you. You must get word to Prince Tzsayn. He can protect you.'

'Ambrose . . .' Catherine began, but before she could say anything more the door burst open and four of Boris's guards ran into the room, swords drawn. Ambrose backed to the window, drawing his sword as well.

Boris strode in with Noyes behind him, his eyes gleaming.

'Well, sister, you continue to surprise me. Meeting your lover under your husband's roof the very day before your wedding?'

Ambrose stepped forward. 'We are not lovers. I am Princess Catherine's guard. Sworn to protect her.'

'Protecting her! Bringing disgrace upon her, you mean.'

'I was not alone with Ambrose, and we were merely talking,' Catherine said. She made a subtle sign with her hand, and Ambrose saw Sarah nod and slip out of the door behind Boris.

'Well, there's no time for talk now.' Boris turned to Ambrose. 'My father wants you back in Brigant to pull you apart limb from limb, but I fear I will have to disappoint him.'

Ambrose felt his blood rising. 'You, or your men? I seem to remember the last two you set against me didn't pose too much trouble.'

Boris sneered. 'Then let's see what happens with four. Take him!'

Ambrose swung his sword up but, before Boris's guards could attack, Catherine darted in front of him, saying, 'No, Boris! Not again.'

'Out of the way, sister! You shame yourself.'

'It's you who shame me!' And she stepped forward so that the point of one of the guards' swords was against her chest.

'No, Catherine!' cried Ambrose.

The guard looked uncertain and began to lower his blade, but Boris stepped forward, pulled Catherine out of the way and threw her roughly to the floor as he shouted, 'I said, take him!'

Ambrose knew he had to get the numbers in his favour as quickly as he could, and he swung to the nearest assailant and cut across his sword arm. The man staggered back. The next guard aimed a clumsy cut at Ambrose's head but he ducked beneath it, his sword opening the man's throat. He parried the third guard's strike, but the fourth was already outflanking him. Ambrose fell back, taking the fight away from Catherine, who was still sprawled on the marble floor. Boris's men came forward. And then the room was full of noise, the stamping of boots and shouts in Pitorian as blue-haired soldiers surrounded them, and Ambrose had never been so happy to have a spear pointed at him.

'Drop your weapons, in the name of His Highness Prince Tzsayn!'

Ambrose dropped his sword, and the other men did so reluctantly. Boris's blade was still sheathed by his side.

From behind the crowd of soldiers stepped another man. He was young and slim and wearing a coat of blue silk. Prince Tzsayn. Ambrose had heard the rumours of his scarred face and indeed it was a strange sight: one side handsome, the other looking like melted wax.

Tzsayn walked over to Catherine, saying, 'It seems I was right: you are more familiar with warriors than me, Your Highness.'

He held out his hand, she took it, and he gently helped her to her feet.

Ambrose forced himself to stay still. He should be the one to take her hand, to help her rise, and he was sure now that that was what she wanted too, but the look she flashed him was enough to hold him in place. There was nothing he could do. He closed his eyes for a moment and breathed deeply. Catherine was safe. He had delivered his message. Whatever happened next was out of his hands.

'Can you tell me what is happening here, Your Highness?' Tzsayn asked Catherine softly.

Boris snarled a reply. 'This man, Sir Ambrose Norwend, is a wanted traitor. He's to be returned to Brigant for trial and execution.'

Tzsayn turned sharply to Boris, an exaggerated look of surprise on his face.

'Ah, Prince Boris, I didn't see you there. It seems we're all going a little blind, as I am sure you would have helped your sister had you noticed she'd fallen to the floor. Perhaps I am seeing this wrong too, but Sir Ambrose does not seem particularly willing to return with you.'

Boris sniffed. 'He thinks he can do as he likes instead of as the king demands.'

'Oh dear. He sounds like a true villain.' Tzsayn looked at Ambrose for the first time with a swift, searching gaze. Ambrose held it for a moment, then bowed his head.

Tzsayn leant to Catherine. 'What do you say, my lady? Is he a villain? I'm tempted to think that in this case Prince Boris might be right.'

'My father demands that Ambrose return to Brigant, that is true, but I fear that if Boris were to escort him Ambrose would not complete the journey alive.'

Tzsayn nodded thoughtfully.

'Well, I have a simple solution to the immediate problem. As Prince Boris will not be returning to Brigant until after our marriage, I suggest that, in the meantime, Sir Ambrose is kept safely and securely in my custody.'

Ambrose began to hope that he would make it out of the room alive after all.

Boris bristled. 'That won't be necessary, Your Highness. My men can ensure he is secured.'

Tzsayn shook his head. 'I don't wish this *villain* to cause any more trouble before my wedding day. He is my prisoner, until I decide otherwise.' Tzsayn turned to Ambrose. 'Have you anything to add, Sir Ambrose?'

Ambrose flicked his eyes towards Catherine, but her own held no clues for him. He stepped forward proudly. 'Prince Tzsayn, I am no villain. I had no desire to fight here, but was forced to defend myself against Prince Boris's men.'

Tzsayn cocked his head. 'But why are you here at all?'

Ambrose hesitated. With Boris and his men in the room, he could not reveal the truth. It was for Catherine to pass on the news he'd given her.

'I was here to speak with Princess Catherine about . . . an urgent matter.'

'Which is?'

'Which is for the ears only of Her Highness and those she chooses to trust.'

Tzsayn blinked, then nodded. 'I see. Take him away.'

Ambrose felt each of his arms clasped by one of the blue-haired guards.

'To the dungeons, I hope,' Boris said, jaw set.

'Well, I'm hardly going to have him sent to my private rooms, am I?' Tzsayn replied. 'Now, please excuse me, but my lady looks a little distressed. I think fewer men and fewer swords will improve the appearance of this room no end.'

Ambrose resisted the urge to struggle as he was pushed out and down the corridor. How stupid he had sounded! An urgent matter for the princess's ears only! He couldn't have made it look more like he'd had some secret rendezvous with Catherine if he'd tried. Had his clumsy words destroyed Tzsayn's trust in her at the very moment Catherine was going to need it most?

Down and down the guards took him. It really was a dungeon that he was going to. The walls here were bare stone, the steps narrow and worn. A guard pulled open a heavy wooden door to reveal a small cell beyond. The light from the corridor illuminated a crude wooden bed, a table and chair. Ambrose was pushed inside and the door was shut and bolted behind him, leaving the cell black and silent. Until the scurrying sounds began.

Catherine

TORNIA, PITORIA

I will be loyal to Brigant and my father.
Pledge sworn by Princess Catherine of Brigant
on her sixteenth birthday

The room was cleared of all the guards, but Tzsayn, Boris, Catherine and her maids remained. Tzsayn walked over to Ambrose's sword, which still lay on the floor, and peered at it as if he'd never seen one before.

'I must say, with every passing moment I'm more excited about our forthcoming marriage. I'm sure it won't be dull at all.' He turned to Catherine. 'However, I think we should find somewhere else to discuss what just happened. I'm desperate to hear all about Sir Ambrose.'

He took Catherine's arm gently but firmly and escorted her to the door.

'We'll go to the Blue Room and have some tea, I think. Will you join us, Prince Boris? You drink tea, I presume?'

'I've no desire for tea at this moment,' replied Boris tersely.

'Then it's just us, my lady,' Tzsayn said to Catherine.

A short time later Catherine and Tzsayn were seated at a small round table in a room decorated with beautiful pale blue and white tiles. Sarah and Tanya sat nearby, pretending to talk to each other, but Catherine knew they were listening intently to her conversation.

Catherine tried to roll her shoulders discreetly to release the tension there. Tzsayn seemed calm. Too calm for a man who had just discovered his fiancée with another man. She tried not to imagine what might have happened had he come in earlier to find Ambrose gently brushing her tears away.

And now Ambrose was in a cell. But at least he was alive.

'So, do you want to tell me about this man, Sir Ambrose, before tea or after it?'

Catherine's mind raced. So much had happened. If Ambrose's news was true – and she believed it was – instead of a wedding to unite their two ruling families, Brigant and Pitoria were facing war. But should she tell Tzsayn? How? And would he believe her? The trust between them was a fragile thing, new and untested. Better to strengthen it first with the truth – as far as she could tell it.

'Sir Ambrose was my bodyguard in Brigant.'

True.

'He is an honourable man from a good family.'

Also true.

'He has never done anything wrong, except defend himself successfully against Boris's men.'

He's kissed my hand and touched my face, but that isn't so wrong . . .

'He would never do anything to harm me. In fact, he risked his life to come here today.'

'Need I ask why, or is the way he looks at you all I need to know?'

Catherine hesitated, blushing.

'Ambrose is honourable. And I . . . I have never done anything that I should not.'

'I'm not sure he is and I'm less sure you haven't.'

Catherine protested, 'Your Highness, I –'

'I apologize,' interrupted Tzsayn. 'That was glib. I can see you're upset. You care for him very much?'

Catherine swallowed. 'It's not that . . . not just that. I do care for him, I admit it.' She glanced up at Tzsayn but his face was unreadable. 'But I know my duty and I have not jeopardized it with a foolish love affair. At this moment my distress is for another reason.'

Tzsayn seemed surprised. 'Can you tell me the reason?'

'I'm . . . There's something more. Something bigger, but . . . I'm not sure what to do about it. I'm torn between my duties . . .'

'Your duties to whom?'

'To Brigant and my father, and to you, Pitoria and my life here.'

Before she could say more, the servants arrived with the tea. Catherine straightened her back and sat in silence while they set out the urn, glasses and lemons, trying desperately to imagine what her mother would advise. After what seemed like an age, the servants left. Tzsayn poured two glasses of tea and placed one before her.

'Catherine, the only advice I can offer is that you must do what you think is right, what you believe in.'

But what do I believe in?

To betray her father, her country, was wrong. But so were her father's plans. He had lied to her, deceived her. Let her believe in a marriage and a future that was nothing more than an illusion. King Arell and Prince Tzsayn had shown her more kindness and honesty in her few days in Tornia than her father had done in her whole life, but that didn't mean her loyalties should change. Or did it?

Catherine felt her eyes beginning to prick with tears. 'I've been so naive. I thought I could come to Pitoria and win people over with a few dresses and a flower. I wanted to be liked – loved – by the people. My father rules by fear and I wanted to do the opposite. We Brigantines have a certain reputation – you implied as much yourself . . . I'm used to warriors. I'm used to fear and hate and being on my guard day and night against a wrong look or a misplaced word.' Catherine took a breath. 'I'm sorry. I'm not looking for sympathy, just trying to explain myself.'

Tzsayn reached out and took her hand, saying, 'I'm honoured that you trust me enough to do so.'

'People expect Brigantines to be aggressive, violent . . . to bring fear. I wanted to change that. I hoped that people might see me differently. But perhaps I'm wrong to even try. Perhaps people should be afraid of us.'

Catherine drew a shuddering breath as she made her choice. Slowly she pulled her hand free from Tzsayn's, slipped it inside one of the slashes in her dress and took out the letter.

'This is the message Ambrose just handed to me. My father is gathering an army in the north of Brigant. He's going to invade Pitoria. These are his orders, under his seal. Ambrose stole this and brought it to me because he knows the danger I will be in when the fighting begins.'

Tzsayn was still, so still he might have been carved in stone. Then he took the orders and read them. And then read them again.

'This is not a forgery? This is definitely your father's seal?'

'Yes. And Ambrose has seen the soldiers. He believes the wedding is –' she drew another deep breath, forcing herself to say it – 'a diversion. A means to ensure that all the lords of Pitoria are here in Tornia, far from their lands in the north.'

Tzsayn's scarred hand that held the paper trembled, but whether with fear or anger Catherine couldn't say.

'Your father would do this? Risk everything on war? Risk his own daughter's life?'

'It's exactly the sort of thing he would do.'

'He has shown himself to be the warmonger my father always feared. And you have shown yourself to be better for Pitoria than I could ever have hoped.' Tzsayn rose swiftly. 'Thank you, Catherine. I need to talk to Ambrose about this before I speak to my father. I won't hand him back to Boris.'

'What will happen to Boris and his men?'

'If Brigant does attack, they are enemy soldiers. They'll be arrested.'

'And . . . what am I?'

Tzsayn took her hand again. 'You and your maids are my guests. You have risked and sacrificed much to tell me this, Catherine, and in return I offer you my protection. I will ensure you are all safe, no matter what happens.'

He turned and strode from the room.

Catherine felt light-headed. Whatever else she had done, right or wrong, she was certain she had brought about her own ruin.

She could not stay in Pitoria; Tzsayn could never marry the daughter of his enemy. She could never go back to Brigant, to the father who betrayed her and whom she had betrayed in turn. She had set herself adrift. And she'd be adrift in a country at war with her own: hated, not loved.

She had never felt more alone. The only comfort she had was the thought that Ambrose had risked his life to help her.

March

March was first aware that they were close to Pravont from the sounds of voices and someone chopping wood and, behind it all, the roaring of the river. The noises carried a long distance, which was a reminder to be as quiet as possible. They approached through a small thicket of trees and, as they got nearer, they saw roofs and woodsmoke and then houses and a few people.

'I can't see any sheriff's men,' Edyon said.

'Maybe not,' Holywell said. 'But if they had a poster of you at some remote inn they'll have one here.'

'Possibly,' Edyon said. 'But this is the north. They hate interference and being told what to do by southerners. They hate sheriffs. They hate everything that isn't northern.'

'We're not northern,' March said.

Edyon grinned at him. 'No, you're *foreign*, which is even worse. But here being wanted for murder might not be such a black mark.'

'Well, I don't think we should go in there bragging about it, Your Highness,' Holywell replied. All the time he was peering through the trees.

'Maybe it's best to go in at dawn, when it's quieter,' Edyon suggested. 'Or maybe evening, when people are tired and not so curious.'

'Or lunch, when they're all eating?' Holywell added.

Edyon nodded. 'That's a good point.' And March wasn't sure who was being more sarcastic.

'So?' March asked. 'Which will it be?'

'The time is right,' Holywell said, looking at March. 'But it's your turn. Take the horses to the stables first, get them fed and see if you can buy another one to carry provisions. We need food to last a week; that should get us to Rossarb. And find out anything else you can.'

'But why me?' March complained. 'My Pitorian is the worst. I'm clearly not from around here.'

Holywell's eyes flicked from Edyon to March. 'If we see you're in trouble, we'll come and get you out of it.'

March knew Holywell would, but still it seemed the wrong plan.

'Unless you've got another idea?' Holywell added.

'You or Edyon could do it better.'

Holywell nodded. 'I could do it better, but could you rescue me better?'

'So you think I'll need rescuing?'

Holywell sighed. 'No, March. I think Edyon will be too southern for these folks, but I have a feeling they'll take to you. You're a man from the mountains, like them.'

March swore in Abask.

'Excellent. I'm glad we're in agreement.' Holywell smiled mirthlessly and turned away.

March's stomach twisted uncomfortably. Ever since the inn, Holywell had been behaving oddly. He seemed to have lost patience with Edyon and was shorter with him now, less courteous and deferential. And he seemed irritated by March as well, since the night with the midges when March and Edyon had shared the smoke.

Now March felt as if there was another reason why he was being sent into the village. It was almost as if Holywell didn't want to leave him and Edyon alone together, which was ridiculous. He was perfectly capable of looking after the prince and keeping up their deception. If anyone was risking that, it was Holywell by not hiding his feelings better. He was sure Edyon had noticed the change in his demeanour too but not said anything. How long until he did?

Nevertheless, March left them both under the trees and led the horses down to the village. Pravont was the biggest settlement they'd seen since Dornan but it was still a village, not quite a town. A woman stared at him as he approached. He nodded once as a greeting and she returned a similar nod and then turned away.

'Wait, please!' said March in his best Pitorian. 'Where are the stables?'

The woman looked at him and said, 'Eh?'

'The stables?'

The woman shook her head. March wasn't sure if she couldn't understand his accent or was just being difficult. He indicated the horses and said, 'Stable,' louder. The woman nodded and pointed to her left.

March led the horses down the lane the woman had indicated. He passed a few more people and there was a bit more nodding but no one spoke.

He followed the trail of hay and smell of manure to the stables, which were large and not just for horses. In fact, there were a few horses, a few more cows and a lot of goats. A woman was sweeping. She didn't stop as March approached.

'Good day. My horses need food and water.'

The woman looked up, saying, 'What?'

March repeated his request, pointing at the horses. What did she think he'd want!

'Where are you from?' she asked.

'Abask.'

'Never heard of it. They all got eyes like that there?'

March couldn't be bothered. He said, 'No, everyone else's are shit brown.'

The woman smiled. 'You can leave your horses.'

'Thank you. I'll come back for them later.'

'Horses ain't no good on the plateau. It's too cold and too steep.'

'Thanks for the advice, but I'm not going up to the plateau.'

'No? You have another reason for being here?'

March shrugged but then smiled. Holywell was right. These people did remind him of home.

'In Abask we ride horses in the mountains. Even in winter they cope.'

'This isn't Abask. Though I admit most of the men here have shit-brown eyes, and shit for brains too. Anyway, you'll need a mountain pony to carry your provisions. And you go on foot.'

The woman told him where to buy provisions and that she had a pony he could buy for five kroners, less a kroner for each of his horses. March knew that their horses were worth more and suspected the pony was worth far less, but he wasn't in a position to argue. Besides, he liked the woman. And it was Holywell's money.

At the trading post he bought food and blankets, a thick coat, a jacket, a woollen shirt and some trousers. It was good to have clean clothes. But Holywell and Edyon also needed clothes. He added two more of everything to the pile. The man who made out his bill didn't comment, at least not about that. He said, 'You'll be needing harpoons?'

'Harpoons?' March didn't understand the word.

'You're going over the river?'

March hesitated. Holywell had given Edyon lots of grief for saying where they were going but it seemed fairly obvious. He didn't have time for a reply anyway.

'Across the river's demon territory. You'll be needing harpoons.'

March shrugged. 'Sure. Three harpoons.'

The man nodded and went through a door behind the counter and returned with three long wooden harpoons with barbed metal tips. On seeing what they were, March said, 'I'm not going hunting.'

The man laughed. 'No, but the demons will be hunting *you*.'

'Oh, right. Is three enough?'

'If it's not, you'll be dead anyway.'

March looked around the store. It was small but well stocked. 'Do many people go up to the Northern Plateau from here?'

The man shook his head meaningfully. 'No one ever does. Not as far as I know.'

March smiled.

He headed back to the stables and on the way stopped at a small inn. Inside was one room with tables and a bar, which was so small that the man behind it filled it. He asked, 'Beer?'

March sat down. 'And food.'

'There's soup and there might be a pie ready, if you're lucky. If you order both, you'll save six kopeks.'

'Both then.'

The man stuck his head through the door and said something that sounded like it could be his order.

March sipped his beer and soon got his soup. 'Is there bread?'

The man shook his head. 'Polecake is three kopeks.'

'Fine.' March had no idea what polecake was and he was surprised to see the man reach up and pull a black disc from a pole that hung above the bar. He threw it over to March, who caught it. It was like a hard, thick biscuit.

'Break it on to the soup,' the barman said.

March did as instructed. The polecake was dry but absorbed the soup and added flavour. 'Good,' he said.

The man watched him eat, then took the bowl and brought him a huge chicken pie and asked where he was from, to which March replied, 'Abask.' The barman had never heard of it so he told March about his knees. His knees ached. Then he informed March that the man in the trading post would rip him off, at which March nodded and said, 'And the woman at the stables.'

March paid and remembered he was supposed to ask about the sheriff's men. It was hardly subtle but he felt increasingly confident that the people of Pravont knew how to be discreet.

The barman nodded. 'Sheriff's men were here a few days ago. They wanted us to set up a roadblock on the bridge over the river. We told them where they could put their roadblock, and it wasn't on the bridge.'

March laughed and thanked the man and a short time later he was leading his mountain pony out of Pravont and back to where Holywell and Edyon were waiting.

'That horse has shrunk,' said Holywell. 'And where are the others?'

'Too steep and cold for horses where we're going,' replied March, bristling slightly.

Holywell grunted and started checking the provisions strapped to the pony.

Edyon smiled and said, 'Your new outfit suits you, March.'

March tugged at his jacket awkwardly. Edyon paid him compliments all the time and, even though it made March feel self-conscious, he realized he didn't want Edyon to stop. He said, 'I've got new clothes for us all.'

As Edyon put on his warm jacket, he asked, 'What are the clothes like in Calidor?'

'Um, similar. But different.'

Edyon laughed. 'Not the most helpful description. But maybe you can tell me about more important things. You know my father. Can you tell me about him, his friends, his court? What should I expect?'

March knew Edyon would be hopeless in the prince's court. He was too unguarded, showed his feelings too quickly and too easily. But then Edyon wasn't going to court. He was going to a dungeon in Brigant. Possibly he'd be tortured. Probably. He'd certainly never see Calidor or his father. Nor his mother either. March imagined her waiting for a letter from her son that would never arrive.

March forced a smile on to his face. 'Of course, Your Highness. Let me tell you about your father . . .'

Tash

PRAVONT,
PITORIA

Tash ordered the polecake and soup, and the pie and a large beer for Gravell. Then Gravell added another pie for himself.

'Best food in the world here,' Gravell said, as happy as Tash had seen him in weeks. 'We'll get our smoke back and hunt a few more demons while we're at it.'

'Have you told Flint that you'll have to pay him later?'

They'd used the last of the money the day before and hadn't eaten since.

Gravell sighed. 'Money, money, money. That's all you talk about.'

'It's not money that I'm talking about but the lack of it.'

'And whose fault is it that we have no money?'

Tash wasn't sure it was totally her fault that the demon smoke had been stolen, and she had done her best to get it back, but she didn't want to argue about that again. It didn't solve the basic problem of having no money anyway.

Flint brought the food over and stood by the table as Tash broke her polecake over the dish and stirred it into her soup.

'How's it going, Gravell?'

'Ups and downs, but it's good to be here, Flint,' Gravell said. 'Good to get some decent food.'

'Where've you come from just now then?'

'Dornan. Full of fucking thieves.'

'Ay, that's true. You had a problem, huh?'

'Someone stole my goods. We think he – they – might have come north. Come through Pravont as it happens.'

'Stole your stuff? Bastards.'

'That is exactly the right word, Flint. *Exactly* the right word.'

Tash pulled out a poster of Edyon that she'd taken from one of the roadblocks. She handed it to Flint, saying, 'This is one of them.'

Flint shook his head. 'Murdered one of the red tops, eh? Well, I've not seen him here.'

'He's with two other men: one young, the other your age. They're foreign.'

Flint dragged over a stool and sat, his voice low. 'There was a young fella came in two days ago. Spoke Pitorian but so bad I could hardly follow him. He had the strangest accent. And weird eyes. Foreign for sure. But he was alone.'

Flint dropped his voice even lower and continued, 'Then two other men came through yesterday. Red tops. From Dornan, they said, but I know southerners when I see them. They headed over the bridge, I hear. Hope the demons get them.' Flint turned and spat on the floor. 'Scarlet-haired bastards.'

'They're following the youngster?' Gravell asked.

'That's my guess.' Flint stood. 'They stayed the night and left at dawn with an early breakfast they insisted I make 'em. That was this morning. You'll track 'em easy enough. Stomping around like all bloody southerners do.'

'Thanks, Flint,' Gravell said. 'I owe you. And . . . I'll have to owe you for the food too.'

Flint put his hand on Gravell's shoulder. 'Not a problem, my friend. You can have a room too if you want. Pay me next time. I know you're good for it.'

Tash looked out of the window. It would be dark soon. Flint was right that it was too late to set off now, but she knew Gravell would be moving at full speed at dawn.

The day was clear and bright and the tracks were easy enough to follow. After his cheerfulness the day before, Gravell was in a serious mood. It was clear that the sheriff's men were following the tracks of what looked like two or three people and a pony. Tash was uneasy: hunting demons was one thing, chasing down Edyon and Holywell was another, but following the sheriff's men into forbidden territory didn't feel right.

'What do we do if we catch them up?' she asked. 'The sheriff's men, I mean.'

'What do you mean, *if*?'

'When, then?'

'Then we go past them, without them noticing, which'll be a doddle as they're southerners and not familiar with this territory, and then we'll catch up with Edyon and his friends.'

'And what if the sheriff's men catch up with Edyon first? I mean, I know they're southerners and stupid and all that, but they have got a head start.'

'Edyon and his friends have already done for one sheriff's man; I doubt they'll worry about doing for a couple more. With any luck, the red tops will take at least one of them out, so the survivors will be easier pickings. And if the sheriff's men kill them . . . well, at least I'll get to spit on Edyon's grave.'

Edyon

NORTHERN PLATEAU,
PITORIA

'I'd like to see a demon,' Holywell said.

Edyon didn't want to see a demon. He wanted to see a building, a warm fire, a blanket and a soft bed. Or he'd like to see the sun and, most importantly, feel its warmth. They were marching on fast, and he was struggling to keep up. He was tired, cold and hungry, but mostly he was cold. He was glad of the fur-lined jacket March had bought, and the woollen shirt and the hat, but Edyon wished he had bought thick socks too. His feet hadn't been warm for two days. At night he warmed them by the fire and hugged the bottle of demon smoke for further warmth. He would have liked to have hugged March instead – he was sure they could find ways to keep each other warm – but his handsome man had gone cold in a different way, keeping his distance and glancing at Holywell whenever Edyon found an excuse to touch him.

'What do they look like, Your Highness? Do you know?'

Edyon shrugged. 'There are lots of stories. Some say they're like humans, only bigger and faster. And redder.'

'Redder?'

'They're supposed to be the colour of the smoke.'

'Your smoke's purple.'

'Yes, so perhaps this smoke came from a purple demon.'

Perhaps, Edyon mused, that was why this smoke was different, why it had this strange power to heal.

'Purple or red, they don't sound that dangerous,' said Holywell.

'Oh,' Edyon added, 'and they have sharp teeth and a strong dislike of human company.'

Holywell laughed. 'Sounds like a man I used to work for.'

'You're in a good mood, Holywell,' Edyon said.

'We're making good speed now, Your Highness. In less than a week we'll be at the coast.'

It had taken them a day to climb the steep slope to the plateau, but Holywell was right: the going was relatively easy now. The land was strangely, emptily beautiful. There were lots of trees but not much else – no people and no signs of demons, though Edyon didn't know if demons left signs. There were plentiful animal tracks – deer and rabbits and wild boar – but really the only outstanding feature of the place was that it was cold. It was the beginning of summer and yet it was colder than winter in southern Pitoria.

'So why is it that no one comes here, Your Highness?' Holywell asked.

'Too bloody cold,' March interjected.

Edyon glanced over at March, who'd hardly spoken since breakfast. He was wrapped up so tightly that Edyon couldn't see his face.

Edyon said, 'I imagine the cold does help keep people away, but it's forbidden because of its history. It used to be a place where people came to hunt, then gold was found in one of the rivers about a hundred years ago. They say all you had to do was paddle around and pick up gold nuggets with your toes.'

'If they weren't frozen off first,' Holywell said.

'Or if the demons didn't get you,' Edyon replied. 'They were said to protect the land; that's one of the old myths about them. Anyway, the story goes that they killed some miners and so demon hunters were employed to protect them. The demon hunters killed the demons, and that's when they discovered the smoke and started selling it to the towns further south. Some people made a lot of money, but eventually the gold began to run out and soon there were rival groups fighting over the good mines that were left. So the king sent his son, Prince Verent – he'd be the grandfather of the present king – up here to investigate the problems.

'But they say Prince Verent fell under the spell of the demon smoke. He was obsessed with it. Instead of using his men to sort out the fighting, he rode north, hunting demons and killing them for their smoke. He went further and further and refused to turn back. Eventually he disappeared into the snowy wastes. Some say he's still going north. After that, King Randall, Verent's father, decreed that no one should go on to the Northern Plateau and possessing demon smoke became a crime in Pitoria. The law hasn't changed since.'

'The law might not've changed but some people still go hunting the demons,' Holywell said. 'They can't be that fearsome if your little girlfriend from Dornan hunts them.'

'I'd rather not find out,' Edyon said. 'Unlike you, Holywell, I've no desire to see one.'

'You're not even curious, Your Highness? It'd be a fine tale to tell your grandchildren.'

'I've no desire for fine tales *or* grandchildren. At the moment I'd be happy with a warm fire. And if we do see a demon I suggest we run.'

'I'm sure you're not such a coward as you suggest, Your Highness.'

'Running seems sensible rather than cowardly.'

'You said they were fast. Shouldn't you stand your ground and fight?' Holywell asked. 'That's the point of the harpoons, isn't it? And throwing a harpoon is difficult when you're running away.'

Edyon bristled at the barely concealed scorn in the older man's voice. 'I suppose you're right, Holywell. I hadn't really thought about it.'

'We should stand together, Your Highness. If you run, you'll be the demon's dinner, I think. And I wouldn't want that.'

Edyon wasn't convinced that Holywell was being entirely truthful.

'You think you can throw the harpoon on target, Your Highness?' Holywell asked.

Edyon was almost too tired to reply. 'I'm sure I'm as good with a harpoon as I am with a sword, which is to say, not good at all.'

'We should practise then. And always walk with one. You too, March.'

With a grunt, Holywell threw his harpoon. It struck a tree, which Edyon supposed he was aiming for, and stuck there, quivering.

March passed a harpoon to Edyon. He squirmed slightly. Fighting – any kind of physical exercise, really – had never been his strong suit. He didn't want to look like a weakling in front of March, but both men were staring at him now, waiting.

Gritting his teeth, Edyon pulled back his arm and threw, trying his best to look strong, but the harpoon skittered a short way along the ground and Edyon wished that a demon would hurry up and carry him off so he could stop feeling like a fool.

March turned away and Edyon cursed inwardly.

'Well, Your Highness,' said Holywell smoothly. 'Shall we try that again?'

March

NORTHERN PLATEAU,
PITORIA

Edyon flung his harpoon again. It flew a short distance and landed butt first in the snow. The prince was not improving.

Edyon blushed and ran forward to pick it up. Holywell shook his head, aimed his own harpoon towards Edyon's back and made as if to throw it, before adjusting the direction at the last moment and hurling it hard past him. Edyon let out a stifled cry as the weapon slammed into a tree to his left.

March balanced his own harpoon in his hand. Back in Calidor, he had seen men throwing spears at jousts, and Holywell had a similar technique. He waited until Holywell had retrieved his harpoon before raising his own, positioning his legs, pointing with his left hand at where he was aiming, and threw. It sailed through the air, not as far as Holywell's but at least in the direction he'd been aiming, which was more than could be said for Edyon's.

'Not bad, March,' Holywell said. 'All that waiting on tables and carrying platters of grapes has strengthened your arm.'

March kept his face impassive, just as he had done back at court whenever a high-born lord or lady insulted him. He didn't understand why Holywell wanted to provoke him, but he was determined not to rise to the bait.

He turned to Edyon instead. Edyon threw again and nearly speared the pony, which reared up with a frightened squeal before trotting out of the way.

'For fuck's sake!' Holywell muttered.

'Sorry,' Edyon said. He was bright red with shame. 'Sorry. Can't get the hang of it.'

'Show him, March. Before he kills one of us,' Holywell said. 'Or himself.'

March crossed over to Edyon.

'First get the harpoon balanced in your hand.'

Edyon nodded, but the weapon was still waving like a reed in the wind. March moved behind Edyon and put his arms round him, demonstrating. 'Like this. So it's still.'

The wave became more of a weave.

'Better. Now, when you throw, you need to use your whole body, not just your arm. Your back and stomach muscles too. Tense your stomach. Use your other arm to aim.'

Edyon threw again and the harpoon went further than before but still landed harmlessly, tail first. He retrieved it and took up his position to throw again.

'Stand with your leg further forward. Use your body more. Take your time.' March moved closer, pressing his leg against Edyon's to move it forward.

Edyon froze, and March was suddenly aware of their closeness. He could feel Edyon's back pressing against his chest. He wanted to move and stay at the same time. March swallowed. 'Try again.'

Edyon's next throw was better.

'Good!' March stepped away.

'Thanks,' said Edyon. 'You're a good teacher. Do they use spears in your country?'

'In Calidor the foot soldiers use spears. Prince Thelonius is an excellent swordsman.'

'And in Abask?'

March turned his head away. 'Abask doesn't exist now.'

Edyon looked at him. 'But in the past?'

'I'm not sure.'

'I think you do know but you don't like talking about it.'

'What's the point? It's gone now.'

'What about your family? Do they serve the prince too?'

'They're all dead, Your Highness.' That shut him up. 'Shall we try aiming at that tree this time? Pretend it's a demon.'

'We can aim, March, but whether I shall hit it is another matter . . .'

By the end of the day most of Edyon's harpoons were at least landing point first, though he never did hit the tree he was aiming at.

'Well,' said Holywell, drawing out the word appraisingly. 'March and I might be able to hit a demon, if it came to it.'

'Let's hope they only attack in pairs.'

'Very funny, Your Highness.' Holywell sounded unamused. 'Did your *books* tell you if they travel in groups?'

Edyon frowned. 'Oh, hadn't I told you that, Holywell? They always come in *hordes*.'

Edyon met Holywell's gaze and, for once, didn't look away.

March realized he was smiling.

*

They made camp as they had done each day so far. First getting a fire going and then eating, sleeping and taking turns to watch for demons or bears or sheriff's men. Whoever was on guard kept the fire going. Every morning, as it got light, they boiled water for porridge and Edyon cooked the eggs, which March thought he was good at, but Holywell scoffed his share down without comment. Then they packed the things on the pony and started out. The plateau was huge and featureless; the map was no use – all they could do was keep heading west. Holywell thought it would take a week to get to Rossarb if they kept at a decent pace. And Holywell's idea of decent was tough. They stopped only at midday, for water and a snack of nuts and fruit. They collected dry wood as they walked, so that by evening there was enough for a fire.

Now March lay as close to the fire as he could, but despite his exhaustion it was hard to sleep for the biting cold. Holywell had taken the first watch and he came over and shook him.

'Your turn.' He spoke in Abask.

March sat up. He might be on guard but he wasn't going to move away from the fire. Holywell sat down close to him. 'How are you getting on with our charge?'

Edyon lay on the far side of the fire, asleep. His jacket bulged where he held the smoke bottle against his chest.

'Fine. He'll be useless in a fight, but you know that.'

'I also know that he likes you.'

March felt an uncomfortable prickling in his scalp but forced a casual shrug. 'Must be my winning personality.'

'You know what I mean. He likes men. Likes men a lot. It's not right.'

'He's the son of a prince. Princes do a lot of things that aren't right in my experience.'

Holywell spat. 'He's no prince. He's a soft, spoilt bastard, and soon he'll be a soft, spoilt prisoner. Don't get too pally with him.'

March didn't need Holywell to tell him what to do. 'I'm a servant. Why would I be pally with him?'

'Servant be damned,' hissed Holywell fiercely. 'You're an *Abask*. Remember why we're here and why he's here. We don't owe him anything. We haven't made an oath to protect him, like Thelonius did to the Abask people. We are exacting our payment for his father's treachery.'

'Yes. I know. Edyon is the son of our enemy. I'll never be his friend.'

'Or anything else.'

'Or anything else.'

Holywell patted March on the shoulder. 'Good. I'll sleep now. Make sure His Royal Highness takes his share of the watch.'

March got up and stamped his feet as he paced round the fire. He remembered the fires he used to make with his brother, and the time they had streaked their faces with soot and hunted each other through the mountains outside their village, and how they had fallen asleep together that night in their father's arms, in the fire glow of their simple home.

He looked at Edyon, his features golden in the light of the fire. Another face, another fire, another world.

All March's family were dead because of this man's father. No, he would never be Edyon's friend.

Ambrose

TORNIA,
PITORIA

In the darkness of his cell, Ambrose was thinking about his sister.
Anne would have been held in a similar cell before they executed her.
She would have been cold and alone, as he was. Perhaps she had rats
for companions too. And perhaps her fate would now be his. Would
Prince Tzsayn see him as a man of honour who had brought news
that might save his kingdom – or a rival to be rid of? Had Princess
Catherine even managed to share the news he'd risked so much to
bring her? Would she be able to get away before the invasion?

His thoughts were interrupted by the rattle of the cell door. A
soldier came in – one of Tzsayn's blue-haired men – and bowed.

'Would you kindly follow me, Sir Ambrose?'

Ambrose blinked, in surprise as much as at the sudden brightness of the soldier's lantern. This wasn't the sort of invitation
he'd been expecting. But he certainly wasn't going to let it pass.

'With pleasure.'

They climbed the winding stairway from the cold stone
dungeons to a warmer place: a room that was finely furnished with

a bed, table and chair. There were windows, but they were barred and, after the soldier left, the door was locked from the outside.

Still, Ambrose was pleased he didn't have to share this room with his friends the rats, and as he lay down on the bed he allowed the faint spark of hope within his heart to spread. This was a good sign, surely? Was it Catherine's doing somehow? Whoever was behind it, you didn't move a prisoner from the dungeon to whatever this place was if you were just planning on cutting their head off.

And yet ... the situation remained perilous. Aloysius's invasion would be starting within a few hours. And who knew what would happen to anyone when the war began! His thoughts were again interrupted by the blue-haired soldier, who opened the door to let in a visitor.

'Prince Tzsayn.' Ambrose stood and bowed.

Tzsayn sat on the chair and motioned the guard to leave. There was a long pause.

'Sir Ambrose, I must thank you for the information you have brought us.' In his scarred hand Tzsayn held the orders that Ambrose had stolen from Lord Thornlee. 'You have risked much.'

'And yet I appear to be your prisoner. Though this is a much more pleasant cell than the one I was in earlier.'

Tzsayn smiled. 'I'm sure you understand that I needed to appear firm in front of Prince Boris. And afterwards I needed to speak to Princess Catherine and find out more about you. Now I think I have your measure. So I should ask you what you wish to do. If I were to open that door, where would you go?'

Ambrose hesitated. He wanted to go to Catherine, of course, but he could hardly say that to the man to whom she was betrothed. So he said, 'I'm not sure.'

'Well,' said Tzsayn, 'you have some time to consider. I'm not going to open the door just yet.'

'So I'm still your prisoner.'

'You're my guest,' Tzsayn demurred, 'and in my home. You'll have the best food and wine. There will, however, be rather limited freedom, at least while Boris is also in my home.'

'And may I ask what you are going to do with the information I gave to the princess?'

'I'm riding north tonight with a few hundred men. More will follow.'

'Aloysius has thousands.'

'Yes, but, thanks to you, we know he's coming. Messenger birds have been sent to all the northern forts, warning them of the attack. If they can't check Aloysius at the border, they'll fall back to Rossarb. The castle there can be held by a hundred men against a thousand. The important thing is for me to get there quickly. I can't do that with a large army.'

'And what about Boris? Have you found out more about his involvement?'

Tzsayn shook his head. 'I could confront him but he'd deny everything. And it would alert him to the fact that we know their plan. He may have means of getting word to his father, and that would destroy any small advantage we may have. I assume his plan is to slip out of Tornia unnoticed during the wedding celebrations to join his forces in the north.'

'And what is *your* plan for *him*?'

'We have a watch on him and his men at all times. For the moment, that is all we can do. Until Brigantine troops cross the border, we are not at war, and he is still my guest and future brother-in-law.' Tzsayn stood to leave. 'Which reminds me – you haven't asked about the wedding.'

Ambrose couldn't help but smile. 'You're riding north to do battle with Princess Catherine's father. I assume the wedding is off.'

'Not at all. Delayed, that's all. When this war is over – if war it is to be – we will be married. Catherine has proved her loyalty to me and to Pitoria. Once I have dealt with her father, I will return and then the wedding can take place.'

'So the only thing standing between you and Princess Catherine is a war with her father.' Ambrose smiled again. 'Good luck with that.'

Catherine

TORNIA, PITORIA

The marriage of Princess Catherine to Prince Tzsayn is to benefit both Brigant and Pitoria.

Betrothal agreement between King Aloysius of Brigant and King Arell of Pitoria

Catherine had been pacing her rooms since she had told Tzsayn about the invasion. He had gone to talk to King Arell and Ambrose, and now he returned, looking pale and tired.

'What news?'

'I've spoken with my father. He thinks delaying the wedding is appropriate. It can't go ahead tomorrow.'

Catherine was less surprised by the news than by the flicker of disappointment it caused. Marriage had been her goal for so long. Now, in an instant, it was gone. She said, 'I understand.'

'Obviously it's impossible for us to marry until we know beyond doubt the truth about this invasion. Besides, there's a practical consideration – I won't be here to be married. I'm going to ride north with my troops tonight. We'll hide the fact that I have left – an announcement will be made that I am ill. My health is known to be precarious, so most people will believe it. I miss numerous engagements, though missing my own wedding is extreme, even for me.' Tzsayn gave a rueful laugh.

'Catherine, what you have done today may have saved thousands of lives. It may have saved my kingdom. My father and I are grateful beyond words. You have proved beyond any doubt that you would make a great queen of Pitoria. But you have also earned the right to make your own decision about that. Once I have dealt with your father, I will return and offer you a choice. If you wish to marry me, I will gladly honour our betrothal. If not, I will release you to do as you will. If there is another man with a greater claim on your heart, I will not stand between you.'

Catherine's mind whirled and for an instant she thought she might faint. She felt free, freer than she had ever known, and yet at the same time strangely bereft. Tzsayn's offer was extraordinary. To allow her to make her own choice – of husband, of country, of future – was beyond all her expectations. And yet, even as her heart sang out *Ambrose*, her head was full of Tzsayn and the pure and simple kindness of his words. She hadn't ever considered *wanting* to marry him, but now, for the first time, she could see what sort of husband he might be – considerate, respectful and wise – and how they might rule Pitoria together.

Faced suddenly with the prospect of a life that was entirely her own to decide, words failed Catherine. She could only nod and say, 'I understand. Thank you.'

Tzsayn nodded too, a small furrow lining the uninjured half of his brow as if he had been hoping for more. If so, he recovered quickly.

'Before I go, I wanted to ask if you can tell me anything further about what your father is planning. Why would he invade? Why in the north? Any information you have could be crucial.'

Catherine shook her head. 'I have no other information, Your Highness. I wish I did. None of it makes sense to me. For so many reasons it makes no sense. My mother has always said my father's only real ambition is to retake Calidor. That everything he does – everything – should be seen in that light. But I cannot see how this invasion might help that aim. If he wants Calidor, why waste men, money and time on a war with Pitoria? Could he just want plunder? Brigant is . . . not as wealthy as it once was. Is there anything in northern Pitoria that is of value?'

'The north is the poorest part of the country. There's nothing there but snow, trees and demons.'

'Demons.' Catherine remembered Lady Anne again. 'Demon smoke. Boys . . .' She paused. 'Could my father want to use the demon smoke in some way?'

Tzsayn shook his head. 'It relaxes you, makes you happy, makes you sleep. It's not a tool for war.'

This was just as Sir Rowland had said. 'But the demons themselves, they sound fearsome.'

'Yes, but they can't be tamed . . . can't be used in an army. Why do you ask about them?'

Catherine wanted to tell him about the execution of Lady Anne, but that would bring the subject back round to Ambrose, so she shook her head.

'Just a thought.' But her father *had* bought the smoke. Lady Anne *had* made the sign. Could she have known about the invasion? Could that be what she was warning about? In that case, though, why not make the sign for war?

'Well, perhaps the only way to find out is to ride north,' said Tzsayn. 'I must go, Catherine. My father's guards are watching Boris and his men. Boris is on a hunt this afternoon and there's a feast afterwards, but he will hear of my "illness" by tomorrow morning. I wouldn't like to guess what he will do then. He cannot wait for me to recover or he will be caught in Tornia when news of the invasion arrives. He may decide to leave and try to take you with him.'

'Whatever I do,' vowed Catherine, 'I am not going back to Brigant.'

'I am glad to hear it. My men will be outside your door at all times. If you need anything, think of anything that might help, if you need to send me a message – ask them.'

'One final question: where's Ambrose?'

'Safe and comfortable. I won't harm him.'

'I'd like to see him. He's done nothing wrong and risked much to help us.'

'He has, but he is safer kept where he and Boris won't meet. I don't want to risk another fight.'

Catherine had a feeling that was not Tzsayn's main concern, but she had no reason to demand to see Ambrose other than her desire to see him. She said, 'I'm glad you're concerned for his safety. It's his information that is helping Pitoria.'

'And for that I will always be grateful. Once Boris has departed, you may see Ambrose, with your maids present, of course.'

Catherine curtsied. 'Thank you, Your Highness.'

Tzsayn took her hand and drew her to her feet. He pressed his lips to her fingers, turned and was gone.

On the morning of the next day – her wedding day – the messages began arriving early: two from Boris, demanding to know what was happening, and one far more eloquent and polite from Sir Rowland, who, in essence, wanted to know the same thing.

Catherine sent a reply to each, saying that she had heard Tzsayn was ill and the wedding was delayed but nothing more. A short time later Sarah opened the door and said, 'Your brother is here to see you, Your Highness.'

Catherine knew this was coming, knew Boris would blame her for any delay; she just had to ensure he didn't suspect she knew of the invasion. She took a calming breath and said, 'Show him in.' But Boris was already pushing past Sarah, his face red with fury.

'What the fuck is going on?'

'Good morning, brother.'

'Don't fucking *good morning* me. This is not a fucking good morning; it's a fucking mess. Delaying the wedding – it's unheard of! I've seen Arell. He's all apologies and "you know my son has a delicate disposition". I've demanded to see Tzsayn and his bloody *delicate disposition*, but got no joy with that, of course.'

'If Tzsayn's ill, there's nothing we can do.'

'*If* being the operative word. He'd better be on his fucking deathbed.'

'Well, I'm sure it's only a delay of a few days, brother. You told me yourself that Tzsayn has physical weaknesses. King Arell has been nothing but enthusiastic since we arrived and Tzsayn himself has seemed to warm to me too.'

Boris's look changed and he eyed Catherine suspiciously. 'And yet yesterday the husband-to-be found his bride with her lover.'

'No, brother. He found me thrown to the floor and your men with their swords drawn, spoiling for a brawl in the king's home as if it was a roadside tavern.'

'Don't try to deflect the blame. What did you tell Tzsayn about Norwend?'

Catherine sighed extravagantly; she'd rehearsed this speech and needed to get it right. 'I told him the truth, of course, as we ladies must with our future husbands. I explained that Ambrose was considered a traitor in Brigant. That he had bested two of your men a few weeks ago and that you must carry the shame of that. Prince Tzsayn didn't appear to have any problem believing the truth of it.'

Boris advanced on Catherine and she stepped back. 'Going to throw me to the ground again?' she said.

He stopped and snarled, 'You haven't answered my question. What did you tell Tzsayn about why Ambrose was here? *Why was he here?*'

Catherine smiled and flicked some invisible dust from her skirt before raising her eyes to meet Boris's. 'He loves me, brother. An emotion impossible for you to understand, I know. And he wanted to see me before my wedding. Love makes men do strange things. I believe Tzsayn is falling a little in love with me too. He believes nothing has happened between me and Ambrose, except that Ambrose has declared his love. So that leads me to believe that Tzsayn has delayed the wedding either because he is genuinely ill or because he is having second thoughts about having a brother-in-law who is rapidly becoming a joke in Pitorian society.'

Catherine advanced on Boris now, pointing at him as she hissed, 'Why would I risk marriage to a prince for a love affair with a wanted man? I'm not the fool here, Boris. I've gone to great lengths to prove to the king, the prince *and* the people of Pitoria that this marriage is my heart's one true desire. If the marriage goes ahead I'll be the future queen of Pitoria; if it doesn't I'll return to Brigant in shame. I should be marrying the prince of Pitoria today; instead I'm stuck here with you!'

Boris stepped back from Catherine's tirade and she was pleased to see he was genuinely shocked. He went to the door. 'If I find this delay is because of you . . .' Then he was gone. As the door slammed behind him, Sarah, Tanya and Jane in unison gave the sign to 'Go and keep going!'

Catherine turned from them and sighed with relief. Her heart was pounding, but it certainly didn't seem as though Boris suspected that Ambrose had news of the invasion – for once she was pleased that Boris believed Ambrose was her lover.

Catherine had only just recovered herself when Sir Rowland arrived.

'I'm not sure what is happening, Your Highness. Prince Boris is furious. He insists that if the wedding doesn't go ahead today he must have assurances from Tzsayn, in person, that it will happen tomorrow.'

Because any longer than that and word of the invasion will be out, thought Catherine. *His plans are crumbling, but what will he do about it?*

'And if he doesn't get those assurances?'

'The wedding will be off. He'll leave and take you with him.'

Catherine felt weak at the thought of that. She was determined that she'd never go anywhere with Boris again.

'Well, I believe Tzsayn wants the wedding to go ahead, as does King Arell,' she said with false brightness.

'Perhaps, Your Highness. But I should tell you that there are rumours that Tzsayn is not ill but has fled the castle. Some say his men were seen leaving in the night.'

'Why would he do that? On the eve of his wedding!'

Catherine was sure her acting skills were not up to much and Sir Rowland's reply – a flat 'I don't know, Your Highness' – convinced her that he wasn't convinced. 'But, whatever is going on here, I'm concerned for you, Your Highness.'

'Thank you again, Sir Rowland. However, I'm sure the wedding will go ahead. I trust Tzsayn. Though of course I'm sad about the delay and his illness. Perhaps you can use your influence to spread a positive tone about the situation among the wedding guests, that the wedding will happen soon?'

'I'll overflow with positivity,' Sir Rowland replied with a smile. 'I shall go and spread it around.'

'Thank you.'

He turned to leave but then added, 'There is one other thing, Your Highness. I've made enquiries about the demon smoke, but I've learnt nothing new.'

Catherine smiled. 'Oh well. Perhaps it was nothing after all.'

But Catherine was sure Lady Anne's message was linked to her father's invasion. She just had to work out how.

Ambrose

TORNIA,
PITORIA

The morning after Tzsayn left, Ambrose decided to test his promise that he'd be treated well, so he asked the soldier guarding the room for food, drink, clean clothes and water to wash in. They were all brought quickly, along with soap and towels. He was even given his sword and daggers, taken from him after the fight with Boris's men. At first Ambrose was amazed his weapons had been returned – until he realized there was nothing he could do with them. If he hurt or even threatened any of Tzsayn's men, he'd have no future in Pitoria. He had no option but to stay where he was.

Tzsayn was irritatingly good at this. He was irritatingly good at a number of things, it seemed. The way he'd controlled Boris, the way he'd arrived in time to stop the fight, and – most irksome of all – the way he had helped Catherine to her feet, as if only he was entitled to do it. Tzsayn was a prince and behaved like it. He, Ambrose, was nothing in comparison: the second son of a provincial marquess. In fact, he had to remind himself, he could hardly even call himself that. He was a wanted man. A proclaimed traitor. And powerless.

But he was still a soldier. He felt that too. He'd much rather be up in the north than lying on a soft, warm bed, even if that meant fighting against Brigantines. He wasn't sure he could call himself a Brigantine any more, even if he wanted to. He was a man of no country, but that didn't mean he had no honour or no loyalties. His loyalty would always be to Princess Catherine. He could still fight for what he believed in. He could fight for her.

This should have been Catherine's wedding day, but instead it would go down in history as the day Brigant invaded Pitoria. Tzsayn would still be two days from reaching the border, but Aloysius and his thousands of men would already be on Pitorian soil. All day, Ambrose stood at the window, staring north, as if his eyes could cross the hundreds of leagues to the border and catch a glimpse of the struggle unfolding there.

I should be there, damn it, not stuck in some guest room in Tornia.

As night fell, the sound of music echoed distantly through the castle.

Ambrose knocked on the door and his guard stuck his head into the room.

'What's happening with the music?'

'Some entertainment for the wedding guests,' the guard replied, closing the door again. 'Got to keep them occupied somehow.'

Ambrose wondered what the guests were thinking. Did they believe Tzsayn was ill? Or did they imagine he'd just got cold feet? Did any of them suspect the truth – that something larger was afoot? Boris might, he supposed. Brutal and cruel the prince might be, but he was no fool. He had planned this wedding like a military operation. What would he do now it was all going wrong?

Ambrose frowned.

A military operation . . . The more he thought about it, the stranger it seemed that Boris would be such a passive player in this great invasion plan. Boris was a warrior; his place, like Ambrose's, was on the front line. And yet he had chosen to be the one to give his sister away in marriage. To sit at a feast while his father stood on the battlefield. It seemed . . . unlikely. Yes, the wedding was necessary as a diversion to get the northern lords of Pitoria away from their lands, but there was no honour in it. Not like the honour of combat. That was the honour Boris craved – the honour of spilt blood and fallen enemies.

And Noyes was here too; he was the king's spymaster, but he also had a small team of elite fighters. Why had Noyes come to Tornia? He wasn't needed for the wedding. So why could he be here?

Ambrose felt a chill settling upon him. Could there be another reason for Boris insisting that all the lords were here? So that he could make an attack on them? It would be risky – very risky – but Boris would love the idea of attacking noblemen rather than ordinary soldiers. The prestige from such a fight, from a victory, would be huge, but what would be the tactical advantage?

And suddenly Ambrose understood Boris's plan, as clearly as if the prince was whispering it into his ear: while the nobility of Pitoria gathered for the wedding of their prince, Aloysius's army would cross the border, overrunning the north, which would be unprepared with its lords absent; and then, at the very moment when decisive leadership was needed in Tornia, Boris would strike, killing King Arell, Prince Tzsayn and as many of the Pitorian lords as he could, before fleeing the city to join his father.

It was ambitious and a little insane, but what two words better described King Aloysius of Brigant?

Ambrose ran to the door, banged on it and shouted to the guard, 'I need to see the king.'

The guard opened the door and laughed. 'The prince said to get you whatever you asked for, but that might be a little difficult.'

'There's going to be an attack on the king's life.'

The guard shook his head. 'He has his guards around him. No one will get through.'

'Can you take a message to him?'

'Forget it.'

'What about taking a message to Princess Catherine?'

'One thing the prince was clear about was that you weren't to see her.'

'I don't want to see her; I want to give her a message. He didn't forbid that, did he?'

'Fine. Write her a letter.'

Ambrose made his message short and to the point.

Boris is planning to kill the king tonight. Warn him.

He handed it to the guard and said, 'Make sure she gets it immediately.'

The guard left, locking the door behind him, and Ambrose went back to his post at the window. A while later the guard returned.

'Her maid took it and said she'd give it to her. I can't do more than that, sir.'

Ambrose lay down but couldn't rest. His mind was racing. The more he thought about it, the more certain he was that tonight was the night Boris would attack. This would have been the wedding night, when everyone was drunk and tired and off their guard. But the situation had changed. There had been no wedding, not yet. Boris might wait a day if he believed the story that Tzsayn was ill and that the wedding would happen tomorrow.

Or would he?

No. Not Boris. He wouldn't delay. The schedule was set. Aloysius's army would already be at the border – there would be no time to get a message to them to tell them to wait. The lords were here, and so was the king. Boris and Noyes would have their escape plan worked out. The attack would go ahead tonight.

At that moment, Ambrose heard a shout. It was distant, muffled. Maybe someone had had too much to drink. There was another shout. Then another. Then more.

It was happening. The attack on the king.

And, to his horror, Ambrose remembered his letter to Catherine. *Boris is planning to kill the king tonight. Warn him.*

He had sent her into danger.

Ambrose grabbed his sword and banged on the door. The guard opened it with an exasperated '*What now?*' and Ambrose pulled him into the room as he leapt past, slammed the door behind him and ran towards the shouting.

Catherine

TORNIA,
PITORIA

*Killing the leader provokes chaos and fear: that's
always a good start.*

War: The Art of Winning, M. Tatcher

At sunset, Catherine retired to her bed but couldn't sleep. If all had
gone to plan, this would have been her wedding night. Instead she
was there alone, Tzsayn was riding north and Ambrose was
somewhere 'safe' in the castle. Her father was invading this peaceful
country and that had been his plan all along. She was nothing to
him, at least no more than a pawn in his game. Tomorrow was her
seventeenth birthday; it should mark the start of her new life. Well,
it certainly was going to be that, though not the one she had been
envisaging. But then she had never wanted to be married to a man
she'd never met, nor to be locked away from the world like her
mother. She thought she wanted to be loved by the people, but one
setback and she was already having doubts.

A scratch at the door and Sarah came in with a note. 'From Ambrose, Your Highness.'

Catherine almost snatched the letter from Sarah's hand.

Boris is planning to kill the king tonight. Warn him.

Catherine dressed quickly and set off with Sarah to find the king. They had to go up numerous flights of stairs to reach his apartments, which were in the largest tower of the castle.

'Princess Catherine!' said the king's chamberlain, a portly man with a waxed moustache, emerging from a side room. 'It's a rather late hour for visiting. Is something amiss?'

'I must speak with the king.' Catherine's tone was pure princess.

The chamberlain looked puzzled but bowed. 'Of course, Your Highness.'

Catherine and Sarah were ushered through to a huge marble-floored room. Large glazed doors opened on to a balcony. The king stood looking through them and out over the city of Tornia.

He turned and Catherine curtsied. King Arell looked weary but dignified.

'I owe you thanks for your information about the invasion, Princess Catherine. I apologize for not seeing you before now, but there has been much to organize.'

'And I'm afraid I have more information, Your Majesty. I believe Boris, my brother, is planning an attack on you. I –'

Before she could say more, she saw a movement on the balcony behind the king. She pointed and said, 'Are they your guards?'

The king turned as the windows behind him burst open. Four men dressed in black ran in, daggers in their hands. Catherine shouted the alarm and a moment later two of the Royal Guard rushed in through the door. But the men in black were already across the room. One assailant grabbed the king by his arm, spinning him round, and another stabbed at his back.

King Arell fell with a cry. His guards ran forward, slashing at the king's attackers with their swords, but with a splintering of glass more black-clad assassins smashed in through the windows. They swung on thin dark ropes and with a jolt of horror Catherine remembered the night on board ship during her crossing to Pitoria, when she had seen Boris's men climbing ropes in the rigging in the dark.

One of the assassins moved towards Catherine, dagger held low. She backed away, heart thumping with terror. Then, impossibly, Ambrose was beside her, sword in hand. He flashed a glance at her, long enough to check she was unharmed, then darted forward, his blade a blur as he cut down her assailant.

The king was still on the floor, blood running from his back, but more guards were pouring into the room now, and the assassins were being driven off. Catherine pressed herself into a doorway, trying to keep out of the way.

Ambrose advanced on the assassins. 'Drop your weapons.'

One of the men spat at him. 'We'd rather die, traitor. And we'll take you with us.' He rushed forward with one of his comrades. Catherine was safe in her doorway but Sarah was standing closer, frozen with fear, and one assassin stepped to her and slashed her across the neck with a dagger as he passed. She looked at Catherine and clutched her neck as blood spurted through her fingers.

Catherine screamed as Sarah's body fell to the ground, a pool of blood growing around her face. Keeping low, Catherine ran to her maid. Sarah's mouth moved but no words came, just a dribble of blood.

Ambrose sidestepped his attacker and chopped down into the man's shoulder, almost severing his arm, before whirling his sword round in a reverse sweep that took off another attacker's head.

Catherine was shaking. She felt like she might be sick. Sarah's body was pale and surrounded by a pool of dark blood. Her own hands and clothes were sticky with it. Then Ambrose was beside her, hugging her close, and then forcing her to look into his face. 'You're safe now, Your Highness. You're safe.'

'Sarah. They killed Sarah.'

'I know. I'm sorry, I'm sorry.'

She clung to his arm as more guards ran in, bending over the king and shouting for a surgeon.

'Is he alive?' she asked.

But no one answered. There were bodies everywhere Catherine looked. Purple-haired guards and black-clothed assassins. Ambrose guided her to a chair. 'You're shaking.'

They sat together as a surgeon arrived and the king was hurriedly lifted from the floor and carried into his bedchamber.

Her father had done this. Killed all these people. Killed Sarah.

Then another of the king's men arrived and took charge, ordering the bodies be removed. Ambrose wanted to look at the faces of the assassins, but he was reluctant to leave Catherine even for a few moments.

'I'm just shaken. But I know I'm safe, Ambrose. Do all you can to help.'

Catherine watched him as he walked among the bodies. How many dead were there? Too many. Again she looked over at Sarah. Catherine couldn't think at all. Couldn't get her body to move. She could only look. There was nothing else to do.

Ambrose came back to sit with her. 'Two are Noyes's men; the rest are Boris's.'

'All are my father's men. He's responsible.'

As Catherine shivered and shook, Sir Rowland arrived.

'Thank goodness you're safe, Your Highness. The Lord Chamberlain told me you were here. He said the king had been attacked.'

Sir Rowland was pale and his jacket was slashed – and not because of the Pitorian fashion. It had blood on it too.

Ambrose answered, 'Yes. The king is badly hurt. But what happened to you?'

'I was in the great hall for the feast, when men arrived dressed in black. They attacked the guests and the servants . . . anyone in their way. There are many dead. Five of the lords at the feast have been killed, twelve wounded and many servants, all unarmed. It was a massacre.' Sir Rowland had tears in his eyes.

Catherine swallowed hard. 'Tzsayn and I were meant to be in that room. It should have been our wedding banquet. Do you think they'd have tried to kill Tzsayn if he was here?'

Sir Rowland nodded grimly. 'I do, Your Highness.'

'They would have killed me too then.' Her father and her brother.

'Boris probably intended to take you back to Brigane.'

Catherine shook her head. 'No. They had no thought for me at all. Me or my maids.'

Catherine stood as Ambrose backed respectfully away. She'd known Sarah for six years. Sarah – the most sensible, most reasonable, most calm of her maids – had been cut down like an animal. Suddenly she wanted to be far from that room, safe with Jane and Tanya.

Sir Rowland said, 'The assailants were all Boris's and Noyes's men. None have been caught alive.'

'And Boris?'

'There's a search out for him, his men and Noyes. If they are clever, and Noyes is nothing if not clever, they will already be out of the city and on their way to the coast. This was all well planned; they'll have their escape route thought through.'

Catherine turned to Ambrose. 'And this attack confirms that the invasion in the north is true.'

'What?' asked Sir Rowland.

Ambrose briefly explained. 'This – all this – the wedding, everything, is a diversion. Aloysius is invading Pitoria even as we speak. That is why Tzsayn left.'

Sir Rowland shook his head. 'Why am I surprised?'

'Fortunately Tzsayn is unhurt, and riding north to repel the invasion,' said Ambrose. 'Many of the lords are still alive too, and with luck the king will survive.'

'But if he doesn't –' Sir Rowland looked at Catherine – 'you will be in great danger, Your Highness.'

'I'm already in danger. I came here with Boris,' Catherine said, her voice low and furious. 'I brought him and fifty other assassins *into the royal palace*. If the king dies, I will be blamed. People will think I was party to the plan. I've won many people over but I'll lose all that favour faster than I gained it if there's a war with my father. We must go to Tzsayn. We'll only be safe with him.'

'Run, you mean?' Ambrose looked concerned. 'But they will think you're guilty.'

'Everything I've done makes me look guilty. For now, I need to be with Tzsayn.'

'He'll be halfway to Rossarb. It's a long, hard ride.'
'I can ride well enough. You know that.'
'And your maids? They'll not be safe here either.'
Catherine nodded. 'We all go.'

March

NORTHERN PLATEAU, PITORIA

Holywell was in a foul mood and he was forcing the pace. They had covered little distance over the last few days as they crossed a flat expanse of icy rock riddled with gaps. Some gaps were narrow enough to step over, others were not, and all that could be done was to go along, or back, until a way through could be found. The wind was harsher and colder. Thankfully they were now in the shelter of the thin trees, but they had been five days on the plateau, food was running low and the cold was relentless.

'Look!' March pointed to a large fallen tree just to their left. It was dead and rotting, with broken branches scattered around. Most of the wood was dry and perfect for the fire. He called to Holywell, 'There's plenty of wood here. We can load the pony up.'

Holywell, who was leading the pony, didn't even turn, but muttered something to Edyon.

Edyon hesitated, then ran over to March.

'What did he say?' March asked.

'Something about the noise carrying and that if you didn't stop shouting he'd use you for harpoon practice.'

March hadn't shouted very loud, but sound did seem to carry a long way here in the still air.

'And I think he wants me to do the job of the pony.' Edyon smiled.

'We're all supposed to stay together and we're all supposed to collect wood.' March set his harpoon down. He said, 'If you load up my arms with the bigger pieces, then bring the harpoons, Your Highness, we'll have enough wood for tonight.'

Though if Holywell had stopped, they would have had enough for two nights.

Edyon piled the wood up to March's chin and asked, 'More?'

'Yes. Thank you, Your Highness.'

'I wish you wouldn't keep calling me that, March. We're travelling companions and fugitives from the law together.' Edyon picked up a couple of branches and the harpoons. 'And wood collectors.'

March half smiled. 'But I am a servant and you are the son of a prince.'

'Yet hardly princely material.' Edyon sighed. 'What do you think my father will make of me?'

'You're his son. I'm sure he'll see your strengths.' March thought this was probably true. Though Edyon seemed naive, he was also intelligent, charming and patient. March had had to wait on many worse gentlemen.

Anyway, said the hard voice in his head, *he'll never meet his father, so what does it matter?*

March slowed to let Edyon go ahead, so that he could avoid continuing the conversation, and that's when he thought he felt something.

He stopped. *What* was *that?*

He took a step back.

And then another.

The something he felt was warmer.

The forest was cold and still, but here it definitely felt warmer. He looked up, wondering if the sun had broken through the clouds, but it was as overcast as ever. He was in a small natural clearing and he was standing at the bottom of a slight hollow in the ground. Edyon was well ahead now. March wanted to call to him, but shouting wasn't a good thing. He looked around, trying to work out if anything else was different, and a piece of wood began to slide from the top of his pile. March tilted it to try to prevent it from falling, but his arms were tired, the wood was heavy, and it fell to the ground. March bent his knees, keeping his back straight, but as he fumbled for it another piece fell, and as he swung the pile round the rest of it toppled out of his arms.

He looked up. Edyon had stopped and was watching him. March swore. He held his arms open to indicate *this is ridiculous* and then bent down to retrieve the wood – and felt the warmth again, but stronger now, on his face and hands. He put his palm on the ground, and was surprised to find it was as warm as skin. And it seemed like the ground had a glow to it, a red tinge to the earth and dead leaves.

He looked up at Edyon and wanted to tell him. But tell him what? And then he realized.

The red tinge. The warmth.

'Oh shits.'

March looked up at Edyon and didn't know if he should shout or run or stay still. In the end, he moved slowly, almost tiptoeing out of the hollow, and when he was clear of it he ran to Edyon, grabbed him by the arm and dragged him along, saying, 'Let's get away from here.'

'What is it?' Edyon was going slowly and looking back.

'I don't know but I think it might be something to do with demons.'

Edyon picked up his pace and ran.

Holywell had stopped a short distance ahead and was looking at them.

'What's up? Where's the wood?'

'I think there are demons here,' March blurted.

Holywell looked around. March did too. And so did Edyon. Everything was as still and silent as ever.

'Demons or not, we need to keep moving.' Holywell nodded to the rock face to his right. 'This place is too enclosed.'

Edyon pointed to the rocks, eyes wide. 'Something just moved there. Something red.'

March snatched his harpoon back from Edyon, his eyes fixed on the rocks, but he saw no movement. No sign of any demon.

Holywell muttered, 'March, keep your eyes behind us. We're going to keep going, but slow.' He had his harpoon held back, ready to throw. 'Stay alert. And stay close.'

March did as he was told, his heart racing.

They'd only gone a few paces when Edyon shouted, 'There!'

March spun and Holywell was unleashing his harpoon at a figure who'd stepped out from behind a tree. The man dodged. Holywell didn't. And suddenly there was a spear in his chest, the dripping point poking out of his back.

Edyon yelped as Holywell dropped to his knees. The weight of the spear pulled him forward and he fell on to his side. Unmoving. Dead.

March looked up to the rock face as a second spear came towards him. Then Edyon slammed into him, knocking him out of the weapon's path. March staggered and raised his harpoon. One man was standing on the top of the rocks; the other – the one Holywell had seen – was down at his level. They both had scarlet hair and were holding long knives. The one on the rocks jumped down and they both moved forward.

March backed away. These were sheriff's men, excellent shots with their spears and probably good fighters with their knives.

'Stay near me. Don't let them get close,' he said to Edyon quietly.

'H-Holywell's dead.'

'Yes.'

'What do we do?'

'I'm trying to think. They haven't got any more spears. If we stay together, we look stronger. Hold your harpoon up.'

'Yes. I won't run. I'll stay with you.'

'It's two against two. We have harpoons. Make them count.'

The men were approaching slowly. March knew his chances of hitting them with his harpoon were low, and Edyon's were, well . . . Still, he said, 'You can do it, Edyon. Remember how we practised.'

'This is crazy,' said Edyon. 'I can't throw.' And he dropped his harpoon.

'*What? No!*'

Edyon took a step forward, arms in the air, saying quietly to March, 'You throw. I'll talk.'

Edyon

NORTHERN PLATEAU,
PITORIA

Edyon knew that he couldn't fight. He couldn't hit one of these men with a harpoon even if they stood still directly in front of him. He couldn't throw, but he could talk.

'I'm Edyon. Son of Prince Thelonius of Calidor.' He opened his jacket and pulled out his gold neck-chain. 'This is proof of who I am and who my father is. If you attack me, you attack Calidor.'

The men stopped and looked uncertain. The older one said, 'You're wanted for murder, whoever your father is.'

'I've murdered no one. Nor has my man, March. And yet we have been attacked by you without warning.'

'You're in forbidden territory. I don't need to give warnings, but I'll give you this one now: if you don't surrender, we'll attack again. Get your man to drop his weapon.'

'So that you can kill us like you've killed my other servant? I think not. Perhaps you can lower your weapons first. As a sign of goodwill.'

The older man shook his head. Thick scars traced his jaw; he didn't look the kind of man to show or expect leniency. 'That will not happen, sir. I'm here with the sheriff's authority. But if you are who you say you are, and you come with us peaceably, perhaps the sheriff will look kindly on you.'

'I'm not interested in the sheriff's kindness. We are innocent of murder.'

'Well, if we stay like this we'll all freeze to death.'

The leader motioned to the other man and they began to move forward again.

March threw his harpoon at the younger man, but he rolled to the side and the harpoon landed in the earth behind him. March immediately snatched up Edyon's harpoon. The older man was now running at Edyon, arms pumping, knives glinting. Edyon retreated as swiftly as he could, but the sheriff's man was too fast and too close. March came between them, swinging his harpoon at the running man. It all happened so quickly.

The running man veered, but March sidestepped in the same direction and the harpoon plunged into the scarred man's side. He was still moving; March moved round with him, impaling the man further on to the barbs, but also driving him towards Edyon, who tripped and stumbled backwards. The scarred man stopped and wavered, then fell sideways, his blood spreading out and sinking into the snow.

But even as relief washed over him Edyon heard a strange, terrible screech. He looked up and saw the younger man, armed with two knives, coming at March, who was now unarmed and backing away to Edyon's left. But the screech came from a red figure that was running out of the trees from the right, faster than a charging bull.

The demon, for that's what it had to be, bowled into the sheriff's man, tossing him into the air like a child. It turned in an instant and, as the sheriff's man fell heavily to the ground, the demon pounced on him, gripping the man's head, twisting and wrenching until it ripped from the body with a sickening crunch. The demon tossed the head into the air, spinning scarlet drops of blood. Then it turned to March and screamed.

March stood frozen. He had no weapon, no chance.

The demon stepped towards March. Edyon had to do something.

'No!' Edyon shouted. 'No! No!'

And he ran, flapping his arms, at the demon.

The demon turned to Edyon and stood to its full height. It was huge.

'Oh shits,' Edyon murmured, skidding to a halt.

The demon sprang towards him. It was stunningly fast and Edyon knew he was about to die. The demon leapt and Edyon fell over backwards, tripping over his own feet as the creature surged through the air –

And was taken in the chest by a harpoon.

The impact of the blow knocked the demon sideways, and its huge body landed heavily in the snow beside Edyon.

I'm alive! I'm still alive!

The demon screamed again, pulling the harpoon free and staggering to its feet.

'Fuck! Fuck!' Edyon scrambled back.

Another harpoon flew from the trees and struck the demon's stomach. And then another caught it in the chest again, bowling it over. This time it didn't get up.

'Thank fuck! Thank fuck!'

A big man – *Gravell!* – a harpoon in each hand, ran out of the woods and stood over the demon as if waiting to see if it was going to move again. The girl appeared too. She took the harpoons from Gravell and he took a bottle out of his jacket.

March took a step towards his harpoon, but Gravell merely said, 'If you pick that up, you're a dead man.'

March went still. He looked over to Edyon, who was trying to get up but his legs wouldn't move. He'd nearly died. Nearly died twice. And lying on the ground before him was a demon. And – *Oh fuck! Oh fuck!* – he was still alive.

Gravell and the girl crouched down over the demon, as if waiting for something. Then a wisp of pink smoke started to rise out of the demon's mouth and into the upturned bottle that Gravell held. The wisp grew thicker, becoming redder and then purple and orange. Soon the bottle was full of swirling smoke, but more and more seemed to pour out of the demon and none escaped. It was as if the bottle was sucking the smoke up.

Finally the flow became paler and thinner and then there was no more. Gravell put a stopper in the bottle, kissed the glass and handed it to the girl. He pulled one of his harpoons from the demon's body and walked towards Edyon.

Tash

NORTHERN PLATEAU,
PITORIA

It was a mess. Three men were dead and now Gravell was advancing on Edyon.

March took another step towards his fallen harpoon.

Tash warned him, 'If you try to get the harpoon, you'll only make Gravell madder. All we want is our smoke back.'

'No,' Gravell snarled, 'that's not all we want. I want my demon smoke back and I want his balls on a platter.' Gravell pointed at Edyon.

'I've seen them, Gravell, and I honestly don't think I'd bother,' Tash said.

'This isn't a joke, girl. He's a thief. He needs to be punished.'

Edyon held out his hands placatingly. 'Gravell, sir, I am truly sorry I stole your demon smoke. If you want to kill me I can't stop you, but I suggest you do it quickly because I think I might be about to die of shock anyway.'

Gravell didn't move and Edyon continued in the most pathetic voice Tash had ever heard. 'I know it was wrong, and I have sworn that I will not steal again. I'm a changed man.'

'You mean you've given up thieving and moved on to murder,' said Gravell, gesturing to the bodies of Holywell and the sheriff's men.

'We were only defending ourselves, sir. We are not violent men.' Edyon struggled shakily to his feet. 'I'd like to make amends for the trouble I've caused you.'

Tash said, 'Perhaps if we had the smoke back, that might reassure Gravell of your good intentions.'

'It's in the pack on the back of the pony.'

Gravell snorted. 'What pony?' And, sure enough, there was no pony to be seen. Tash knew there had been one, though; they'd followed its tracks for the last five days. Gravell knew it too but seemed determined to make Edyon wet his pants.

Edyon looked around, flustered. 'It must have run off when the fighting started, but it won't have gone far,' he pleaded.

'Tash, go and find this pony – if it exists. I'll watch our two thieving murderers.'

'We can look together,' Edyon said.

'Tash can look. You can get on your knees and wait.'

Tash ran off and quickly found the pony tracks and, only fifty paces further on, the pony itself, quietly rubbing its haunches on a stunted tree. She approached it cautiously but it was more tired than afraid and she stroked it and spoke to it a little. In its pack was the demon smoke. The bottle still looked full of swirling purple smoke, but from the weight she could tell there was only about half left and she grimaced. She wasn't sure how Gravell would react to this latest development.

She led the pony back. Edyon and March were kneeling in front of Gravell, their hands held in the air. Gravell loomed over them like a mountain, arms folded round a harpoon, two more beside him with their points in the ground.

'I've found the pony,' Tash said, and immediately felt foolish as that was rather obvious.

'What about the smoke?' Gravell asked.

Tash held up the bottle.

'How much is left?'

'Umm, maybe half.'

'*Half?*' Gravell roared.

Edyon yelped. 'I used it to help March. He was wounded.'

'What do you mean, *help March*?'

'The smoke, sir. I used it to heal him.'

'Is everything that comes out of your mouth a lie, boy?' Gravell said this as he swung the harpoon so that the wood hit Edyon's arm. Edyon screamed in pain.

March started to get up and Gravell landed a backhand slap that sent him reeling, blood dripping from his nose.

'If you move again without my say-so, next time I'll use a harpoon. Get back on your knees.'

March spat on the ground and stared up at Gravell with venom, but he did as he was told.

Tash ran forward. 'Hurting them won't bring the smoke back.'

'Maybe not, but it's making me feel better.'

Gravell jabbed the butt of the harpoon into Edyon's shoulder. 'You stole my smoke, dragged me halfway across the country and got me tangled up with the sheriff's men. I need repaying. Fifty kroners for the smoke you stole and fifty kroners for my trouble.'

'We'll pay you for the smoke we've used and nothing more,' March snapped. 'Twenty-five kroners.'

It was the first time Tash had heard him speak. His accent was strange, not like anything she'd heard before.

'And you have twenty-five kroners? Not that I'm accepting it's enough.'

'We'll get it.' March stared such an evil stare that she thought Gravell might hit him again.

'I have money. I have money.' Edyon spread his arms. 'Not fifty kroners, but you can take what I have.' He rummaged in his coat and pulled out his purse.

Gravell took it and tipped the money out. 'There's not even ten kroners here.' He shook his head.

Edyon said, 'Fine. Fine. You can have this.' And he pulled a gold neck-chain from beneath his jacket. 'It's worth a hundred kroners at least.'

'No,' March said. 'Not that. He can't have that. Holywell has money. And his knives are worth a lot. You can have them. Not the chain.'

Tash went to look at the gold chain. It was beautiful but she knew they shouldn't take it. She remembered that Edyon hadn't taken it off, even in the bath. It obviously meant more than just its weight in gold. The smoke wasn't of personal value to Gravell. It wasn't fair. She went back to Gravell and spoke quietly.

'We don't need the chain. We can sell the knives in Rossarb. We'll get a good price for them there. Really this is a good deal. We have the knives, what's left of the smoke they stole and this other bottle. You've not even had to dig a pit.'

'I like digging the pit.'

Tash tried hard not to sigh. 'Well, we can come back after Rossarb and you can dig the best pit ever. By then we'll be well fed and rested thanks to the money from all this smoke. Then we can head back to Pravont, repay Flint and eat as many pies as we can. Sounds like a good summer to me.'

Gravell rolled his shoulders. 'I'm taking the chain *and* the knives.'

'You always told me not to be greedy.'

'I'm not being greedy. I'm taking something he really values. It's the chain or his balls.'

Tash rolled her eyes. 'Fine. Fine. Take the chain.'

Gravell turned back to Edyon and March. 'It's your lucky day, boys. Tash here wants me to let you live. I'm taking the knives and the gold chain.'

'No!' March shouted, rising again, and Gravell ripped a harpoon from the ground and struck him so hard across the head with the shaft that March collapsed.

'The foreign boy can speak; shame he can't listen.'

Tash took the knives from Holywell and the sheriff's men. It didn't feel good. She'd never stolen from people before and this felt like stealing. Edyon was still on his knees and handing over his gold chain to Gravell, who put it in his jacket with hardly a glance. Edyon turned back to March, who was unconscious on the ground.

Within no time she and Gravell were setting off west. Moving fast. Leaving the boys with the pony. They'd probably survive, Tash told herself. But she felt bad. She'd never felt bad about anything she'd done before. She followed Gravell and said nothing.

Late in the afternoon Gravell turned to her, saying, 'You're quiet.'

Tash didn't reply.

They carried on, but before long Gravell stopped and said, 'Out with it.'

Tash stopped too. 'What?'

'Something's bothering you. Spit it out.'

'You know what it is. We shouldn't have taken the gold chain or the knives. You've always told me not to be greedy, but that's greed, taking them.'

'It's not greed; it's teaching them a lesson.'

'And making a lot of money in the process. Very convenient. Well, if you can be greedy, so can I. The pie man in Dornan pays better than you. I'm going to work for him after this.'

'The pie man, *not greedy*? He's as fat as a pig.'

'Food is different to gold chains and knives.'

Gravell shook his head. 'Greed is greed. You want me to show you how ungreedy I am? Watch this!' And he threw the gold chain and the knives on to the ground. 'There. I don't want them. I just don't want those boys to have them.'

Tash stared at the chain and knives.

'Well? Is that all right with you, missy?'

Tash wanted to hug Gravell, but she just smiled at him and said, 'It's better. But the gold chain belongs to Edyon. He should have it.'

She bent down to pick the chain up. The complex swirl of gold in the pendant was beautiful and now she saw that it was a ring contained within thorns.

'Well, if you're suggesting I go back and return it to him you're asking just a bit too much.'

Tash put the chain in her empty leather purse and tied it in her special hiding place, among the dreadlocks at the back of her neck. 'I'll find a way of returning it to him one day.'

March

NORTHERN PLATEAU, PITORIA

March woke to cold and a throbbing head and it took a moment for him to remember what had happened. Gravell had hit him. Hard. Twice. He felt his head and found a large lump. It wasn't bleeding but his hair was matted and wet. He sat up.

'Take it slowly,' said Edyon's voice. 'I put snow on your head where he hit you. I'm not sure if it was the right thing to do.'

'I'll be fine. Thank you,' March croaked.

Edyon was sitting beside him. The pony was tied to a tree, but there was no sign of Gravell or the girl.

'Have they gone?'

'Yes,' said Edyon, handing March his water bottle. 'They left us with the pony. There's food in the bags. I was about to start a fire, but now you're awake I think we should get out of here, if you can walk. I don't know if one demon means more demons, but there are the bodies too. It's not a great place.'

March got to his feet. He felt a little light-headed, but mainly he was cold. 'Which way?'

'They went west. I think they'll be going to Rossarb. If we follow their tracks they should lead us there. And hopefully they'll kill any demons in our path.'

It sounded sensible. March didn't have a better idea and going back the way they'd come might lead them to more of the sheriff's men.

'I'd like to bury Holywell, but we don't have a spade and the ground is frozen solid,' Edyon said.

'He wouldn't care. He might even prefer to be left in the open.' March went over to Holywell's body.

It could easily have been March with a spear in his chest. March pulled the spear out and rolled Holywell over. His eyes were open, the icy blue even paler than when he was alive. March dropped to his knees, wondering if he really was the last of the Abasks now.

Edyon came over and said, 'I'm sorry about Holywell. I know he didn't think much of me, but no man should die like that.'

March nodded. He took a breath and moved closer to Holywell and felt his body, looking for anything of value, anything that might be useful. Gravell had taken Holywell's knives and money, but there was a thin silver chain round his neck with a crescent moon hanging from it, the old symbol of Abask.

'Should we send that to his relatives?' Edyon asked. 'I mean, does he have a wife or children?'

'No. He was alone.' March took the chain. 'I think he'd want me to have it. I might take it to Abask for him. Bury it there.'

'That would be good. He was a hard man, but I'm sure he'd appreciate your kindness. You'll miss him?'

March nodded. 'He was a true Abask. We were brothers. Yes, I'll miss him.'

And what do I do now, brother? What do I do with the prince's son? This boy who healed me when I was hurt? Who trusts me? Who makes me feel –

March rubbed his face hard. Holywell had kept his own plans to himself. All March knew was that they were to take a ship from Rossarb to deliver Edyon to Brigant. But which ship? Sailing to which port? And who was the master Holywell had mentioned? All the knowledge he needed was locked inside Holywell's head, gone forever. He needed a new plan.

One thing hadn't changed – it was freezing cold on the plateau. They needed to get to Rossarb as quickly as possible. He could work out what to do on the way.

He could do that, but he could do no more for Holywell. He didn't even want to cover his face or close his eyes. He thought Holywell would prefer to be looking at the sky.

'You're right, Your Highness – we should get moving. Gravell will probably travel fast.'

March took a last look around to see if there was anything else to take. He went over to the demon. It was a red and orange colour and quite magnificent, even dead.

'He's beautiful, isn't he?' Edyon said as he came to stand by March. 'I thought I was going to die.' Edyon's voice was serious. 'I've never . . . I mean, I travel with my mother buying and selling furniture. This is all new to me.'

'I've spent all my years as a servant to a prince, pouring his wine and running his bath. It's new to me too.' March hesitated but then had to say it. 'You distracted the demon. It would have killed me if you hadn't done that. It was brave of you. Thank you, Your Highness . . . Edyon.'

Edyon's face lit up with a smile that warmed March's heart.

'I'm sure you'd have done the same for me. You certainly stood up to Gravell, not that it made any difference in the end.'

March wasn't sure what he'd have done if the circumstances had been swapped. But he hated that Gravell had taken Edyon's chain and the prince's ring, the proof of who Edyon was. March knew what it was like to be cut off from your own past.

'Let's collect some of that wood. We'll need it later.' March led the pony back to the hollow where he'd dropped the branches. It looked different somehow. He couldn't see the red glow any more, but he felt the earth and it was still warm.

Edyon was watching him and March said, 'I think this is where the demon came from. I don't know how. Before it had a red glow. That's gone now.'

'You don't think there are more of them here?'

March shrugged. 'I'd guess they live alone. For all his strength and prowess with a harpoon, even Gravell wouldn't want to take on more than one demon at once.'

'I didn't really believe in demons,' Edyon said. 'Even when I used their smoke I didn't believe in them. They're too incredible. And even after seeing one, nearly being killed by one, I'm still not sure what to think.'

'It's because they're from another place. From in there.' March pointed at the ground.

They collected the wood and set off at a steady pace. March's head was swollen and the cold was as biting as ever, but he was sure that if they followed Gravell's tracks they'd reach Rossarb. They might get cold and hungry along the way but they'd cope with that.

But then what?

He could take Edyon to Brigant and try to deliver him to Aloysius himself but . . . how could he do that to Edyon now?

He had saved March's life. March's thirst for revenge on Thelonius had never wavered, but betraying a man who'd risked his own life to save yours wasn't right. No, he couldn't take Edyon to Aloysius.

So then what?

Perhaps letting Edyon return to his father was the best revenge on Thelonius – the great warrior would get a son who couldn't fight. But March knew he was doing a disservice to Edyon. He was braver and more principled than most of the lords he'd come across.

March was not like Holywell. He didn't know the world – he had never left Calidor. He had no friends, no one to turn to for help. Now even Holywell was gone. March felt the chain with its crescent moon inside his glove and made a promise to Holywell.

I'm sorry, brother. I can't betray Edyon. But I will get our revenge on Thelonius, for you and all of Abask. I will not fail our people.

Catherine

TORNIA,
PITORIA

In summary, avoid being captured at all costs.
War: The Art of Winning, M. Tatcher

'Gather your things. We're leaving,' Catherine told her maids as she entered her chambers.

Ambrose and Catherine had left King Arell's rooms, marching quickly through the castle, which was in uproar, though no one hindered them. Sir Rowland went to arrange for horses to be prepared.

Tanya and Jane had locked the door, forcing Ambrose to knock three times before they would open it. Now they stood in the sitting room, faces pale.

'But where to, Your Highness?' Jane asked. 'Not back to Brigant?'

'No, never back there,' Catherine replied. 'Boris and his men have attacked King Arell and many other lords. Some are dead.

The king is badly injured. We are in danger here. Ambrose is going to take us north to Prince Tzsayn. He will protect us.'

But will he? His own father, stabbed by my brother's men . . .

Catherine forced her doubts away, only to be confronted with the question she had been dreading.

'Where's Sarah?'

For an instant, Catherine couldn't find the words. Then she forced them out, her voice cracking.

'Boris's men killed her.'

Jane's hands flew to her mouth. 'But . . . why would they do that?'

Ambrose shook his head. 'Because they care nothing for others.'

'Because they're Boris's men,' Tanya said furiously. 'And Noyes's men too, no doubt.'

'They're all my father's men. He is the source of all this death,' Catherine said. 'But we are no longer with my father, nor with Brigant. We're with Pitoria, King Arell and Prince Tzsayn, and the better for it.' She did believe that – she had to believe it. 'And so we must go to the prince. There's no time for us to grieve. We must be strong. Sarah would want that.'

Tanya and Jane got straight to work and made small packs of clothes for Catherine and themselves. Catherine made sure she had her jewellery. With no coin to speak of, she knew they might need it to trade with on the journey.

A short time later Sir Rowland returned with a man with white hair and one of the blue-haired guards the prince had allocated to her before he left.

Sir Rowland introduced the men, saying, 'Geratan and Rafyon will help us leave the city and make our way north to join Prince Tzsayn.'

Rafyon bowed and reassured Catherine by saying, 'We will go with you wherever you go, Your Highness. Prince Tzsayn said that we were to protect you, and it's not safe here for you now. There's myself and my nine men, and Geratan and his troop.'

At this, the white-haired man stepped forward. He was tall and slim and powerfully built, and Catherine recognized him as one of the dancers who had accompanied her on her progress to the city. He bowed elegantly.

'We dyed our hair to show our allegiance, Your Highness. We still have white hair; we are still your men.'

Catherine could hardly believe it. 'You know that Boris, my brother, has killed many Pitorians?'

Geratan nodded. 'We know, Your Highness. And we all know Prince Boris for a cruel and proud man. We saw his behaviour on our journey here. And we saw yours. Your kindness to the people, your interest in our ways. We know you are not like your brother. Prince Tzsayn wishes you to be safe and so do we.'

Catherine again felt tears fill her eyes, but this time they were tears of gratitude.

'However,' Sir Rowland said, 'everyone knows that Boris is responsible for the attack and some of the lords are saying that you must be involved. In the prince's absence, Lord Farrow has taken charge. For the moment all he has done is to forbid you, your maids and myself from leaving the city. But if the king dies Farrow will take the law into his own hands before Tzsayn can return.'

'Farrow hates me. He's always seen me as a Brigantine warmonger.' It was as she had feared, but at least she could now be certain she was making the right choice in leaving. 'We're ready to go.'

Rafyon nodded. 'Good. I have horses waiting outside the castle. There is a tunnel, known only to a few people. It's used by the prince on occasion to escape the court undetected when His Highness is . . . unwell.'

Catherine smiled. 'When he's bored, you mean? It sounds perfect.'

'We must be swift. I will lead. Geratan will stay at the rear.'

Tanya put Catherine's cloak over her shoulders, then she and Jane picked up their bags. Catherine took one last look at her room, wondering if she'd ever return. Even in their haste, the irony did not escape her. For so long she had dreaded the journey to meet Tzsayn. Now she was flying to him. It was the only way she and her maids would be safe now.

They set off, not creeping along as Catherine had imagined, but walking swiftly and boldly, cutting through rooms and side doors, keeping to the quieter corridors, meeting only two servants, who stepped smartly to the side.

They went to the terrace where Catherine had first spoken to Tzsayn. That was only two days ago but felt like years. Once outside, Rafyon went ahead to check the route was clear. They waited in silence. Ambrose stood close to Catherine, protecting her, she realized, with his body. She wasn't sure it was necessary but she couldn't deny it felt good to be close to him. Tanya and Jane were holding hands. They both looked pale and terrified. Catherine signed *Strong* and Tanya forced a smile.

Rafyon appeared at the far side of the terrace and beckoned them, and once again they were moving, but faster now, almost running through the paths of the rose garden to the water garden, then down steep stone steps to a wooden door hidden behind the branches of a large bush. Sir Rowland went ahead and Ambrose grasped Catherine's hand as the darkness of the tunnel hid them. Rafyon lit a lantern but, apart from a faint glow showing how low the stone roof was, it didn't much help them find their way. Luckily the floor was smooth and even, paved it seemed, but also descending more and more steeply.

Catherine tripped on Ambrose's boots and he said, 'It's easier if we walk side by side.' He put his arm round her shoulder, pulling her to his body. Catherine had never felt a man so close to her, and her pulse quickened even more.

Within a few moments they stepped out into a cobbled alley. Sir Rowland turned and seemed surprised to see Ambrose holding Catherine, but before he could say anything Ambrose suddenly pushed Catherine away from him with a cry of alarm.

Two men in black jumped down from the wall above, one landing on Rafyon and the other on Ambrose. The four men tumbled to the ground in a tangle of limbs. Catherine pressed herself against the wall by the tunnel entrance, backing into Tanya and Jane. Sir Rowland pulled a long knife from his jacket and, with surprising speed and strength, stabbed the man grappling with Ambrose.

Rafyon rolled to the side and his assailant stood, saw that his comrade was dead and scrambled back up the wall he'd jumped from. He twisted to face Catherine and threw one of his knives. Tanya yanked Catherine back into the tunnel as it clattered against the wall where she'd just been standing. Then she heard a cry of pain. She hoped it was the assailant but could see that Sir Rowland had dropped to his knees.

Catherine clung to Tanya, and Ambrose was beside her, eyes wide. 'I thought he'd got you. I thought . . .'

'But what of Sir Rowland?'

Rafyon was with him and he looked up at Ambrose and shook his head. Catherine went to the ambassador and knelt beside him, taking his hand, but his eyes were already fixed and still.

Rafyon was looking up the wall. 'One of them got away, Geratan. See if you can catch him. We'll wait here.'

Geratan nodded, quickly scaled the wall and disappeared.

They waited in silence. Jane was crying and holding on to Tanya. Catherine remained bent over Sir Rowland's body. Another wasted life. A man of kindness and wisdom destroyed by her father.

When Geratan returned, jumping lightly down into the alley, he shook his head. 'I caught a glimpse of him, far ahead of me. I couldn't catch him. He's gone.'

Rafyon turned to Catherine. 'We must go on. It's not far to the horses. I'm sorry, but we must leave Sir Rowland's body here. There's nothing we can do for him now.'

Catherine nodded. There would be time to mourn him later. Ambrose again grasped her hand and they ran after Rafyon. They went down one alley after another, twisting and turning until all sense of direction was lost. Catherine's heart was beating so hard she thought she'd collapse, but she forced herself on and they turned into a courtyard – and there were the horses!

With them stood more men, some with the blue hair of the prince's guard and an equal number with white hair. Ambrose swept Catherine into his arms and carried her the last ten paces; she clung to him and looked over his shoulder, realizing that they were now well outside the castle walls, its great central tower high but distant. Ambrose lifted her on to her mount, and she had to let him go.

He leapt on to his own horse. 'Stay close to me, Your Highness. We don't stop for anything.' And he set off fast.

Catherine looked quickly around. Jane and Tanya were already mounted, so Catherine kicked her horse and they raced after Ambrose, clattering down the street, the blue-haired soldiers shouting for people to make way.

Catherine was exhausted. She was used to riding but not like this. Tanya and Jane had not said a word of complaint, but Catherine knew they must be feeling as bad as she was. The soldiers had been trying to keep the ladies' spirits up with encouraging tips – 'Try to relax a little' and 'No need to grip so hard'. Timid Jane never replied, but Tanya struck up a conversation and was disappointed that the men didn't know the name of her horse, so she called it Boris. One of the soldiers laughed and said, 'It's a mare.'

'Yes, but if I call her Boris I don't feel so bad when I kick her.'

It was well after midnight when Rafyon called a halt. Bone-weary, the fugitives dismounted from their equally tired horses with barely enough energy to build a small fire and share a few mouthfuls of bread.

Afterwards, Tanya, Jane and Catherine lay down and rested. Catherine looked to Ambrose and he caught her eye, but then turned away to answer Rafyon. Catherine watched them talk. Ambrose's hair half hid his face, which was serious for the most part but then broke into a smile at something Rafyon said.

Catherine forced herself to close her eyes. She shouldn't spy on Ambrose; she was riding to meet Prince Tzsayn. But despite their exhausting journey Catherine couldn't sleep, her mind too full of the day's events, Sir Rowland dead and the assassins in black waiting for her – or were they waiting for Prince Tzsayn? She was sure that Noyes was behind it. The dead man was one of his, and finding out about Prince Tzsayn's secret tunnel and lying in wait at the end of it was more Noyes's style than Boris's.

Not wanting to think of it any more, she lay silently, hoping for sleep, half listening to the men talk about the attack on the castle and their escape. She was drifting off when one of Rafyon's men called out, 'Sir Ambrose! We hear you're close to being the perfect soldier. But it's obvious to us that you've got just one glaring fault.'

Ambrose asked, 'What's that?'

There was jeering, as if Ambrose should know. Catherine braced herself, assuming they would say it was that he was Brigantine.

'What's his problem, boys?' called Rafyon.

The men chorused back, 'His hair's not blue!'

Catherine smiled and slept.

Ambrose

WEST COAST ROAD, PITORIA

The second day on the road north from Tornia, they came to the first roadblock. The soldiers changed position to ensure Catherine and her maids were protected on all sides, and Ambrose rode forward with Rafyon to find out what was happening. He assumed the checkpoint was to stop Boris, though in truth it didn't look like it could stop very much at all: there were two men at the barrier, which was merely a pole supported on each side by a stool, but it was official, as one of the men manning the post had the scarlet hair of the sheriff's men.

The red-haired man saluted Rafyon and explained. 'We're checking on all who are travelling south, sir. One of our men was murdered in Dornan a few days ago.'

'Has Prince Tzsayn passed this way?'

'Yesterday, sir. With many of his men. A fine sight. They were travelling fast.'

'As we must too.'

'May I ask, sir? The white-haired men? I'm not familiar with which lord they represent.'

'That is the white of Princess Catherine of Pitoria, the future wife of Prince Tzsayn and your future queen.'

The sheriff's man peered back at Catherine and Ambrose looked back too. Catherine's small figure was upright on the horse. She looked as strong and dignified as ever. Though he knew she must be exhausted and worried, she didn't let that show.

News of the invasion reached them later that day, from travellers coming south. A huge Brigantine army, thousands strong, had crossed the border, scattering the Pitorian defenders and advancing on Rossarb. Ambrose knew the Brigantines would have no pity on anyone in their way; they gloried in fighting and despised prisoners.

Catherine closed her eyes for a moment and said, 'I had hoped that somehow it was all a mistake, but it's true. Pitoria and Brigant are at war.'

Ambrose nodded. 'I've spent all my life training and expecting to fight for Brigant. But now . . . perhaps I'll be fighting against them.'

'Could you do that? Fight against your own countrymen?'

Ambrose wasn't sure. 'Brigant is still the country of my father and my brother. But it's no longer my country.' He turned to Catherine. 'I don't know where I belong any more.'

Catherine met his gaze. 'I recognize that problem.'

'My only certainty is that I swore to protect you and that's what I'll do. I will ensure you get safely to Tzsayn.'

But then what? It was clear that Tzsayn didn't want him around, and he had no idea what Catherine wanted. She cared for him, he was certain of that, but what could he offer her? Nothing in comparison with what the prince of Pitoria could.

They rode on for a while in silence before Catherine said, 'I need to tell you something. I've been thinking about my father and the reasons for his invasion. I believe your sister may have learnt something of his plans.'

Ambrose replied without thinking, 'She knew of the boys at Fielding, and they seemed to know about the invasion.'

'What? What boys?'

Ambrose told Catherine about his doubts about the reasons for Anne's execution, his journey to Fielding and the boys' camp. He ended by asking, 'But what makes you think about Anne?'

'She gave me a message at her execution. Three signs. I couldn't see the last one properly, but the first two were the words "demon smoke" and "boy". Do you know what the third word might be?'

Ambrose shook his head. ' "Boy" must relate to the boys at Fielding. But "demon smoke"? Is that even a real thing?'

'My father bought some. I believe it is real. Though I still can't quite believe in demons.'

'But I can believe Anne knew something. That's why she was in Fielding.' Ambrose looked at Catherine. 'It was nothing but murder. She knew something and Aloysius killed her because of it.'

'Her death has not been in vain though, Ambrose. She gave me the message. Because of her, you went to Fielding, and because of that you learnt about the invasion.'

'Small comforts.'

'Yes, small comforts.' She leant over and put her hand on his arm. 'I wish I'd known Lady Anne.'

Ambrose smiled, tears in his eyes. 'I wish it too.'

That second night they rested at an inn, paying for their stay with one of Catherine's sapphire earrings, probably worth more than the building itself and everything in it. Catherine didn't seem to care. She said, 'Make sure there is enough food for everyone and the horses too. And for our journey tomorrow.' And she disappeared into a room with her maids.

Ambrose took his turn to guard and patrol the perimeter of the building. No one had caught up with them from Tornia, so it was impossible to know whether King Arell was alive or dead, if Lord Farrow was in control, or if his men were riding in pursuit of the fugitive princess, but Rafyon and Ambrose agreed that they should take no chances.

On the third night they made camp away from the road. While the food was being cooked, Tanya and Jane sat with the men they had befriended over the course of the journey. Catherine sat a little apart and Ambrose went to her, saying, 'We'll arrive in Rossarb tomorrow.'

'You've done well to get us here safely, Ambrose.'

'I can't say I'm happy about it, Your Highness. Your father's army has advanced quickly. We'll be closer to the fighting than I'd hoped. But Rossarb is where your husband is.'

'Prince Tzsayn is not . . . We are still only betrothed, but . . .' Catherine turned her head aside. 'Prince Tzsayn has released me from my obligations. He says he still wishes to marry me, but only if I'm willing.'

Ambrose was surprised. 'And are you?'

'He's an honourable man. I confess . . . I like him. I admire him.'

'That doesn't answer my question.'

Ambrose heard the hardness in his voice and hated it. But he hated still more to think that Catherine even *liked* Tzsayn.

Honourable Tzsayn. Admirable Tzsayn. The prince and his horrible habit of doing everything well.

'I need to think. All my life I've known that I'll marry the man my father chose for me. Now suddenly I'm free to choose for myself. It's a strange feeling. And in truth I'm not sure I feel free at all. There is a war. I'm running from Lord Farrow.' She paused. 'But if I were truly free to choose –' she blushed and looked down, then back up again, her eyes meeting Ambrose's – 'there is no one more honourable and true than you, Ambrose.'

'You'd . . . choose me?'

'There is no one that . . . I mean, being with you these few days has been . . . Oh dear, speaking of love is difficult.'

'Love?'

Ambrose was lost for words. Without thinking, he lifted her hand and kissed her fingers. He kissed each one, wanting to kiss her hand and arm and more.

Catherine pulled her hand away. 'Please, Ambrose.'

He gazed at her. 'Speaking of love is difficult, I agree. Kisses are easier.'

'Really?' And Catherine lifted his hand and kissed the back of it. And then each finger and his thumb.

And Ambrose leant forward and whispered in her ear, 'There is no one that I love but you, nor will there ever be.'

Catherine

ROSSARB,
PITORIA

Honour and Fidelity.

Motto of the Prince's Troop

The closer they got to Rossarb, the more people they encountered fleeing south, each providing increasingly alarming news. The best was that Prince Tzsayn had reached Rossarb and was fortifying it; the worst was that Aloysius's army was established on Pitorian soil, advancing on Rossarb and burning and killing all in its path.

Catherine wondered again why her father was doing this. The land she was now riding through was poor: a few scattered houses and villages, small fields with stubby crops. Was he truly coming because of the demons? Or was her father himself some sort of demon, bent on killing and destruction for their own sake?

Rafyon came to ride beside Catherine. 'We'll reach the coast soon, Your Highness, and then you'll be able to see Rossarb. It's a fishing port. There's a small castle and an old walled town round it. If the town is under attack, the troops will barricade the streets and remain within the walls. If they can't hold the town, they'll fall back into the castle. I was stationed there once. Not one of my most exciting deployments.'

Catherine gave a mirthless smile. 'Unfortunately this visit is likely to make up for that.'

As the road approached the coast, the thin sea mist that hung in the air thickened into a fog. Soon Catherine couldn't see more than twenty paces ahead. The air was still and silent, but she was sure she'd glimpsed a dark figure run across the road ahead of her, then another, and then a few more. Catherine tried to tell who they were from the colour of their hair, then realized they were wearing helmets.

Brigantine helmets.

For a moment the fog parted and Catherine made out many small boats pulled up on the beach, with tens, maybe hundreds, of soldiers spilling out of them.

'Brigantines!' she cried, pointing.

Ambrose swore. 'They're taking advantage of the fog to get a foothold on this beach and cut off the town. The soldiers in Rossarb may not even know they're landing. We have to warn them.'

The gap in the fog had revealed the soldiers, but it had also revealed Catherine's small group. Some of the Brigantines were already running towards them.

Ambrose drew his sword. 'Whatever happens, Your Highness, ride as hard as you can to Rossarb. Don't look back.'

Catherine urged her horse on, but more Brigantine soldiers were already pouring on to the road ahead. Ambrose galloped forward, slashing at them and forcing a passage through, but then his horse squealed and fell, a spear jutting from its neck.

Ambrose rolled free, shouting, 'Keep going! Don't stop!'

And Catherine galloped through the gap he had forged, Jane and Tanya either side of her, Rafyon and Geratan behind. She glanced back and saw another man running at Ambrose before they were lost in the thickening mist.

She kicked her horse on, fear choking her. Ahead she saw the dark grey outline of a stone building. Where was she? Was this Rossarb? Surely it had to be. Her horse stumbled and slowed with exhaustion and Catherine looked around, but the mist was thick behind her and she could see no one, not her maids or her guard or Ambrose.

Her horse came to a halt at the wall and shuddered. It wouldn't even turn so she dismounted and ran forward, shouting for help.

A blue-haired head appeared over the top of a stone parapet.

'Raise the alarm!' she shouted. 'There are Brigantines on the beach! They're coming!'

A stream of profanities was her answer, but then came the sound of a great gate creaking open and further along the wall a stream of soldiers emerged and ran towards the beach. Surely there were enough to repel the Brigantines?

But where were her men? Ambrose? Tanya and Jane?

The sounds of fighting were distant and grew fainter, but she wasn't sure if that was a trick of the fog. For what seemed an eternity Catherine stood, heart hammering in her chest, as slowly the mist thinned and the scene before her was revealed.

There were horses standing and a few men, but the ground was covered with bodies. The first person she recognized, stumbling towards her, was Tanya, who was carrying a sword covered in blood. Then she saw some of Rafyon's men. All had blood on them. One approached Tanya and took the sword from her, and she leant into his shoulder, weeping. Then Rafyon appeared, leading his horse and limping. And behind the horse was another figure that Catherine recognized immediately.

She started to run to Ambrose, then checked herself. He looked weary but unhurt. She went to Rafyon.

'Is this all that's left of us?' Catherine didn't want to ask but had to. 'Where's Jane?'

One of the men said, 'I'm sorry, Your Highness. She was hit by an arrow and fell from her horse.'

'Might she be alive?'

'I went to her.' He shook his head. 'I'm sorry.'

Catherine was in a daze. First Sarah, now Jane. Gentle, kind Jane. Catherine had brought them both to this country and now they were dead. There was just her and Tanya left. Tanya came to stand by Catherine but she didn't speak and Catherine couldn't think of what to say. She wanted to crumple to the ground, but she had to stay strong. She took Tanya's hand and held it tightly.

Rafyon said, 'The Brigantines have fallen back to the beach. We need to check for the wounded, quickly, and we'll find Jane, bring her body. You should go to the castle, Your Highness. If it's any comfort, we made a difference today. Had we not been here, the Brigantines may have taken the town by surprise.'

Was that a comfort? Some. But Catherine wanted everyone safe.

'I'm going nowhere until everyone is accounted for.'

There were just fourteen standing with her, so six men were missing.

Rafyon nodded. He gave instructions for his men to search the battlefield quickly. They all looked exhausted but moved away, bending over bodies.

Ambrose and Geratan stayed with Catherine and Tanya.

'My first battle,' Catherine said numbly.

Geratan said, 'And mine.'

'Mine too,' said Tanya. 'And my last, I hope.'

But Catherine suspected there would be more.

The men returned, one carrying Jane's body. Another of Catherine's men was alive but would probably not survive the day. The rest were dead.

'We should go and find Tzsayn,' said Ambrose quietly. 'It isn't safe here.'

Catherine gave a nod and Rafyon led the way through the open gates of Rossarb towards the castle. The cobbled streets were damp and cool, though the sun was now shining brightly. Soon she'd see Tzsayn again, which meant not seeing Ambrose. Or did it? Catherine didn't know. She couldn't think about that now. Her mind felt numb still, her thoughts whirling in an unformed mess that she couldn't put in order.

They passed through a barricade made of doors and tables, makeshift but high, deep and strong. Beyond it, Catherine was surprised to see a few townspeople carrying bundles of belongings towards the small grey-stone castle that stood at the centre of the town.

'I thought most people had left,' Catherine said, her voice barely above a whisper.

'Some have fled south,' replied Ambrose, 'but not all will be willing or able to leave. They'll take refuge inside the castle, where it's safer.'

The castle gates were open but guarded by several blue-haired men.

They saluted Rafyon and one asked, 'Who's that with the white-hairs?'

'Princess Catherine – Prince Tzsayn's betrothed.'

'Here?' The soldier sounded surprised. He stepped out of the way to allow them to enter.

They passed through into a courtyard where they waited while Rafyon spoke to the guard. Tanya sat down and so did some of the soldiers. Catherine wanted to sit too, but princesses don't sit on the ground. Eventually another blue-haired man appeared. Catherine recognized him as one of Tzsayn's bodyguards.

'Your Royal Highness.' He bowed deeply. 'We were not expecting to see you here. Your father's army will arrive at any moment to lay siege to the town. This is not a safe place for you.'

'There are no safe places for me,' replied Catherine, exhaustion threatening to swamp her. 'This is as good as any. I have news for my . . .' Catherine caught sight of Ambrose in the corner of her eye. 'For Prince Tzsayn.'

The guard blinked. 'The prince is out viewing the town defences. I will send word to him that you are here. Until he returns, may I show your and your maid to somewhere you can rest? Your men can wait here. I'll see that they are well looked after.'

Catherine and Tanya followed the guard through a doorway and up a set of narrow stone stairs to a simple wooden door. He opened it and stood back, saying, 'I will bring the prince as soon as I can.'

'Thank you.' Catherine and Tanya entered and closed the door behind them. Tanya immediately turned the key. That was a new habit.

Catherine lay on the bed. She wanted to sleep, but her mind still seemed to be galloping through mist. Whenever she closed her eyes, she felt the cold of the fog slipping round her. The stab of terror at the moment she lost sight of Ambrose. And what must Jane have felt, alone, abandoned . . .?

'Jane was alone. I said we'd stay together,' Catherine murmured.

'It's not your fault, Your Highness. Col was with her. He's another who died. They were ahead of me and got the worst of it. Legion was with me. He didn't leave me. Col didn't leave Jane.'

'You've got to know the men well these last few days,' said Catherine with a weak smile. She had been too busy with Ambrose and thinking of her father's plans to pay much heed to the men. They'd been charged to protect her – to die for her – and some of them had.

'They're all good men.' Tanya's face crumpled then and she cried. 'Were good men.'

Catherine went to embrace Tanya, but still her own tears didn't come. She thought instead of her father and her brother. They were not good men. They were mad. They had chosen to start a war – they, who knew better than she the full horror and pain of it. They'd lived through one and yet they wanted more. But it was Jane who'd died. Sarah and Jane, Sir Rowland and Col, and the others, nameless to her, who had given their lives on the beach.

And because of what? Catherine was determined to find out.

Edyon

NORTHERN PLATEAU, PITORIA

Edyon and March had been following Gravell and Tash's tracks for three days. It wasn't as hard as Edyon had feared. Mostly there was snow and Gravell's giant footprints were easy to spot. They took it in turns, one looking for tracks while the other led the pony and collected wood, though they had agreed never to stray far from each other and, if anything felt strange, be it warm ground or whatever, they would abandon the pony and run together.

On the morning of the first day after the demon attack, March was following the tracks when he shouted, 'Look what's here!' He held up Holywell's daggers. 'But why have they left them?'

Edyon smiled and shrugged. 'I've no idea. But perhaps we can sell them. Money from them and the pony will pay for food, and a boat to Calidor, wouldn't you think?'

Edyon remembered Madame Eruth's words about the path to riches, but then there were warnings about death being all around, and that was certainly true when the demon attacked.

But perhaps he was through that now. Death was behind him and ahead lay foreign lands and a happier future.

March nodded and put the daggers inside his jacket, just as Holywell had done. It made Edyon shudder and he remembered something else Madame Eruth had said, about the handsome foreign man: *he lies too.*

So much of what Eruth had foretold had come true, but that part had not. Had March lied about something? He resolved to ask, maybe tonight. Maybe . . .

Suddenly March turned round and smiled. It wasn't often that March showed emotion in his face but he was beaming.

'Please tell me you're smiling because you can see the end of the plateau.'

March's grin widened. 'I'm smiling because I can see the end of the plateau.'

Edyon noted that March hadn't called him 'Your Highness' and was sure it wasn't because he was being rude but because they had become friends at last. He came forward to stand by March. Then his smile faded.

'They went down *there*?'

Ahead of them, the land dropped away abruptly down a steep and stony slope. In places, the slope gave way to a sheer cliff. A network of paths so narrow Edyon could barely see them zigzagged among the scree.

'Mountain goats,' said March knowledgeably.

'Will the pony make it, do you think?' asked Edyon anxiously.

'Will *we* make it? That's the question. I'll lead the pony. You find the way down.'

Edyon set off and found to his relief that it wasn't as hard as it looked. The footing was loose but dry. Some of the paths led to dead ends, cut off by landslides or rockfalls, but Edyon only had to retrace his steps a few times, and with each step down he was feeling more positive and a lot warmer.

The map placed Rossarb just at the edge of the plateau. They could be there for lunch ... and have a bath ... a proper bed for the night. Edyon picked up speed. But, as his mind wandered, he lost his footing and slid, only saving himself by flipping on to his stomach and digging his toes in. He looked up to find March peering down at him, his usually unreadable face creased with laughter.

Edyon smiled back. How come he always managed to make a mess of things? Always when March was watching. Since Holywell's death, March seemed to have brightened, as if freed from some unseen burden. Edyon had hoped it might make March more receptive to his flirtatious remarks, but the Abask still seemed embarrassed by every compliment. Well, perhaps tonight, in a real room – with a real bed – things would be different ...

At the bottom of the slope they reached a narrow, fast-flowing river. The ground was flat and grassy and a thick mist made it difficult to see, but Edyon could smell the tang of salt in the air and could just make out the walls of a town ahead.

'Rossarb!' he cried, turning to March. 'We made it! Never had a doubt.'

March grinned at him. 'Nor I.'

'What do we do first?'

'Sell the pony.'

'Oh yes. Sell the pony. Then a meal, then a bath. A hot, hot bath. And then bed and sleep for a full day.'

As they carried on walking, past several small farmsteads, March said, 'It's very quiet. Where is everyone?'

'Perhaps there's a festival on and everyone's gone into town.'

'Perhaps,' agreed March, but he didn't sound convinced.

As they got closer they joined a road that led to a small gate set into the stone town wall. Four blue-haired soldiers were manning it.

They both slowed. March asked, 'What does the blue hair mean? Are they sheriff's men? Are they looking for us even here?'

'Blue is Prince Tzsayn's colour. They're his soldiers. Though I don't know what they're doing this far north.'

'Shall we go back?'

But it was too late for that. The soldiers were rushing forward, spears out. Edyon put his hands up and the soldiers dragged him and March through the gate and thrust them roughly against the inner wall.

'Who are you? What are you doing here?'

Edyon's mind worked quickly. He could hardly admit they'd come from the forbidden territory of the Northern Plateau, but then he remembered the map and Rossarb's proximity to Brigant. He smiled brightly.

'We've just arrived from Brigant. We're traders but we were robbed on the main road. Hence our rather shabby state. We were afraid we'd meet more villains, so we skirted round to the east to come into town this way.'

Edyon glanced up at the soldier's face. He looked incredulous.

'Just come over the border today?'

'This morning, yes.'

The soldier stared at them both, then peered closer at March's ice-blue eyes. 'You came over the border too then?'

March replied, 'My friend just explained where we've come from.'

'What? I can hardly understand you. Where's that accent from?'

'Look,' Edyon interrupted, 'what does it matter what his accent is? He's with me. We're here on business.'

The soldier turned to Edyon and poked him in the chest. 'I wasn't talking to you.' He swung back to March and poked him in the chest as he asked, 'So? Where exactly are you from?'

March knocked the man's hand away. 'Abask.'

'Abask? Isn't that part of Brigant?' And the guard poked March's chest again and said, 'And what is it that you're carrying under here?' He ripped open March's jacket to reveal his knives.

'Armed to the teeth,' the guard said. 'And from Brigant.' The guard nodded to his comrades. 'You're under arrest.'

'Arrest? What for?' protested Edyon. Surely word of the sheriff's man's death hadn't reached all the way to Rossarb?

'Smelling like shit.'

Edyon tried to smile. 'But that's not a legal offence.'

The soldier leant forward and said in an exaggeratedly innocent voice, 'Oh, I'm sorry – isn't it? Well, better add spying.' And he turned to March and poked him hard, saying, 'And for being Brigantine. And for carrying weapons into the city.'

March smacked the soldier's hand out of the way again and the soldier said, 'And resisting arrest.'

And he punched March hard in the stomach, doubling him over.

Another soldier grabbed Edyon's arms and tied them behind his back, ignoring his protest. As he was pushed down the road Edyon looked back to see March being dragged along behind.

Something had gone horribly wrong.

Catherine

ROSSARB,
PITORIA

*Rossarb was once the richest town in Pitoria, a home
of gold miners and demon hunters.*
A History of the North, Simion Saage

Catherine's rooms in Rossarb were a sharp contrast to those in
Zalyan Castle. There were three connecting chambers: a sitting
room, bedroom and study, all simply furnished and small. The
sitting room was her favourite as it had tall, narrow windows on
three sides. The views to the west were stunning, with the blue
water of the bay and beyond that the distant hills of Brigant. The
flat land around the bay was now occupied by the Brigantine
army, which had swept over the border like a wave, to lap at the
walls of Rossarb.

Her father's army looked impressive, Catherine thought grimly.
There were dozens of rows of tents, temporary stables, blacksmiths'
forges and armourers. The bustle of the Brigantine war machine.

And somewhere among them was her father. What was he doing now? Planning an attack? Eating his dinner? Thinking of her? Catherine had never been close to her father, but now more than ever he felt like a stranger, just a man she vaguely knew. And she was ashamed of him. He'd betrayed her, shown the worst side of the Brigantine character: warlike and devious.

Catherine turned away and crossed to the north-facing window. She'd glanced out of it earlier and only seen cloud, but now mountains were revealed, mountains like Catherine had never seen. They were dark, almost black, and snow-capped, and amid them rose an area of land that wasn't peaked and pointed but flat and vast. The Northern Plateau. Demon country. Even from this distance it looked strange and wild and beautiful.

Did her father intend to go there? Did he want the demons for some reason? If so, Rossarb certainly seemed a good base of operations. But what was he really after? Lady Anne had signed 'demon smoke', 'boy' and something else. It made no sense, but Catherine could not shake off the feeling that she held almost all the clues needed to solve this puzzle, but just couldn't put them together.

She had been in her rooms all day. From the window that looked east she had seen Tzsayn stride out into the courtyard, leave on horseback and return a few hours later. The Brigantine army also had arrivals and departures. As well as the army that had invaded by land, her father seemed to be sending more troops by ship across the bay. Catherine couldn't see where they were landing but felt certain they were the support troops for the soldiers her party had encountered on the road. They would be strengthening their beachhead to the south of Rossarb, threatening the coastal road she had ridden along from Tornia. Rossarb was surrounded by sea to the west and the Brigantine army to the north. Unless more Pitorian troops arrived soon to relieve the defenders, Rossarb would be encircled and cut off.

It was dark when there was a knock at the door. Catherine was hoping it would at last be a message from Tzsayn but was surprised to see not a messenger but the man himself. The eye on the scarred side of his face was red and half closed. He looked exhausted. Catherine was certain she was not at her best either.

'Princess Catherine, I'm sorry I couldn't see you sooner. It's been a busy day. I hear you came through the battle to reach us.'

'Yes, we saw some of it. I lost one of my maids and some of the men were killed too.'

'I heard that. I'm sorry. It's not been a good day for us. Your father's men have captured the beach and intend to cut us off and take Rossarb. They'd have taken her already, though, if it wasn't for the warning you gave us.'

'And you can defend Rossarb?'

Tzsayn nodded. 'It's small but the walls are strong. We should be able to hold out until reinforcements arrive from Tornia. Even so, this is not a good place for you to be.'

'What drove us to leave Tornia was not good either. As well as the invasion, my father planned an assassination. Boris and his men aimed to kill you and your father on the night of the wedding; when the wedding was postponed, they attacked anyway. Your father was injured and a number of lords were killed.'

'Yes, I've had the news by bird.'

Catherine hesitated. 'And? Is your father, is the king . . .?'

'Alive? Yes. But not out of danger.' Tzsayn sat down on one of the wooden chairs, suddenly looking much younger than his twenty-three years. 'I hear you were with him when it happened, and that I have to thank Sir Ambrose for the fact that you and my father weren't both killed. I wish I'd been there. I wish I was there now.'

Catherine sat next to Tzsayn. 'I'm sorry for what has happened to your father. It seems I underestimated my own.'

Tzsayn grimaced. 'He is quite special, isn't he? He sends assassins to my wedding and his army into my land. He's killed many of my people, tortured and maimed others, taken two forts and now threatens to take Rossarb.'

'Special indeed.'

'But he won't take it,' vowed Tzsayn, clenching his scarred hand into a fist. 'I have the support of the people. They hate and fear your father.'

'You have my support too, for what it's worth.'

'It is worth a great deal to me, Catherine.' Tzsayn smiled at her. Then his face fell. 'But this invasion still makes no sense. The attack on my father makes no sense. Even if Boris had succeeded in killing him and half the lords of Pitoria, Aloysius couldn't conquer the kingdom. His army here isn't large enough, and there are no signs of another invasion further south. He must want something *here*, but what? Why?'

'I still think it's something to do with demon smoke,' said Catherine. 'But I cannot fathom what that is.'

The prince stood. 'Well, whatever he wants, I intend to stop him getting it. Now, alas, I have more issues to attend to before I retire.'

'One final question, Your Highness. May I ask about my men?'

'*Your* men?'

Catherine blushed. 'I realize that Rafyon and the Prince's Troop are yours but they have looked after me well for the last few days.'

He smiled. 'And I hear your own men chose to follow you out of the city. Well, they shall all be your men from now on. All *your* men are being housed in the barracks. Including Sir Ambrose.' He went to the door and then turned. 'I think they should all have their hair dyed white. Short white hair would look good. Particularly on Ambrose. I can arrange for a barber.'

Catherine smiled but, as ever, she wasn't entirely sure that Tzsayn wasn't being serious.

Edyon

ROSSARB,
PITORIA

It was dark and cold in the cells. And smelly: a mix of stale piss and worse. Edyon crouched with his back to the door, not wanting to encounter anything that might be lurking in the dark corners. The door was of thick wood, but there was a tiny barred window in it, through which Edyon could see more doors. Though he'd shouted for March, there'd been no reply.

When they took Edyon from his cell the first time, he went meekly along. He was taken to the room at the end of the corridor. The interrogator was a slim man with blue hair and a thick scar across each cheek. He told Edyon, 'All you have to do is answer my questions truthfully.'

'I'll do my best.'

The questions started off reasonably enough: questions about his name, where he was from and where he was going. Edyon wasn't totally truthful, but really this was none of the man's business.

Then came the less reasonable questions. 'You're a spy, aren't you?'

'No. And who would I be a spy for anyway? Spying on what?'

'Who sent you?'

'Nobody sent me.'

'Who is in the Brigantine camp?'

'Um, I've no idea what you're talking about.'

'What are your orders?'

'I don't have any orders. No one has given me orders. This is ridiculous!'

That was the first time the scarred man hit him: a punch to the stomach.

Edyon had managed to croak, 'I demand to talk to your superior officer.'

The scarred man laughed and punched Edyon again. This time Edyon fell to the floor.

The scarred man bent low and hissed, 'You're a spy. Sent by the Brigantines.'

'And you're a fool with blue hair, sent by the *prince* of fools!'

He'd been kicked for that, and punched some more. He was left on the floor for some time, then dragged back to his cell, where he fell into a strange sleep, full of dreams of Madame Eruth, swirling smoke and the demon.

The second time they came for Edyon, he resisted as best he could, which only made his next beating worse. The questions were the same and he couldn't think of any other answer than: 'I'm not a spy.'

When he was back in his cell, he shouted to March, desperate for the sound of a kind voice. But to no avail. Finally Edyon lay on the floor, shivering and listening, until sleep found him again.

The third time they came for him, he was too tired and cold to resist. It was pointless. He was taken down the corridor to the same room as before.

This time it wasn't empty.

March hung in the centre of the room from chains attached to his wrists. He was bare-chested and bloodied. His body was covered in cuts, blood pooling on the floor at his feet. His eyes were open but unfocused, his lips split and puffy.

The interrogator turned to Edyon. 'Ready to tell me the truth this time?'

Edyon couldn't tear his eyes off March.

He is in pain, so much pain. I cannot see if he lives or dies . . .

Damn Madame Eruth and damn her foretelling.

'I told you before: we're not spies,' he forced himself to say. 'We're not even *from* Brigant. I'm from Pitoria. This is my country. March is from Calidor.'

'He's Abask. All the Abasks were taken to Brigant after the last war.'

'He lives in Calidor. He's a servant to Prince Thelonius. He's not a spy. He's with me. We're travelling to Calidor.'

The interrogator walked to the table and picked up a large metal hook.

'What are you doing?' Edyon's voice rose to squeaking pitch. He couldn't believe this was happening. 'Please! I'm sorry if I was rude. But I'm telling the truth. Do you think we'd have such a bad story if we were spies?'

'You've come from the Brigantine camp.'

'We came from Goldminster. We got the route wrong.'

'I thought you'd only just come across the border from Brigant? That's what you told the guard on the gate.'

'I . . . I . . .' Edyon couldn't think clearly, his lies tangling together around the point of the metal hook as the interrogator took a step towards March.

'Stop! Just stop, please! We . . . we were lost. We . . .'

Your future has many paths. You must make a choice. And thievery is not always the wrong one. But you must be honest.

Madame Eruth's words now came back to him clearly and he knew he had to tell the truth.

'We came from Dornan, from the fair. There was a fight. I . . . I hurt someone. We were trying to get to Rossarb, but they were following us, so we went on to the Northern Plateau. That's where we were coming from when the guards caught us.'

'The only people who go into the Northern Plateau are demon hunters. You doing a bit of demon hunting on the side?'

Edyon almost laughed but he knew he would sound hysterical. 'Do I look like I hunt demons?'

'You're just a spy then.'

'I'm *not* a spy. Please listen to me. *Please!*'

The scarred man shook his head and placed the point of the hook against the skin under March's arm.

'No! No! Stop!' Edyon screamed, lunging forward, but he was pulled back by two guards.

March's eyes fluttered open and he aimed a feeble kick at the interrogator, but there was no strength in it. The interrogator pressed down on the hook, and a tiny spot of blood beaded out against March's skin. Edyon's stomach turned and he thought he might be sick.

You must be honest . . .

'I'm the son of Prince Thelonius of Calidor,' Edyon found

himself saying. 'This man is helping me get back to my father. If you hurt him again, I'll –'

'You'll what?' The man turned; the disdain in his voice silenced Edyon. 'So now you're from Calidor, too? Not from Pitoria?'

And the interrogator turned back to March and sank the hook into his chest.

March howled.

'Stop it!' screamed Edyon. 'I am the prince's son! There were demon hunters on the Northern Plateau. They took my proof – the prince's ring. I had it on a chain but they stole it, Gravell and the girl, they stole it.'

The room fell suddenly silent, apart from March's low, agonized moans. The interrogator's face was calm. He appeared at last to be listening, to be believing.

'A ring . . . on a chain?'

'Yes,' said Edyon. 'A gold seal. An eagle with a green emerald. Please. That is the truth. It's the seal of Calidor. I am Prince Thelonius's son.'

The interrogator turned to Edyon's guards, his face still giving nothing away. 'Take these two back to the cells. Find the men who arrested the demon hunters and bring them to me.'

'Gravell and the girl?' Edyon could hardly believe it. 'They're in here?'

But the man's only reply was to throw the hook across the room so that it clattered to the floor.

March

ROSSARB,
PITORIA

It was so dark and cold, but Edyon's voice was soothing him and Edyon's hand was holding his. March's head was in Edyon's lap, and he could tell Edyon was crying. His mouth was parched and he couldn't move without making the pain worse. He was tired, so tired, but couldn't sleep. He knew there was no hope. He could feel his life ebbing away.

At first he just wanted it to be over, to hurry up and die. But then he remembered all the lies he'd told Edyon. It was his fault that Edyon was here, in this dungeon, with these men and their fists and their boots and their hooks. If it wasn't for him, Edyon would be on a ship now, on his way back to Calidor and the life of a prince. He needed to tell Edyon, to explain what he'd done and why. Maybe Edyon would forgive him. He tried to speak but his throat was so dry. He didn't have the strength. All he could manage was, 'I'm sorry.'

Edyon told him not to be sorry and he talked about the journey they'd make together when they were released. He said something about a crossroads and how they'd soon be on the way to Calidor, and how when they were there they'd be warm and well fed and lying on feather beds. They'd travel through Calidor together, seeing the whole country, and Edyon would meet his father, the prince, and do his best to be honest and not so cowardly, and March was angry at that so he forced more words out, not caring that they hurt.

'You're not a coward.'

His voice was so wrecked he hardly made sense, but Edyon said, 'You're the brave one.'

And then Edyon carried on with his story. How they'd go to Abask and stay in the mountains there, and March would show Edyon all the places from his childhood. And March tried to remember them but they were just fractured images of mountains and sky. But then he saw his brother Julien there and he felt relieved.

He was going home at last.

Tash

ROSSARB,
PITORIA

Tash had been sitting in a cell for two days.

After all the years of avoiding sheriff's men, it was soldiers who had got them. Tash felt there was something wrong as soon as she saw the checkpoint at the gate. There were never any checks in Rossarb; it was a tiny place, with a few bored soldiers normally. But now it seemed to have half the Pitorian army within its walls, and by the time they'd realized that it was too late. The soldiers had stopped them, found the demon smoke and that was that.

Gravell had tried to fight, but there'd been too many of them, even for him. Tash had tried to run, but the soldiers had been too close. One had grabbed her by her dreadlocks and pulled her back so hard she thought her head would come off. And, while her head had stayed on, the purse containing Edyon's gold chain had fallen out. The soldiers had taken the smoke and the chain and dragged Gravell off somewhere. Then she'd been thrown into the cell with a load of other women who were in for theft or prostitution, Tash guessed. The cell stank. There was a bucket for pissing in that hadn't been emptied for a day.

'So why are you here, sweetheart?' another prisoner, called Nessa, asked.

'For being stupid.'

'Well, ain't that the truth all over?' Nessa replied.

'Why are there so many soldiers in Rossarb?' Tash asked. 'The place is full of them.'

'To fight, of course. Haven't you seen 'em? There's a whole army of Brigantines just over the river.'

'I didn't come that way.'

'Ahh. You came the cold way, was it?' Nessa laughed. 'The high way? I recognize you now. You're with that demon hunter, Gravell.'

'Might be.'

'I remember him. Lousy tipper. They got him too then?'

Tash didn't reply.

'Shame. Nice fella really. Lashes and a year's hard labour for possession of demon smoke; the gallows for demon hunters.'

'Thanks for reminding me.'

'Well, if we get lucky, the Brigantines'll take the castle and let us all out.'

'Can't see that happening.'

'Nor me, luv, nor me. But we live in hope. Got nothing else.'

At that the cell door was unlocked and the gaoler shouted, 'Get up and get ready to move! All of you! You've got new accommodation.'

The women gave a mix of cheering and mocking comments about moving to the inn or the soldiers' barracks.

The man replied, 'You're not far wrong. You're going to a nice room in the cellar of the barracks. These fine lodgings here is reserved for enemy soldiers.'

'Is there ale in the cellar?'

'Course there is, darling. Gallons of it. Now hurry up and get moving.'

Tash followed Nessa along the corridor, up the narrow stone stairs and into the castle courtyard. There was only the gaoler in front and one guard behind. They both had short spears, but they hadn't chained her hands as they had done the adult prisoners' as the manacles were too big and she could slip her hands out of them.

Tash blinked as her eyes adjusted to the light of the courtyard. This was her one chance to make a dash for it. The women weren't hurrying, despite the shouts from the gaolers. At the front of the line, Tash could hear Nessa loudly demanding a rest in the fresh air. One of the other women was already sitting down on the cobbles. There were soldiers in the courtyard, but not near the gates, which stood open. If she could get out of the castle she'd be able to find a hiding place. She'd have to come back to find a way to free Gravell, but the first thing was escape.

The gaoler was prodding the woman sitting on the ground and Tash's eyes met Nessa's. She smiled and walked past Tash, saying, 'I see you eyeing the gate. You'll have to be fast if you try it.'

Tash smiled. 'I'm fast enough.'

Nessa said, 'Be ready then.' And she walked towards the gaoler, complaining loudly. 'We need water and fresh air! None of us has had a drop to drink for a day. It's torture. Amy there is pregnant.'

The gaolers were both looking the other way. Now was her chance! Tash ran directly for the gates.

She'd got halfway before the gaoler shouted, 'Stop her!'

She'd got three-quarters of the way before she saw the soldier running at her from the left, but he was much slower than a demon, and she knew she could get away from him. She'd make it through the gates easily.

Then she reached the gates and came face-to-face with four guards who were stationed on the other side, out of sight from inside the courtyard.

'Shits!'

She swerved and doubled back and heard laughter as the soldiers chased her. This wasn't like running from the boys in the bathhouse. She ran up some steps but one of the men leapt up to block her path. She jumped down, dodged past another and went back for the gates. But two men had stayed there and they advanced on her, so she veered round and ran for the castle keep itself. Perhaps she could find a way out through there.

As she reached the door of the keep, though, it opened and Tash barrelled straight into a woman, who fell backwards with a scream. Tash tripped, her feet tangling in the woman's skirts, bounced off the door frame and back into the waiting arms of a Pitorian soldier.

Catherine

ROSSARB,
PITORIA

*The demon hunter was asked about his methods and how
he came by the smoke. He said the secret would go with
him to the grave and I agreed that that would be soon.*
Sheriff's notes on the arrest of Jonyon Burgens

Catherine had been sitting in her rooms all morning watching
men die.

Early in the morning, a small flotilla of Pitorian ships had gone
out from Rossarb to attack the Brigantine ships ferrying fresh
soldiers across the bay. From her distant vantage point, Catherine
thought their struggle appeared like an awful game: tiny figures
sending out flaming arrows, other tiny figures putting out the fires,
and some men falling in the water. The transport of Brigantine
troops was being slowed but it hadn't been stopped. Catherine
couldn't face watching any more.

'I'm going to see my men,' she told Tanya, who smiled for the first time that morning.

Catherine made the best she could of her appearance and told Geratan, who was guarding her door, to lead the way. They went down the narrow, winding steps of the castle. Geratan opened a door, and Catherine was about to step out into the courtyard when a young girl ran straight into her.

Catherine was knocked backwards with a short scream of surprise as the girl ricocheted off her and through the door. Geratan grabbed the girl, who kicked him in the shin. He threw her to the ground with a curse.

Tanya asked, 'Are you hurt, Your Highness?'

'No, just surprised.'

Catherine realized that ever since the attack in the king's rooms she was more easily startled, but this was ridiculous. Screaming in public – because of a girl. Hardly the behaviour of a princess. She took a breath and smoothed her dress and stepped out into the courtyard.

The girl was on the ground, a thin line of blood running from her forehead. She couldn't be more than twelve years old. Her hair was long and blonde and in thick ropes that were matted and tangled like a bird's nest. Her skin was a dark honey colour and when she opened her eyes they were the deepest blue, reminding Catherine of Tzsayn's blue silk jacket. The girl certainly wasn't like anyone she had seen before.

As the girl sat up, a man came over, shaking a heavy ring of keys.

'Right, you,' he said to the girl. 'Get back with the other prisoners!'

Catherine looked around. A group of women sat on the far side of the courtyard. One was complaining loudly about being thirsty.

'Who are they?' Catherine asked.

'Criminals and low-lifes, my lady,' replied the gaoler. 'We're movin' 'em out of the cells to make room for Brigantine prisoners.'

'Can you give them some water at least?' Catherine said. 'They look half dead.'

It looked like this request was too much for the gaoler's mind to take in. Geratan told him, 'The princess means for you to get the prisoners water. Now. I'll watch this one.'

The gaoler grunted, but he set off for the well. Catherine crouched down next to the girl.

'What's your name?'

The girl looked up. 'Tash. What's yours?'

'Catherine.'

'You foreign?'

'I was born in Brigant but I'm Pitorian now. And proud to say so. What about you?'

'I was born in Illast, I think. But I've travelled all my life. Not so much now, of course – now I'm a prisoner.'

'May I ask why you're a prisoner?'

'Do I get water as well? Or just a lot of questions?'

'I'm sure I can get you water.'

'And something to eat?'

Catherine smiled, impressed by the girl's confidence. 'Yes, I think so. Geratan, find this young lady some food.'

Tash stood up and brushed herself off. Catherine wasn't tall, but this girl was tiny.

'So?' Catherine asked. 'Why are you a prisoner?'

'I've not done anything wrong,' Tash said. 'A case of mistaken identity.'

One of the soldiers smacked her across the top of the head. 'Don't lie to Her Highness.'

'Hit me again and I'll . . .' Tash glared at the soldier, then kicked him.

'No more hitting or kicking, please,' Catherine said.

The soldier said to Catherine, 'She's a demon hunter, Your Highness. And a natural-born liar too.'

'A demon hunter! At *her* age?'

Tash shrugged. 'I'm a natural-born demon hunter, as it happens.'

Catherine couldn't help but laugh. She still wasn't sure she believed in demons but the girl herself was like no one she'd ever met before.

A soldier brought the food and Catherine had them set up a table at the side of the courtyard in the sun. Ambrose had arrived too and Catherine felt him watching her as she sat opposite Tash while the girl munched through the dried apples and cheese. Their eyes met for a moment and she felt a bloom of warmth in her cheeks and forced herself to turn away.

Tash squinted at Catherine and asked, 'Who are you again?'

'I'm Catherine. Princess Catherine, formerly of Brigant, now of Pitoria.'

'Oh. Right. Should I curtsy or something?'

'Strictly, yes. But I'll let you off. I'm not that fond of curtsying myself.'

'Your father? Is he the king of Brigant then?'

'Indeed he is.'

'The vicious one.'

'He has that nickname and that reputation.'

'Oh well. You can't choose your family, as they say.'

Catherine certainly wouldn't choose her father or Boris. She asked Tash, 'Where's your family?'

Tash shrugged. 'Gravell's my family now.'

'Gravell?'

'My partner.'

'Your demon-hunting partner?'

'I never said I was a demon hunter.'

'Actually, you said you were a natural-born demon hunter.'

Tash looked irritated at that and stuffed more cheese in her mouth.

As the other women prisoners were being led away, Catherine was reminded of Lady Anne being led on to the scaffold. Women in chains, and always men holding the other end . . .

And thinking of Lady Anne reminded her of something else. Here at last was someone who might know something about demon smoke.

She said to Tash, 'I've never really believed in demons. Can you tell me what they're like?'

Tash carried on eating, eyes down.

'What do they look like, for example?'

'I don't want to get myself into more trouble.'

'Well, you've already admitted to being a demon hunter. Anyway, if it's just you and me, two ladies, talking, I don't see how that can lead to any trouble. And I'm sure I can get you more food and water.'

'Freedom is what I need. For me and Gravell.'

'That's a little harder, but I could get food and water to Gravell too, if he's in the cells here.'

Tash looked up quickly. 'He is. And they treat us all like sh– I mean, they treat us badly. They'll send us to the gallows and we don't do any real harm and Gravell is soft as butter at heart.'

Catherine couldn't quite imagine a demon hunter being as soft as butter in any respect, but she nodded and said, 'I'm sure he is.'

She turned to Ambrose and said, 'Can you bring some milk? And bread and honey.' She turned to Tash. 'Do you like honey? I love it.'

Tash nodded.

When the milk was brought, Tash drank a large cup of it, wiped her mouth and belched. Then she watched Catherine sip her milk and drizzle honey on to a torn piece of bread. Tash copied Catherine and sipped her next cup of milk slowly.

Catherine smiled kindly but her mind was on how to get Tash to talk. Perhaps she should sound more like a potential customer.

'I've heard that you can inhale the smoke from demons. Do you do that too? Do you think I could try it?'

Tash looked alarmed. 'You don't want to do that.'

'Oh, why not?'

'It makes you silly and sleepy and if you take too much you lose days of your life. Some can't stop using it once they start.'

'And that's its only use?'

'It's warm. And beautiful to look at. All red and purple and orange, never stops swirling around. Like it's alive. Gravell says it's the demon's soul that escapes from their mouths.'

And again Catherine was reminded of the sign Lady Anne made. She'd done it for a reason. She'd looked at Catherine and made the sign and then looked at the king. Catherine had a sudden feeling that perhaps Lady Anne knew that her father was going to betray her. She felt dizzy at the idea, though somehow it felt right.

'You all right?' Tash asked. 'You look a bit sick.'

Catherine nodded and tried to recover the conversation. 'So the smoke is red and orange?'

'Yeah. And purple sometimes. It varies. But it's all beautiful.'

'I'd love to see it.'

'The soldiers took ours.'

'There's some here? In Rossarb?' She turned to Ambrose. 'Can we get it from whoever took it from Tash?'

Ambrose summoned another soldier and spoke with him.

Tash sighed. 'I suppose you're going to throw me back in the cells now I've told you everything?'

Catherine smiled. Tash had hardly told her everything and she very much wanted to learn more.

'I can't stop them taking you back there now, but I'll do my best to help you get out. You have my word on that.'

It was late in the evening before Prince Tzsayn returned to the castle. Catherine knew he'd spent all day on the town walls and she had watched for his return from her rooms. As soon as he rode into the courtyard she ran down with the intention of intercepting him, then slowed, smoothed her dress and held her head high as she stepped outside.

'Good evening, Your Highness. May I speak with you?'

Tzsayn looked even more tired than he had done the night before, but he said, 'Of course. Join me.'

He led her to a small dining room where a table was set and food was brought to them promptly.

'May I ask how the defence of Rossarb is going?'

'The walls are strong, but your father is tightening the siege. His men captured the road to the south today. Some of our reinforcements arrived before then, but not enough, and the rest have had to fall back.'

Catherine felt her chest tighten. 'So we're cut off?'

'I'm afraid so. All I can do now is try to hold out until further reinforcements get here. When Lord Farrow arrives with his men, they'll cut through the siege lines and relieve the town.'

'How long?' she asked quietly.

Tzsayn puffed out his cheeks and ran his scarred fingers through his hair.

'Three days.'

'Can we do it?'

Tzsayn grimaced. 'Aloysius's men tried to storm the town walls twice today, once from the south, once from the west. We threw them back, killed a hundred men probably, but lost a dozen of our own. Their army is growing all the time as Aloysius ferries more men over from Brigant. They can afford losses like that. We can't. I fear we cannot hold the town and will have to retreat into the castle. We can hold that until Farrow gets here, I'm certain, although if Aloysius's army occupies the town it will be a bloody business to dislodge them.' Tzsayn leant back in his chair with a sigh. 'But enough gloomy news. What have you found to occupy yourself today?'

'Well, that is why I wanted to speak with you.'

'And there was I thinking that you dashed down to meet me for my charming company.'

Catherine smiled. 'Of course, that too, Your Highness.'

'Hmm, of course. So what is it you want to discuss?'

'I've been thinking about what my father wants. None of us have been able to guess his motive for this invasion. So perhaps it's something we would have no reason to know about.'

'I'm afraid I'm a little tired for riddles.'

'My father bought some demon smoke last year. I found records of it in his accounts.'

'You think he's been smoking it?' Tzsayn chuckled bitterly. 'That would explain a lot.'

'No. My father never even drinks wine. But nor does he ever spend money without a reason and this smoke cost him two hundred pounds. There's something else too. I need to tell you about Ambrose's sister and a place called Fielding.'

Tzsayn frowned but listened quietly as Catherine told him about Lady Anne's execution and the signs she'd made and the boys at Fielding.

'"Demon smoke" and "boy" was the message?' Tzsayn said. 'I don't understand how this could relate to your father's invasion.'

'No, but if we knew more about the smoke then we might understand.'

'And how can I help? From my vast knowledge of demons?'

'Well, actually, there are two people in your custody with first-hand knowledge.'

Tzsayn's face soured. 'Demon hunters, you mean.'

'Yes. I met one of them, a young girl, by chance today. She knows about demons. I think she might shed some light on what my father is after.'

'You can have her brought to you. Don't go to the cells.'

'I've spoken to her, but she won't tell me more unless she's free.'

'No.' Tzsayn shook his head. 'She's a criminal.'

'She can help. It's a chance to find out what my father is up to. A small chance, I grant you, but it will cost you nothing to let her go.'

'Apart from the fact that she's broken the law.'

'She's a child. A royal pardon would, I'm sure, encourage her to share her knowledge.'

Tzsayn sighed. 'And what's to stop her running away once she's out of the cells?'

Catherine spread her arms. 'Run where? You just said yourself, we're cut off.'

Tzsayn nodded ruefully. 'Fine, she can have her freedom. And you can have her. Learn what you can. Perhaps it will help.'

'Thank you, Your Highness. There is her partner too, a man called Gravell.'

'No.'

'But he may know more.'

'A child I can just about pardon; a grown man, I cannot.'

Catherine lowered her head. 'Thank you for the child then.'

'I hope she appreciates her luck in finding such a considerate princess.'

'And such a considerate prince.'

Back in Brigant, no one would be released from gaol at Catherine's request. She would learn what she could from Tash tomorrow and, if needs be, she'd question Gravell too. She could always go to his cell for that. However, for now, she wanted to help take Tzsayn's mind off his troubles with talk of something lighter.

'The girl is from Illast originally, I think. Her hair is the most amazing I've ever seen. It's long and tangled like thick rope. I've never seen the like of it before. Her skin is dark and her eyes are a stunning blue. Even deeper than the blue of your silk jackets.'

'It sounds like she's swept you off your feet.' The prince smiled again.

Catherine laughed. 'Actually, that is exactly what happened.' Before she could say more, a servant entered and bowed to Tzsayn.

'Karl asks permission to see you, Your Highness.'

The prince rubbed his eyes. Catherine saw again how tired he was. 'Where is he?'

'Outside, Your Highness.'

'Excuse me,' the prince said, turning back to Catherine. 'It seems there is more work to be done.'

Catherine nodded. 'I'll leave you then. Thank you for agreeing to my request.'

As she left the room, a man in the corridor bowed as she passed. He had a scar down each of his cheeks and was holding a thick gold chain.

Edyon

ROSSARB,
PITORIA

March was dying. Of that, Edyon was sure. And this time there was no way to stop it.

After Edyon had told the scar-faced man he was the son of Prince Thelonius, both he and March had been taken back to Edyon's cell. They were given bread to eat and water to drink, but March couldn't eat. Edyon tried chewing the bread to make a paste to feed him but it was hopeless. He dribbled water into March's mouth and talked to him and that was all he could do.

I cannot see if he lives or dies . . .

Perhaps Madame Eruth couldn't, but Edyon could. It felt like death was in the room with him.

So Edyon talked and talked and held March's hand. He had asked for some cloths and water to clean the wounds and eventually the door opened.

The man in the doorway didn't have either bandages or water, but he was holding Edyon's gold chain. He was so beautifully dressed in blue silk and shining silver armour that Edyon wanted to laugh at the awful joke of it as he and March lay on the ground in a cell where even the air was filthy.

'I believe you claim this gold chain is yours.'

'Yes, it's mine.'

'Can you tell me how you got it?'

Edyon was almost too tired to speak. But he gave a short version of his story, from birth to his arrival on the cell floor.

The man stared at him. 'There are many questions I have for you but they can wait until you have more strength.'

'I'm telling the truth.'

The man nodded. 'I believe you are, Edyon.'

And with a flick of his fingers four soldiers came into the cell. 'They'll take you to a better room. I'll send a surgeon for your friend. We'll talk again later.'

The soldiers tried to lift March, but he tightened his grip on Edyon's hand and Edyon knew he shouldn't let go. The soldiers told him to give them room, but the man in blue silk spoke quietly to them and then they worked around him. Somehow they got March on to a stretcher and carried him out of the dungeon into the cool air.

They crossed a stone courtyard into a large keep and to a room with light and furniture and a large fire. There, a man wearing a white tunic cleaned March's wounds and bandaged them while Edyon still kept hold of March's hand.

'Who was that man? The one in the silk?' Edyon asked, though he had a feeling he knew, from the terrible scars that had covered the left side of his face like melted wax.

'That was Prince Tzsayn, sir, and I'm his personal physician. He's asked me to do whatever I can to help you.'

Edyon didn't know what to say. Was this all happening because they believed that he was the son of Prince Thelonius? Clearly they no longer thought he was a spy. Edyon felt the faintest spark of hope. Then his eyes fell on March, his face pale, breathing shallow, and the spark died.

'And March? Can you help him?'

'I'll do what I can. But he's very weak and his wound is deep.'

Edyon wished he still had the demon smoke. That would cure March. The only thing he'd ever stolen that had been useful, and he'd lost it again.

But Gravell and Tash were here in the castle. The prince must have got the chain from them, so he must have the purple demon smoke too. It was a pathetically hopeless chance but he had to say it.

'The demon smoke! That will heal him.'

The physician shook his head. 'Demon smoke doesn't heal.'

'It does; I've seen it.'

The physician raised his eyebrows. 'Was this after you'd taken some, sir?'

'It will work, I promise you.'

'Impossible. And, anyway, illegal.'

'Listen,' said Edyon. 'Two demon hunters were caught as they came into Rossarb. They had my gold chain, which holds the seal of my father, Prince Thelonius.' Edyon thought it wouldn't do any harm to name-drop. 'They also had some purple demon smoke. It cures wounds. I've seen it. I've used it. And now I need you to get it. My friend's life depends on it.'

'I know you want your friend to live, sir, but this smoke won't help him. It may ease his passing, if he can smoke a little, but –'

'Find it,' said Edyon firmly. 'The prince told you to do everything you could. If March dies I will blame you. Either bring me the smoke or bring me the prince. Now!'

Catherine

ROSSARB,
PITORIA

*History often forgets that King Stephen, one of Brigant's
most well-loved kings, was born out of wedlock.*
                  Brigant: A Detailed History, T. Nabb

The morning after discussing Tash with the prince, Catherine
had obtained the girl's freedom and, at Tash's insistence, had
allowed her to go to see Gravell in his cell, provided that two
soldiers stayed with her at all times.

'She can run fast. Watch her,' Tanya had warned with a smile
as they left.

Shortly afterwards Ambrose arrived at Catherine's rooms
carrying a small canvas sack. There was a purple-and-red glow
coming from it and she couldn't help but feel excited.

'The smoke? You've got it?'

Ambrose pulled out not one but two bottles and held them up.
One was full of red-and-orange smoke. In the other, the smoke

was purple and glowed more brightly. He held the purple bottle out to her, saying, 'Be careful. It's hot.'

Catherine took it and was surprised by the weight of it, although the heat was gentle rather than fiery.

Could this strange smoke really be the reason her father had invaded Pitoria? It certainly wasn't anything ordinary. But how could it be useful to him?

'Are you handling illegal goods, Sir Ambrose?' Prince Tzsayn said as he entered the room. 'The penalty for possessing demon smoke is a year's hard labour.'

'Would I have to go to prison as well?' Catherine held up the bottle of purple smoke.

Prince Tzsayn grinned. 'Fortunately I'm in a position to pardon you, fully and completely.' He came to her and took the bottle.

'I got these from your guards, Your Highness. They'd taken them from two prisoners.'

'The demon hunters, I assume,' Tzsayn said, looking to Catherine.

Catherine nodded. 'As I explained, I think the smoke might be the reason my father is invading. But I'm not much wiser as yet.'

The prince held up his bottle. 'I've not seen smoke this colour before. It's normally red, like the one Sir Ambrose is holding.'

'Perhaps Tash can explain the difference,' Catherine offered.

'Let's hope she has some use,' the prince replied. 'However, I'm not here this morning to discuss smoke. There's something else you should know. Two men were arrested while trying to enter the town just before the siege. The guard thought they might be spies. Under interrogation, one of them claimed that his father is Prince Thelonius of Calidor.'

Catherine shook her head. 'Thelonius has no children – his sons both died recently.'

'I should have said, this man was born out of wedlock. Illegitimate but still a son. He says he never knew his father's identity until a few weeks ago. He told me Prince Thelonius sent him a token to show his good faith and prove his story was true – a ring designed to sit within a pendant. He was travelling to Calidor to meet his father. This son may be a bastard, but it's possible that Thelonius wants him to be recognized and legitimized.'

Tzsayn held out a gold chain.

Catherine took the chain. It was heavy and thick, and from it hung a complex pendant in the design of thorns. Set inside the thorns was a ring.

'It's Prince Thelonius's royal seal,' Tzsayn said simply.

Catherine sank into a chair. 'But that would mean . . . he's my cousin.'

'And, if legitimized, the future prince of Calidor.'

Catherine was in a daze. She looked up at Tzsayn. 'What's his name?'

'Edyon Foss.'

'A Pitorian name.'

'Yes. His mother was – is – Pitorian.'

Could it be true? Her cousin? Her father had always claimed that her uncle was a dishonourable coward. It would be no surprise if such a man was to have been unfaithful to his wife. Then again, her father had proved himself to be dishonourable in his dealings over Catherine's marriage. If Edyon's story was true, then it sounded like he had been left in the dark about his parentage all his life and was only now being summoned to his father because the prince needed an heir after the death of his legitimate children. Edyon, like Catherine, was being used by his father. She wondered if he would turn out to be as manipulative as Thelonius seemed to be. She'd have to see for herself.

Catherine gripped the arms of her chair and pushed herself to her feet.

'I want to see him.'

Tzsayn put up a hand to stay her. 'Soon. His companion is gravely ill, I'm sorry to say, because of the treatment received from my interrogators. You must see him of course, but now is not the right time.'

There was a heavy knock on the door and Tanya moved to let in a man wearing a white tunic. He was breathing heavily and between gasps for air he spoke.

'Halfway round the castle ... never knew it was so big ... then up a thousand steps ... for a fool's errand.'

Prince Tzsayn went to the man. 'Gregor, is it bad news about March?'

Gregor looked up, seemed surprised to find himself in the prince's presence, then bent over again and Catherine wasn't sure if it was a bow or a wheeze.

'Your Highness. My apologies.' Gregor took some more deep breaths and stood. 'You said to do ... whatever I could for the patient.'

'So why are you here and not tending him?'

'The little prince wants demon smoke. He is most insistent. I've been twice round the castle trying to find it. The guards said they'd given it to Sir Ambrose. But finding Sir Ambrose is not so easy.'

'Well, he's here and he has the smoke. But why does Edyon want it?'

'He says it can heal his friend's wounds.'

'The smoke can *heal*?'

'No, Your Highness. It's absolute nonsense of course, but Edyon insists it's true.'

Catherine's mind whirled. *But what if it isn't nonsense? What if the smoke really can heal wounds? Is this what my father is after?*

Tash

ROSSARB,
PITORIA

'Oi, big man! You've got a visitor.'

Gravell was sitting on the floor of a cell every bit as cold, miserable and smelly as the one Tash had been in. But when he saw Tash in the doorway, his hairy face cracked into such a huge smile he might have been in the finest palace in Pitoria. Tash ran to him and hugged him.

Gravell lifted her up and said, 'Good to see you, missy.' And he hugged her back so hard she couldn't breathe.

When he gently put her down Tash could feel tears in her eyes, but she couldn't let him see that, so she wiped her face across his stomach and took a breath before forcing a smile and looking up.

'How are you keeping?'

'How do you expect, in this shithole? Did you escape or something?'

'Or something with bells on! I've got a royal pardon and I'm helping Princess Catherine. She wants to learn about demons.'

Gravell laughed, then checked Tash's face. 'You're serious? Princess who?'

'Catherine. She's betrothed to Prince Tzsayn. That's how come I got a royal pardon.'

'Very nice too.' His eyes narrowed. 'You're not giving away any of our secrets, are you?'

Tash shook her head. 'No. And I'm not exactly free. The whole town's surrounded by Brigantines, so I can't leave, even if I want to. But at least I'm not in these stinking cells. I've tried to get them to let you out too but they won't do it. They say I'm a child and that's different.'

'It is different. You shouldn't be in here.'

'Neither should you.' She remembered the food. 'I've brought some apples and nuts and cheese. I can bring you some food every day. They've said I can do that.'

'That's good.'

'And I've been thinking,' continued Tash, lowering her voice so the two guards who had accompanied her to the cell couldn't hear. 'There is a chance you'll be able to escape. The Brigantines are building up to a big attack. When they do you'll probably be moved out of the cells to make room for soldier prisoners, just like I was. If you get out – I mean, *when* you get out – and I'm not with you, I'll meet you at the bottom of the path that leads up to the plateau. The one we came down.'

Gravell sniffed. 'Sounds like a good plan.'

'I think it'll work. You just need to be ready.' And she hugged Gravell again and didn't let go of him until the gaoler said her time was up.

As she left the cells and went back through the castle courtyard, Tash saw the prince and princess, with Ambrose walking behind them carrying a canvas bag that glowed red and purple.

The princess summoned her over. 'Tash, come with us. We're going to use the smoke.'

Typical, Tash thought as she fell into step behind them. *It's illegal for me and Gravell to have it, but princes and princesses can smoke as much of it as they like . . .*

Edyon

ROSSARB, PITORIA

The physician had left and Edyon paced the room, then returned to March and took up his hand again. It was cool, too cool, like the life was leaving him. He needed the smoke! Where was the damn physician? Would he even find the smoke? The soldiers could have smoked it all for their own pleasure or let it escape and drift away, or . . .

Edyon went to the window, but there was no sign of the physician.

'Hurry up! Hurry up!'

He went back to March and took his hand again, feeling tears prick his eyes. 'It'll be all right. We'll get the smoke and I'll heal you and we'll be on our way to a land of riches before you know it.'

But Edyon knew that was a lie. Death *was* all around. And it was all his fault. If only he'd not stolen the smoke in the first place. If only he'd not killed the sheriff's man. He lifted March's hand to his lips and kissed it, saying, 'I'm sorry, March. I'm sorry.'

The door opened and Edyon sprang to his feet. However, it wasn't the physician who stood on the threshold but the prince, and he was holding the bottle of purple smoke.

'I believe you wanted this.'

Edyon had to stop himself from snatching the bottle from the prince's hands. 'Yes, Your Highness! I know it's illegal, but it has healing powers. It will save March. I've used it before.'

Tzsayn held out the bottle. 'Show us.'

And by this time Edyon could see there was an 'us'. More people had crowded in through the doorway. The physician, a young woman dressed beautifully in a pale grey silk dress, an incredibly handsome soldier with long blond hair and, pushing to the front of them all, Tash. Edyon wasn't sure if he should laugh or cry.

Edyon took the bottle and went back to March. He held the bottle upside down, eased the cork out and breathed a small wisp of smoke into his mouth. He leant over March and held his lips above the worst wound made by the hook.

The smoke was hot and dry in his mouth and swirled around the wound, but also it seemed to seep into his brain. Edyon held his position, his body shaking, until he could hold his breath no longer. Then he released. The smoke curled up and away, and everyone watched it rise. The young woman reached out to touch it but the prince held her hand back as the smoke climbed to the ceiling and then crawled across it to the corner of the window, where it found a crack and seemed to be sucked through.

'That's impossible!'

The physician's exclamation pulled everyone's attention back to March. The terrible wound was already sealed and bloodless.

The young woman took her hand from the prince's and moved forward to March's side.

'It's . . . it's healed.'

'Yes.' Edyon felt himself smile.

The physician bent forward to inspect March's skin. 'I've never seen anything like it.'

'It heals bruises as well, if you have a bath with it.' Edyon laughed at the memory. He needed to control himself but he was too happy. 'I'm sorry. Using it this way does make you a little light-headed!'

'Oh, now I get it! That'll explain my ankle!' Tash said. 'I've never smoked it, or had a bath with it. But I hurt my ankle when we caught that demon and put the bottle near the swelling. The next morning my ankle was better. I thought it was odd, and thought that maybe my ankle hadn't been so badly hurt after all. But I remember feeling good the next day.'

Edyon had almost forgotten Tash was there. He laughed again. 'The last time I had a bath was when I met Tash.'

'Yes. Imagine if that hadn't happened. We'd be happily eating pies in Dornan right now,' Tash said, and folded her arms. 'And the smoke would be with me.'

Edyon wasn't sure where he'd be. The room was spinning and he could hardly think, but March was healing – that was all that mattered. And he felt so good. He went to Tash to hug her. He wanted to hug everyone. He pulled Tash to him and lifted her up.

'Ow, don't be so rough!'

'Sorry.' Edyon remembered he had fought the sheriff's man back in Dornan and he gently put Tash down and said to the prince, 'You've got to be careful with this stuff. It makes you stronger too. Watch this.' And to demonstrate he went to a heavy wooden chair in the corner of the room and lifted it above his head, but the prince didn't look that impressed and Edyon felt foolish and embarrassed and also a little annoyed. Why didn't anyone ever take him seriously? And he smashed the chair down as hard as he could. It shattered against the flagstone floor with an ear-splitting crash, cracking the flagstone too.

Silence filled the room.

Edyon laughed. 'Well, it was the ugliest piece of furniture I've ever seen. Though I do feel the need to sit down.' And he sank to the floor.

'Did you see that?' exclaimed Tzsayn to the physician. 'He smashed that chair like it was nothing.' He bent over the flagstone, tracing the crack in it with his fingertip.

The physician was bent over the flagstone too. 'It heals and it gives strength! I've not read or heard of this before. Is it only the purple smoke that does this?' He turned to Edyon, but Edyon just shrugged.

Tash said, 'I think so. It's from the younger demons, the purple ones.'

'And how long does the strength last?' the physician asked.

No one replied. Edyon thought about his harpoon throwing; he'd certainly lost his strength by then. He said, 'A day? Something like that. Not forever anyway.'

The young woman said, 'But still long enough to fight a battle. The smoke would be a great asset to an army, I imagine.'

The prince said, 'Giving great strength for the fight and instantly healing their wounds after. Ready to repeat the next day. That army would indeed be formidable.' He looked at Edyon. 'Assuming the soldiers don't collapse and fall asleep.'

'Perhaps it must be taken in small doses? Who knows – we've still much to learn about it! But this has to be what my father is after,' the young woman replied. 'And that's why his army is only big enough to hold the north of Pitoria. He's not here to conquer the whole kingdom – he only needs access to the Northern Plateau. He's come for the purple smoke.'

Ambrose

ROSSARB, PITORIA

Ambrose, Tzsayn, Catherine and Tash had left Edyon with March and gone to the courtyard of the castle.

'I'd like to test the smoke,' Tzsayn said.

Ambrose smiled. 'That's a year's hard labour, Your Highness.'

Tzsayn grinned back. 'Actually, I was thinking you should try it. First see if it'll heal a cut. Then we'll test your strength.'

Ambrose didn't hesitate. He took his dagger and made a cut across the pad of his thumb. Tzsayn passed him the bottle and Ambrose let out a wisp of smoke that he sucked into his mouth. He put his mouth over the cut.

He was soon feeling light-headed; the smoke was alive, swirling around in his mouth and into his mind. When he breathed it out, he watched it rise up and swirl away into the sky.

'Rather disappointing if you don't mind me saying, Sir Ambrose.' Tzsayn was peering at the cut, which still bleeding.

'Would you like to try?' Ambrose offered the bottle back to Tzsayn. He did the same exercise and his cut too failed to heal.

'Well, it worked on Edyon, March and Tash. Let me try,' suggested Catherine.

'No!' said Tzsayn and Ambrose simultaneously, before they turned to glare at each other.

'I think I should. I understand now. Lady Anne's message was "demon smoke" and "boy".'

Tzsayn said, 'Catherine, whatever you're thinking, you're not a boy.'

'Neither are you. You're a man. Edyon and March are younger than you and Ambrose, and it worked on them. And it worked on Tash too. So I think boy or girl doesn't matter but age does. Now give me the dagger and let me try.'

Ambrose reluctantly held out his dagger and Catherine took it and gently nicked the tip of her thumb, then took the smoke and inhaled some. Ambrose and Tzsayn were both silent as she held her lips over her thumb. They were all still for a long moment, then Catherine breathed out and the smoke rose away. She peered at her finger, then held out her hand. The wound was gone.

'I could feel it! It was moving as if the smoke was seeking out the cut.' Catherine laughed. 'And I'm feeling a little dizzy.'

'But do you feel stronger?' Tzsayn asked.

Catherine shrugged. Then she laughed again. 'I've always wanted Ambrose to teach me swordplay. Perhaps now is the right time to try it.'

Ambrose smiled and glanced at Tzsayn, saying, 'The side effects of this drug are certainly revealing.'

'She may have the strength to best you, Sir Ambrose. That would certainly be an interesting side effect.'

Ambrose remembered the boys at Fielding besting him. It surely had something to do with the smoke. 'Perhaps I can teach you to throw a spear, Catherine.'

Tzsayn raised his eyebrows but summoned a soldier, taking his spear.

Catherine clapped her hands excitedly. 'Wonderful!'

Tzsayn handed the spear to Catherine, but he seemed more than happy to show her himself how to throw. Ambrose watched as Tzsayn moved each of her fingers to hold the spear firmly, and then showed her how to stand, and then, more slowly than ever, with his arm supporting her, how to hold her arm back and throw.

Catherine was smiling and laughing occasionally and Ambrose paced around, wishing he'd just taken a spear himself. She had wanted him to teach her the sword.

Finally she was ready and Tzsayn stepped away from her. But Catherine said, 'Ambrose should throw first. Then I'll see if I can match him.'

Another spear was brought and they moved to the far side of the courtyard. Ambrose threw the spear towards the far wall with all his strength. It struck the cobbles just in front of the wall.

'Not bad. Nice technique,' Tzsayn said. 'Let's see if the lady can beat you.'

Ambrose took a deep breath and managed to stop himself from rolling his eyes.

But then he was amazed. Catherine threw. Her technique was not perfect at all and the spear wobbled in the air, landing harmlessly tail first, but she had matched the distance that he had thrown – almost exactly, in fact.

Catherine laughed and clapped her hands. 'With practice I think I could get it over the wall.'

'My turn!' Tash shouted.

Catherine, Tzsayn and Ambrose turned to see Tash holding the bottle of smoke.

'Gravell told me I shouldn't ever inhale this stuff, but, well, if the princess has, and anyway it's just this once.' And she inhaled the smoke, held it in and then breathed out a long stream of it. She picked up a spear, twirled it in her hand, banged its base on the paving, took a few steps and launched it.

Ambrose gaped. Tash's technique was good but that could not account for the distance. The spear flew high across the courtyard and was still rising as it sailed over the battlements, thankfully to land harmlessly in the river or possibly even beyond it.

Catherine grinned. 'I think the ladies have won the tournament.'

Ambrose said, 'And I think I know my sister's full message.' He looked at Catherine. 'There were hundreds of boys at Fielding, all training to fight.'

Catherine said it: ' "Demon smoke", "boy", "army".'

Ambrose added, 'Though it appears the smoke works on boys and girls.'

'My father would never have girls in his army. But it seems that the younger the boy or girl, the better the effects of the smoke. It doesn't work on you, on grown men, at all.'

Ambrose thought back to the boys on the beach at Fielding. 'Yes, the boys I saw ranged from twelve to fifteen or sixteen at the most. They clearly had great strength and speed but were developing technique. And with demon smoke they'd be more than a match for any army. They could take Calidor. And possibly Pitoria too.'

March

ROSSARB,
PITORIA

March awoke to the touch of something cold on his back. He tensed, waiting for the bite of the hook, but instead a familiar warm, soothing tickle began to spread across his skin.

'Don't move!' Edyon's voice. 'You've got a few cuts here that I missed this morning. I'm using a cup to hold the smoke. Seeing if it works better.'

'And?'

'Hard to tell.' March felt soft fingertips stroke his back, then Edyon said, 'But I prefer the old-fashioned method.' And he pressed his lips against March's skin.

When March woke again, it was to the sound of Edyon's voice, saying, 'He's sleeping now, but much better, Your Highness, thank you.'

Your Highness? Was there another prince in the room?

March lifted his head a fraction from his blankets to see a petite and delicate fair-skinned and fair-haired young woman dressed fashionably in the palest of grey silks, standing with a man dressed in a blue leather jacket. That had to be Prince Tzsayn. March rested his head back, closed his eyes and listened.

'And I have to thank you,' said Tzsayn. 'By bringing us the smoke, you've helped uncover the truth behind this invasion. However, the reason I'm here now is to properly introduce you to Princess Catherine, formerly of Brigant, now of Pitoria.'

'Oh! I mean, I'm honoured, Your Highness.'

'And I'm honoured and pleased to meet you . . . cousin.' The princess's voice was light and musical. 'Circumstances were rather . . . *unusual* earlier, so we couldn't be introduced then.'

Edyon gave an embarrassed cough. 'Yes, my apologies. I was a little worse for the effects of the smoke.'

'You weren't the only one! But it seems you are recovered now.'

'Yes, thank you. Though I feel foolish, even without the smoke. I'm not really used to this. I've only just discovered who my father is. March was sent to take me back to him.'

'I'd like to hear about your life and your journey. It certainly sounds eventful.'

'And, from what I understand, I can say the same for you. Or can I? I'm not even sure what I can say to a princess.'

At that, the prince said, 'And I'd like to hear from March. I wonder how his wounds feel. They're certainly looking better.'

March thought back to the man who'd hit him and cut him, his stupid questions and ridiculous accusations. He remembered hanging from the ceiling. He remembered the hook. That man was working for this prince.

He opened his eyes.

'I'm feeling better,' he said. 'Though, if I see the bastard who did this to me, I'll gladly sink a metal hook into his chest.'

The prince nodded. 'Then I'll make sure your paths don't cross again.'

It was that simple for a prince. But, March realized, nothing was truly simple.

The princess looked at March and smiled graciously. She was very beautiful. 'March. We'll let you recover in peace. Edyon, I hope we can talk more soon.'

After they'd gone, March watched Edyon plump up the pillows on his bed. Edyon had saved his life on the plateau and risked his own to do so. And then, somehow, he had saved him again. They were brothers now, but still that didn't feel right. Edyon had held his hand in the cells. Touched him gently, more gently than he'd thought possible. Put his lips to his skin.

And March had liked it.

Edyon was sitting cross-legged on a small bed in the corner of the room, inspecting his chain and the ring it contained.

'Thank goodness they found this. It's what convinced them we weren't spies.'

March scoffed. 'Common sense would have told them that in the first place.'

'History shows that, in times of war, sense of any kind is thin on the ground.'

'And did the princess tell you how the war is going?'

'I genuinely forgot to ask, but there aren't many cheerful faces around here.' He smiled at March. 'Except for mine. You're alive, I'm alive, we're not in a cold cell.' He picked up an apple. 'We have food, clean clothes.'

'Speak for yourself. I'm naked under here.'

Edyon raised an eyebrow. 'I know. Who do you think undressed you? We may all be killed tomorrow, but at least we can enjoy today.' He bit into the apple.

'Well, I'd like some clothes. If Rossarb is going to be overrun by Brigantines, I can at least run away with my dignity intact.'

Edyon threw him some trousers and held up Holywell's silver necklace. 'I got them to bring this as well.' And he went to March and fastened it round his neck.

It was funny how quickly things changed. Three weeks ago, when he'd arrived in Pitoria, March had hated Edyon, even though they had never met. Two weeks ago he'd found him foolish, naive and frivolous. Now Edyon was helping him dress. March wasn't sure what he felt for Edyon, but he knew one thing: he couldn't betray him to Aloysius. Edyon did not deserve that fate.

March and Holywell had tricked Edyon into leaving his home and his mother. Brought him to this town surrounded by danger. If they survived, March knew what he had to do: he had to help Edyon get to Calidor, even though March could never go with him. So March had a choice: to tell Edyon the truth and leave him, or tell him a lie and leave him.

No, nothing was simple. But he knew he should tell the truth. He wanted Edyon to be a true prince and for that there should be no lies.

Catherine

ROSSARB,
PITORIA

The sign for 'traitor' is a vertical palm with all four
fingers bent closed at the second joint, while the thumb
stands out.

Signing, G. Grassman

Tash was sitting on the floor, playing a game of draughts with Tanya. Catherine had been trying to learn as much as possible about demons now it seemed certain her father was planning to use their smoke. But how was he going to find them? How many demons were there? Were they easy to hunt? Catherine had asked Tash these things, but she had just shrugged and said, 'If Gravell was free like me I'm sure he could tell you all this. It's because of our smoke that you've found out about the boy army.'

Catherine knew she'd done well to get Tash released and didn't hold out much hope of doing the same for Gravell, so she was continuing the slow process of befriending Tash, hoping that the odd piece of information might be revealed.

'So you don't remember your parents?'

'I remember being starving and being beaten.'

'And Gravell doesn't starve you or beat you?'

'He swears at me. Probably less than I do at him, though.'

'So would you say you were equals? I was told the women in Pitoria are more liberated than in Brigant.'

'Yeah. I'm completely liberated.' Then she mock-muttered to herself, 'Wish I was liberated from this shitting castle.'

'And I hear that some women here in Pitoria own property and have their own businesses. Is that what you want?'

Tash shrugged and moved her draught. 'I suppose. I tried the pie business once. But I prefer demon hunting. With Gravell I have a good life. Money. Travel. Inns with beds better than in here. Baths. Plenty of food. I don't want for more.'

'That's what you spend your money on? Or does Gravell pay for all those things?'

'Gravell pays mostly.'

'Ah, not so liberated then.'

'I work equal to him. I do all the dangerous stuff. I draw the demon out. I'm the bait.' Tash shut up abruptly, then said, 'I'm losing this game with all this chatter.'

'What are demons like?'

Tash hesitated. 'Big, fast and red.'

'Red or purple?'

'Mostly red. I think it's the younger ones that are purple. They look like humans, but it's hard to say how old they are. Anyway they're all sort of beautiful.'

'Beautiful! I thought they'd be terrifying.'

'Oh, they're that too.' Tash shrugged. 'If you had one coming after you, you'd not be thinking much about how beautiful it was. You'd be concentrating on running. Finding the best path back to Gravell. Luring the demon is serious. It's life or death. Not a game.'

Catherine nodded. 'I was in my first battle two days ago. I know what you mean about concentrating. I was focused on my horse and myself and the route ahead.'

Tash leant her head back against the wall and studied Catherine. 'You're not how I thought a princess would be.'

'How so?'

'You're more . . . normal.'

'Oh well, and there was I thinking I was special,' Catherine replied, laughing.

Just then there was a knock on the door: a soldier with a message from Tzsayn asking Catherine to come to him immediately.

Catherine looked at Tash and said, 'Maybe not so normal, to be invited to see a prince.'

Tash shrugged again. 'Is Edyon a prince too?'

'Not exactly.' Catherine stood and Tanya smoothed her hair and helped arrange her skirt. Catherine wanted to discuss the demon smoke further with Tzsayn, perhaps have another go at getting Gravell's release. If Tash was there perhaps they'd make more progress. She said, 'Tanya will accompany me and, Tash, you will come too.'

'And the two soldiers outside, no doubt,' Tash said.

'Indeed,' Catherine replied.

In the great hall, Catherine was surprised to see several senior soldiers, including Rafyon, who looked different with his hair dyed white, though Catherine realized she was smiling to see it. Ambrose was with him and she was smiling too that his hair was still the natural blond that she preferred. The sight of him, his armour polished brightly, made Catherine feel stronger. Across from Ambrose she spotted Edyon and March. It seemed that Prince Tzsayn was treating Edyon with the courtesy he would afford a legitimate son of Prince Thelonius. Or was it because he was Catherine's cousin? Whatever was going on Catherine put aside her idea of discussing Gravell: this meeting looked much more serious. Tzsayn sat on an ornate chair at the far end of the room, flanked by guards, reminding Catherine uncomfortably of her last audience with her father.

Catherine approached and Tzsayn rose and came to her, taking her hand and escorting her to a chair to his right, where the queen would sit. He spoke quietly. 'A messenger has arrived from your father. He insists that you and Ambrose are here before he speaks.'

Catherine had an ominous feeling. If the message was for Ambrose as well as her . . . she dreaded to think of what shame or embarrassment her father might seek to create.

'We both know the message will be bad,' continued Tzsayn. 'That is why you are sitting here beside me. We are betrothed. You have my protection.' He held his hand out for her to take.

Catherine put her hand in his and said, 'Thank you, Your Highness.'

The warmth of Tzsayn's hand was a comfort, but she felt Ambrose's eyes on her as she took her seat beside him.

The great doors to the hall opened and the messenger entered. However, it wasn't just one messenger – it was five: four men carrying a huge square wooden box with another in the lead wearing the uniform of her father's guard. His jacket arm was folded over the end of his stump.

'It's Viscount Lang. He fought Ambrose a few weeks ago; that's how he lost his hand.'

Catherine's own hand tightened round Tzsayn's as Lang stepped forward.

'I am sent on behalf of King Aloysius of Brigant to agree terms for the surrender of Rossarb. King Aloysius believes that his whore of a daughter, Catherine, is with you, as is the cowardly scoundrel who constantly fawns at her heels, Sir Ambrose Norwend.' Lang made a show of looking at Catherine. 'I see the whore is present.'

Tzsayn's face was impassive. 'Princess Catherine is an honourable lady and my betrothed. Whoever insults her insults me.'

'I stand in your hall under a flag of truce. You can kill me, if you dare. I am not afraid to say what I know to be true,' Lang sneered. 'Is Norwend too cowardly to show his face?'

'Sir Ambrose is here,' Tzsayn said, motioning Ambrose forward. If Tzsayn's face was a picture of studied calm, Ambrose's was a mask of fury. Rafyon stood at his shoulder, eyeing Ambrose anxiously, as if worried he might have to hold him back.

Steady, Ambrose, Catherine thought. *It's only words.*

'Then I can deliver my message. King Aloysius has surrounded this pitiful town. He may capture it at his whim. When he does, he will have no mercy. He will kill all within its walls: men, women, children. All will die.' Lang paused. 'However, His Majesty may be persuaded to be merciful. The people of Rossarb will be allowed to leave the town unharmed, including yourself, Prince Tzsayn, if you give the king something he wants.'

'And what would that be?' Tzsayn asked.

'The whore and the coward.'

Catherine sucked in her breath.

'Call the princess a whore again and I will kill you where you stand!' Ambrose shouted. His sword was half out of its scabbard as he took a step towards Lang, but Tzsayn stayed him with a sharp gesture and Rafyon was blocking his path. Trembling, Ambrose thrust his sword back into its scabbard, though he didn't step back.

Catherine forced herself to look calm, though her blood was burning as fiercely as Ambrose's.

I should have known. He wants revenge and won't stop until he gets it.

For her father there could never be forgiveness or reconciliation. He'd think nothing of parading his own daughter through the streets to the scaffold. But Tzsayn would never agree to such a thing.

The silence stretched until Catherine could not help but glance sideways at the prince. His gaze was fixed on Lang.

Was he considering it?

Ice filled Catherine's veins. Tzsayn was an honourable man, she was sure of it. But the safety of all the people of Rossarb was at stake. If he could hand over Catherine and Ambrose – two foreigners – to buy the safety of his people, why wouldn't he? Her father had sold her to Pitoria as a distraction, a means for him to make war. Why should Tzsayn not sell her back to buy peace?

After an eternity, Tzsayn stood.

'If King Aloysius is so sure of taking Rossarb, let him try. Our walls are strong, our soldiers ready. I see this message as a confirmation that he knows his position is weak, not strong. He knows that he could attack Rossarb and fail. After all, he's well known for failure in war, isn't he?' Tzsayn's voice rang out across the stone-flagged floor of the great hall. 'I will not hand over my betrothed or her bodyguard to that butcher.'

Lang stiffened. 'Prince Tzsayn, we both know your reinforcements have not arrived. We have closed the road from the south. We can take Rossarb whenever we wish, but many men will die, on both sides. That can be avoided for the price of just two lives. Send them to us and no one else will be harmed. You have until midnight tonight to deliver them.'

Lang stepped to one side so the wooden box was in full view.

'As a sign of his intent, King Aloysius sends you a gift.' Lang looked at Ambrose. 'He knows that the coward and the whore betrayed Brigant. And he knows who helped them. Traitors and cowards are equally damned.'

He pulled a metal bolt from the top of the box and the sides fell with a crash to the ground.

'Look away!' Tzsayn snapped to Catherine.

But it was too late.

Within the box stood a large black metal cross on a stand. It was the height of a man. Attached to the horizontal bar were a pair of human hands, one at each end. Mounted on the top was a human head. The cross was constructed so that the opening of the box disturbed the metal contraption, making the head nod and hands sway as if alive.

The face was unrecognizable, beaten and disfigured, the lips sewn together, but the golden hair was unmistakable.

Ambrose staggered forward and dropped to his knees. The room was silent except for the strange keening, groaning sound coming from him.

Catherine had to look away. She wanted to forget what she'd seen. What must they have done to him before he died? Tears spilled out of her eyes. Her father had done this. How could anyone do this?

'Who is it?' Tzsayn asked grimly.

Catherine only just managed to answer.

'Tarquin Norwend. Ambrose's brother.'

Ambrose

ROSSARB, PITORIA

My brother is dead.

Murdered. Tortured. Tongue torn out, lips sewn up, hands cut off. All while he was still alive. And what else besides?

Through his tears, Ambrose saw Lang's smirking face. He should have killed him that day in Brigane. He lurched to his feet but Rafyon was holding him back.

'No, Ambrose. That's what he wants.'

'It's what I want too!' And he pulled free of Rafyon.

Lang stepped back, fumbling for his sword, but more blue-haired men blocked his path and pushed Ambrose back.

Ambrose tore at the men, but they held him fast.

The room was roaring with noise, but above it all Tzsayn ordered, 'Get everyone out of here. And that contraption too.'

Lang pointed at Tarquin's mutilated body. 'It took days for him to die. I had the pleasure of watching.'

Ambrose roared in anger again but the soldiers' grip was unbreakable.

Tzsayn was standing now. 'Get out, Lang! And think yourself lucky I treat you with more honour than you treated that man.'

Lang and his men retreated to the door.

'You have until midnight,' were Lang's parting words.

And then they were gone and the doors were slammed shut behind them.

Ambrose watched as they took the metal contraption and the remains of his brother away.

'I swear I will kill them all,' he said to Rafyon. 'Aloysius. Boris. Noyes. Lang. All of them.' He tore free of the soldiers holding him. 'I will have my revenge.'

'I believe you, Ambrose. But now, please, try to calm yourself.'

But how could he be calm? His brother was dead. Who knew what Aloysius was doing to his father – left alone, two children dead and the last survivor marked as a traitor? He would take his father's lands, take everything.

Ambrose screamed in fury again and then sank to his knees.

The next voice he heard was calm and quiet. Tzsayn knelt on the floor beside him.

'I'm sorry, Ambrose. For you and for your brother. Let me assure you that I would never send you or Catherine to Aloysius. I'd not send anyone to him – he's a monster.'

Ambrose didn't know what to say. He couldn't think. He sniffed and realized his face was covered in tears.

'Catherine tells me your brother was an honourable man.'

Ambrose looked up at Tzsayn. 'He was the best. The best brother, the best son.'

'He helped you steal the orders for the invasion?'

'Yes. With no thought for his own life. He only wanted to help me. And this is his reward.'

'I'm going to summon everyone back in. I need to explain my decision not to surrender. There may be some who consider two Brigantine lives worth giving up. Will you speak too? If you're able?'

'I'd rather fight than speak.'

'There will be time for that soon enough, but for the moment I need your words.'

As the room filled again with Pitorian soldiers, Ambrose wiped his face and took some breaths to steady himself.

Tzsayn spoke first. 'Aloysius has invaded our country, killed and maimed our men, and now demands that we leave Rossarb so he can do with it as he wishes. He insults Princess Catherine, to whom I am betrothed. He insults Sir Ambrose Norwend, who saved the life of my father a few days ago and has risked much and given up much for Pitoria. And, most disgusting of all, Aloysius has tortured and executed Ambrose's brother, who risked all and gave all to help Pitoria. I'd like Ambrose to tell you about his brother.'

Ambrose took a few steps forward. He looked at the sea of faces and for a moment wasn't sure he could speak. But then he thought of Tarquin's smile and he knew what he wanted to say.

'Tarquin Norwend was the most honourable man I've ever known and a man I'm proud to call my brother. He was the gentlest, kindest and most considerate of men. With his help I discovered Aloysius's plan to invade Pitoria, and with his help I obtained the evidence of the invasion. My brother believed Aloysius was acting dishonourably by planning to attack a peaceful neighbour. But Tarquin was always honourable, and for that he has been tortured and killed.' Ambrose turned to face Tzsayn and said, 'And I will avenge my brother.'

For the first time since the box was opened, Ambrose looked at Catherine. She was pale and dignified and holding tightly to Tzsayn's hand. Perhaps that was as it should be. He no longer knew.

He had no tears in his eyes now. He turned back to the room and continued, 'Aloysius insulted me and his own daughter, Princess Catherine. I was a soldier in the Royal Guard, sworn to protect her. I will never break that oath; that is still my duty. But her father, whose natural duty should have been to protect her life with his own, betrayed her and sent her here so that her wedding could be a distraction to his invasion. He is a fiend and never to be trusted. And so now I add to my oath. I will protect Princess Catherine and I will do all I can to fight for Pitoria.'

Tzsayn stood now.

'Some of you may believe we can negotiate with Aloysius. We cannot. His behaviour is monstrous. This man, this honourable man, Tarquin Norwend, a Brigantine, gave his life to help us Pitorians. And we Pitorians owe it to him to fight on. Pitoria has been invaded by a maniac. He may frighten us, horrify us and threaten us, but if we surrender we lose more than our heads. We lose our humanity.'

A few of the soldiers and lords shouted, 'Agreed!' and 'Hear! Hear!'

'Aloysius is a maniac, but he is still only a man. A man who lost his last war. He is not indestructible. Our reinforcements will be here tomorrow and then we take the fight to Aloysius. Until then, we double the watch. Aloysius wanted a reply by midnight tonight and I say to him that I will not surrender my loyal friends but fight for every inch of my country with you, my fellow Pitorians.'

Tash

ROSSARB,
PITORIA

Tash had thought demons were scary but men could be just as bad. The head in the box had nearly made her sick, the smell almost as awful as the sight of it. King Aloysius sounded like a madman. It was hard to imagine that someone as nice as Princess Catherine could be his daughter. Prince Tzsayn wouldn't give Aloysius what he wanted, that was obvious. That meant the Brigantines would attack. But that also meant that perhaps she and Gravell had a chance of escaping during the chaos of the battle.

When they got back to the princess's rooms Tash went to the window and looked out at the Brigantine army. Their camp was the size of the Dornan trade fair twice over. If it came to a fight, Tash was pretty sure the Brigantines would win, and she had no intention of ending up with *her* head in a box.

The courtyard below was abustle with preparations. Aloysius had given Tzsayn until midnight to hand Catherine and Ambrose over, and Tash couldn't imagine he'd be the patient type. Tanya was already packing a bundle of things in case the castle fell and they had to flee.

'If there's an attack, what will happen to the prisoners in the cells?'

Tanya ignored her. 'We need food. I learnt that from my last escape from a castle. I'll go and get some. You stay with the princess.'

Catherine was at the other window, her red-rimmed eyes unseeing. Tash crossed over to her. 'Please, tell me: what will happen to Gravell?'

'I don't know, Tash.'

'He's a good fighter. He could help. They should release him.'

'I've asked for his release before, Tash. The prince won't trust him.'

'Well, I'm not leaving here without him.'

'Hopefully none of us will have to leave. The town walls are strong and the castle walls are stronger. Reinforcements will be here soon.'

Tash huffed quietly. The princess spoke fine words but she was still getting ready to leave.

As night fell, the three of them dined together. Tash had thought the princess would eat separately, but she sat with Tanya, who talked about the soldiers, but Tash now wanted to ask her own questions.

'So, Princess Catherine, you're still betrothed to the prince even though he's at war with your father?'

'Yes.'

'And you seem to like him and he seems all right. I mean, you handled that whole head-on-a-wobbly-spike thing pretty well. And he's not bad-looking, at least from one side. And he's a prince and going to be a king, which I guess is good. So that's all fine and dandy.'

'Indeed,' Catherine replied, as Tanya hid her smile with her hand.

'And Ambrose – he's just a handsome soldier, sworn to protect you with his life.'

Tanya went still.

Catherine said in a too-calm voice, 'He was one of my body-guards in Brigant. All of them swear to protect their royal charges.'

'I don't see any of the others around here, though.'

'There's a reason for him being here. The invasion.' Catherine fanned her face.

'Hmm. So you've known him a while?'

'A few years.'

'And you seem to like him too. I mean, as well as Prince Tzsayn.'

'I'm quite capable of liking more than one person at a time. I like a lot of my men. I mean, in the sense that they're good men. I mean, good soldiers.'

'I guess that makes sense. You're a princess. Why limit yourself? Have it all.'

Tanya seemed to have a coughing fit at this.

'That isn't what I meant at all!' Catherine got to her feet, saying, 'I could do with some air.' She went to the window and said firmly, 'I care for Ambrose – he's loyal and I trust him. But I'm betrothed to Tzsayn. It's as simple as that.'

'So you're going to marry Tzsayn?'

Catherine hesitated. 'As you mentioned yourself, he's at war with my father at the moment, so . . .'

'As simple as that then,' Tash said. She got up to look out of the window too. It was a clear night, many stars in the sky. The fires of the Brigantine army were burning brightly, like stars on the earth. She said, 'You know, these windows are very narrow and very high. No one can get in through them, even if they had ropes to scale the walls. But we can't escape through them either. If this tower was attacked, we'd be trapped.'

Tanya butted in. 'Will you shut up? We're not being attacked. The princess explained that. The Brigantine army would have to fight all the way through Rossarb before it reached the castle.'

'Unless they scaled the castle walls from the river,' Tash said. 'Isn't that what you said they did in Tornia?'

Catherine froze. 'They did.'

'And wasn't that castle supposed to be impregnable too?'

No one replied.

Tash muttered, 'It must be about midnight. I bet your father's not one for waiting much past deadlines.'

'Waiting for the deadline will be agony for him,' the princess replied.

It was a moment later that shouts came from below.

Tanya and Catherine looked at one another and then out of the window but they could see little in the dark.

Geratan rushed in. 'The Brigantine army has breached the town walls and set fire to the buildings. And others have somehow found their way inside the castle walls too. They've killed Lord Reddrian. Ambrose says you must stay here with the door locked. He and the rest of your men are going through the castle searching for the assassins. Baranon and I will remain here with you.'

'And Prince Tzsayn?'

'He's fighting on the town walls.'

'And how is that fight going?'

Geratan hesitated. 'Your Highness, we must be prepared . . . I mean . . .'

'Shits!' cursed Tash. 'We're all going to end up with our heads on poles.' She paced around the room looking through each window, but eventually she went to sit with the others.

They were mainly silent, listening to the distant sounds of fighting.

Geratan said, 'There's a lot of waiting in war. Waiting and bad food.'

'And a lot of dead men,' Tash added.

Geratan shot her a look, so she got up again and went over to the window.

The fires in the Brigantine camp were as clear as before and the stars as bright, but now there was also a flickering yellow light, much closer and from below.

Tash said quietly, 'I think the castle is on fire.'

Geratan swore under his breath and ran to the window as a billow of smoke rose past it.

'We need to leave, Your Highness.'

Tash picked up her bundle and was ready to go. Geratan led the way. Catherine, Tanya and Tash followed, with the other guard, Baranon, bringing up the rear. As they descended the stairs, the smoke became thicker and flames came from one room they passed. At the bottom, Tash could see the doorway that led to the courtyard, but before they could reach it Tanya screamed as a man in black ran out of the smoke with a knife. Geratan grappled with him and they slammed together into the wall.

Tash pushed Tanya, saying, 'Go! Get past them!' And she took the princess by her wrist and pulled her out into the courtyard. Tash looked back and saw Baranon slit the attacker's throat with his dagger. It wasn't like killing a demon. Blood spurted out, covering Baranon, and the man didn't scream but choked and grabbed at his neck.

The courtyard was dark and smoky and it was hard to work out what was happening. The fire was spreading fast. If Gravell was still locked in the cells, he'd die. Tash had to get him out. She set off for the cells but was immediately grabbed by a strong arm round her shoulders, lifting her off the ground. She kicked out and struggled.

'Calm yourself,' Rafyon said, and set her down. 'Stay with the group, miss. It's safer together.'

'But Gravell's not in the group; he's in the cells. I'm going to get him out.'

She squirmed free and hared off through the smoke and swirling sparks. Rafyon shouted some orders and Geratan and Baranon followed her as she ran down the steps.

There was no sign of the gaoler – bloody coward would have fled at the first sign of trouble – but the keys to the cells hung on a wooden peg in his room.

'Come back, Tash!' Geratan shouted. But Tash had already snatched up the keys and run to Gravell's cell. He was at the door as she opened it. Tash grabbed his hand and pulled him into the corridor. She threw the keys to Geratan and said, 'You can deal with the others. We'll see you outside.'

She ran back to the courtyard, Gravell behind her.

'Shits!' Gravell said as they got outside.

The fire had got worse. Ambrose and Rafyon were standing over bodies at the entrance to the castle. Tash and Gravell joined the princess in a group of white-haired men and among them she saw Edyon and March, who seemed completely recovered from his injuries.

'Rossarb is lost,' gasped Ambrose as he ran up to them. 'The Brigantines have broken through the western barricade. We're cut off from the prince. We have to find a way out ourselves.'

'What do we do?' Tash asked Gravell.

'Stay with everyone else until we're safely out of this mess,' Gravell replied. 'Then find our way up to the plateau. The Brigantines won't follow us there.'

'I wouldn't be so sure,' muttered Tash.

'What do you mean?'

'I mean, they've come for the demon smoke. That's why they're here.'

Gravell shook his head. 'That makes no sense.'

'Sense or not, that's what's happening.'

And then they were off and running, out of the castle and into the streets. Tash and Gravell stayed near the front, close to Rafyon, who seemed to know the side roads well. They headed south-east and had almost reached the town wall when they spotted a group of Brigantine soldiers ahead. Rafyon drew his sword but turned his head and shouted, 'Not this way. Go back. Go back!'

The Brigantines moved towards them slowly, one man throwing a spear that sailed over Tash's head. There was a scream from behind her. More spears were launched, landing in the people behind her. The screams and shouts were frantic and Tash was pushed forward towards the Brigantines. 'No,' she yelled. 'Go back. Go back!'

But there were too many people in the narrow alley. Tash looked for another way out, or even up, but there was nothing. One of the Brigantines ran forward, his spear levelled at her throat. Tash had nowhere to go. She was trapped between soldiers on either side. Everyone was trapped. Then she felt Gravell's hands on her shoulders, turning her, and somehow she knew what he was doing.

She screamed, 'No!' but he was too strong, curling his body round her like a shield as the spear point pierced his side.

Gravell grunted and staggered. The spear was embedded deep in his chest. With one pawlike hand, he grabbed the Brigantine soldier by the neck and snapped it with a wrenching twist, hurling the body back and scattering the rest of the Brigantines. Now the crowd behind him began to move, but too late.

Gravell fell to his knees and Tash put her hands to his face. 'No, no, no!'

He looked at Tash and said, 'Run, missy. Run!'

'No!' screamed Tash. 'Get up!' And she tried to pull him to his feet.

'You can't move me, missy. You go.'

There was fighting all around her now but Tash didn't care. She didn't care about anything but Gravell. But what could she do? She clung on to his jacket and put her mouth to his ear, telling him, 'I'm not going without you. I'm not going *anywhere* without you.'

'Just don't go back to that fat pie seller in Dornan. You're better than that.'

Tash shook her head, tears pouring down her cheeks. 'I'm working with you. Always.'

'Good girl,' said Gravell, and he closed his eyes and his body slumped sideways.

Tash stood, disbelieving. And then arms grabbed her again and lifted her up and away from Gravell, and all her kicking and screaming was no use at all.

Catherine

ROSSARB,
PITORIA

War is often seen as the end, but often it is a new beginning.

War: The Art of Winning, M. Tatcher

The smoke was choking, tears stung Catherine's eyes and she coughed and spluttered. All she could do was keep hold of Ambrose with one hand as Tanya clung to her other.

Catherine was afraid, not of the Brigantines but of what Ambrose might do. Ever since he'd seen Tarquin's body, he'd been different. Distant. Hurt beyond words. He'd not spoken to her, but something about him had changed. And yet he was here, pulling her through the alleyways of Rossarb. She glimpsed others, some of her men, Edyon and March, Rafyon carrying Tash, who had stopped kicking and was now just sobbing quietly.

Finally the smoke cleared. They were at the eastern edge of the town, then through the last barricade, through the walls and leaving Rossarb behind. The night was dark and the road quickly became no more than a stony path. The only sounds were their laboured breathing and the river roaring to her left.

They were climbing, Catherine realized, the slope becoming steadily steeper and steeper. This path had to lead up to the Northern Plateau, to demon territory.

They carried on up the slope, Ambrose gripping her hand tightly, almost too tightly. At one point she stumbled and, like lightning, he turned to catch her but then carried on as fast as before. Finally, in a hollow in the hillside, they stopped.

Behind, there were dark silhouettes of people straggling up the hill, and beyond them, through the trees, Catherine could make out a bright orange glow.

Tanya said, 'The whole town must be in flames.'

'My father's legacy. Destruction.'

Catherine shook her head and felt tears fill her eyes.

'Will they come after us?' Tanya asked. 'Or will they think we're with Prince Tzsayn?'

'They'll come, sooner or later.'

Her father would never stop. He'd never forgive. For those he deemed traitors, he would give no quarter, not even to Catherine. Especially not to her.

Catherine pulled her shoulders back. Her father could try to do to her what he'd done to Lady Anne, but she would fight back. She knew what he wanted now, and she would do everything she needed to do to stop him getting the purple demon smoke and leading his boy army against his peaceful neighbours.

And yet, in her heart, Catherine wanted to do more than that. She recognized now her own ambition, and for a brief moment she had a vision.

Her own army, white-haired, well armed and strong as demons. Marching to war against her father.

Places and Characters

BRIGANT

A war-hawkish country.

Brigane: the capital
Norwend: a region in the north of Brigant
Fielding: a small village on the north-west coast, where Lady Anne was captured by Noyes
Castle Tarasenth: the home of the Marquess of Norwend

Aloysius: King of Brigant
Isabella: Queen of Brigant
Boris: Aloysius's first-born son
Catherine: Aloysius's daughter; betrothed to Prince Tzsayn of Pitoria; sixteen years old, turning seventeen
Harold: Aloysius's second-born son
Noyes: the court inquisitor
Sarah, Jane and Tanya: Catherine's maids
Peter, Viscount Lang, Dirk Hodgson, Sir Evan Walcott: members of the Royal Guard

The Marquess of Norwend: a nobleman from the north of Brigant

Tarquin: the Marquess of Norwend's first-born son

Ambrose: the Marquess of Norwend's second-born son; member of the Royal Guard; twenty-one years old

Lady Anne: the Marquess of Norwend's daughter; executed as a traitor

Sir Oswald Pence: Lady Anne's friend, now deceased

CALIDOR

A small country to the south of Brigant.

Calia: the capital

Abask: a small mountainous region, laid waste during the war between Calidor and Brigant, where the people are known for their ice-blue eyes

Thelonius: Prince of Calidor, younger brother of King Aloysius of Brigant

Lord Regan: Thelonius's oldest friend

March: servant to Prince Thelonius; Abask by birth; sixteen years old

Holywell: works for Aloysius as a fixer, spy, killer; Abask by birth

Julien: March's older brother, now deceased

PITORIA

A large, wealthy country known for its dancing, where men dye their hair to show their allegiances. The wissun is a white flower that grows wild throughout most of Pitoria.

Tornia: the capital
The Northern Plateau: a cold, forbidden region where demons live
Charron: a port town
Westmouth: a port town
Dornan: a market town
Pravont: a village on the edge of demon territory
Rossarb: a northern port with a small castle
Leydale: home to Lord Farrow

Arell: King of Pitoria
Tzsayn: Arell's son; Catherine's fiancé; twenty-three years old
Sir Rowland Hooper: the Brigantine ambassador to Pitoria
Lord Farrow: a powerful lord who distrusts Catherine and all Brigantines
Rafyon: one of the prince's guard and most trusted of his men
Geratan: a dancer

Gravell: a demon hunter
Tash: Gravell's assistant; born in Illast; thirteen years old

Erin Foss: a trader
Edyon: Erin's son; a bastard; seventeen years old
Madame Eruth: a fortune teller

ILLAST

A neighbouring country of Pitoria, where women have more equality, being able to own property and businesses.

Valeria: Queen of Illast, many years ago

Acknowledgements

Writing *The Smoke Thieves* has been a complex process that began a few years ago. It started with an idea – one of those ideas that get you so excited that it's vital that you tell someone immediately. In this case I stopped my car by the side of a country lane and rang my agent, Claire Wilson.

'Father and son – demon hunters,' I said.

'Love it!' she replied.

However, getting from the idea to a novel was far from straightforward and I struggled to develop the story. Eventually, I realized that I wasn't that interested in demon hunters, but what I really wanted to do was to tell the story of two strong female characters. So the father and son morphed into a man and a girl – Gravell and Tash – and I developed the character of a princess who is privileged and yet also a second-class citizen because of her sex.

Catherine is a girl of intelligence, wit and courage, who begins to realize her potential (in both senses of that phrase) as she grows up and assesses the men around her and wonders how hard can it really be to rule. Her character was inspired in particular by two famous women – Elizabeth I of England and Catherine the Great of Russia – but also by all the examples of strong women I had grown up with. I was brought up in a family and educated in a school where women dominated in numbers, and where I was encouraged to work hard and believe I could achieve anything a man could (occasionally while doing it backwards, as the old Ginger Rogers joke goes). My thanks to all those inspirational women in my family, my school and my working life.

There have been a number of strong women and men who have helped me in the writing of this book. Thanks to my agent, Claire Wilson, and to my editor, Ben Horslen, who encouraged and supported me through the whole process, especially during the dark days when it was all getting too complicated and difficult. Thanks to all at Penguin Random House, including Tig Wallace in editorial, Ben Hughes in design (for his wonderful map and covers), Wendy Shakespeare, the most kind and supportive copy-editor ever, and the world's best rights team. Thanks to everyone at Viking in the US and in particular to my editor, Leila Sales – a wonderful, strong female character if ever there was one! Huge thanks to my family and friends. And my heartfelt thanks to all the wonderful fans of *Half Bad* who have supported my writing, often made me smile and occasionally brought me to tears of happiness.

And finally thanks to you for reading *The Smoke Thieves* – it's a lot easier to keep writing a book when you know that someone is going to read it.

A PRINCESS

A SOLDIER

A HUNTER

A TRAITOR

A THIEF

THE SMOKE THIEVES

Audio edition available now

Listen to an audio extract here:

soundcloud.com/puffin-books-uk

 @sallegreen   www.penguin.co.uk